# Contents

**Section III: Lessons Learned From Data Analysis**



**Section IV: Reflections on the Future**



**Conclusion**



**Appendix**

# Preface

**R. Eugene Rice**

*Director, AAHE Forum on Faculty Roles & Rewards*

If you want to know about post-tenure review in American colleges and universities, this volume and the two companion pieces to be published shortly will provide the best resources available for some time to come. If you want to establish a process for reviewing and renewing tenured faculty in your institution — to get a feel for the pros and cons and find out what the viable options are — this is where thoughtful ideas and practical examples are readily accessible.

When members of the general public debate the work of college and university faculty, tenure looms as a particularly contentious issue. On campus it is not tenure itself that is most contentious, but wide differences do focus on how to go about regularly reviewing the quality of the work of tenured faculty — the time it requires, its primary purposes, and how the process ought to be organized. The essays in this volume provide concrete, experience-based answers from programs across the country selected because they represent examples of the best practice available. And, they are written by those who have emerged as national leaders in the struggle to forge campus-based programs that both work and make sense.

In 1992, the American Association for Higher Education entered into the growing national debate about the priorities of the professoriate by establishing the Forum on Faculty Roles & Rewards — a program that sponsors an annual national conference, issues publications on faculty-related matters, and periodically initiates special "lines of work." Thus, when tenure and the discussion of alternative career paths emerged in the spring of 1994 as a major issue of concern and media attention, the Forum launched a number of inquiries into various aspects of the changing academic career. The project was called "New Pathways: Academic Careers for the 21st Century."

Phase one of the New Pathways project produced 14 studies of different dimensions of faculty work, ranging from tenure to part-time faculty. These New Pathways Working Papers generated widespread discussion — and some rather sharp controversy — about the future of academic careers. In phase two we wanted to move beyond the study of faculty careers to an action phase, to concrete practice on campuses. We chose to target issues that serve as key leverage points in the academic career, issues that have the potential for making individual faculty careers more vital and, at the same time, for providing institutions with the flexibility needed to anticipate and respond to a changing educational environment.

Among the New Pathways studies from the inquiry phase that attracted the most attention was Christine Licata and Joseph Morreale's *Post-Tenure Review: Policies, Practices, Precautions* (Working Paper No. 12). Persuaded by the strength of their work, we chose to make post-tenure review a central focus of the New Pathways project's second phase, "From Inquiry to Practice."

Maintaining the vitality of senior faculty is a critical challenge, and post-tenure review both as an occasion for serious career planning within a changing institutional context and as a faculty development process has the potential for making a significant difference. Post-tenure review is also a promising response to the recent call for faculty accountability and the press for institutional flexibility and responsiveness. With tenure-track faculty, however, the case for a post-tenure review process that works effectively is hard to make. In some state systems, it is seen as nothing more than a cynical ploy to stem the threat of a legislative assault on tenure. Clearly, the kinds of experiences with post-tenure review set forth and analyzed in the essays in this volume are what is needed. Everything from statewide policy choices to everyday practice in disciplinary departments can be informed by the accounts found here.

In addition to the detailed reports of campus-based experience with post-tenure review, this volume reflects the collective exchange — in conference settings and online — of many people, including most of those doing the writing here. Christine Licata has been unusually effective in establishing communities of practice around the concern with post-tenure review. She has worked with sectors of higher education (e.g., community colleges, state universities, liberal arts colleges), with state systems, and with disciplinary and professional associations. Then, representatives from all of those groups have been drawn together at assemblies on post-tenure review that she and AAHE convened before our annual Conference on Faculty Roles & Rewards.

Two of the essays, Shirley Clark's lead account of the experience of the Oregon University System and William Plater's concluding essay "A Profession at Risk: Using Post-Tenure Review to Create an Intentional Future," began as keynote addresses to those assemblies and were subjected to intense debate and critique. Christine Licata's work in this area is a stellar example of how to establish a national dialogue that is well-informed and genuinely open to diverse perspectives. She has also ensured that the discussion is rooted in concrete campus experience and is data based.

Having been involved with the post-tenure review component of the New Pathways project from the beginning, and having spent time on campuses interviewing faculty and academic administrators participating in post-tenure review processes, I can conclude that many of the debilitating mistakes immediately evident on many campuses would have been avoided if those responsible for developing the processes had been introduced to the "stories" available in these essays.

Their lessons to be learned about change in an academic setting are particularly instructive. The significance of peer review in evaluating faculty is underscored again and again. The leadership role — from provost to department chair — is thoughtfully addressed. Cautions about the tie to other faculty review policies and practices are especially important; the neglect of this policy continuum frequently undermines post-tenure review endeavors. William Plater's sage comments on the importance of building an ethic of collective responsibility will become increasingly central as we continue to grapple with the review of tenured faculty and move toward a better integration of faculty priorities and institutional mission.

In addition to Christine Licata's work on post-tenure review, I want to acknowledge the national leadership of Joseph Morreale in helping to shape the New Pathways agenda on this project. He contributed to both the early conceptual work and the challenging follow-through with campuses — the site visits, the reviews of proposals, and the collaboration with professional associations. The introductory and concluding essays of this volume by Christine and Joseph frame the disparate examples of best practice on campus in a way that provides coherence, identifies counterproductive strategies, and envisions new directions to be explored.

Tenure is not going to be abandoned. It is now fully evident, however, that the percentage of faculty holding full-time, tenure-track appointments is decreasing — in the last 10 years, quite dramatically. Maintaining the vitality of the tenured "core" of our faculty is going to become increasingly important. The future of our institutions will depend on it. The lessons learned from these essays move us in the right direction.

# Acknowledgments

Our work together on post-tenure review began in 1996 when we joined forces to collaborate with the American Association for Higher Education (AAHE) on the New Pathways initiatives. This has been a fruitful and dynamic union. We are grateful to R. Eugene Rice for recognizing the need to include post-tenure review in the array of New Pathways topics, for being an incredibly engaged scholar with us every step of the way, and for consistently providing us with enthusiastic encouragement. We also thank The Atlantic Philanthropies and an anonymous donor for their generous support of these efforts. Without it, this project could not have taken flight.

We are indebted to the contributing authors of this volume, as well as to the faculty, staff, and administrators on their campuses with whom they worked to move their projects from drawing board to storyboard. Their task — and ours — has been to create, first and foremost, a volume based on practices and full of resources. Our objective from the start was to make this publication useful to those in the field who might benefit from the successes and failures of others who walked a similar path. Our authors have met this charge admirably and have been responsive to deadlines and our requests for further editing.

We are grateful to Bry Pollack, director of publications at AAHE, for her wise counsel about volume organization and her help with hundreds of other editing details. She really took this volume to new levels.

A word of special thanks to the exceptional support staff on our home campuses: Sydney Long and Kelli McIntee-Shaw at Rochester Institute of Technology/National Technical Institute for the Deaf and Eleanor Fein at Pace University. These individuals kept us on track so we could, in turn, keep the publication on track.

Only we know how much they have contributed to the success of this endeavor.

Our campus CEOs saw value in our work with AAHE and heartily endorsed it. These individuals — visionary leaders in higher education — were patient and, more than that, were proud of the work we were involved with and the risks we were taking. We wish to recognize the unwavering support we received from Dr. Albert J. Simone, president of Rochester Institute of Technology; David A. Caputo, president of Pace University; and Dr. Patricia D. Ewers, president emeritus of Pace University.

We also wish to thank Dr. James J. DeCaro, Dr. T. Alan Hurwitz, and Dr. Marilyn Jaffe-Ruiz for the many kindnesses they extended to us on our home campuses during the time we were involved with AAHE's New Pathways Project. Their interest in our work and their accommodations of our schedule were greatly appreciated.

Over the past five years, we have worked with thousands of dedicated faculty and administrators. All were striving to better understand post-tenure review and sensitively shape an appropriate approach on their campus. Our work with these colleagues has deepened our knowledge and enhanced our appreciation for how difficult change can be, especially when transformational in nature. We have most assuredly learned more from them than they learned from us, and we dedicate this book to them.

Finally, we would like to thank our spouses, Dr. Barry R. Culhane and Barbara L. McAdorey. Their love and support made this journey enjoyable. Their patience and understanding made it doable. Their good humor kept the work in balance. Their encouragement helped us make it to the finish line! We now look forward to capturing missed moments with them.

C.M.L.
J.C.M.

November 2001

# Introduction

**Christine M. Licata and Joseph C. Morreale**

A man is not idle because he is absorbed in thought.
There is a visible labor and an invisible labor.

— Victor Hugo

## Converging Conversations

Victor Hugo's words aptly describe the work of full-time tenured faculty. In our lifetimes, we have seen a sea change regarding faculty work, from great respect and admiration to questioning its value and relevance. Some of this change in attitude is attributable to a general attack on higher education — especially concerning its increasing public cost — and part of this change derives from resentment toward privilege, i.e., tenure. When one reviews the state of higher education in the 1990s, one sees a curious contradiction: Public confidence in faculty work fell to an all-time low and skepticism about faculty productivity reached an all-time high, yet higher education and faculty work were recognized as critical to the future of the nation, even the world. An ever-louder public demands accountability of higher education in general, and particularly of its most important resource, full-time tenured faculty.

Some commentators have referred to this era as a time of faculty bashing, such as *New York Times* education writer William H. Honan: "Faculty bashing is on the rise. It used to be a whisper, but now people speak it loudly" (Honan 1998: 32). A former trustee of a large state system repeatedly attacked tenure as an "absolute scam that insures lifetime job guarantee rather than academic freedom" and said that "he never spoke to a single individual outside the academy who thought that tenure made sense" (Carlin 1999: A76). As attacks on faculty work echoed across the country, legislatures in a few states (Florida, Arizona, Oregon, and Texas) seriously considered abolishing tenure. Some pundits attributed the public's disenchantment with tenure to a growing chasm between business and academic cultures. Rising expenses and shrinking revenues prompted boards of higher education institutions to question certain fundamental features of the academic model. Trustees cautioned administrators that university budgets had to be balanced by other means than increasing tuition. Such corporate solutions as re-engineering and reallocation were suggested. What remains unclear is how corporate solutions could and should be applied to academe. As articulated by a board member of a Midwestern university:

> In my view, many American universities need to commit themselves much more seriously than they have done so far to a similar process (i.e., reinvention) — keeping the best and changing the rest. (Mahoney 1997: B4)

If we think such redesign efforts are waning, one only need review the newest approach to corporate performance reviews. Termed "ranking systems," this practice requires supervisors to rank employees from best to worst and then use this ranking as the blueprint for downsizing or making room for new talent. Despite questions about the legality of this practice, the Ford Motor Company, Sun Microsystems, Cisco Systems, and General Electric have launched their own version of the top-to-bottom ranking strategy — each hoping to recruit talented new hires in a slower economy without increasing the size of the workforce (Jones 2001). Employee performance and measurement issues, whether in the corporate or education venue, are not likely to go away.

What the past decade did was fuel serious conversations about faculty review and renewal practices, and the initiation of policies designed to demonstrate that the way faculty work and measure performance makes sense to those outside academe. By questioning the tenure system, policymakers demanded to know not only what we measure, but how we measure what is valued and rewarded. The tenure system survived, but in the process, faculty evaluation and development programs were significantly overhauled. Post-tenure review, as we know it today, grew in numbers because such reviews represented intentional and deliberate efforts to ensure that tenured faculty were performing at institutional standards and in accordance with tenure expectations.

## Growth of Post-Tenure Review

Defined as a "systematic, comprehensive process, separate from the annual review, and aimed specifically at assessing performance and/or nurturing faculty growth and development" (Licata and Morreale 1997: 1), most post-tenure review policies were formulated to respond to this call for greater accountability. By the 21st century, post-tenure activity was under way in some form or other in 37 states, ranging from required by the entire state system, or adopted within selected public institutions, or at least on the drawing board in others. The private sector is more difficult to quantify, but a recent Harvard University study places the number of private institutions with such policies at about 48 percent (Trower 2000).

Some institutions used this period to go beyond issues of performance review and rethink the career trajectory and professional renewal needs of tenured faculty. In doing so, some policies placed developmental opportunities at the center of the expected outcome. What motivated this formative approach was the realization that human development and career development theories carry an important message to organizations — such as academe — where job security is high and retirement is uncoupled from a mandatory age: As workers age, their interests, energy, and motivation change. Continued vitality and well-being depend on creating a good match between institutional needs and individual needs. Because the needs and interests of mid-career and late-career faculty differ from early-career faculty, professional review and development are important to refresh a career and continue contributions to the institution. Bland and Bergquist (1997) helped promote this framework and reminded institutions that senior faculty are largely ignored when it comes to development.

While in the minority, a few institutions and systems chose to develop policies without external pressure to do so. Most of these institutions had more time to craft policy objectives not only to meet the need for accountability but also to inspire faculty to think prospectively about future directions and new interests.

Regardless of whether these policies were driven by external or internal stimuli, campuses examined how information from the reviews would be used, and decided whether their policy's intent was summative, formative, or both. A "summative" review is a review of retrospective performance leading to a personnel action or consequence (positive or negative). "Formative" reviews identify areas for growth, and lead to prospective planning.

## Post-Tenure Review Terminology

When we discuss post-tenure review, we make a distinction between "periodic" and "episodic" review. Periodic review occurs automatically for *all* tenured faculty — usually every five to seven years — and is conducted *in addition to* the annual merit review. The episodic, or "triggered," approach, in contrast, uses the annual review for all faculty to determine whether a more intensive review is warranted. This closer look occurs for the few whose performance is below standard. A third approach — one in which the annual review is significantly altered to include peer review and a range of reasonable outcomes — is also defined as post-tenure review by some institutions.

Generally, when triggered reviews are used, they tend to be more summative, with the chair or department head completing the annual merit evaluation and a peer committee conducting the more intensive review, if needed. Every policy carries its own nuances, though, and most portray the intent of the review as both summative and formative.

In the mid 1970s, the early practitioners of tenured faculty review policies (California State University System, Oregon University System, Carleton College, and Earlham College) focused principally on formative purposes. Sanctions following the review were rare. Today, however, policies have expanded on what "consequential" results should flow from the reviews. In the majority of cases an unfavorable review requires an improvement plan; a favorable review results in promoting professional development; and in a very few cases (the University of California System, Georgia State University, and Coastal

Carolina University) a highly favorable review means merit rewards may follow.

## Continuing the Dialogue: The New Pathways Project

Recognizing the dearth of documented institutional experiences in designing programs for senior faculty review, the American Association for Higher Education (AAHE) used its New Pathways Project to assist faculty and administrators to meet external mandates or investigate current review policies, in anticipation of needed changes.

This present volume grows out of the experiences of institutions that worked with AAHE under its New Pathways aegis. The institutions represented here successfully competed for AAHE minigrants to help their campus or system start, maintain its momentum, or experiment with novel approaches to tenured faculty review and development. AAHE provided support to 34 "institutional projects with promise." While 13 projects report out here, a complete listing of all of the projects is found in the appendix. We encourage you to review the nature and scope of the full range of projects and to contact the identified institutional liaison for further information and discussion.

In this book, we have brought together some penultimate examples of the adoption and implementation of post-tenure review, both in systems of higher education and at specific institutions. The 13 institutional examples offer a variety of insights into post-tenure review as described by faculty and administrators who participated in their institution's work.

The volume is divided into sections focused on similar contextual themes: (1) system-level issues and lessons (some of which represent unionized settings); (2) lessons learned for departments, chairs, and faculty; (3) lessons learned from data analysis; and (4) reflections on the future of the post-tenure review movement. This organization provides a context. Regardless of organization, the underlying objective in each commentary is to inform the field and provide experience-based recommendations about building effective evaluation/development programs, making mid-course adjustments, and choosing one approach over another.

This current volume is written by individuals who directly labored in the post-tenure review vineyard, so the fruit of their efforts should provide insight to provosts, deans, and department chairs who carry evaluation responsibilities and who wish to affirm or improve their current practices. Faculty leaders should also find this volume useful because a compelling theme that cuts across every chapter is the importance of peer involvement every step of the way including in the review itself. Policymakers at various levels are also encouraged to take in the lessons recounted here, because they tell an evocative story about policy evolution. Finally, higher education faculty and doctoral students may find this work valuable because of the opportunity it provides to become familiar with some of the critical evaluation issues and particularly to clarify areas for further research.

## Common Themes

As you read each experience recounted here, you will notice some common themes and challenges. We believe there are four overriding themes, and each one represents an important juncture for an institution about to initiate change in faculty policies. The first theme, **Critical Beginnings**, refers to the cultural traditions that must be considered when setting up an environment conducive to change. The second, **Strategic Checkpoints**, recognizes that there are important times to "pause" along the change route to assess whether the necessary conditions for implementation are in place. **Intentional Intersections,** the third theme, suggests that changes in one policy can affect other policies and norms and that such convergence must be anticipated and coherently integrated. The last theme, **Future Pathways,** directs attention to the value of ongoing reflection and prospective thinking during and after the initiation of policy changes. Here the emphasis is on whether intended results actually occur, whether unintended consequences strengthen or diminish policy intent, and whether changes in the path or the destination are warranted.

These themes cut across institutional type and evaluation models. We point them out to you at the outset because we believe these themes provide important texture to the conversation we wish to engender. Regardless of whether or not your institution currently has a tenured faculty review policy, the underlying motifs here have relevance to any change effort and most especially to those aimed at faculty performance, development, and reward.

There are a variety of approaches taken, and the authors write candidly about their experiences. This is a conversation about post-tenure review realism, not idealism. While we have our own views on this topic, on the pages that follow are the voices of those who are plowing the field and who wish others to know the contour of their efforts.

Listen carefully to the four themes that unfold and note particularly the many shared experiences.

## Critical Beginnings

### *Faculty Grassroots Involvement*

Faculty support what they help create. This is the motivating mantra emanating from every institution represented. In particular, through the experiences of Idaho State University, Indiana University Purdue University Indianapolis, Arizona State University, the University of Kentucky, Drexel University, the University of Massachusetts, the Texas State University System, and the Georgia State University, one sees different approaches for how faculty support is obtained. In these settings — some of which are governed by collective bargaining agreements — faculty involvement went beyond mere validation and was carefully built into the negotiations. Respect for the institutional context was always the centerpiece.

The terms "negotiating culture," "negotiating collaboration," and "negotiating compromise" can be heard throughout the accounts told by the University of Nebraska-Lincoln, the California State University-Long Beach, the University of Massachusetts System, and Oregon University System authors.

### *Summative Versus Formative*

The flashpoint of any conversation about post-tenure review occurs around the question of whether a policy should have consequences including rewards, remediation strategies, sanctions (a summative review), or be limited to professional/career development ends (a formative review). In this volume, we see Drexel University, Winthrop University, and California State University-Long Beach intentionally avoid linking the review to rewards; Georgia State, Idaho State, the Virginia Military

Institute, and the Oregon University System make a direct connection. Drexel and California State University-Long Beach describe processes mainly participative and formative in nature, seeking reflection and renewal as their objectives. Charles Walker and William Plater provide a solid conceptual basis for why such formative reviews hold the greatest benefit for faculty.

The other institutions discuss and include formative results in their policy portfolio, but also require an improvement plan if performance is below standard. Many policies (Indiana University Purdue University Indianapolis, Arizona State University, Winthrop University, Texas State University System, the University of Kentucky, and the Georgia State University) even mention allowable sanctions to be considered if there is no improvement within a reasonable amount of time. Drexel University, Idaho State University, and the Virginia Military Institute colleagues advise institutions to have clear purpose(s), communicate the purpose(s) often, and be prepared — regardless of clarity — to reiterate frequently with faculty what the purpose(s) are of the review.

***Peer Review Patterns***

William Plater argues that peer review is the defining feature lending credibility and legitimacy to tenure and to post-tenure review. He asserts, "What is neither seen nor understood is not valued. As faculty work becomes more public, so will tenure — through peer review." Interestingly, while peer review was not initially mandated in the Arizona State System, one of the recommendations made after the first round of review was to require it. The Oregon University System — as do others — remands the peer review option to each campus and unit to decide how review should be operationalized. At the University of Kentucky, either the chair or a peer committee conducts the consequential review. In other settings, peers have a major role in either the review or the creation of the development plan. Peer review is crucial to ensuring the process is self-regulated.

***Leadership and Engagement***

Implicit in most reports — and strongly explicit in a few — is the need for leadership of the post-tenure review process during formation and particularly implementation. The role of department chairs is essential to providing consistent application. Senior-level administrative engagement is equally paramount.

Applegate/Nora (Kentucky) caution that the proper leadership team must be in place to elicit trust in the system. Barr (the Virginia Military Institute) suggests leadership from above the dean's level must expect and be willing to spend significant time and energy on the post-tenure review process if it is to be meaningful to faculty. Henry (the Georgia State University), Hunter/Lawson (Idaho State University), McLean/Callarman (Arizona State University), and Janousek/Dick (California State University-Long Beach), each in their own way, affirms the pivotal role academic leaders play to ensure policies achieve their objectives. Achievement occurs only through the active engagement of leadership.

## Strategic Checkpoints

### *Ritualistic Compliance*

Two systems (Oregon and Arizona) and two institutions (Winthrop University and Indiana University Purdue University Indianapolis) experienced the dichotomy between the intentions of the original mandates and the reality of implementation. Implementation in these four settings — and even after one year in the Massachusetts University and Texas State University systems — shows how key policy aspects can be lost and/or policy gaps uncovered. When promised funds to support development or rewards are not forthcoming, compliance can become ritualistic. While local control of implementation is the norm in all of the institutions reporting here, those who tracked policy interpretation — such as the Arizona State System, Massachusetts System, Texas State University System, and Georgia State University — found local control does not guarantee fair process or wise judgments. Policy interpretation across the university or system was uneven, fragmented, and/or divergent. "The devil is in the details" as one contributor notes, and oversight of implementation cannot be ignored or forgotten.

### *Setting Performance Benchmarks*

One of the most difficult and time-consuming processes described by our authors is setting performance criteria and standards. As demonstrated at Indiana University Purdue University Indianapolis, Winthrop University, Arizona State University, the University of Nebraska-Lincoln, and the Texas

State University System, the issue is where the bar is to be set. Is the emphasis on what is acceptable and unacceptable? Or is the emphasis on a performance scale that delineates well above minimum performance and can be used to reward high-level performers? The experiences of Indiana University Purdue University Indianapolis and the University of Nebraska-Lincoln portray the conundrum of establishing credible and measurable performance benchmarks.

#### Chair Development

Another compelling issue is repeated realizations about the need for chair training and orientation with respect to faculty evaluation. Indiana University Purdue University Indianapolis and the University of Nebraska-Lincoln present substantive ideas about approaches, strategies, and resources to assist chairs to prepare themselves for complex evaluation duties. Two authors even question whether the traditional rotating chair process should be re-examined, given the responsibilities chairs are asked to assume and the need for a longitudinal chair perspective, especially with reviews that span five to seven years.

A corollary need for orientation and training for peer reviewers was demonstrated through the experiences of California State University-Long Beach, Winthrop University, and Georgia State University.

#### Assessing Outcomes/Tracking Implementation

Throughout the individual institutional reports, one sees heightened attention to the need for assessing whether procedures are working, how faculty perceive the process, and — in the case of Georgia State University and Arizona State University — what results the reviews show in terms of development activities, career redirection, and retirements.

Five years ago, assessing outcomes and tracking implementation would not have occurred. The University of Massachusetts System describes a novel approach to oversight: an oversight committee comprising representatives from the Commonwealth's executive office, the university board of trustees, and the president's office. Chairs and faculty have tracked implementation within the Arizona State University System, Winthrop University, Texas State University, and the Virginia Military Institute, and are planning to do so at the University of Kentucky. Several campuses have already made or are planning to make mid-course corrections. Campus leaders place great importance on monitoring and measuring review outcomes and their impact. This also leaves the door open for policy refinements and modifications to increase the efficiency and effectiveness of the practice.

## Intentional Intersections

### *Policy Convergence*

Many authors emphasize the importance of nesting post-tenure review within the institution's matrix of performance review and development procedures or, as Plater suggests, the policy continuum of "hiring to retiring." Applegate/Nora refer to this strategy as "piggybacking" on current evaluation systems. The University of Kentucky faculty, they say, already felt "over-evaluated." So post-tenure review was integrated as seamlessly as possible into the current evaluation system. Clark (Oregon University System) concludes that the "refreshed" approach to post-tenure review in that system "fits generally with the direction of large-scale system-wide change of the past decade." Within the Arizona system, post-tenure review was directly linked to the annual review and also to academic program review procedures. The University of Nebraska-Lincoln broadened the focus to include the creation of supportive work environments to enable faculty to achieve their highest level of performance. Called the "faculty roles initiative," this effort is preventive and aimed at "instituting changes to enhance faculty vitality before systemic problems result in declining faculty productivity." Drexel University joins individual professional renewal with department renewal. Georgia State University and the Virginia Military Institute purposely link post-tenure review with reward (merit) policies, and Idaho State University plans to do the same.

Most institutional experiences recognize that regardless of approach, post-tenure review brings renewed focus to annual review practices. The triggered model ratchets up the importance of fair and systematic annual review procedures; the periodic approach — because it usually refers to annual review results — adds value to the annual review process.

#### *Ethic of Collective Responsibility*

Stated in different ways by different authors, post-tenure review makes each faculty member's work more known to other faculty and thus has the potential to also make the needs of the academic unit more public. This shared knowledge can lead to a sense of collective responsibility for meeting departmental and institutional missions or, as Plater frames it, adapting "the values we associate with individual work to the work of the unit." He sees post-tenure review as helping preserve values and missions of an institution through shared responsibility of the faculty for the well-being of the whole. Henry (Georgia State) believes much the same. He suggests post-tenure review can contribute strongly to this ethic of collective responsibility which "is essential for the ongoing vitality of the university." This philosophical position lies at the base of Drexel's approach as well.

Differentiated workloads, or differentiated workload profiles, are discussed in Georgia State University, Arizona State University, Indiana University Purdue University Indianapolis, the University of Nebraska-Lincoln, Winthrop University, and the University of Kentucky chapters. Reflecting on the 25-year experience of the Oregon University System with post-tenure review, Clark suggests institutions visit the concept of the "responsive university" (Tierney 1998). She also suggests that evaluations should be linked to development to enable multiple career pathways. She says, "Post-tenure review needs to function in such a way that mutual loyalties are increased and mutual needs are met."

#### *Preservation of Tenure*

Some authors have chosen to discuss tenure, its value in academe, and its relationship to post-tenure review. Post-tenure review is not a re-tenuring process in the institutions represented in this volume. In fact, the term "post-tenure review" was deliberately avoided when policy language was crafted by Georgia State, Indiana University Purdue University Indianapolis, the University of Massachusetts, the University of Kentucky, the Texas State University System, the California State University System, Drexel University, and the Virginia Military Institute.

The commentaries from authors at Arizona State University, the Oregon University System, and Indiana University Purdue University Indianapolis (Plater) address ways in which they believe post-tenure review will preserve tenure. Both Clark and Plater assert tenure must change to keep pace with the evolving purposes of higher education. They see post-tenure review as a means to affirm tenure by transforming it. Clark states "tenure must work better or at least be perceived as working better." Plater purports "tenure will be irrelevant if faculty are not held responsible for adapting to a new knowledge, to a more competitive marketplace, and to serving a clientele where learning continues throughout life instead of through a career." Accordingly, Plater believes "tenure must be functional and valuable to be preserved, and if it serves a pragmatic end then it can surely be measured and assessed and reported through post-tenure review."

In Arizona, Texas, and Massachusetts, post-tenure review was a compromise to avoid legislative action abolishing tenure. In these three states, post-tenure review has forestalled interference in issues surrounding tenure — at least for now.

## Future Pathways

We invited William Plater and Charles Walker to discuss the future of faculty work life and faculty vitality. Each brings a different perspective.

Charles Walker (St. Bonaventure University) provocatively suggests that post-tenure review is not sufficient to improve faculty vitality. He believes "post-tenure review that focuses only on individual faculty member performance will not lead to improved faculty vitality. What is needed is comprehensive review of the work and work conditions of faculty." He describes a model of faculty well-being and the necessary conditions for faculty to experience high levels of well-being. In his analysis, for post-tenure review to effectively promote faculty well-being, it must be embedded within a comprehensive program of faculty development seeking to improve not only the individual faculty member but also the environmental conditions of his or her work.

The concluding article by William Plater (Indiana University Purdue University Indianapolis) takes the longer term view of post-tenure review. Plater concludes, "if we are purposeful, we can use our current experience in preserving tenure, and our understanding of the forces of societal change, to make post-tenure review the very means of invigorating and reviewing the profession." Plater concludes with six questions:

1. How can post-tenure review take advantage of the growing importance of teaching in universities and colleges?

2. How can post-tenure review help us develop effective means of differentiating the responsibilities of individuals from one another and for each of us over time?

3. How can post-tenure review shape our thinking about the placement of aging faculty with new kinds of appointments?

4. How can post-tenure review become a factor in helping preserve the values and mission of an institution through the shared responsibility of faculty for the well-being of the whole — transcending and enduring beyond changes in the office of the chair, dean, provost, or president?

5. How can the purpose of post-tenure review shift to continuous improvement for all and away from pruning the deadwood of isolated, ineffective individuals?

6. How does the responsibility of individual academic citizenship — surely an obligation of tenured faculty — get assessed in post-tenure review?

Surely these questions deserve our attention. And as we move beyond examining current practice to seeking process improvement, these questions demand thoughtful answers.

As you reflect on the following experiences, remember context matters and that what plays well in Massachusetts may not play well in Minnesota. Keep in mind that some of the institutions and systems represented here are modifying procedures. It is probably accurate to also assume that by the time this book is published many of the lessons learned by individual campuses will have turned into action. California State University-Long Beach, the Virginia Military Institute, and the Texas State University System have already begun process enhancements.

Our authors welcome your follow-up questions, and we have provided email addresses for that purpose. We encourage you to continue the conversation started here with our authors and to use this volume as a tool to inform your own institutional programs.

## References

Bland, C.J., and W.H. Bergquist. (1997). *The Vitality of Senior Faculty Members: Snow on the Roof, Fire in the Furnace.* ASHE-ERIC Higher Education Reports, no. 7. Washington, DC: The George Washington University, Graduate School of Education and Human Development.

Carlin, J.F. (November 5, 1999). "Restoring Sanity to an Academic World Gone Mad." *The Chronicle of Higher Education,* p. A76.

Honan, W.H. (January 4, 1998). "The Ivory Tower Under Siege." *New York Times* (education section), p. 32.

Jones, D. (May 30, 2001). "More Firms Cut Workers Ranked at Bottom to Make Way for Talent." *USA Today,* pp. B1–B2.

Licata, C.M., and J.C. Morreale. (1997). *Post-Tenure Review: Policies, Practices, Precautions.* New Pathways Working Paper Series, no. 12. Washington, DC: American Association for Higher Education.

Mahoney, R.J. (October 17, 1997). "Reinventing the University: Object Lessons From Big Business." *The Chronicle of Higher Education,* pp. B4-B5.

Tierney, W.G. (1998). *The Responsive University.* Baltimore: The Johns Hopkins University Press.

Trower, C.A., ed. (2000). *Policies on Faculty Appointment.* Bolton, MA: Anker Publishing Company.

# Section I:
# System-Level Issues and Lessons

# Ahead of Our Time at the End of the Trail? Post-Tenure Review in the Oregon University System

**Shirley M. Clark** [1]

## Birth of a Policy

In recent years, interest in post-tenure review has been intense. An American Association for Higher Education (AAHE) survey found that in more than 37 states, public systems of higher education had established post-tenure policies and procedures or were in the process of doing so; 77 percent of those policies were initiated after 1992 (Licata 1999). My state of Oregon is one of the earliest adopters of post-tenure review, dating back to 1973.

How did this prescience come about? Why in recent years have we schemed and strategized our way toward a "just-in-time" reaffirmation of post-tenure review in the Oregon University System?

Tenure is just as subject to scrutiny as other inventions of the academy. Interest in reexamining it arises periodically when pressures from outside groups converge with our desire to induce changes in faculty behavior toward greater responsiveness. Thus, at an earlier time of intense national focus on tenure in the 1970s, the Board of Higher Education for the eight public universities in Oregon undertook a six-month study. The process culminated in a decision to require post-tenure review. Interestingly, post-tenure review was not a leading concern going into the study: A presumed lack of rigor in and short length of the probationary period, the lack of clarity in reduction-in-force policies, and excessive "tenuring in" of the institutions were more pressing issues. The board declined to impose a quota on tenured faculty, directed that reduction-in-force policies be developed, and lengthened the probationary period from three to five years.

Board members decided to adopt post-tenure review for two reasons: (1) the public image of and public support for higher education, and (2) the direct positive benefits of review to the institutions. The public image, as elaborated in a report to the board, was of a tenured faculty member "protected against the rigors of a competitive world," an image that "cannot be exorcized merely by declaring it to be an errant aberration of the uninformed" (Oregon State Board of Higher Education Committee on Academic Affairs 1973: 1). The institutional benefits anticipated as a result of post-tenure review would include (1) evidence of the productivity of the majority of faculty, (2) a stimulus to faculty performance and subsequent recognition, (3) a way to identify faculty in need of professional development, and (4) a means to gather evidence to demonstrate cause for those few faculty moving toward negative sanction or termination.

As with most faculty personnel policies in the Oregon University System, the board provided latitude for developing a range of specific institutional policies within its overall policy framework. A policy in the form of an Oregon Administrative Rule (OAR) was subsequently adopted. The text of the rule follows.

> Post-Tenure Review
>
> (1) Tenured faculty members shall be evaluated periodically and systematically in accordance with plans developed in the institutions.
>
> (2) Institutional plans for post-tenure reviews shall include, but not necessarily be limited to:
>
> (a) a statement of the objectives of faculty post-tenure review and evaluation;
>
> (b) a statement of criteria to be used in evaluations, the nature and kinds of data that will be accumulated, and the method of data collecting;
>
> (c) a designation of persons making evaluations;
>
> (d) a designation of the frequency and regularity of evaluations;
>
> (e) a description of the institutional plan for relating post-tenure reviews to the faculty reward system, such that appropriate recognition for excellence can be provided;
>
> (f) a description of the institutional plan to deal firmly but humanely with situations in which the competence or the vitality and drive of a particular faculty member have diminished to such an extent that the resources of the faculty

> career support program are unable to provide the stimulation or help necessary to return the faculty member to a fully effective state. (OAR 580-021-0140) [Oregon State Board of Higher Education 2000: 15]

Two other Oregon Administrative Rules include references to post-tenure review:

> Specific provision shall be made for appropriate student input into the data accumulated as the basis for . . . post-tenure review. (OAR 580-021-0135[3], Criteria for Faculty Evaluation) [Oregon State Board of Higher Education 2000: 15]

> Faculty members shall be provided written information that includes . . . criteria to be used in evaluating the faculty member in connection with . . . post-tenure review. . . . (OAR 580-021-0005[3][A], Appointment Procedures) [Oregon State Board of Higher Education 2000: 1]

The tenor of the original board rule was in keeping with currently recognized objectives of good post-tenure review policy: that is, it balanced the formative emphasis with the potential for disciplinary sanctions to be imposed, if necessary.

## Institutionalizing an Innovation

Each institution through its shared governance mechanisms developed and implemented post-tenure review policies to coexist with pre-tenure reviews, promotion reviews, and annual reviews for salary adjustments and other purposes. Over time, post-tenure review in Oregon became invisible to outsiders as it was woven into the organizational structures of the campuses. Invisibility may be a positive and inevitable result of institutionalization of any innovation. Ideally, the innovation should be incorporated, absorbed, and owned by those who manage it and are affected by it. A cynic (or a realist?) might say that, for accountability purposes, the board responded to public critics of the tenure system by conducting a study, taking a stand, approving a new rule, and issuing a press release. The public could be reassured that tenure was no faculty sinecure in the Oregon University System.

Complicit with this process, institutional leaders and their governance groups could "virtually adopt" post-tenure review by proclaiming it to be in place without doing a great deal about it (Birnbaum 2000: 11) There is, after all, a history of virtual institutional responses to board mandates of "foreign import" solutions to pressing issues (Birnbaum 2000: 12). New management directives that have their roots in business practices (e.g., total quality management, zero-based budgeting, responsibility-centered management, enrollment management, performance funding) are difficult to apply to core processes in our enterprise because they do not seem to gel with academic culture or fundamental purposes (Birnbaum 2000). Virtual adoption, whereby the form but not the substance of an innovation is implemented, offers a response without *significantly* changing. This can be a valuable survival tool in a world that, as Peter Ewell observed, "increasingly wants colleges and universities to engage in visibly businesslike practices" (1999: 15).

It is difficult to know definitively what unfolded in the Oregon University System between the mid 1970s and the late 1990s regarding post-tenure review. Like personnel practices in many settings, it became routinized and pro forma in some institutions. Assuming this occurred, a justification or two might be offered. The System experienced ongoing fiscal austerity constricting faculty development resources and meaningful merit salary increases, thus making post-tenure review "dry" of rewards or career assistance. Alternatively, perhaps faculty and administrators were not persuaded any value was added; therefore the process was ritualized.

## A Strategic Response to a Changing Environment

By the late 1990s, the environment regarding tenure — nationally and in Oregon — was changing. We had successfully buffered our faculties from occasional bashing and intrusive statutory directives in the biennial legislative context of the early 1990s. Strong board support for a System-wide academic productivity and educational reform initiative helped. This initiative provided small grants to faculty to undertake curricular revisions and distance education experiments, the results of which we showcased to appreciative legislative committees. A defining moment, however, came in 1997 after a presentation to the board by one of the campuses on the rigor of its probationary review process. Several board members in one-on-one conversations with System officials said they had no doubt of our high standards for hiring and for the award of tenure. What concerned them was what happened to faculty after achieving tenure, because several decades would pass before retirement occurred. This concern — a message, really — was then carried by System officers to our eight campus provosts, and thus began a conversation among us at monthly meetings that ran for more than a year.

We learned from one another that, at some level, all institutions were carrying out post-tenure review on established cycles. On most campuses, little or no data on reviews and outcomes moved beyond the deans of colleges and divisions. Provosts received limited information except about the occasional "problem" faculty member for whom a workplan was developed or who might be heading toward a sanction for cause. No provost could recall an instance of a faculty member who was terminated for cause as a result of post-tenure review (not that this could happen directly anyway under the board's policies). Provosts unanimously believed that "counseling out" was the more time-honored, humane, effective, and less-costly method of obtaining a seriously problematic faculty member's voluntary resignation or retirement. There was concern about the relative dearth of both resource rewards and policy "teeth" in the post-tenure review process. There was awareness that the board's, the legislative, and the national focuses on faculty performance review were heating up. In turn, provosts began conversations with faculty leaders on their campuses by suggesting the time was right to review existing policies and procedures for their responsiveness to current conditions on the campus and external concerns. When asked on occasion by board members, "What's going on with post-tenure review?" we could tell them honestly the issue was on our agenda, the provosts were asking their faculty governance groups to review current practices, it was under discussion in the Interinstitutional Faculty Senate, and we would be coming to the board with a report and recommendations in due time.

These interlocking conversations were galvanized by an event near the end of the 1997 legislative session. A proposal to abolish tenure summarily for K–12 public school teachers in Oregon and put the teachers on three-year contracts was "stuffed" into a school reform bill and was quickly passed by both the state Senate and the House of Representatives. A legislative leader subsequently turned to our director of government relations and said, in effect, "Don't think this gets you off the hook; higher education is next." This event — and the accompanying warning — was useful to us as leverage when campus faculty expressed doubts about the seriousness of public concerns.

As we prepared for the 1999 legislative session, the chancellor, the director of government relations, the provosts, and our office decided to complete our report and recommendations to the board as a preemptive strike before the session began in January. We went to the board in December 1998. The board's discussion of post-tenure review received generous and positive press coverage; the director of government relations reported on this as "putting our house in order" in his regular newsletter to all legislators. Although the board's discussion was generally laudatory of the report and its recommendations, four areas of concern were raised.

- Reaffirm the importance of tenure explicitly;
- Affirm and support the career-development aspects of post-tenure review;
- Clarify that salaries could be adjusted downward as well as upward at the next contract notice period as a consequence of reviews; and
- Insert language to identify explicitly in the policy the existing rules that apply to personnel actions for cause.

Clearly the last two concerns were intended to sharpen the teeth of the policy, and were reported in exactly those words in the state's major newspaper the next day.

Prior to the December 1998 board meeting, the Interinstitutional Faculty Senate had deliberated on the proposed changes. Some senators preferred to revise the post-tenure review policy to focus only on faculty development, but other senators insisted on a revision incorporating sanctions. They referred to the need for levers to ensure that nonproductive, nonresponsive colleagues who create workload, reputational, and other issues for departments would be sanctioned. We returned to the board in February 1999 for final action on the revisions. One institution's American Association of University Professors (AAUP) chapter had submitted AAUP's policy statement on post-tenure review as evidence that Oregon's policy should limit consequences to developmental assistance. Several board members voiced their disagreement with AAUP's policy statement.

The board adopted revisions to the applicable Oregon Administrative Rule as follows.

Post-Tenure Review

(1) Tenured faculty members shall be evaluated periodically and systematically in accordance with guidelines developed by each institution.
(2) The purposes of post-tenure review are to:
 - assure continued excellence in the academy,
 - offer appropriate feedback and professional development opportunities to tenured faculty,
 - clearly link the level of remuneration to faculty performance, and
 - provide accountability to the institution, public, and Board.
(3) Institutions shall develop post-tenure review guidelines in accordance with the objectives and guidelines promulgated in IMD 4.002, OAR 580-021-0135(3), and OAR 580-021-0005(3)(A). (OAR 580-021-0140) [Oregon State Board of Higher Education 2000: 15]

The board also adopted a new Internal Management Directive (IMD) preserving and extending the language of the 1973 policy, as follows:

Post-Tenure Review

Recognizing that the quality of higher education is inextricably tied to the quality of faculty, the Board reaffirms its commitment to tenure, academic freedom, and maintaining an environment that supports sustained performance in teaching, research, and service. Further, the Board recognizes the rigorous, multi-year review process to which probationary faculty submit prior to the awarding of tenure, as well as the numerous ways in which tenured faculty performance is reviewed thereafter (e.g., student ratings of instruction, peer review of scholarly work, competitive sponsored research grants, juried exhibits, and artistic performance). Nevertheless, for the purposes of more comprehensive review after tenure has been conferred and in accordance with the purposes stated in OAR 580-021-0140, each institution shall develop post-tenure review guidelines, which shall be filed with the Chancellor's Office. Institutional guidelines shall include, but not be limited to:
(1) a statement of post-tenure review objectives;
(2) a statement of criteria to be used in evaluations, the nature and kinds of data that will be accumulated, and the methods of data collection;
(3) a designation of persons making evaluations;

> (4) a designation of the frequency and regularity of evaluations;
> (5) a description of the institutional plan for relating post-tenure reviews to the faculty reward system, so that annual salary-adjustment decisions (i.e., increase, no increase, decrease) will reflect the results of performance evaluations;
> (6) a description of appropriate formative opportunities (e.g., professional development plan, faculty career support program [IMD 4.001]);
> (7) a description of the institutional plan to deal firmly but humanely with situations in which a faculty member's competence or vitality have diminished to such an extent that formative opportunities are unable to sufficiently stimulate or assist the faculty member's return to a fully effective state. Personnel actions for cause shall be implemented in accordance with OARs 580-021-0320 through 580-021-0470 (IMD 4.002). [Oregon State Department of Higher Education 1999: 23-24]

Tenure came under a new attack. Early in the legislative session, a former student at one of our universities persuaded a legislator to propose a bill to end tenure in Oregon's community colleges and the Oregon University System and to place faculty on three-year contracts after a probationary period. The chair of the House Education Committee allowed the proponent of the measure to testify during a hearing. Our director of government relations spoke briefly in opposition, including in his testimony our attentiveness to revision of the post-tenure review policy. The committee was satisfied and permitted no additional hearings on the bill (which died in committee). There were no other attempts to abolish or alter tenure during the 1999 session.

We had dodged the bullet. More importantly, we had reaffirmed tenure and refocused attention within the campuses on post-tenure review, consistent with the board's larger focus on performance measurement. We were also advocating — successfully as it turned out — for gubernatorial and legislative support of our new budget model, which is strongly performance and accountability based. Common themes were interwoven among our strategic initiatives; there was deliberate policy convergence based upon as much mutual agreement as we could mobilize.

## Key Elements of Institutions' Policies: A Differentiated Response

The institutions had some differentiation in their individual policies. Seven institutions [2] were in the process of revising their institutional policies concurrent with our collective work with the board on the System-wide framework policy. Portland State University, Southern Oregon University, and Western Oregon University have unions, so their post-tenure review policies are embedded in collective bargaining contracts, which subsequently had to be renegotiated. Eastern Oregon University, Oregon Institute of Technology, Oregon State University, and University of Oregon, which do not have unions, spent substantial faculty senate time on post-tenure review policy revisions in 1998 and 1999. By and large, the changes made were subtle and consisted more of procedural refinements and additions of broadly worded outcomes than of substantial departures from past practices. However, Eastern Oregon University changed its schedule of reviews by adopting a "triggering" mechanism; this was the most significant departure in timing. Oregon State University undertook the most intensive faculty senate deliberations, and settled on the most specific listings of faculty development resources as well as potential sanctions.

Some distinguishing and common features of the revised policies, as implemented by the campuses, are shown in the table on pages 28-29.

## Lessons Learned

### *1. Early Adoption*

There are advantages to early adoption of a policy innovation; for example, it provides a basis of experience from which to build and does not have to be sold as an unproven strategy to skeptical faculty. If the policy was virtually adopted, however, it probably is not being followed systematically and its benefits may be marginal to individuals and their institutions. This argues for a periodic review of how your policy is being implemented, and modifications made based on the findings.

### *2. Timing*

Academic managers, like comedians, learn that timing is critical, since issues have a way of rising and waning in cycles. When an issue is not timely, it is difficult to initiate the decision-making process and keep it focused until the issue is resolved (Julius, Baldridge, and Pfeffer 1999). Transcending the status quo is

## Table: Oregon University System's Post-Tenure Review Policies: Differentiated Responses

**Eastern Oregon University**
*Timing:* triggered by unsuccessful biennial professional development plan
*Criteria:* mission specific
*Reviewers:* dean/division chair
*Outcomes:*

- personnel adjustments (e.g., salary, assignments, or promotion are affected)
- professional development
- improvement plans

**Oregon Institute of Technology**
*Timing:* every six years; if unsuccessful, another review within two years
*Criteria:* mission specific
*Reviewers:* faculty peers
*Outcomes:*

- recognition
- improvement plans
- alternate career counseling or early retirement
- sanctions (e.g., merit salary increase withheld, ultimately termination)

**Oregon State University**
*Timing:* annual and five-year reviews
*Criteria:* mission specific
*Reviewers:* unit head/faculty peers
*Outcomes:*

- personnel adjustments
- professional development plan and resources
- sanctions (e.g., reduction in rank, reassignment, ultimately termination)

**Portland State University**
*Timing:* every five years or earlier, depending upon the professional development plan
*Criteria:* mission specific
*Reviewers:* faculty peers
*Outcomes:*

- recognition

- personnel adjustments
- career support fund for improvement
- review committee reports to unit head if professional development plan is unsatisfactorily completed

**Southern Oregon University**
*Timing:* annual professional plan and activities report/third-year full evaluation
*Criteria:* mission specific
*Reviewers:* department chair/faculty peers
*Outcomes:*

- reward/recognition
- if problems noted, a plan of action developed
- sanctions (e.g., provost takes appropriate action)

**University of Oregon**
*Timing:* substantive review every three years/major review every six years (the latter review is done in depth and includes peer committees)
*Criteria:* mission specific
*Reviewers:* unit head or dean/faculty peers
*Outcomes:*

- personnel adjustments
- other rewards (e.g., additional research or clerical support, recognition)
- career support if needed
- other alternatives (e.g., altered career plan, early retirement, sanctions per other rules)

**Western Oregon University**
*Timing:* every three years
*Criteria:* mission specific
*Reviewers:* division chair, in consultation with faculty peers
*Outcomes:*

- personnel adjustments
- improvement plans
- sanctions of increasing severity for unsatisfactory performance (e.g., reprimand, suspension, salary increase denial or reduction, discharge)

more likely to be achieved if an issue is receiving local, state, and national attention.

#### *3. External Pressures*

Public institutions are vulnerable to pressures from external groups making policies and laws to govern them and providing necessary resources to support the institutions. Offensive strategies crafted by institutions themselves that suit and support academic culture and specific missions are more likely to work, and can deflect externally imposed solutions to perceived problems. Academic managers and faculty change agents can use the reality factor of external threat to advantage in overcoming inertia in the change process.

#### *4. Policy Convergence*

In Oregon's case, a revised and refreshed approach to post-tenure review fits within the direction of large-scale System-wide change of the past decade. The board adopted performance goals in the mid 1990s, took a positive stance on supporting faculty and learner productivity, and adopted a new performance-based budget model. A proficiency-based admission standards system for undergraduates is nearly developed. Thus, the common priority theme of performance and accountability should be reflected in all institutional policies and procedures, not just those pertaining to tenure.

## Conclusions and Considerations

Oregon's experience as an early adopter may have relevance for others who are attempting to shore up their tenure systems in a turbulent environment while addressing real and imagined problems that have excited the public. Our experience with this cyclical nature of criticism toward tenure also suggests four important considerations for institutions as post-tenure review policies are developed or revamped.

#### *Concern With Deadwood*

The hue and cry concerning tenure is not about academic freedom, though new threats to academic freedom arise every year. We could develop a long list of faculty ideas unpopular in some quarter for which a call to silence or sanction the faculty member is made. By and large, the concerns focus on so-called deadwood and faculty productivity. It is hard to dispel the notion that the tenure system protects and shields unmotivated and unproductive individuals, even though no evidence shows that higher education institutions have a larger portion of unproductive professional employees than do businesses or other organizations. We have some faculty, of course, who are stuck in their careers for a variety of reasons, or who have signed off. But for most faculty, their extended professional socialization, their professional pride, the typically rigorous probationary process that precedes the award of tenure, and the constant feedback through student evaluations and peer reviews of scholarly work provide clear indications of what is expected and whether they are measuring up.

The higher education community has a moral and organizational obligation to deal with our unproductive members. In many institutions, it is lack of courage, not policy, and a strong distaste for conflict that prevent us from taking action to deal with egregious offenders. To design a post-tenure review process exclusively for this purpose displaces the opportunity to assist the majority of faculty with their career development, and thereby increase their productivity, their satisfaction, and their commitment to the institution.

#### *Opportunity to Affirm Tenure*

Post-tenure review is a way to affirm and transform tenure. This is not an easy sell. In spring 1999, a faculty senator at one of our institutions said to his governance colleagues:

> . . . Justifiable demoralization has led to something else on this campus: suspicion. I wish this were not true. . . . But over the past year I have heard many faculty whom I greatly respect tell me that they actually believe the impetus to reform post-tenure review policy, for example, was the result of a dark administrative plot to undermine academic freedom, and to create a sharp tool with which to excise faculty members without cause. (University of Oregon 1999: unpublished testimony)

It is naive to think that faculties at large will embrace post-tenure review with enthusiasm. However, understanding is growing that public institutions, in particular, are functioning in a consumer/performance/results-oriented environment and that there are some things we must do at least at the ritualistic level if not at the restructuring-reinventing level.

### *Mutual Obligations*

We must challenge ourselves to move beyond this legitimate, if limited, level of response to consider what Tierney (1998) and others propose in advocating for the concept of the "responsive university." Evaluate we must — and we do — but couple evaluation processes with professional development plans tied to institutional goals and plans (Bland and Bergquist 1997). Is it unduly utopian to think that we can aspire to develop more supportive cultures where individuals and institutions mutually obligate? In the words of two members of the Oregon State Board of Higher Education at the December 18, 1998, meeting:

> We're trying to change a perception as opposed to demonstrating that we know how to punish professors. I think that some of our discussion centers not so much around the process of review, but the desire of everybody to make sure that we have competence, that we have excellence in development, that people are given the opportunity to respond to deficiencies or actions, and, ultimately, the product we're providing is supported by a review process that allows for that kind of change. The goal is not the review process; the goal is competence and excellence. (Oregon State Board of Higher Education 1998: 604)

### *Tenure Evolution*

The venerable institution of tenure needs to change to keep pace with other changes in 21st-century universities and society. The basic framework remains, but we should ask: How does it serve the evolving purposes of higher education in the new era? New generations of students and faculty? New forms of scholarship and service? New relationships with the external environment? Each of these questions requires a separate study, or a stream of studies, to answer.

Take, for example, the new generation of faculty and what its characteristics portend for the future of the academy, academic work, and tenure systems. The new generation includes more women, more persons of color, more foreign born, and a growing proportion of new hires in professional versus core programs (Finkelstein, Seal, and Schuster 1998). By implication this suggests generational differences that need to be deliberately thought through in the evaluation as well as the socialization of faculty, since there are categorical discontinuities created. Another significantly changing dimension is the shrinking proportion of faculty, full-time or part-time, who are invited into the tenure system because of an organizational determination that more flexibility is needed in personnel arrangements.

The faculty is changing and diversifying and so are its career pathways. Tenure does not seem to dominate and define the career trajectory as much as it has in the past. The framework of tenure must work better — or at least be perceived as working better — or institutions may quietly reduce its scope further in favor of more transient appointments. Post-tenure review needs to function in such a way that mutual loyalties are increased and mutual needs are met. But how it is structured should be customized by each individual institution and its faculty with career development and growth as the preeminent purpose.

## Notes

1. Shirley Clark has served as vice chancellor for academic affairs of the Oregon University System since 1990. Previously, she held faculty and administrative positions at University of Minnesota. Clark's educational background includes B.A. and M.A. degrees in sociology from Bowling Green State University and a Ph.D. in sociology from the Ohio State University in 1961. Clark's academic interests are in the sociology of education and higher education. She has written widely on educational reform issues, professional development, gender issues, and faculty vitality and institutional productivity. (Contact her at Shirley_clark@ous.edu)

2. One institution, Oregon Health Sciences University, became an affiliated institution in 1995 and no longer falls within the board's purview for fiscal, administrative, and personnel purposes.

## References

Birnbaum, R. (January/February 2000). "The Life Cycle of Academic Management Fads." *The Journal of Higher Education* 71(1): 1–16.

Bland, C.J., and W.H. Bergquist. (1997). *The Vitality of Senior Faculty Members: Snow on the Roof, Fire in the Furnace.* ASHE-ERIC Higher Education Reports, no. 7. Washington, DC: The George Washington University, Graduate School of Education and Human Development.

Ewell, P. (November/December 1999). "Imitation as Art: Borrowed Management Techniques in Higher Education." *Change* 31(6): 11–15.

Finkelstein, M.J., R.K. Seal, and J.H. Schuster. (1998). *The New Academic Generation: A Profession in Transformation.* Baltimore: The Johns Hopkins University Press.

Julius, D.J., J.V. Baldridge, and J. Pfeffer. (March/April 1999). "Memo From Machiavelli." *The Journal of Higher Education* 70(2): 113–133.

Licata, Christine. (November/December 1999). "Precepts for Post-Tenure Review." *Trusteeship* 7(6): 8–13.

———. (1999). *The Status of Post-Tenure Review Within State Systems of Higher Education.* Report. Washington, DC: American Association for Higher Education, New Pathways II Project.

Oregon State Board of Higher Education. (December 18, 1998). *Minutes, Meeting #679: 548–640.* Eugene, OR: Oregon State Board of Higher Education.

———. (March 2000). *Oregon Administrative Rules.* Eugene, OR: Oregon State Board of Higher Education.

Oregon State Board of Higher Education Committee on Academic Affairs. (1973). *Tenure in the Oregon State System of Higher Education: Objectives and Proposed Administrative Rules for Governing It.* Eugene, OR: Oregon State Board of Higher Education.

Oregon State Department of Higher Education. (March 1999). *Internal Management Directives.* Eugene, OR: Oregon University System.

Tierney, W.G. (1998). "Tenure Is Dead. Long Live Tenure." In *The Responsive University: Restructuring for High Performance,* edited by W.G. Tierney, pp. 38–61. Baltimore: The Johns Hopkins University Press.

University of Oregon. (April 14, 1999). Unpublished Statement of a Faculty Senator Read to the University Senate. Eugene, OR.

# Post-Tenure Review in Kentucky: A Clash of Cultures

**James L. Applegate and Lois M. Nora** [1]

The most practical advice we can give at the outset to those implementing a post-tenure review system is to not underestimate the depth of change the creation of such a process requires for most campus cultures. Post-tenure review can take many forms. Some demand more change than others. A developmental system requiring all tenured faculty to review their work plans in light of their own and the institutional goals creates the greatest demand for "transformational change": that is, pervasive change over an extended period to intentionally alter institutional assumptions and behaviors. A "triggered" post-tenure review system involving only those faculty who demonstrate performance problems over time demands at best a more "isolated" form of change that deeply affects a limited area of the institution. At the least, triggered systems represent an "adjustment": an adjustment of current procedures that, while revitalizing, does not have deep or far-reaching effects on faculty roles and rewards (Eckel, Hill, and Green 1998).

At the University of Kentucky, our AAHE-assisted effort at transformational change through implementing a comprehensive developmental post-tenure review system failed. Instead, we succeeded in creating a significant, but more isolated, change with a triggered post-tenure review process (see the text of the policy at the end of this chapter). In addition, our work contributed to a state-wide effort producing post-tenure review systems at many institutions. This chapter outlines the changes we attempted and the lessons learned along the way.

## Underlying Assumptions That Inhibit Change

Certain assumptions in existing faculty roles and rewards systems inhibit implementing a developmental, inclusive post-tenure review system. Faculty autonomy in defining their work is a deeply held value. Faculty research and teaching activities are largely self-determined. Evaluation processes focus on doing things right; i.e., the quantity and quality of work produced. They seldom consider whether the right things are being done.

A second assumption is that whatever faculty do will be evaluated in a reactive way. Faculty work is evaluated over a specified period of time using traditional criteria that seldom change. These traditional criteria are often inconsistent with evolving institutional goals. For example, we may rely on student evaluations of teaching when our aim is to motivate faculty to develop new teaching strategies to reach a more diverse student body. We count publications when we want to promote research that seeks truth and innovation. The next evaluation period begins without clear expectations for what specific activities or areas of improvement will be pursued beyond the vague notion that faculty will engage in some forms of research, teaching, and service. Whatever that work turns out to be will again be evaluated using the same criteria retrospectively. These are what Schein (1992) calls underlying assumptions at the inner core of our institutions.

A comprehensive post-tenure review system focused properly on faculty development demands that campuses rethink these assumptions. It requires a proactive evaluation system focused on setting goals and planning as the basis for evaluation. It also requires the integration of the goals of individual faculty members with program, institutional, and even state-wide goals for higher education as the basis for the direction and evaluation of faculty work.

Many faculty are only vaguely aware of program and institutional goals. Strategic planning, creating engaged campuses, becoming a learning organization, and similar topics occur at administrative levels without the full involvement of faculty. Faculty then become concerned when these "administrative" agendas they had no part in creating are now part of evaluations of their work. Any post-tenure review effort must conceptually challenge these underlying assumptions about the definition and evaluation of faculty work if it is to succeed.

## Eleven Lessons Learned

What follows outlines some of our lessons learned in practical terms. Our observations may require translation depending on the nature of the institution and its culture(s). The University of Kentucky is a research institution with a land-grant mission. It includes a large medical campus and a community college. During post-tenure review development, the university was taking aggressive steps to improve its research reputation in traditional terms. In addition, the entire Kentucky higher education system was receiving new funds linked to initiatives designed to better serve the state's economy. The post-tenure review effort followed a campus-wide initiative revising the promotion and tenure system to reward multiple forms of scholarship. A pilot triggered post-tenure review system had been in place in our largest college for several years when we started this process. The dean at that time had introduced that pilot. It sparked vigorous debate. The program itself was due for review as we began our process. Few, if any, faculty had undergone review under the pilot program. Anecdotal evidence suggested the pilot had motivated some faculty retirements. We hoped to institute a developmental system for all faculty with much greater impact. Unfortunately, the pilot created the expectation that the campus-wide effort would replicate the pilot.

### *Lesson 1: Post-Tenure Review Efforts Should Be Faculty Led*

As in some other states, the post-tenure review effort in Kentucky began with legislators questioning tenure. While no legislative mandate was created, institutions were asked to report on progress in developing post-tenure review systems. At our institution — as at many others in our state — faculty leadership responded, convinced that an institutionally derived policy was preferable to legislative fiat. The University of Kentucky Senate, comprising faculty, students, and select administrators, applied for the AAHE post-tenure review grant and led the effort on campus. In addition, a council of senate faculty leaders from across the state worked to coordinate work at other public colleges in the state. We believed a faculty-driven process gave the best chance to secure faculty support and ownership of the resulting policy.

On the other hand, it is vital to keep campus administration informed. Key administrators were involved at every post-tenure review campus event. They reviewed drafts of the policy during its development. When we brought external consultants to campus [see lesson six] they met with the president, his cabinet, deans, and chairs to put our effort in a national context and describe best practices. If you do not involve key administrators throughout the process you risk committing enormous energy to gain faculty buy-in to a policy that could founder on administrative concerns. Our governing board was purposefully not engaged in the process until the policy had campus-wide support. Of course, on campuses where the governing board initiates the post-tenure review effort, more board involvement will occur.

**_Lesson 2: Have the Proper Leadership Team in Place_**

Policy development and strategic implementation are critically dependent on the quality of the leadership team. The leaders should be selected from among those who will be affected by the policy, and should reflect the diversity of faculty on the campus. Our leadership group had representatives from our medical campus and community college, two different cultures. The leadership team also comprised representatives from our largest college (the College of Arts and Sciences), our American Association of University Professors (AAUP) chapter, and the present and incoming leaders of our university senate. Without this breadth of perspective we would have failed to create a policy workable across the campus. Not one of us fully understood the complex ways any policy would need to be adapted across sectors. None of us could have anticipated and addressed the variety of faculty and administrative concerns that arose.

At the same time, we worked to keep the leadership group at eight to 10 individuals, the optimum size for team functioning. We would not recommend a large body to lead the effort; instead, involve other campus groups as you progress. A group of 25 "leaders" attending meetings irregularly to engage in substantive discussions is a recipe for inaction.

**_Lesson 3: Separate Post-Tenure Review From Loss of Tenure_**

Post-tenure review is about proactively setting goals as the basis for evaluation, faculty development, and overall effectiveness. Most campuses have procedures in place for removing tenured faculty for incompetence, failure to perform duties, or unethical behavior. Make clear from the outset that post-tenure review and existing termination procedures are different things. If post-tenure review fails, then in-place termination procedures — with all their appeals and safeguards — may be required. However, post-tenure review aims to improve the performance of productive faculty and prevent the failure of nonproductive faculty. An institution that properly defines post-tenure review embraces the principle that people are its most important asset and puts resources into developing those people.

### *Lesson 4: Focus on Post-Tenure Review as a Method of Preserving Tenure and Drawing Support for Faculty Development*

While post-tenure review processes and existing termination policies must be clearly differentiated, post-tenure review is an attempt to infuse greater accountability into the tenure system. It provides an answer to critics who see tenure as lifetime job security even in the face of incompetence. Post-tenure review also allows for significant change in the types of work that tenured faculty do over a career, including nonvoluntary changes (e.g., requiring an ineffective teacher to focus his or her work on outreach or research).

For these reasons, the idea of post-tenure review did not sit well with some traditional tenure advocates. Most faculty realized that without these modifications, the real reason for tenure — the guarantee of academic freedom — is obscured and tenure itself could be lost. The leadership team shared materials to support this argument during post-tenure review meetings, as well as posting them on the university senate post-tenure review web page.

From the outset the leadership team realized that post-tenure review could be a potent mechanism to increase support for faculty development within our existing faculty roles and rewards system. In a policy addendum, estimates were included of the costs to train faculty, chairs, and deans to implement the system and to support: (1) successful faculty whose review suggested additional support would advance or refocus their work in productive ways, and (2) faculty experiencing difficulties so that improvement plans could be implemented. Making faculty development the centerpiece of your post-tenure review policy is both correct and politically wise. Faculty development requires a concrete, dollar-centered discussion between campus administrators and faculty to clarify the focus of post-tenure review and the required level of financial commitment. In

Kentucky, post-tenure review was a state-wide undertaking, leading to the creation of a $1-million faculty development fund provided from the state government for all public institutions of higher education. Too often post-tenure review policies focus on "sticks" as motivators (e.g., loss of tenure, forced job redefinition). Increased support for faculty development identifies "carrots" relevant for the majority of faculty members.

### *Lesson 5: Engage the Entire Campus Community*

We recommend organizing campus-wide symposia, discipline-based meetings, web sites, and other activities to engage the entire campus community in post-tenure review discussions. We held campus-wide symposia, sponsored meetings (with food and drink) in each college, organized special events for chairs and deans, and regularly reported to the university senate and the president's cabinet. We created a web site of resource materials, such as examples of post-tenure review policies at peer institutions, and held online debates of various issues as they arose throughout the process. This helped us understand concerns, engage new administrative and faculty leaders as they came on board, and created a sense of ownership by those who ultimately approved and implemented the policy.

### *Lesson 6: Use Outside Expertise*

In retrospect, one of the smartest things we did was involve experts from outside the institution in our process. At our campus-wide symposium representatives from other research universities, other community colleges, and staff members from the Association of American Medical Colleges and AAHE's post-tenure review project shared experiences and facts about post-tenure review. Faculty from sister institutions in Kentucky developing post-tenure review policies also were involved. This helped our faculty and administrators see post-tenure review as part of a national agenda for change in higher education. It reassured our campus that we were not out on a limb responding to idiosyncratic pressures from selected legislators.

In addition to the symposium, we made sure each of our experts had separate, focused meetings with the pertinent constituencies. Each expert was held in high regard by that constituent group. The consultants took the time to carefully listen to and answer many questions and concerns raised in these small groups. And since we convened them early in the policy development process, we were able to refer to their ideas to defuse objections as similar concerns continued to reemerge with various groups. The AAHE post-tenure review grant itself lent additional credibility to our work — a contribution as valuable as the dollar support it provided.

***Lesson 7: Create a Flexible Policy***

Though you may not have a medical center, community college, and research campus to encompass with your policy, you will need to create a flexible policy that can be adapted to the variety of faculty evaluation systems and value structures that characterize different parts of your campus. A one-size-fits-all policy will not work. Our most dramatic example was the medical campus.

Like a number of other universities, the University of Kentucky includes an academic health center, the Chandler Medical Center. Despite geographic proximity (the medical center and main campus abut each other), the cultures of the two campuses are not the same. These cultural differences stem from the unique clinical service (patient care) mission of the academic health center, and affect perceptions about tenure and faculty evaluation. These differences had the potential to create distrust and undermine our policy development process.

For example, there is general agreement across our university that tenure is intended to protect academic freedom and not intended to guarantee a salary or job in the absence of productivity. But most faculty associate a tenured position with a certain job and a specific salary. However, this is not true of clinical faculty members in our College of Medicine. These faculty members — many physicians — typically have only a small portion of their salary linked to the status of tenure. The majority of the salary is negotiated annually with the faculty member's chair and is based on such factors as research, education, and patient care. These salary practices have developed for a number of reasons and are critical to the successful functioning of the medical campus. Tenure remains highly coveted among medical faculty, but not for financial reasons.

Another significant difference is the nature of work assignments. The critical nature of patient care contributes to different expectations regarding assignments and evaluations in clinical departments. Because clinical care obligations must be met as an overarching priority of the clinical faculty, assignments are more susceptible to change and the role of the chair in directing faculty work is significant. Faculty members are evaluated frequently and mission-sensitive productivity measurements are used. Salaries may be adjusted accordingly. Evaluating faculty based on program goals is well accepted in the medical campus culture, unlike on traditional research or teaching campuses.

As a result of these differences, the post-tenure review policy development committee had two groups of faculty and administrators with dramatically different perceptions of the meaning of tenure and the role of ongoing evaluation in determining salary. The policy development process had the potential to be inhibited by these differences, particularly if clinical medical faculty focused on the "salary security" of other tenured faculty in the university, or if that group of tenured faculty focused on "salary size" of the clinical medical faculty. At the same time, the project provided a mechanism to enhance understanding across the two groups of faculty.

Involvement of the diverse groups of faculty lengthened the development of post-tenure review policy. However, the benefits of using an inclusive process outweighed the difficulties created. The issue brought diverse constituent groups together and increased cross-cultural understanding.

The process helped ensure that the final policy incorporated concerns of all critical constituent groups. For example, the final policy triggers post-tenure review of a faculty member after two consecutive negative performance reviews without identifying a set time in which those reviews would take place. This language allowed most colleges to maintain their biennial review of tenured faculty members (the maximum amount of time allowed between reviews according to university administrative regulations) but also allowed the College of Medicine to maintain its mandatory annual review of all faculty members.

#### *Lesson 8: Piggyback on Current Evaluation Systems*

Faculty on most campuses already feel enough time is spent on evaluation. Post-tenure review evaluations are seen as "one more evaluation to do." This was a concern of some faculty and administrators from the beginning of the process. The post-tenure review committee worked to integrate post-tenure review evaluations as seamlessly as possible within the current evaluation system.

Thus we proposed that information on faculty goals and future plans be incorporated into mandatory retrospective reports on work to date. University regulations already require peer involvement in those reviews, so the same peer process (with department chair involvement) was used for the post-tenure review component. The three-person peer committee-would first meet to approve the faculty member's plan to address the post-tenure review, and subsequently to verify its completion, or at worst three years later to mark its failure (see the policy). The AAUP was especially sensitive to the need to put peer evaluation at the center of the evaluation process to minimize the chance for abuses of academic freedom. We were careful to link our work with current AAUP positions on post-tenure review. We staggered post-tenure review evaluations so only one third of the tenured faculty are involved in any one evaluation cycle.

Several visiting colleagues from peer institutions were asked to address the burdens imposed by a post-tenure review system. They spoke about their initial concerns, but ultimately realized the process was workable. They also described how post-tenure reviews contributed to greater faculty awareness of colleagues' work and improved team building within departments.

Despite these efforts to minimize administrative burden, the objection to post-tenure review as one more evaluation remained an obstacle to acceptance. Many faculty saw no reason for the proactive component, especially if they were receiving good retrospective evaluations of their work. Some university faculty were uncomfortable with aligning individual faculty research and teaching goals with program and institutional goals. They sensed a potential loss of autonomy and were concerned about infringement on academic freedom. For the medical center and the community college faculties, goal integration was acceptable.

We discovered that despite existing rules requiring the use of peers in evaluation, the system in practice had minimal peer involvement. So the creation of peer evaluation teams with meaningful responsibilities for helping faculty develop and assess plans was, in fact, a "new" element. Ultimately, faculty were only comfortable with a proactive, peer-driven, planning process for the small minority of faculty whose merit evaluations demonstrated significant performance problems over two successive evaluation periods. The majority never saw the benefit of such a process for all tenured faculty. A broad system remained, in their eyes, too great an administrative burden. This concern proved fatal to implementing a broad-based post-tenure review program.

We wondered whether the "one more evaluation" argument was a cover for other, less articulated concerns. As others have noted, post-tenure review raises the stakes in the faculty evaluation process. Since current evaluation systems are tied to minimal differences in salary increases, they are tolerated even if they are perceived as flawed, irregular, and vague. If tenure is perceived as at stake, things change. Flaws in the system seem more threatening. We still recommend minimizing administrative burden by integrating post-tenure review into current evaluation processes. Realize that in doing so you inherit whatever problems are inherent in that system. The result may be a post-tenure review policy development process catalyzing reform of the entire campus faculty evaluation system.

#### *Lesson 9: Build in Staff Training and Program Assessment From the Outset*

The complaint that faculty and faculty who become administrators are ill-prepared for management roles is well known. Constructive, rigorous evaluation of any employee — especially faculty peers — is difficult. Campuses with effective programs in place to help faculty, chairs, and deans develop these skills are the exception. Building staff training for post-tenure review will address broader needs on your campus. Just as post-tenure review can highlight problems in the faculty evaluation process, it also raises the level of concern about peers' and administrators' evaluation ability. This concern is legitimate, and regular training for the changing cast of people involved in post-tenure review evaluations should be carefully designed and funded from the outset.

As post-tenure review becomes an issue for increasing numbers of campuses, the demand for data on its outcomes also increases. We found ourselves constantly confronted with questions about the impact of post-tenure review on other campuses as we advocated implementation. At that time the evidence for post-tenure review's impact was scarce. Thanks to AAHE, that situation is improving. Still, to contribute to national efforts and to improve your own policy over time, workable, targeted assessment plans need to be in place from the outset linked to the goals of your particular policy. This is not an easy task.

If the goal of your policy is truly faculty development and improved performance, then counting the number of terminations or retirements attributable to post-tenure review is not appropriate. Still, some will want that data. Process data are also valuable: the number of faculty undergoing review and the resulting performance improvement should be reported. We also required regular brief reports from department chairs on the effects of post-tenure review. We hope these reports would capture the more intangible effects of post-tenure review (such as increased awareness of colleagues' work, collaboration, and team building).

In the original draft of the policy we included addenda with procedures for implementation including (1) training of peers and administrators, and (2) regular assessment of the effectiveness of the policy. We planned to use a part of the AAHE grant we received to do the initial training and built evaluation in as a regular part of institutional research activities.

***Lesson 10: Take Trust Seriously***

A substantive change in the faculty evaluation system demands a certain level of trust among all parties. Without trust, worst-case scenarios of potential abuses of the system take on added credibility. Trying to create a system that precludes hypothetical abuses by hypothetical administrators with the worst of intentions is impossible. Minus a reasonable level of trust, any form of transformational change can feel like jumping into the abyss. Several incidents, unrelated to post-tenure review, placed administration and faculty at odds during the time we were developing the policy. This contributed to faculty reticence to make significant changes in the way they were evaluated by administrators. Assess the trust level on your campus at the outset. Develop strategies to take into account the changing nature of the relationship between administrators and faculty.

***Lesson 11: Build Continuity Into the Process***

Recognize that the road from development to approval to implementation is a long one. Faculty and administrative leadership will change. Put people on your leadership team who provide stability over time and make sure new leadership is brought into the process along the way. We succeeded in sustaining commitment over the several years it took to enact the policy. In the final stages, however, some of the key proponents of post-tenure review had left leadership positions. Some of the plans for training of faculty and administration to do post-tenure review never materialized. How this will affect the quality of post-tenure review reviews is unclear at this time.

## Conclusions

Our preferred post-tenure review policy called for a basic change in faculty evaluation from a retrospective, individualistic system to one that was proactive and focused on the integration of individual and program/institutional goals. We could not accomplish that transformational change, though we made steps in that direction. We could not overcome resistance to the perceived burden of additional evaluation processes.

In the final analysis, however, we were able to implement a sound triggered post-tenure review policy across a diverse set of academic cultures. We did so with strong faculty support: The vote for approval in the university senate was almost unanimous. Our work helped stimulate and form post-tenure review policies now in place at almost every other public university in the state. Legislators seem satisfied. We hope post-tenure review, following a substantial revision of the promotion and tenure system, was another step in a transformational change in the way faculty and administrators define, evaluate, and reward faculty work. The environment of higher education is changing. Faculty deserve credit for varied forms of scholarship. Faculty productivity needs to be better linked to institutional goals — and the public good. State governments and administrators must invest resources to support development of faculty across their careers. Faculty, like those they teach, must be lifelong learners. Properly done, post-tenure review can help faculty and institutions meet these challenges.

## Note

1. James L. Applegate is vice president for academic affairs for the Kentucky Council on Postsecondary Education and a past president of the National Communication Association. Previously and during the initial phases of the post-tenure review process in Kentucky, he was chair of the University Senate Council and a department chair at the University of Kentucky. Applegate received a B.A. from Georgetown College (Kentucky) and an M.A. and Ph.D. from the University of Illinois-Urbana/Champaign. His research interests include individual and cultural influences on the development of people's communication ability and factors affecting change in higher education. (Contact him at jim.applegate@mail.state.ky.us)

2. Lois Margaret Nora is professor of neurology and associate dean for academic affairs and administration at the University of Kentucky College of Medicine. Nora received her M.D. degree from Rush Medical College in Chicago and her J.D. from the University of Chicago. She completed her postgraduate training in neurology and electrodiagnostic medicine at Rush-Presbyterian-St. Luke's Medical Center and her fellowship in clinical ethics at the MacLean Center at the University of Chicago. Her research interests include the interface of medicine and law, and the impact of environment on faculty and student productivity and success. (Contact her at Lmnora1@pop.uky.edu)

## References

Eckel, P., B. Hill, and M. Green. (1998). *On Change: En Route to Transformational Change.* Washington, DC: American Council on Education.

Schein, E.H. (1992). *Organizational Culture and Leadership.* 2nd ed. San Francisco: Jossey-Bass.

| UNIVERSITY OF KENTUCKY ADMINISTRATIVE REGULATIONS | IDENTIFICATION AR II-1.0-11 | | PAGE 1 |
|---|---|---|---|
| | DATE EFFECTIVE 12/16/00 | SUPERSEDES REGULATION DATED | |

**TENURED FACULTY REVIEW AND DEVELOPMENT POLICY**

This policy is designed to provide definitive guidance to units in supporting tenured faculty to increase their productivity and to identify and address problems in performance.

**This policy builds on the current system for conducting regular performance or "merit" reviews, as defined in AR II-1.0-5, of tenured faculty for purposes of salary increases. It requires the following:**

A Consequential Review process must be instituted for any faculty member receiving successive unsatisfactory performance or "merit" reviews in a "significant area of work". For the purposes of this policy, a significant area of work is defined as a Distribution of Effort Agreement greater than 20% in the areas of instruction, research or service. The review is summative in nature and requires a plan to improve performance within a specified period.

Upon recommendation of the department chairperson and approval of the dean, a faculty member subject to evaluation under this plan may be exempted if there are extenuating circumstances (such as health problems). A decision by the chairperson not to recommend such exemption may be appealed to the Dean. A Consequential Review will not be undertaken until the final disposition of any appeal.

The Dean shall notify the faculty member and department chairperson of the initiation of a Consequential Review process and of the procedures of the review.

For a faculty member selected for Consequential Review, the department chairperson shall prepare a review dossier in consultation with the faculty member. The faculty member has the right and obligation to provide for the review dossier all the documents, materials, and statements he or she believes to be relevant and necessary for the review, and all materials submitted shall be included in the dossier. Ordinarily, such a dossier would include at least the following: an up-to-date vita, a teaching portfolio, and a statement on current research or creative work. The chairperson shall add to the dossier any further materials (prior evaluations, other documents, etc.) he or she deems relevant, in every case providing the faculty member with a copy of each item added. The faculty member shall have the right to add any material, including statements and additional documents, at any time during the review process.

The Consequential Review will be conducted by the department chairperson, or at the request of the faculty member by a three-member ad hoc committee consisting of tenured faculty members including one member selected by the Dean, one member chosen by the faculty member, one member selected by the college faculty.

It is not the purpose of the Consequential Review to evaluate the performance of the faculty member but rather to develop a plan to remedy the deficiencies indicated in the performance reviews. It is the responsibility of the department chairperson to recommend the plan that has been developed to the Dean for approval and to monitor the implementation of the plan approved by the Dean. Ideally, the plan should grow out of an iterative collaboration among the faculty member, department chairperson and Dean. The review should be completed within 60 days of notification of the initiation of the review.

It is the faculty member's obligation to assist in the development of a meaningful and effective plan and to make a good faith effort to implement the plan once it is adopted. In the event that the faculty member objects to the terms of the plan, the faculty member may appeal to the appropriate Chancellor. Once the appeal has been resolved, the resulting plan will be implemented.

The plan must:

1) Identify the specific deficiencies to be addressed
2) Define specific goals or outcomes that are needed to remedy the deficiencies
3) Outline the activities that are to be undertaken to achieve the needed outcomes
4) Set timelines for accomplishing the activities and achieving the outcomes
5) Indicate the criteria for annual progress reviews
6) Identify the level and source of any funding which may be required to implement the development plan.

The faculty member and his or her department chairperson should meet each semester to review the faculty member's progress towards remedying the deficiencies. A progress report will be forwarded to the Dean.

Further evaluation of the faculty member within the regular faculty performance evaluation processes of the University may draw upon the faculty member's progress in achieving the goals set out in the plan.

When the objectives of the plan have been met, or in any case no later than three years after the start of the plan, a final report will be prepared by the department chairperson and given to the faculty member. The faculty member will be provided an opportunity to comment on the report if he or she wishes. The faculty member's input will become part of the report submitted to the Dean. If the chairperson states that the objectives of the plan have not been fully met and the faculty member disagrees, the three-member ad hoc committee of tenured faculty members involved in the development of the plan shall be reconvened. If a person who was part of that three-member ad hoc committee is no longer available to serve, his or her successor shall be chosen in the same manner as the original person was chosen. The three-member ad hoc committee will then meet and prepare a report for the Dean. Both the chairperson's report and the report of the three-member ad hoc committee shall be forwarded to the dean, together with any written comments that the faculty member wishes to add, for the dean's final decision.

In those cases where serious deficiencies continue to exist after the Consequential Review plans are completed, dismissal for cause procedures may be initiated.

Each academic unit may create a process for a Developmental Review of tenured faculty, consistent with criteria in AR II-1.0-1, that includes setting individual faculty goals in collaboration with unit chairpersons, deans, and senior faculty colleagues. These reviews should be incorporated into the current performance review process for tenured faculty to minimize administrative burden.

Each chancellor and dean shall develop a process for allocating additional funds as appropriate to provide necessary support for faculty members undertaking a Consequential or Developmental Review.

Each dean shall prepare annually a summary report on cases resulting from the implementation of the Tenured Faculty Review and Development Policy in that college and transmit the report to the chancellor.

AR II-1.0-11.doc

# Tracking Evolving Meanings: Five Years of Post-Tenure Review in Arizona [1]

**S. Vianne McLean and Thomas Callarman** [2]

## The Gauntlet Is Thrown

In a neater, tidier world, we could state exactly what problems a policy change was designed to address. And after implementation, we could objectively determine the success of the new policy in resolving those problems. But this is not a neat and tidy world, and in the case of the Arizona University System and its post-tenure review policy, it has been difficult to reach consensus on both the definition of the problem and the effectiveness of the solution.

To comprehend the Arizona experience of post-tenure review, it is essential to understand something of this context. Within the universities in the 1990s, change had been proceeding at its usual measured pace. Potential modifications to personnel policies were being debated, some pockets of innovative practice in workload allocation policies were developing, and faculty evaluation processes — including mandatory annual reviews and merit pay determinations — were stable, if disparate in terms of rigor. University administrators had only occasional concerns with poorly performing faculty members, and these were seen as part of life in the academy. Serious sanctions such as suspension or dismissal were almost never invoked as responses to these performance problems.

In mid 1995, this stability was disrupted when the Arizona Board of Regents, concerned about the performance levels of faculty members, inserted itself in the development of personnel evaluation and management policy. The two pillars of these universities' personnel systems — the time-honored principle of tenure as a fundamental protection of academic freedom, and the principle of self-governance by university faculty — were identified by the regents as key components of "the problem," as they threw down the gauntlet and decreed that neither of these principles could be guaranteed into the future.

The regents' decision was immediate and far-reaching. For those faculty leaders and administrators present at that meeting, the realization that tenure might be abolished in Arizona was chilling. For those not present, the event had different meanings. Was it an example of the unwelcome intrusion of political appointees into the universities' business? Was it a call to arms for the faculties — the catalyst that sent university communities with little history of workplace agitation into industrial turmoil? The faculty leaders and senior administrators of the three Arizona universities took some time to make sense of this event. The groups met at length and crafted a shared set of interpretations.

Although the loss of tenure would be disastrous for the universities, we decided the time for confrontation had not yet arrived. While the risk to tenure was communicated to members of the faculties — through national and local media, as well as the academic senates — the parties decided to consider several options.

For months, the fate of tenure stayed unresolved. In January 1996, a respected consultant led a regents study session in which regents expressed the specific problems with which they were concerned and explored options for addressing those problems. The most important outcome from this discussion was their acceptance that post-tenure review could be a way to address their concerns; thus, the abolition of tenure could be avoided.

The feasibility of crafting a post-tenure review policy acceptable to both the regents and the universities remained to be seen. Would the outcomes of this policy address the problems the regents raised? Despite these misgivings, the regents allowed the universities and their faculty governance systems to draft a policy, while retaining the right of veto if the policy did not meet the regents' requirements.

For nearly one year the faculty leaders and administrators, in conjunction with Arizona Board of Regents staff, argued through many different policy options. Faculty leaders and administrators consulted with regents individually and collectively on many occasions. Several insights emerged from this experience in terms of personnel policy development and some valuable lessons were learned about implementation.

## Key Insights From the Policy Development Phase

### *Administrative Leadership Matters*

The senior administration of the universities provided excellent leadership during this process. They enabled faculty governance and their elected leaders to "do the heavy lifting" on policy development, and they ensured that communication across the "great divide" of administration and faculty governance was frequent, open-minded, and characterized by a high level of trust. They spoke publicly and enthusiastically about the leadership being provided by the faculty's leaders, and expressed their support for the emergent policy positions, both individually to regents and in response to formal reports made to regents meetings. Thus it was possible to present a unified position to the regents on every dimension of the policy.

### *Grassroots Faculty Involvement Matters*

As faculty leaders, we used every means to involve members of the faculty. A key part of these early meetings was developing consensus on a set of principles underlying any post-tenure review policy. These principles helped assess a range of policy dimensions, which often conflicted. Email updates and newsletters were used on several campuses to keep faculty informed, and many debates occurred at the senates or in subcommittees.

### *Regents' Engagement Matters*

Faculty leaders also engaged regents on a personal level. We visited their offices and homes to better understand their perspectives. Even after the January 1996 workshop, it remained unclear which specific problems the individual regents were hoping post-tenure review would address. Through conversations one-on-one or in small groups, gradually we compiled a list of these concerns, and were subsequently able to address them all, either through post-tenure review itself or through other policies. The unintended consequence of this process was that faculty leaders and regents came to know each other well, and a new era of mutual respect and increased trust was established. We came to realize that the success of this policy development phase was due to the personal relationships as much as to the emergent policy.

In February 1997, the Arizona University System had a post-tenure review policy ready for implementation in all three universities. It is a complex policy, with many dimensions, but (1) it satisfied the principles established by the faculties; (2) it was seen as a useful contribution to academic personnel management by the administrators of the universities; and (3) it was deemed acceptable by the regents. The regents reserved judgment on whether it would address all of their concerns with faculty performance, and they required a comprehensive annual report.

## What Did the Solution Look Like?

### *Combined Triggered and Periodic Approach*

Using the typology developed by Licata and Morreale (1997), the Arizona post-tenure review policy can best be described as a combination triggered and periodic approach. An unsatisfactory performance rating either in one element of work or in overall work performance in an annual review (based on 36 months of performance data) can *trigger* a required improvement plan. If the unsatisfactory performance is limited to one area of work, this is called a *faculty development plan* and generally the faculty member has one year to address that area of performance. A more serious *performance improvement plan* is invoked either when a faculty member is found to be performing at a generally unsatisfactory level across all dimensions of work, or when a faculty development plan has failed to lift performance in the prescribed area to a satisfactory level. The duration of this more serious plan can be up to three years. If performance is not lifted to a satisfactory level by then, a case can be made for dismissal on the grounds of chronic poor performance.

### *Dean-Level Audit*

Once every five years, a faculty member's performance data are considered in a dean-level audit process. This periodic review serves several purposes. From the faculty leaders' and administrators' perspectives, this review was an audit of the annual review process. The policy allowed several meanings for this review to coexist — a check on the fairness and accuracy of the judgments made by the peer reviewers and department chairs who conduct the annual reviews. From the regents' perspective, this was a way to involve senior managers in the evaluation process and to provide a second, higher level of performance review.

***Link to Academic Program Review***

The final component of the process involves a link between academic program review and post-tenure review. From the beginning, some regents were adamant that reviews of faculty performance must include reviewers external to the university. Under the pre-existing guidelines for *academic* program review, the external review team was required to consider the contributions of individual academic staff to the program area(s) under review. With the advent of post-tenure review, the program review team (most of whom are external to the university) are required to include in their report any concerns they have with a faculty member's individual contributions. A faculty member thus identified then would be re-evaluated by the regular peer reviewers used in the annual review process. This link was always an uneasy one for faculty, but it was seen as the most palatable of the small range of options available.

While the policy was more complex than generally believed to be desirable, the regents, administrators, and faculty leaders were confident it could provide a useful tool for administrators to resolve those few chronic performance problems. The policy left the major responsibility for performance review with peers and/or department chairs while ensuring a greater degree of rigor in annual reviews. It reflected a flexible workload allocation stance based on negotiation between department chairs and faculty members, and allowed individual faculty members to place emphasis on different components of the total workload at various times in their careers. It was seen to be reasonably efficient in that it was based on a preexisting mandatory annual review process, so well-performing faculty would see little change with the arrival of post-tenure review. For those few with chronic poor performance, the level of scrutiny would be increased and serious consequences would flow, but for the most part academic staff were not opposed to the "teeth" in this policy. Most believed there were adequate protections against administrative capriciousness in this and other university policies.

## Implementation Challenges

### *Local Control*

The Arizona universities implemented the post-tenure review policy, each in its own way. Further, the policy itself provided many opportunities for local control, so there were additional layers of meanings ascribed at the campus, college, and department levels.

Across the universities, the nature and rate of this implementation process differed greatly, linked only by the regents' requirement for annual reporting of outcomes. On some of the university campuses, campus-level post-tenure review policy statements were adopted; on others, procedural guidelines rather than policies were adopted. At the University of Arizona, the central administration took a high profile by allocating a substantial amount of money to the implementation process for creating a database to track performance data and to support resulting faculty development programs. The administration also started a newsletter to provide updates on the process.

### *Bridging Implementation*

As Arizona State University (ASU) faculty members, we are most familiar with the implementation processes on the Main and West campuses of ASU. From this experience we came to understand one of the dilemmas of faculty-led policy development and implementation. Involving elected faculty leaders in heavy-duty policy development carries many benefits, but there remains a chasm between policy development and policy implementation. Elected faculty leaders' terms typically expire long before the equally demanding work of policy implementation is complete. The rich multilayered and often contradictory meanings of the policy are not immediately evident. They only emerge over time as the policy is lived and renegotiated by the stakeholders. Implementation of a complex policy such as post-tenure review takes years to accomplish fully, and throughout it needs administration champions and a faculty governance system characterized by a strong sense of continuity.

At ASU West, this gap was bridged for one year when the former leader of the faculty senate during the post-tenure review development phase moved to an administrative position that carried responsibility for leading the early implementation process. By mid 1998, this continuity ended. As former senate presidents at Main and West campuses, respectively, we ourselves remained involved in post-tenure review only as researchers and, to a lesser extent, as keepers of the institutional memory. We both continued to monitor the quantitative outcomes reported annually to the Arizona Board of Regents, and began gathering extensive data using text analysis of local-level policy and procedures documents, interviews with faculty and administrators, an email survey of department chairs, and a survey of faculty perspectives. From these data emerged a picture as complex as the policy itself.

## Document Analysis

Our first step in this research was to examine the local-level policies and procedures documents produced to comply with post-tenure review. Some were extensively detailed; others were only a few lines long. One of the first lessons learned from analysis of these documents was the downside of local control. As senators, we had fought to maximize the metaphoric "empty spaces" in the policy, so that local groups could customize it to fit their needs. But these spaces were not always filled in the ways we had anticipated. For example, a few departments had managed to purge any intention of flexible workloads, and had instead inserted a narrow numeric formula for determining levels of workload productivity. Rather than supporting flexible and holistic perspectives on faculty work, as we had intended, they had used the policy to reinforce a narrow slice of academic work. Several local groups had chosen to eliminate peer review, giving away this important principle in favor of performance reviews conducted solely by the department chair. While the majority of departments and colleges had taken more encouraging directions, it was clear that local control does not guarantee wise decisions. In hindsight, it would have been better to hold out for mandated peer review than to rely on local collective commitment to make it happen.

- *Lesson Learned: Local control does not guarantee wise decisions.*
- *Lesson Learned: Peer review is worth mandating.*

Another interesting dimension of these local-level policies occurred in creating benchmarks for performance. Some units struggled with the complexities of creating fair benchmarks in a world of differentiated workloads, and made real progress.

Others sought an easier path, and relied on numeric averaging of scores across each of three 12-month periods of performance data, rather than trying for a more holistic picture of performance over a 36-month period. Similarly, these units seemed to diminish the importance of the self-review, which we had hoped would provide the opportunity both for a long-term prospective view of one's career directions as well as for a short-term review of progress made in the last year.

- *Lesson Learned: Performance benchmarks are difficult to establish.*
- *Lesson Learned: Retrospective and prospective reflections of careers are important.*

There were some creative approaches to writing benchmarks in the procedures drafts submitted for approval. One could not help but conclude that in one or two departments, if a faculty member was warm and breathing, that was sufficient to warrant a judgment of satisfactory performance. When confronted with the dubiousness of their proposed benchmarks, some faculty members had the grace to look a little sheepish, as if they thought it at least had been worth "having a go" at subverting the process.

- *Lesson Learned: Benchmarks for satisfactory performance need to be "real."*

A personal insight gained by one of us during the first year of implementation was the sheer time and diplomatic skill needed to go to local-level groups and attempt to renegotiate those initial proposals for implementing post-tenure review. Those policy "empty spaces," which had looked so valuable through the eyes of an elected faculty leader, looked different when seen as an administrator responsible for making sure this policy worked.

- *Lesson Learned: Implementation uncovers policy gaps.*

## Chair Perspectives

When further data were gathered from department chairs in 2000, the policy had been in place for three years and a new range of insights were gleaned. It was clear that further differentiation of the policy had occurred during this time and a new set of local meanings had grown around it. Some five years after the faculty leaders' group had commenced work on developing the policy, institutional memory of that process had faded. In those difficult and wonderful days when agreements were finally reached through painstaking negotiation involving both university faculty and regents, we might well have concluded "We did it!" Now that feeling had been replaced — at least in some corners of the university — with "They did it to us!" Arizona would not have a post-tenure review policy today if it had not been for the activism of those regents in 1995, but the nature and specifics of the policy are a product of a faculty work group. This piece of history appears to be eroding in institutional memory.

One of the most unexpected local variations on the policy is a new balance between triggered and periodic review. In several colleges of ASU, the decision was made to select performance portfolios for the dean-level audit collectively by department and not individually. This simple decision has had a profound effect on the emergent meanings of post-tenure review. In these colleges, the annual review appears to have changed little as a result of post-tenure review, and has maintained a low profile. What is seen as important is the "dean's review of the department" that now occurs every five years. What is fascinating from the departmental chair data is the way in which the language has shifted to reflect this local reality. Typically, these department chairs now refer to the dean-level audit as "post-tenure review," and to the annual review as something else entirely — a means of allocating merit pay, when available.

These divergent meanings of post-tenure review have revealed that a complex and ill-defined set of problems have yielded a complex and multifaceted set of practices hoping to provide a solution.

- *Lesson Learned: Local implementation leads to divergent interpretations.*

## Results: How Successful Has the Policy Been?

So, how successful has the policy been thus far? For the reasons outlined above, it is difficult to say. The annual data from the Arizona Board of Regents shows that almost all tenured faculty members in Arizona universities (approximately 2,700 people) are now undergoing post-tenure review on a regular basis.

In the annual report to the board in January 1999, there were 36 unsatisfactory ratings in one area of performance, though these faculty were still performing at an overall satisfactory level. Within one year, seven of this group had left the university system, one person successfully appealed the rating, and the remaining 28 people successfully completed a faculty development plan. Also in the 1999 report, 11 people were rated as overall unsatisfactory. Within one year, two of this group had left the university system, five successfully completed a performance improvement plan, and the remaining four were still engaged in a performance improvement process as of January 2001.

In the 2000 annual report, 25 faculty members were found to be performing unsatisfactorily in one area of work, though their performance was still evaluated as overall satisfactory. Five of these had left by January 2001, another 14 satisfactorily completed a faculty development plan, and three others were still engaged in a faculty development plan. Three faculty members had failed to meet the performance benchmarks set in their faculty development plans, so they had been moved to the more serious performance improvement plan. Of the seven faculty who were rated as overall unsatisfactory in that year, four had left the university and three were still engaged in a performance improvement plan.

In the most recent report in January 2001, 16 people had been found unsatisfactory in one (or more) areas of performance, though their overall performance was still rated as satisfactory. One of these faculty members had already left the university, two had their performance ratings modified to satisfactory, and 13 entered faculty development plans. Five other faculty members were found to be overall unsatisfactory in performance, making a total of eight faculty members engaged in performance improvement plans in 2000.

As the policy allows for performance improvement plans of up to three years and with grievance processes taking up further time, no faculty member has yet been dismissed as a result of post-tenure review in Arizona. While substantial resignations and retirements have occurred since the instigation of post-tenure review, it is impossible to attribute individual separations from the university to this policy.

***What Constitutes Success?***

If the problem to be solved was the inability to terminate chronic poor-performing faculty, then either there are none such faculty in the Arizona universities or the post-tenure review policy has failed. However, few regents would claim this outcome reflects the purpose behind the policy. If the performance culture of the university has been enhanced by the advent of post-tenure review; if faculty whose performance is at risk are identified and helped to regain maximum productivity; and if faculty members' own professional growth is better supported by post-tenure review, then by these measures post-tenure review is a successful policy. These benefits are more difficult to demonstrate with measurable outcomes. We tried to get at these data using qualitative techniques such as interviews and open-ended surveys and by soliciting the opinions of department chairs, who carry the major responsibility for post-tenure review implementation.

***Department Chair Perspectives***

**1. Adds value to the annual review.**

In considering the merits of the annual review and dean's-level audit components, most department chairs saw the annual review as valuable, because it helped faculty members "stay on track," and was "a motivator for them to attend to their own performance." Those chairs who preferred the five-year review cited the benefit of greater aggregate performance data. Averaging performance over time was seen as a benefit for several reasons. For those few faculty who had occasional performance problems, it made for a "gentler, kinder system" and provided a measure of protection for the generally well-performing faculty member who might experience a "blip" of poor performance from time to time.

One goal for a post-tenure review system within ASU was to ensure adequate rigor in mandatory annual review processes across the university. Data from chairs on how much their annual review processes had changed since post-tenure review are difficult to interpret, but that may reflect their different starting points. Chairs were almost evenly divided between those who said the process was now much more rigorous and those who said little had changed. Of those who had seen changes, the process was described as being more standardized, more formal, more reflective, and — in one case — as leading to better planning for the following year's work.

**2. Enables flexible workload practices.**

One of the most interesting findings to emerge from these data was the chairs' perceptions of the relationship between more-flexible workload allocations and post-tenure review. Prior to post-tenure review, ASU already had been moving toward policies to enable more-flexible approaches to workload allocation, but these had not been uniformly adopted. In the College of Arts and Sciences, for example, these ideas were widespread. In some other colleges they had barely surfaced. But as the post-tenure review policy was being developed, ASU administrators and faculty leaders were keen to see these ideas enabled — even embraced — within the policy. When asked about flexible workload practices in their departments, almost all department chair respondents indicated this practice was operational at some level. This flexibility ranged from minor adjustments to basically standardized workloads, to major differences across individuals within departments. Despite acknowledging the difficulties of ensuring equity when workloads varied in composition, the chairs were enthusiastic supporters of flexible workload policies, with only one chair holding an opposing point of view.

**3. Creates unintended consequences.**

But from the chairs' viewpoint, post-tenure review had not supported greater flexibility in workloads. Rather, it was seen as the source of even greater administrative burdens, and several chairs mentioned unintended consequences from the intersection of post-tenure review and flexible workload policy. For example, one claimed that post-tenure review had "turned off" the "super performers" and created "nine-to-fivers." Another commented that the intersection had caused the best researchers to "turn off teaching." On the other hand, several chairs commented that the intersection had allowed them to increase the teaching loads of faculty members who were not actively engaged with research, so they were now making a much greater contribution to the overall productivity of the department.

**4. Dubious value as an early warning system.**

The chairs did not find post-tenure review serving as an "early warning system" for faculty members whose performance was at risk. The majority indicated their department either had no need of or already had such support services. One third of the respondents said post-tenure review was not providing an early warning or helping staff address performance problems. One negative response suggested performance problems were deeply rooted in motivational issues and could not be addressed by any form of performance review. Several other chairs indicated they believed peer mentoring and support was the most effective way to improve performance.

**5. Gain:pain ratio remains unclear.**

On the key question of whether the gains from post-tenure review were worth the pain it created, the chairs were sharply divided. Some said it had changed little in their evaluation practices — no pain, no gain. Just over half of the chairs said it was at least "a little better" than what had preceded it, with a few going so far as to say it was "a lot better." But approximately one third concluded post-tenure review was not a good value, because it created a lot of paperwork, wasted time, and at worst damaged faculty morale. Perhaps these somewhat ambivalent feelings were best summed up by two chairs. One concluded: "It causes not much pain, for a little gain." The other concluded the pain of the solution far outweighed the pain of the problem: "Post-tenure review is a sledgehammer to hit a tack!"

### *Changes to Be Recommended*

Our experience of first developing this policy, then studying its implementation and outcomes has yielded some insights into faculty policy change. But the step between insight and recommended actions is a long one. Even with insight, there are no easy recipes to follow in implementing major changes in faculty policy.

Post-tenure review policies are not generic stand-alone models. Their meanings and success inevitably will be context-specific. They may be developed as discrete policies, but as they are implemented, they will take meaning from the universe of policies operating within the institution. The needs they address and the outcomes that emerge will depend not only on the features of this particular policy but on the entire policy context.

In the Arizona experience, having elected faculty leaders involved in the "heavy lifting" of policy development was a successful strategy. But the transition from development to implementation and beyond, to facilitating the operational health of the policy, requires collaboration for the long haul, and this is not easily accomplished.

Implementation needs to be understood as a long-term process; that is, not concluded within a few months or even a year. We need better ways of conceptualizing this phase — understanding that policies are not fully developed at their adoption: They continue to acquire new meanings, new manifestations, as they interact with other policies, and, most important, they are shaped through use by people over a period of years. Policies are not born self-sufficient; their long-term implementation and nurturing require careful planning and ongoing monitoring. Policy implementation needs administrative champions — visible leaders who care about the long-term outcomes and who watch over the health of the policy as its long-term meanings for the institution gradually emerge.

Understanding policy implementation within both temporal and institutional contexts will help embed the policy within the mission and goals of the institution. In this way it can become part of a coordinated suite of policies that does move the institution in a consistent direction. To have policies working against one another not only wastes energy, it is also a major source of frustration for those who must live within the policy environment.

Two specific tasks need to be important priorities for the administrators and/or for the faculty charged with policy implementation.

1. Develop systematic ways to negotiate the inevitable tension between local control and some minimal level of standardization across departments, and
2. Recognize the critical role played by department chairs.

It is in the exercising of the chair's role that most faculty policy changes are enacted. Such changes are time-consuming in an already busy life, and are only one among many important priorities that chairs must juggle. If such changes are to be embedded positively in the fabric of the institution, then chairs need to be thoroughly engaged both with the need for the change and with the task of implementation.

## Conclusions

Is the Arizona post-tenure review system a sledgehammer to hit a tack? Perhaps so. It is certainly a complex and time-consuming performance evaluation system that is needed to address only a small number of chronic performance problems in the Arizona faculties. But it may be that its most important benefits come indirectly, from an enhanced performance culture within the universities, and from its power to verify to those outside the academy the high performance levels of university faculty. When well integrated with flexible workload allocation policies and faculty development programs, post-tenure review has the potential to keep members of the faculty fully engaged with their careers through the cycles of academic life. But its achievement of this potential is by no means assured. The meanings of post-tenure review in Arizona are still unfolding, with no end in sight.

### Notes

1. This chapter contains insights gained through a research project sponsored by the Pew Charitable Trusts and the Project on Faculty Appointments, Harvard Graduate School of Education. AAHE's New Pathways project had a collaborative role with this particular project.

2. S. Vianne McLean was a newly elected faculty leader at Arizona State University West when the Arizona post-tenure review initiative began. She later became associate vice-provost for academic programs and graduate studies, and in that role led a number of policy and performance projects, including the initial implementation of post-tenure review and the development and implementation of an outcomes assessment model. She holds an M.Ed. and Ph.D. in elementary education from ASU and a B.Ed.Stud. from the University of Queensland (Australia). McLean is currently dean of the faculty of education at Queensland University of Technology, in Brisbane, Australia. (Contact her at v.mclean@qut.edu.au)

Thomas Callarman served as president of the faculty senate at Arizona State University Main during the development of the post-tenure review policy. In 1998, he became associate dean of the Graduate College at ASU Main, serving until January 2001. Currently, he is director of the Institute for Manufacturing Enterprise Systems, jointly sponsored by the College of Business and the College of Engineering and Applied Sciences at Arizona State University. (Contact him at thomas.callarman@asu.edu)

## Reference

Licata, C.M., and J.C. Morreale. (1997). *Post-Tenure Review: Policies, Practices, Precautions.* New Pathways Working Paper Series, no. 12. Washington, DC: American Association for Higher Education.

# The View From the Elephant's Tail: Creation and Implementation of Post-Tenure Review at the University of Massachusetts

**Kate Harrington** [1]

Writing about the establishment and implementation of post-tenure review at the University of Massachusetts is like the proverbial description of an elephant by a group of blind men. Each of the blind men accurately describes a piece of the elephant and assumes it to be the whole. There are many "blind men" or constituencies with a point of view about post-tenure review in the university system. There is the "public," including those in state government, and the faculty, faculty union representatives, campus administrators, and central office administrators. This article is written from the perspective of a central office administrator and so represents one point of view. The perspectives of other constituencies are noted to a lesser extent. This chapter describes the establishment of post-tenure review at the University of Massachusetts, the negotiation process in which a post-tenure review policy was achieved, the first year of implementation and subsequent issues, the oversight process, and preliminary responses to the first year of implementation.

## Understanding the Context

The University of Massachusetts is a five-campus system comprising four undergraduate/graduate campuses — Amherst, Boston, Dartmouth, and Lowell — and a medical campus in Worcester. The university system is led by a president, and each campus has a chancellor as its chief executive officer. ("University" will henceforth be used to refer to the system entity.) Faculty on the four undergraduate/graduate campuses are unionized, represented by three different unions (Amherst and Boston faculty share the same union). Contracts typically are negotiated for a three-year period, and a new contract period began July 1, 1998. The university is the employer of record and negotiates directly with its bargaining units such as faculty unions, graduate student unions, professional staff unions, etc. Negotiations are either conducted directly with or overseen by a member of the President's Office. In pre-bargaining discussions in early spring 1998, university administration informed the faculty unions that establishing a post-tenure review policy was a management initiative to be developed and implemented during the upcoming contract period.

For university management, the decision to develop and implement post-tenure review resulted from external and internal pressure. External pressure included the need for public accountability and to answer concerns of legislators and other public figures who perceived tenure as an entitlement to lifetime employment without accountability. The chair of the Massachusetts Board of Higher Education and the secretary for the State Executive Office for Administration and Finance had publicly challenged tenure and faculty work. In a speech given to the Greater Boston Chamber of Commerce in November 1997, the chair referred to tenure as "an absolute scam" that allowed faculty to teach only 12 hours a week and conduct "meaningless research" that was "a lot of foolishness." [2] Internal pressure included some university Board of Trustees members and others who argued that tenure contributed to fiscal constraints, lack of institutional flexibility, and faculty "deadwood."

#### *Contract Negotiations*

The university's announcement of post-tenure review as a management initiative was not well received by the faculty. The announcement was made as a prelude to the start of contract negotiations, which typically begin in mid-spring; contracts expire June 30th of each contract period. However, the governor indicated a reluctance to pay negotiated salary increases retroactively when contracts were not settled in a timely manner. The governor's position was significant, since negotiated contracts must be submitted to the Commonwealth's Executive Office for Administration and Finance for approval. The governor, in turn, requests funding for the negotiated salary increases from the legislature. Thus it became necessary to negotiate a contract that met the governor's expectations within the contract deadline. This meant that there was approximately four months of official negotiations. This time frame pressured the unions, which did not want to lose any portion of a potential salary increase; university management saw this pressure as useful to conducting effective bargaining.

#### *Negotiating Compromise*

The time pressure led to a compromise in negotiating a post-tenure review policy. University management agreed to accept an initial contract commitment by the faculty to the concept of post-tenure review with a provision for re-opening negotiations on the specific campus procedures. The unions agreed to give faculty time to develop positions on the issue and collaborate in designing the review process. A decision was also made to avoid the term "post-tenure review" and use "periodic multiyear review (PMYR)" instead (in this chapter, however, "post-tenure review" will be used to refer to the university's policy). The faculty felt "periodic multiyear review" conveyed a more positive orientation. It was agreed that negotiations regarding specific campus implementation procedures would reopen no later than February 1, 1999, allowing the campuses several months to develop specific procedures.

The university tied a significant salary package to establishing post-tenure review, a critical factor to reaching agreement with the unions. A substantial portion — nearly half — of the three-year salary package offered to university faculty depended on the development and implementation of post-tenure review:

- First-year salary increases (effective January 1999) were contingent on the university and the union reaching agreement on the concept of the post-tenure review process;
- Second-year salary increases (effective January 2000) required the implementation of post-tenure review during that academic year; and
- Third-year salary increases (effective January 2001) took effect only if post-tenure review had been successfully implemented.

### *Negotiating Strategy*

Between July 1, 1998, and February 1, 1999 — when contract negotiations re-opened — the university employed a new strategy in negotiations. During initial negotiations — in which agreement to the concept of post-tenure was achieved — the University's Director of Human Resources, as official representative, conducted the negotiations, with the President's Office Academic Affairs staff (including the author) developing specific language and acceptable parameters. Once the initial agreement had been achieved, President's Office Academic Affairs worked collaboratively with campus representatives on campus procedures, while the university's representative continued to conduct negotiations with the faculty unions. Administration and union representatives met in system-wide meetings to share concerns, discuss key issues, and disseminate draft policies. This sharing of ideas led to similar policies on three campuses with adjustments for specific campus differences (see the attachment at the end of this chapter). These system-wide meetings were not part of the negotiating process; indeed, care was taken that no agreements or commitments be made during these meetings. Funds received from AAHE's New Pathways: Post-Tenure Review "Projects With Promise" program supported these meetings, as well as activities on the campuses to gain faculty understanding and acceptance of post-tenure review and creating viable procedures. The informal meetings enabled all parties to reach an agreement in principle. When negotiations re-opened, they were, to some extent, a formality.

### *Negotiating Collaboration*

Working collaboratively on issues under negotiation was a new approach for both management and unions. University officials involved in the negotiations were nervous during the process, but the successful working relationship between President's Office staff in Academic Affairs and in Administration and Finance lessened these fears. This is not to suggest that all went smoothly and amicably during this period. There was significant faculty resistance to post-tenure review, as well as concern that the unions had agreed primarily for the financial package. Academic Affairs staff were caught in the middle between faculty, who favored a developmental policy independent of existing reward or disciplinary structures, and university board members, who wanted a punitive policy directly linked to existing rewards and discipline processes.

## Policy Guidelines

The agreed-upon system guidelines follow. These guidelines allow campus flexibility in designing procedures consonant with campus mission, union contracts, faculty culture, campus professional development tools (such as existing services through Centers for Teaching and Learning for a sabbatical year), and administrative structures.

### *General*

- Supplements existing reviews.
- Primary purpose is faculty development.
- Reflects all aspects of faculty work.
- All tenured faculty included but exceptions allowed.

### *Process*

- Cycle completes every four to seven years.
- Faculty self-assessments, peer reviews, and external reviews involved as appropriate.
- Multiple levels of review conducted by both faculty peers and administrators above the department level.
- Standards set for satisfactory tenured faculty performance.
- Faculty member outlines long-range goals in relation to departmental and institutional plans and needs.

### *Consequences*

- Develop a professional improvement plan and/or an accelerated schedule of reviews as warranted.
- Future work assignments affected.
- Does not directly reward or discipline faculty, but specifies links to existing mechanisms for both rewards and penalties.
- Specifies circumstances under which procedures for disciplinary action and/or dismissal for cause are triggered.

Specific funds were established in the Amherst and Boston contracts for professional development funds to support professional plans written as part of post-tenure review. Amherst allocated $250,000, with $150,000 in college development funds and $100,000 to the Center for Teaching; Boston allocated $56,000 and $37,500, respectively, in the same manner. Dartmouth's and

Lowell's contracts specified development funds be allocated above existing development funds without naming an amount.

## Implementation

During 1999–2000 — the first year of implementation — 173 faculty, or 10 percent of the tenured faculty, went through post-tenure review. Of them, 158 were rated as "excellent/satisfactory" in performance, meaning no change in direction or emphasis was warranted, nor was improvement needed, beyond what a faculty member may have suggested in his or her own self-assessment. The remaining 15 faculty (nine percent) were categorized as "in need of improvement." This rating indicates a need to make improvements or adjustments to better serve the needs of the department and school or college. Of these 15 faculty, the major issue(s) identified as problematic included research/scholarship/creative activity (11), teaching/advising (5), academic outreach/public service (2), and university service (4); some faculty were cited for multiple issues. Progress on the revised plans will be monitored annually. Five of the 15 faculty received funds to support professional development activities associated with their plans. In addition, approximately half the faculty with "excellent/satisfactory" performance are voluntarily undergoing professional development activities, most of them with the assistance of professional development funds allocated through the post-tenure review process. These faculty identified areas of growth or enhancement of current activities and applied for funds to help them realize their goals. The high number and percentage of faculty pursuing professional development as a result of post-tenure review are testimony to its effectiveness as a developmental process for improving the overall productivity of the faculty.

### *Oversight*

University management and unions negotiated a post-tenure review policy that was primarily developmental and not linked to existing reward and disciplinary structures. There were many — both on the university's board and elsewhere — who felt the policy should have more specific links to dismissal and other sanctions. As mentioned earlier, two key public figures with access to the governor questioned tenure and the value of faculty work. Their view of the university's post-tenure review policy was that it was a "sham" with no effective means to remove non-productive faculty or ensure that faculty work was relevant to the needs of the institution and the state.

To demonstrate the university's commitment to implementing a successful post-tenure review process that would result in specific defined outcomes, the university agreed to the establishment of an oversight committee, comprising representatives from the Commonwealth's State Executive Office for Administration and Finance, the University Board of Trustees, and the President's Office. This oversight committee was charged with (1) monitoring the implementation of post-tenure review, (2) determining whether or not it was achieving its expected outcomes, and (3) approving contingent salary increases. The oversight committee, while not an official part of the negotiated contracts, has played a critical role. Following the first year of post-tenure review, the oversight committee reviewed the data submitted by the campuses. These data comprise demographic information (e.g., age and rank), the results of the review, and the number of faculty undergoing professional development (voluntary or required), as well as the funds provided. In addition, it reviewed a random sample of redacted files from each of the campuses to determine the quality of the materials submitted and the effectiveness of the process. The oversight committee's response to the first-year report was overwhelmingly positive. The Board of Trustees' representative expressed her conviction that the oversight committee allows the board itself to feel more confident that the process and outcomes of post-tenure review are being closely monitored and faculty are being rigorously evaluated. [3]

### Administrative Response

Based on the first year's results, the university administration, the Board of Trustees, and the oversight committee consider post-tenure review to have been successfully implemented and to be achieving its objectives of:

- greater alignment between faculty work and institutional/departmental needs;
- more differentiated work assignments within academic units;
- redefinition of faculty career profile;

- performance improvements among faculty with minor weaknesses;
- increased faculty satisfaction with career progress/institution; and
- reinforcement/improvement of annual review process.

Following are testimonials from a dean and provost, respectively, who participated in the first-year review.

> Preparation and review of the statements [aka faculty self-assessments] led to conversations between faculty and their departments that were useful on both sides. In three cases, the statement forwarded to me is identified as a revision of the one originally received in the department. However, I believe that substantially underestimates the extent of the collegial process used in arriving at the submitted statements. There were many more cases in which faculty members worked informally with the department head or personnel committee as they prepared their statements.

> In the absence of clear institutional guidelines about the criteria for evaluation in post-tenure review, the departments have begun to evolve their own. This probably makes sense, since post-tenure review was conceived as a developmental evaluation designed to improve faculty performance in relation to the needs and mission of the department. The evaluation will become more meaningful as other evaluation processes . . . continue to take shape. Departments are already beginning to articulate their mission, set goals for themselves, and develop measures for assessing their progress. . . . It will thus become easier over time to articulate faculty performance and departmental needs and expectations.

### Faculty Response

Not everyone feels positive about the policy. Using funds from a second AAHE grant, a consultant interviewed a sample of reviewed faculty from each campus on the implementation and outcomes of post-tenure review. A quantitative survey based on the one developed by Christine M. Licata and Joseph C. Morreale for the AAHE New Pathways II project was administered to all faculty who participated in the first-year implementation of post-tenure review. This research shows faculty do not find the process to be particularly developmental nor helpful in focusing future plans. Attitudes were similar across all four campuses, perhaps due to similar policies and academic cultures. On one campus — where post-tenure review has been tied to the academic review process for departments — faculty reported greater clarity in understanding how to link their roles to departmental goals and mission. Faculty did not fully accept that the university needed to respond to external concerns about accountability, and therefore saw the negotiation of post-tenure review with an attractive salary package as a "sell-out" by the unions (O'Meara 2000). Faculty also indicated post-tenure review might serve a need for accountability to the public but they did not believe that post-tenure review resulted in improvements in teaching, research, or professional outreach.

One goal for the post-tenure review process was to limit its time commitment on faculty. While faculty think post-tenure review paperwork is excessive, qualitative information indicates faculty did not find the process as onerous or as time-consuming as anticipated. As the consultant noted, this paradox might be explained by faculty's overall perception that post-tenure review has few positive benefits; without a belief in the value of the process, any amount of time spent will seem excessive.

Faculty suggested the process could be improved by ensuring critical feedback to those being evaluated from "those who matter," that is, the person in a role to influence the faculty member's career through allocation of dollars, space, teaching assignments, and so on. Lack of this feedback led faculty to perceive that the process was not taken seriously. In addition, there was confusion among faculty regarding the availability and/or purpose of faculty development funds designated for post-tenure review. Not all faculty realized these funds were available to assist with a professional development plan even when no changes in direction had been indicated. Faculty also felt that the funds were inadequate to influence significant change.

### *Union Response*

Response from the unions has been mixed. Those involved with the actual negotiation of post-tenure review clearly felt that they had conceded a significant issue to university management. Union representatives understood public discussion of tenure and faculty work required a response from the university, yet the unions were still able to negotiate a policy primarily developmental rather than punitive in nature. Some say post-tenure review carries a high price. Across the University of Massachusetts, the commitment of time and energy to carrying

in the master's program in higher education at Azusa and served as a student affairs administrator on a number of campuses. (Contact her at KHarrington@umassp.edu)

2. James F. Carlin in a November 1997 speech given to the Boston Chamber of Commerce, Boston, MA.

3. Diane E. Moes in October 2000 chair's remarks to the Board of Trustees Committee on Academic Affairs, Student Affairs and Athletics, Boston, MA.

## References

O'Meara, K.A. (June 2000). "Periodic Multi-Year Review of Tenured Faculty: The First Year Implementation." Internal report prepared for the University of Massachusetts. Boston, MA.

University of Massachusetts. (2000). *Periodic Multi-Year Review of Faculty: The First Year.* Boston, MA: Author.

## University of Massachusetts: Comparison of Campus Post-Tenure Review Policies

**Amherst**[1]

*Basic File:* Statement of <2,500 words summarizing activities and goals; updated vita; AFRs[2] for current and last 6 years; teaching evaluations

*Review Process:* Dept Personnel Committee (DPC) and Chair review doc's and recommend to accept or revise statement; Dean concurs

*Categories and Consequences:*

Accepted: With further comments or suggestions optional. PMYR[3] is complete with option for prof devel $

Revised: Statement revised to address issues in consultation with DPC and Chair; option for prof dev $; follow-up review in 3 years with annual progress reports; if insufficient progress, "other possibilities may be discussed"; Dean may refer matter to Provost for initiation of disciplinary action

*Provost's Role:* Receives summary from each Dean including details for all revised plans

**Boston**

*Basic File:* Statement of <2,000 words summarizing activities and goals; updated vita; AFRs for current and last 6 years; teaching evaluations

*Review Process:* Dept Personnel Committee and Chair review doc's and recommend Category I or II; Dean concurs and may override a Cat I finding

*Categories and Consequences:*

Category I: PMYR is complete with option for prof devel $

Category II: Development Plan is created in consultation with DPC and Chair; option for prof dev $; follow-up review in 3 years with annual progress reports; if faculty member does not cooperate, PMYR process concludes and disciplinary action may be initiated

*Provost's Role:* Receives summary from each Dean including details for all revised plans

**Dartmouth**

*Basic File:* Updated vita; annual activity reports and annual evaluations; student evaluations of teaching; 3-page narrative on major accomplishments, long-range plans and their relationship to inst'l plans/needs

*Review Process:* Evaluation Committee, Department Chair, College Dean, College Academic Council, and Provost; three or more levels designate a category

*Categories and Consequences:*

Excellent Sustained Performance: PMYR is complete; eligible for Merit I and II

Generally Satisfactory Sustained Performance with no need for improvement: PMYR is complete: eligible for Merit I and II

Generally Satisfactory Sustained Performance with need for improvement: eligible for Merit I only. Develop a plan for prof devel with approval of Dept Chair, Dean, and Provost; progress reviewed annually until Provost, Dean, and Chair are satisfied plan fulfilled. If not, person is ineligible for Merit II increases until plan fulfilled

Deficient Performance: develop a plan for prof devel. Reviewed annually by Chair and Dean; no merit until move to Generally Satisfactory level; if no improvement in 3 years, Provost may initiate dismissal proceedings

*Provost's Role:* Active role in reviewing every case

**Lowell**

*Basic File:* Statement of <2,500 words summarizing activities and goals; updated vita; regular reviews since last PMYR

*Review Process:* Dept Personnel Committee and Chair review doc's and recommend to accept or revise statement; Dean concurs

*Categories and Consequences:*

Accepted: with further comments or suggestions optional. PMYR is complete with option for prof devel $

Revised: statement revised to address issues in consultation with DPC and Chair; follow-up review in 3 years with annual progress reports; if insufficient progress, "other possibilities may be discussed"; Dean may refer matter to Provost for initiation of disciplinary action

*Provost's Role:* Receives summary from each Dean including details for all revised plans

**Notes:**

1. Amherst and Boston policies were written with management and labor exchanging draft documents and consulting on language and terms; Lowell utilized the Amherst/Boston agreement extensively in developing its policy. Dartmouth did not exchange documents with the other campuses and developed its policy with the union providing most of the contract language based on existing personnel policy.

2. AFR = annual faculty review

3. PMYR = periodic multiyear review

# The Benefits of Pilot Testing: Post-Tenure Review at California State University, Long Beach

**Kelly S. Janousek and Wayne Dick** [1]

## The Challenge

The California State University System Board of Trustees and the California State Legislature mandated post-tenure review in July 1980. By 1983, post-tenure review had become part of the system-wide collective bargaining agreement (see attachment A at the end of this chapter). Each campus wrote its own review process for post-tenure evaluation. Our school — California State University, Long Beach (CSULB) — had each department write procedures for post-tenure review but, to date, there is no official campus-wide policy guiding the process. The reasons why are the basis for this chapter.

As an urban university with 951 full-time faculty, CSULB provides baccalaureate and graduate degrees to more than 30,000 students. The campus favors decentralized governance because of its educational diversity. Academic Senate policy generally defines basic principles but leaves procedures to colleges and/or departments. The long-standing absence of a campus-wide policy by the Academic Senate on post-tenure review is a result of the difference of opinion regarding its basic principles. In fall 1996, the Academic Senate began working on developing a policy, but when the system-wide administration committed to merit pay as its primary instrument to ensure faculty accountability, the opportunity for calm dialogue was lost. The implementation of merit pay seemed to cause unrest and anger in the faculty governance system. Any policy introduced that was personnel-related usually ended up provoking a diatribe on the "evils" of merit pay and its deleterious effect on professorial morale and work output. Basically, putting a stop to the original policy discussion.

Locked in a contentious collective bargaining process since 1998, the California State University system has embarked upon a controversial system of merit pay and annual faculty reviews. A majority of the tenured professoriate view annual faculty reviews and post-tenure reviews as redundant. The resulting controversy has spawned increased hostility toward peer review. The California State University (CSU) system management continues the merit pay system against the objections of the faculty union and of a state labor fact-finding panel. The current merit pay policy, called Faculty Merit Increase, was voted down by a 3 to 1 margin in a general campus-wide election held at California State University, Long Beach, in May 1999. Other campus senates in the system refused outright to implement the initial plan. Contract negotiations have begun concerning a new contract effective July 1, 2001, in an atmosphere of distrust and hostility.

In sharp contrast to the system-wide strife, however, the local campus administration values shared governance, respects faculty bargaining agents, and consults faculty and staff on important campus issues. Over the past decade, peer review for retention, tenure, promotion, and part-time faculty evaluations on campus has been decentralized. Even the disputed merit pay plan is implemented primarily at the department level at CSULB. While harmony will never exist, the campus climate can honestly be described as one of guarded trust.

## The Response

Current post-tenure review policies at the department level at California State University, Long Beach, are based on criteria used in evaluation for retention, tenure, and promotion. The process calls for a current vita and a statement of responsibilities and teaching evaluations, similar to annual faculty reviews for merit pay. The process is summative and offers little opportunity for reflection.

The awareness of the need for change evolved from several sources. The first was the publication in 1992 of an internal study by the Provost's Advisory Commission on the Function and Values of Teaching, Scholarly and Creative Activity and University and Community Service (CSULB 1992). This study introduced the Long Beach campus to new models of scholarship that matched institutional needs. In a large teaching institution, such as CSULB, faculty members begin their career by concentrating on discovery scholarship, but then move in other directions as their careers proceed. This report acknowledged career diversity and spoke to the need for more than a summative post-tenure evaluation. The report summary states:

> Equally important to support of young faculty is recognition of the value of the diverse contributions made by CSULB faculty at all career stages. It is proposed that each faculty member create a renewable Faculty Career Plan that would be used both to formalize the university's commitment to supporting each person's activities and to establish benchmarks for periodic evaluations. (CSULB 1992: iii)

The second was the university president's decision in 1994 to give new untenured faculty release time to conduct discovery research and develop new teaching skills. This pleased new faculty, but it did nothing to assist established faculty. A third source of motivation was the growing pool of aging tenured faculty. The need for mid- and late-career professional development was clear. The new post-tenure review policy offers a chance to support faculty in ways they themselves see as important for developing professionally.

The faculty governance system worked with the Faculty Personnel Policies Council during the late 1990s to develop a campus-wide policy on post-tenure review called the Evaluation of Tenured Faculty policy (see attachment B). The council began by reviewing other post-tenure review policies within the CSU system.

The proposed policy differs from other campus evaluation and review documents in two respects. First, it invites a level of personal honesty that may be impossible in reviews of probationary faculty. Second, it provides for potential rewards for participation. Our project, funded by AAHE, pilot tested this campus-wide policy to determine whether any revisions are necessary before it becomes official. This process will lead to greater acceptance, a stronger feeling of ownership by faculty, and, ultimately, a more powerful instrument for supporting the careers of our faculty and the mission of the institution.

## Project Goals

The main goal of the pilot test was to determine whether this new approach to post-tenure review — a developmental model dependent on trust — can succeed within a climate of strained relations over annual reviews and merit pay. The objective was to catch procedural errors, eliminate cultural insensitivities, ease communication, and use the intelligence and experience present on our campus to improve the policy.

Another goal was to determine the policy's effectiveness in providing professional development for faculty. In particular, to use this policy to stimulate a campus-wide dialogue related to mid- and late-career review and planning. The goal was to work through the participatory campus budget-planning process to fund the professional development component of the policy.

The final goal was to conduct an educational process. The campus culture is strong in consulting during policy development but weak in testing a new policy prior to enactment. We tend to underestimate the training needs of new policies during their formation, never realizing the full impact until after implementation.

## The Pilot Testing

Our study sample consisted of volunteer faculty members distributed over several departments. Volunteers were compensated by a small stipend. The stipend served as an incentive. The number of subjects was limited by available funds. Although official CSU system policy states that post-tenure review must occur at least once every five years, faculty members were given the opportunity to stand for early review if they wanted to participate in the trial.

In November 2000, the Faculty Personnel Policies Council invited faculty to participate in the pilot testing; 23 said yes. We held two open sessions in December 2000 to describe the study and the new policy; some volunteers opted out of the study at that time, citing misgivings about early review or an unwillingness to do the extra paperwork despite the monetary incentive. The official pilot sample settled at 17 faculty. There is at least one representative from five of the eight colleges; one department has four of its five tenured faculty members participating in the pilot test.

We offered two workshops for those who would have to prepare an evaluation document based on the new policy. Although attendance was light, these sessions initiated an important dialogue. Recognizing the importance of training, council members visited participants who could not attend workshops. In this way, every faculty participant received help with the writing process except for one participant who claimed to already know how to write a such a narrative.

The focus of these workshops was to discuss the writing of an evaluation narrative. This activity represented a significant change from current practice, which usually involves the faculty member submitting a current curriculum vitae and a grid of teaching evaluation statistics related to his or her teaching effectiveness. The new evaluation process still calls for a curriculum vitae and student evaluation data, but it also requires a multi-year self-assessment plan. This plan is embedded in a three-part narrative intended to be an honest and unguarded assessment of one's recent professional life in the institution.

> Context: This is a description of the candidate's perceived roles in the department, college, university, community, and profession. It delineates the most important goals toward which the candidate has focused his or her contributions since the last evaluation.
>
> Reflections: This is the place for a faculty member to engage in a personal, contemplative appraisal of his or her recent progress toward professional goals.
>
> Aspirations: This is an opportunity for the faculty member to express cherished professional aspirations and to articulate how to fit them into the context of the department, college, university, community, and profession. It is a place to propose a plan of action for achieving those goals, and a thoughtful assessment of ways in which the candidate's colleagues, department, college, and/or university might facilitate success.

The process of offering training sessions to pilot subjects revealed a need to train the faculty and administrative evaluators involved in the review process as well. We realized it would be unfair to encourage a group of subjects to submit honest and unguarded narratives intended for a developmental process to a committee of evaluators who were expecting a short list of factual data suitable for a brief summative evaluation. The pilot process involved approximately 45 evaluators. The chair and vice chair of the Faculty Personnel Policies Council met with each evaluator and/or team.

## Success/Outcomes

Many of the desired outcomes have resulted. The workshops and visits with participants and evaluators did create a positive campus-wide dialogue. We received vital feedback and headed off some painful mistakes. Some of the participants have reported significant growth from the process. The following is a list of the main discoveries:

### *1. Training Is Important*

There was a "cultural need" met by the workshops and meetings with the faculty members under review and the members of evaluation teams. Training is a key element of a successful post-tenure review system. In most cases, our discussions fostered a tone of open dialogue and listening. They also clarified the goals of this new type of review, and in most cases stimulated enthusiastic participation. This was significant, given the initial resistance to any form of post-tenure review by most faculty members. Most of our volunteers were skeptical, and our initial meetings were difficult.

### *2. Clear Policy Language Is Essential*

The policy as drafted was flawed in many ways. Some language that seemed clear to the council confused many faculty. For example, the term "professional growth" is primarily associated with research in many of our departments and colleges. But the council used this term to include the range of faculty activities. We had also included a place for the evaluators to rate a faculty member's performance as being *excellent, good, satisfactory,* or *less than satisfactory.* This rating was rejected by most subjects and evaluators. The universal reason given was a summative judgment would destroy the atmosphere of open dialogue and the focus on successful formative review.

### *3. Practical Implementation Must Be Considered*

There were many places where the policy simply failed to address practical implementation. For example, the organization, content, and purpose of the narrative evaluation and supporting materials need to be delineated in greater detail. Many departments already have procedures in place for forming evaluation committees that differ from but are consistent with the spirit of the policy. The evaluation committees complained the policy is unclear on the content of a final report. They are also concerned about the time commitment needed for the meetings and discussions with review candidates. This problem needs to be addressed, because dialogue between faculty members standing for review and the evaluation committee is a central feature of the process. Finally, the process of providing rewards for participation needs to be spelled out concretely. The idea of rewarding faculty for serious professional planning is foreign to our campus culture.

Many subjects have already reported on their initial experiences. Most agree that the narrative takes more time than expected, and that the entire process was far more time intensive than the past practice of putting together the curriculum vitae and data. Despite this drawback, many felt the exercise was worthwhile. Many participants noted, both verbally and in writing, that they did not remember the last time they looked at their professional life in such depth, or when they had last considered where they were going and how they planned to get there.

## Conclusions and Lessons: Look Before You Leap

Active dialogue beyond consultation before enactment of policy does seem to improve prospects for successful policy implementation. We feel this post-tenure review policy will work better because of the pilot testing. The Faculty Personnel Policies Council has started modification of the Evaluation of Tenured Faculty policy based on feedback. The requirement for a judgment of *excellent, good, satisfactory,* or *less than satisfactory,* for example, has been dropped. Instead, the final report will include the dialogue between candidate and evaluators. Agreements and differences between candidates and evaluators will be discussed without passing summative judgment on the faculty member's goals and accomplishments. The entire group will work together to develop a positive professional development plan to meet the aspirations of the individual and satisfy the needs of the institution.

The original plan of going to the campus budget-planning committee for support of professional growth has been scrapped in favor of an educational program on the need for such rewards. This education for CSULB faculty will start with campus leadership at an Academic Senate Retreat. The pilot testing revealed peer evaluation and professional development are not connected on our campus. Both entities are well established and valued, but they are not linked in any way. The idea that mid- and late-career faculty are continually called on to fill the teaching, research, and service spaces created by retirements and enrollment expansion is staggering. Many faculty are called to do something they may not be familiar with or experienced in without a chance to retool or retrain. Recognition has come to give support to untenured faculty and is reflected in the Retention, Promotion, and Tenure process. The basis in the Evaluation of Tenured Faculty policy working is a chance for faculty to self-determine their professional development based on what goals they set for themselves.

The Faculty Personnel Policies Council has approached the University Academic Senate Executive Committee to host the fall 2001 Academic Senate Retreat. These annual retreats provide a forum to discuss and plan for projects or programs affecting the entire university campus. The attendees at the retreat include CSULB faculty, staff, and administrative leadership. The retreats have been the starting point for many policy initiatives in the past. The council will lead a discussion on linkages between assessment, learning outcomes, accountability, peer review, and professional development. The discussion will cover the five-year post-tenure review in its new context, evaluation of teaching, other assessments based on annual reviews, and the relationship of all this to the overall professional development of faculty. Such a sustained discussion will help the Faculty Personnel Policies Council re-introduce the Evaluation of Tenured Faculty policy within the larger context of institutional quality assurance, and will enable us to build a case to connect this process to ongoing faculty development.

## Notes

1. Kelly S. Janousek has been on the California State University, Long Beach, faculty for 13 years and is a full librarian. Janousek received her M.L.I.S. from the University of Pittsburgh; she also holds a certificate in paralegal studies from Mississippi University for Women and a B.A. from Western Michigan University. At CSULB, she is the library

representative to the Faculty Personnel Policies Council and co-wrote the application for the AAHE Projects With Promise grant. Her research interests include information in the popular literature on United States Supreme Court decisions, which cumulated in a book published by Scarecrow Press in 2001. (Contact her at janousek@csulb.edu)

Wayne Dick has worked at California State University, Long Beach, as a professor of computer science since 1980. His research interests include information access for the visually impaired and the scholarship of teaching mathematics for computer science. He is the current chair of the Faculty Personnel Policies Council and an elected member of the executive committee of the Academic Senate at CSULB. Dick received his B.A., M.A., and Ph.D. from the University of California at San Diego. (Contact him at wed@csulb.edu)

2. California State University, Fresno. *Periodic Evaluation of Tenured Faculty*, revised February 1995. San Jose State University, Janus Project, Fall 1998. *San Francisco State University Performance Review of Tenured Faculty for Professional Development and Support*, revised March 1998.

## Reference

California State University, Long Beach. Provost's Advisory Commission on the Functions and Values of Teaching, Scholarly and Creative Activity and University and Community Service. (1992). *The California State University, Long Beach, Professoriate Preparing for the Twenty-First Century.* Long Beach, CA: Author.

# Attachment A

## Collective Bargaining Agreement
## Periodic Evaluation of Tenure Faculty Unit Employees

15.29 For the purpose of maintaining and improving a tenured faculty unit employee's effectiveness, tenured faculty unit employees shall be subject to periodic performance evaluations at intervals of no greater than five (5) years. Such periodic evaluations shall be conducted by a peer review committee of the department or equivalent unit, and the appropriate administrator. For those with teaching responsibilities, consideration shall include student evaluations of teaching performance.

15.30 A tenured faculty unit employee shall be provided a copy of the peer committee report of his/her periodic evaluation. The peer review committee chair and the appropriate administrator shall meet with the tenured faculty unit employee to discuss his/her strengths and weaknesses along with suggestions, if any, for his/her improvement.

15.31 A copy of the peer committee's and the appropriate administrator's summary reports shall be placed in the tenured faculty unit employee's Personnel Action File.

# Attachment B

**POLICY ON EVALUATION OF TENURED FACULTY**
**(DRAFT 8/25/00)**

***I. PREAMBLE***

The purpose of this policy on Evaluation of Tenured Faculty (ETF) is to establish the required process* through which tenured members of the faculty periodically reflect on their achievements, rethink their professional goals, and chart their aspirations for the future. In addition, this policy provides a process through which tenured members of the faculty are evaluated and receive constructive feedback from their peers, department chairs and deans to facilitate their continued professional growth and development. These processes are consistent with, and build upon, the main professional standards expected of all faculty, as articulated in the University Policy on Retention, Tenure, and Promotion. [*As per CFA-CSU Collective Bargaining Agreement, Article 15.29 et al.]

***II. EVALUATION PROCEDURES***

A. Tenured faculty members shall be evaluated at intervals of no greater than five (5) years.*
[*As per CFA-CSU Collective Bargaining Agreement, Article 15.29.]

B. Before the middle of the Fall semester, the Office of Academic Affairs shall notify all faculty members who are scheduled for evaluation in that academic year, and shall set the deadlines for all stages of the process. The department chair shall receive a copy of this notification and shall ensure election of an appropriate ETF committee(s).

C. The department-level evaluation shall be completed by a Department ETF Committee, which shall consist of the department chair, two full-time tenured faculty members elected by the department, and a fourth member who shall be selected by the candidate who is being evaluated. The selected member may come from either the faculty member's department or from a related discipline. The department chair and the two elected members shall serve on all ETF committees conducted in the department during a single academic year. A faculty member may not serve on an ETF committee during an academic year in which he/she is being evaluated under this policy but may serve as the selected fourth member on a committee. If a department chair is subject to EFT, a third faculty member will be elected to her/his ETF committee. In units without a chair, there will be three elected committee members. Where insufficient eligible faculty members to serve on the peer committee the department shall elect members from a related discipline(s).

D. The faculty member being evaluated is responsible for collecting and presenting materials for consideration by evaluators. At a minimum, the materials submitted for evaluation shall include a completed EFT Assessment form, a current Curriculum Vitae, and summaries of student evaluations of the faculty member's teaching effectiveness for the period under review. The Multi-Year Self-Assessment Form includes a narrative in three parts:
   - Context: a description of the candidate's role in the department, profession, college and university; as well as the most important goals toward which the candidate has sought to focus his/her professional contributions since the last evaluation;
   - Reflections: a reflective appraisal by the candidate of his/her recent professional goals, achievements, and any obstacles to achievement; and
   - Aspirations: a description of the candidate's aspirations for further professional growth and development in the context of the department, college, university, community and profession, a plan of action for achieving those goals, and a thoughtful assessment of ways in which the candidate's colleagues, department, college and/or university might facilitate their achievement.

E. The Department ETF Committee(s) shall review the materials submitted by the candidate and shall then meet with the candidate for purposes of discussion before completing its written evaluation.

This policy document was i .troduced to the California State University, Long Beach, Academic Senate in fall 2000. The Faculty Personnel Policies

F. The Department Committee's written evaluation shall be on the standard "Evaluation of Tenured Faculty Form," and shall include comment on all three sections of the faculty member's completed ETF Self-Assessment Form including the committee's perception of the candidate's strengths and areas that may need improvement if any.
   1. The committee's evaluation shall include specific recommendations concerning support for the candidate's professional development.
   2. If the committee perceives an area that needs significant improvement, it may initiate specific recommendations.
   3. The candidate shall sign the Department ETF Form and shall have the right to append a written response to the evaluation within seven (7) days, prior to its being reviewed by the dean.

G. Following review of the candidate's ETF Self-Assessment Form, the ETF Form, and the written response of the candidate, if any, the dean shall meet with the department chair and the candidate to discuss the evaluation. This discussion shall include any request for resources by the faculty member and/or the Department Committee, and the purposes to be served by such resources.

H. Following this discussion, the dean shall provide an overall written evaluation and recommendation to the candidate. These recommendations may include specific offers of support and/or resources for the candidate's professional development.

I. If, the candidate accepts support offered by the dean, he or she shall sign a statement agreeing to use of such support for the purposes stated by the dean. If the resources are accepted in whole or in part, however, the candidate shall use them for the purposes stated by the dean.

***III. PROCEDURES FOR SPECIAL EVALUATION OF TENURED FACULTY***

A. If the dean evaluates the candidate's performance as Less Than Satisfactory in a normal Evaluation of Tenured Faculty, the dean may require a special Evaluation of Tenured Faculty of the candidate, prior to the normal five-year interval between such evaluations. The candidate shall comply with this requirement.

B. A special ETF shall be conducted in the same manner as a normal EFT. Candidates in a special ETF shall address the specific areas of concern in his or her narrative. If the dean evaluates the candidate's performance as needing significant improvement, specific actions may be required as part of the faculty member's work assignment.

Council withdrew this version from the Academic Senate in spring 2001. It is currently being revised based on the outcome from the pilot test.

**APPENDIX I:**
**Evaluation of Tenured Faculty -- Candidate's Self-Assessment Form**

Date:

Name:

Department:

I. Context
*In narrative form, describe your role in your department, your profession, your college, and the University.*

II. Reflections
*After considered reflection, discuss the degree to which you have realized your professional aspirations since your last evaluation.*

III. Aspirations
*Discuss your professional aspirations for the next five years. Be as specific as possible. Describe the resources (both material and non-material) that would best enable you to achieve your most important professional aspiration, including the specific uses to which you would put any resources granted in response to your proposal.*

**APPENDIX II:**
**Evaluation of Tenured Faculty -- Department Committee's Evaluation Form**

Date:

Candidate's Name:

Department:

I. Context
*Department Committee's response to candidate's narrative on the candidate's role in the department, profession, college, and the University.*

II. Reflections
*Department Committee's response to candidate's reflections on his/her professional achievements since last evaluation, and materials submitted by candidate to accompany those reflections.*

III. Aspirations
*Department Committee's response to candidate's professional aspirations for the next five years, including a response to the specific resources requested by the candidate to support the candidate's aspirations for the future.*

* * * * * * * * * * * * * * * * * * * * * * * * * * * * * * * * * * * * * * * * * * *

IV. Department Committee's Formal Evaluation of Candidate:
In summary form this Committee evaluates the Candidate as follows:
_____Excellent _____Good _____Satisfactory _____Less Than Satisfactory

Department Committee Members' Signatures:

________________________________ Date __________

________________________________ Date __________

# Section II:
# Lessons Learned for Departments, Chairs, and Faculty

# The Evolution of Post-Tenure Review at Indiana University Purdue University Indianapolis

**N. Douglas Lees** [1]

## The Context

Indiana University Purdue University Indianapolis (IUPUI) is both a complex and venturesome institution, seeming to make it difficult to implement change. Motivated faculty — trying to enhance the national reputation of the institution — and innovative administrators are turning IUPUI into a new model of urban public higher education.

IUPUI was founded in 1969 and has changed from a dual two-year feeder institution to a campus of more than 27,000 students offering the widest array of degree programs available in the state of Indiana. It also houses several professional schools including the Indiana University School of Medicine, the second-largest medical school in the United States. Despite the range of programs and the diverse cultures existing in IUPUI schools, the institution has been largely successful in operating fiscally under responsibility-centered management. [2] In addition, the campus has been farsighted in many ways; for example, we have been working on post-tenure review for more than a decade. That project came to fruition in 1999 with the approval of Faculty/Librarian Review and Enhancement (FLRE), the campus policy on post-tenure review.

## The Policy

Faculty/Librarian Review and Enhancement is an initiated (triggered, selective) post-tenure review policy using the existing structure of the annual review to determine whether a formal review of a faculty member or librarian should take place (see attachment A at the end of this chapter). This approach places responsibility for instituting formal review of underperforming faculty and librarians on the department chair or individuals who conduct annual reviews. Two consecutive years of an overall "unsatisfactory" rating initiates the formal review process. A committee of faculty peers reviews the unsatisfactory rating and, if the rating is upheld, generates a development plan to improve the faculty member's performance. The policy also provides for a voluntary review initiated by a faculty member who requests the formation of a peer committee to facilitate a change in career direction.

Those formulating the policy recognized the need for several follow-up items:

1. Unsatisfactory performance would have to be defined within the contexts of the 18 schools at IUPUI.
2. Each school would have to decide how to form the peer review committees.
3. Each unit would have to develop a set of sanctions short of dismissal for faculty whose performance continues to be less than satisfactory after completion of the development plan.
4. Department chairs and individuals conducting annual reviews would need guidelines and training to equitably evaluate faculty for this purpose.

## Planning for Implementation

These concerns led IUPUI to seek funding from the AAHE New Pathways II project on post-tenure review. A campus implementation team comprising three department chairs, faculty governance leaders, a widely respected faculty member (with no ties to the post-tenure review movement), a librarian, and a member of the IUPUI Office for Professional Development was assembled. The main objectives, as mentioned earlier, were to define unsatisfactory performance, establish faculty peer review committees, and develop sanctions short of dismissal for faculty who fail to meet the expectations of a development plan. Each school formed a committee to develop school policies, with the distinguished faculty member from the campus-wide team serving as a liaison. This process was scheduled for completion in one academic year.

The training objective of the project was to develop a workshop for chairs in which chairs would (1) become fully acquainted with FLRE in the contexts of their own school policies, (2) learn about approaches for conducting rigorous and equitable faculty evaluations during the annual review (annual reviews were employed unevenly across campus, especially for full professors), and (3) become more cognizant of their new responsibilities and of campus resources for faculty development. The contents of this workshop would form the major elements of a campus website (www.iupui.edu/~profdev/flre/) through which IUPUI could share its experiences and outcomes with other institutions developing functional, effective post-tenure review processes. The website is now operating and has five parts:

1. "Information and Documents" contains text of the IUPUI project, a flowchart of the post-tenure review process, discussion of the annual review process, and a listing of faculty development opportunities.
2. "Policies" posts FLRE and the individual school policies.
3. "Case Studies" has four case studies set up to allow comments from those visiting the site.
4. "References" is relevant literature pertinent to post-tenure review and faculty evaluation.
5. "Chair Workshop Materials" are materials from workshops for those unable to attend.

## Developing School Policies

The team liaison to the schools met with representatives of most schools to help them establish performance measures for faculty. The problem the team noted from the outset was that there were few national models for defining unsatisfactory performance. Everyone was struggling to set definitive performance parameters.

One critical role played by the liaison was informing each school that the team was not intending to promote, defend, or champion post-tenure review but rather to help schools implement a new, approved policy. The liaison also assured the school committees that their faculties were empowered to define what was acceptable performance and to make those judgments without external interference. Many meetings began by airing concerns about post-tenure review. This is a necessary first step in the process.

Several months later, most schools complied with the deadline and submitted their policies for administrative review. A substantial percentage of the policies, however, were found not to be in compliance with FLRE and were returned to the schools for clarification and re-formulation. The reasons for noncompliance ran the gamut: failure to define unsatisfactory performance; lack of sanctions for continued poor performance; and violations of the guidelines for composing faculty peer review committees. These initial efforts were viewed not necessarily as failures, but rather as a result of uncertainty as to how to set performance standards and provide for peer review. In some cases, however, the policy could apply only to the most egregious offenders. In other words, the standard for unsatisfactory performance was set too low.

After revisions, most policies were accepted. Currently, most schools have approved policies in place. The newer versions satisfy the committee structure requirements of the policy but, in many cases, the definitions on unsatisfactory faculty performance remain vague.

## Definition of Unsatisfactory Performance

The majority of the school definitions of unsatisfactory performance are similar. Unsatisfactory performance is defined by describing what behaviors in teaching, research, and service qualify as unacceptable. Further, every policy stresses that overall performance must be unsatisfactory, meaning individual areas of poor performance are tolerable. The behaviors are presented as typical criteria and all policies state that other factors may come into play in some circumstances. While individual schools vary, the following list provides a good example of these definitions:

- **Teaching:** Failure to meet scheduled classes, to be available to meet with students outside of class, to report grades on time, to update course content and pedagogy, or to receive satisfactory evaluations by peers, students, and others.
- **Research:** Failure to regularly engage in scholarly research, publishing, or other creative activity, or to remain current in the discipline and contribute to its knowledge base.

- **Service:** Failure to apply disciplinary knowledge and professional expertise to the community and the profession/discipline, or to contribute to effective academic citizenship through service on committees and in other activities or through contributions to the overall well-being of the school, campus, and university.

One school took a different approach. The chair rates all faculty in the three areas of responsibility. Those who have distanced themselves from their peers in all three areas of faculty activity are identified as unsatisfactory.

In both of these models there are challenging elements for chairs. For example: How many instances of the listed behaviors constitute unsatisfactory? How does one define terms such as "regularly," "satisfactory," "current," and "effective?" What would constitute "distancing" from peers?

## Peer Review Committees

The FLRE policy mandated that the peer review committee be elected and exclude administrators at the level of department chair and higher. Schools developed various ways to compose committees. One school chose to have tenured faculty elect three associate or full professors. Another school opted for one tenured full professor (preferred) elected from each department plus two at-large members elected by the faculty council of the school. A third school decided to elect one tenured faculty member from each department to form a pool from which the faculty member under review selects two peers and the dean selects one who becomes the committee chair.

## Sanctions

The listing of sanctions short of dismissal, as called for in FLRE, ranged from deferring sanctions to the dean or vague statements such as they would be "significant and include dismissal," to the listing of specific actions such as salary freezes, loss of travel support, loss of sabbatical eligibility, reassignment of duties, suspension without pay, and salary reduction — a concept without precedent at IUPUI.

## Training Chairs

To design a credible program to train chairs, the FLRE implementation team included chairs from the three largest schools on campus — medicine, liberal arts, and science. These chairs offered the widest range of opinion on training. The nature and content of the workshop have undergone rapid evolution. An outline of the history and elements of FLRE and its implementation procedures has now become more focused on the critical areas of evaluation and faculty development.

The AAHE grant provided for an evaluation of the workshop prototype. In fall 1999, an external consultant and a select group of experienced IUPUI chairs were presented the prototype workshop. Based on their feedback, the workshop was modified and offered in spring 2000. Low attendance (seven) at this workshop indicated the reality of FLRE had not set in for the 100 or so chairs and other administrators who would have to judge whether performance of each faculty member in their unit was satisfactory or unsatisfactory during the next annual review. The second campus offering in fall 2000 drew 18 participants (a full house), with a few others attending ad hoc. The enrollment limit had been set low in response to a recommendation from the outside evaluator. Limiting the number of participants enabled interactive discussions using case studies. The workshop will be offered each semester, emphasizing faculty evaluation and faculty development and using the discussion of case studies to gain practice and insight into these processes.

The current workshop agenda begins with an introduction to post-tenure review from a national perspective; a developmental history of post-tenure review at IUPUI; and a review of due process, academic freedom, peer involvement, appeals procedures, institutional support, and the order of events in the process.

The next workshop section is devoted to faculty evaluation and the annual review process. Some of the highlights of this component are:

- The annual review — This involves a re-focusing of the review process in light of the new consequences inherent in FLRE. It also informs chairs of their expanded role in fostering faculty development.

- Setting performance measures with faculty — The primary objective here is to bring faculty together to decide on what they value and what they expect of themselves and their colleagues in teaching, research, and service. This allows all faculty to know what is important and establishes a basis for equity in the evaluation process.
- Collecting data: form reflects measures — Reporting forms for faculty activities should reflect the measures established by the unit. This reinforces the concept that the process is being conducted fairly.
- The evolution of faculty work.
- Differential expectations.
- Providing feedback — This topic encompasses a critical set of elements in faculty evaluation. It involves verbal and written communication with faculty that acknowledge their accomplishments (equity is confirmed when faculty are credited with meeting the expectations they have set), extends accolades for excellent performance, and provides specific direction and support for performance improvement.
- Faculty development — This lists existing institutional support from the Office of Professional Development and tools available to the chair for fostering improvement (see attachment B).
- Case study — The "Dr. Erratic" case study is used to encourage chair discussion about difficult performance issues (see attachment C).

## Preliminary Impressions

### *Productivity and Faculty Development Are Linked*

On first impression, enhanced, better supported, and more visible programs for faculty development will lead to greater faculty productivity and maximum benefit to the institution. Faculty development programs must be designed to help faculty — all faculty — improve performance. Making these programs available to high-performing faculty will have the greatest impact on the bottom line. The notion that faculty development is only for poor performers will doom efforts for global improvement and will stigmatize faculty who seek to enhance performance.

### *Post-Tenure Review Is a Threat to the Department Environment*

Another impression is chairs are reluctant to identify unsatisfactory performance even when it truly exists. As one colleague put it, "No chair in his/her right mind would ever check the unsatisfactory box on the form." This attitude is rooted in department tradition and the genuine efforts of chairs to create collegial and supportive atmospheres in which their faculty can do their best work. Many faculty believe it is better to tolerate a few poor-performing faculty members than endure the atmosphere of fear, threat, and suspicion many associate with post-tenure review. While this attitude is found only in some units, it nonetheless exists at IUPUI and elsewhere.

### *Policy Flaws and Loopholes Have Been Identified*

Some chairs attending the early workshops believe FLRE is too weak to allow the institution to really unburden itself of chronically poor-performing faculty. Many who attended the first workshops came expecting FLRE would make it possible for them to deal with problem faculty. In one instance, a longstanding poor-performing faculty member acknowledged FLRE but vowed to fight every step of the way, invoking every appeal, and taking the case to the courts if necessary. The entire process could take years: Two years of unsatisfactory ratings start the formal review, development plans typically take two additional years, followed by several years more for the due process appeals. Busy administrators may be reluctant to pursue this arduous road. In addition, other provisions of FLRE were regarded as providing an escape for underperforming faculty.

### *Rethinking Chair Appointments and Chair Support*

Finally, the issue of chair vulnerability has surfaced. In fact, this is addressed in one of the workshop discussions. Clearly, the practice of the rotating chair, found in some IUPUI units, places an individual in a difficult position. When the chair is outranked or even untenured, implementing FLRE with a low-performing senior faculty member can be difficult. In addition, a sympathetic peer review committee or a dean (or a higher administrator) might overturn the unsatisfactory evaluation by the chair. While peer review is designed to protect faculty from arbitrary and capricious decisions by the chair, it can also result in the overturning of the legitimate and thoughtful judgment by a chair. This results in the chair losing all credibility with that faculty member as well as with others who are not performing up to expectations. The chair must walk a fine line and the risk is not trivial.

Most of these issues are yet to be faced in a real way, but the groundwork has been laid. The next year or two should tell us whether FLRE is going to be an effective tool to promote faculty improvement.

## Successes and Cautions

### *Successes*

The IUPUI approach to post-tenure review has been to involve faculty and librarians in both the development and implementation phases. This has helped to defuse some of the initial faculty resistance. A particularly important element has been the attitude of the implementation team. The team approached its work from the perspective of offering assistance in dealing with an approved policy rather than as a champion for post-tenure review. A second area that proved valuable for the institution was the increased emphasis on formative faculty evaluation. We recognized that everyone will be evaluated in a more detailed way, so chairs and individuals charged with this responsibility will need guidance to conduct equitable reviews. Therefore, our chair training is critical in ensuring that the process has the desired outcome of improving institutional performance.

Our advice here is that faculty need to take the lead in the post-tenure review process and that equitable means for evaluating faculty must be established for this to gain any level of acceptance on campus.

### *Cautions*

We have also made some observations that could be called cautions, failures, or truisms about post-tenure review. Some faculty and administrators, both chairs and deans, do not take post-tenure review seriously.

- The use of quantitative models to identify poor-performing faculty is not advisable. Faculty will do the math, sometimes in incredibly complex ways, to generate predictions or "quotas" for the number of underperforming faculty who might be identified.

- Faculty fears run deep and will not dissipate over the short term.
- Questions will emerge that need attention.

How will we report the impact of post-tenure review to external constituents? Will we need a list of dismissals or mandatory development plans in order to satisfy our critics? Will we be able to demonstrate increased institutional productivity as the result of our efforts? These are questions worth answering. Be prepared to answer them.

## Notes

1. N. Douglas Lees is professor and chair of biology at Indiana University Purdue University Indianapolis (IUPUI). His continuing research interests are in fungal sterol biosynthesis and anti-fungal drug discovery. He is also an active contributor to national meetings and the literature on higher education issues related to the work of department chairs. He is a coauthor, with Betsy E. Brown and Susan H. Barr, of three related articles on "Preparing Chairs for Expanded Roles in Post-Tenure Review" in *The Department Chair,* published in the Fall 2000, Winter 2001, and Spring 2001 issues. Lees received his B.A. from Providence College and his Ph.D. from Northwestern University. (Contact him at nlees@iupui.edu)

2. Responsibility-centered management is a budgeting system whereby centers, usually schools or divisions, receive all the income they generate from student tuition and fees, state appropriation (if public), and grant overhead. From these funds the centers must pay all faculty and staff salaries and fringe benefits, make budgets for departments and other components, and pay assessments to campus. The latter include costs for the so-called service units (bursar, registrar, financial aid, purchasing, admissions, building and grounds, campus police, human resources, physical plant, library, travel management, administration, and so on) and special projects. The positive elements include flexibility with funds and the rewards resulting from creative entrepreneurial activity. It provides incentives to make classes accessible to students and promotes the seeking of external funding. The downsides include competing for student credit hours can lead to course duplication and the lack of obvious restraints for increasing campus assessments.

# Attachment A

**NAME:** **DATE:**

**CALENDAR YEAR:**

## IUPUI SCHOOL OF SCIENCE
## ANNUAL FACULTY REVIEW FORM

The Department Chairperson completes this form during the annual interview with the faculty member, files a copy with the Dean, a copy with the Department, and provides a copy to the faculty member. Comments should be brief, informative and made only when applicable.

**I. Review of Performance during the Past Year:**

**A. *Teaching***

**1. Classroom**

**2. Individual and counseling**

**B. *Research including applications for grants & contracts, and awards***

**C. *Service***

**1. School**

**2. University**

**3. Professional**

**4. Community**

**II. Change in Performance over Previous Year(s):**

**III. Goals for the Coming Year:**

**A. *What the faculty member hopes to achieve***

**B. *What the academic unit expects if different from A***

**IV. Recommendations or Suggestions by Faculty Member**

**V. Summary:** Overall comments concerning the total performance of the individual and, where appropriate, prospects for continued re-appointment/tenure/promotion considering the goals of the Department/School.

**VI. Tenured Faculty and Librarian Review:** In accord with the campus policy of Librarian Review and Enhancement, the department chair and dean, (or designee) should note whether the overall performance has been satisfactory with regard to quality and productivity.

**A. Satisfactory or better; no review anticipated:** ______________________.

**B. Unsatisfactory; review needed unless significant improvement occurs; discuss with faculty member:** ______________________.

**VII. We have gone over this completed form together and each has been provided a copy.**

| | | |
|---|---|---|
| ____________________ | ____________________ | __________ |
| Faculty Member | Reviewer | Date |

# Attachment B

## Chair Tools for Faculty Development

During the course of working on the post-tenure review project it became clear that department chairs have been doing a good deal of what one would call faculty development. This finding was supported by a recent IUPUI campus task force report that concluded that faculty development work is distributed at several levels of organization and permeates the institution. The same is likely to be the case on other campuses. Implementing FLRE also predicted that chairs would have to become more proficient and knowledgeable about faculty development in order to raise the productivity level of all faculty including those who may be experiencing problems.

These considerations led to the formulation of a set of tools available to the chair to promote faculty development. While this may not be a complete list and not all strategies will be available in all departments, they at least alert chairs to a few things they may do internally to enhance faculty performance. One key to using these tools effectively is flexibility. This is directed at institutional policies that restrict chairs in setting workloads, using allocated funds, and working outside the immediate department or school environments. Another key to successful utilization is the realization by the chair that management responsibilities need to be accompanied by creative activity in leadership in the change process, in risk taking, and in entrepreneurial enterprises. Here are the chair tools presented as part of the IUPUI workshop.

**Discretionary funds**: Although chairs routinely deny having fiscal resources (They are, no doubt, preparing to be Deans!), virtually everyone has a budget. Even if it is sometimes allocated to certain uses (budget categories), there remains some discretion available to chairs in how it is spent. Choosing to "invest" in faculty who might return more than the investment, in kind or in another form, may be a wise strategy to employ. For example, inviting a renowned scholar to come to campus for a symposium or colloquium may provide the necessary "connection" to gain funding for a member of the faculty. Likewise, supporting a trip to a national meeting may result in new ideas that may bring acclaim to the campus through the establishment of a new interdisciplinary program or center. Technology training may invigorate an ineffective teacher and eliminate student complaints, an outcome worth more than its weight in gold to a beleaguered chair. This investment strategy may have to displace, in some units, an entitlement culture where resources are distributed by formulae.

**Modification of assignments**: A common cause of diminished faculty effectiveness is burn-out. Doing the same thing over and over can take its toll in enthusiasm and performance. Likewise, changing student demographics and behavior, changing interests of funding agencies, and changing disciplinary goals may disenfranchise faculty and make it difficult for them to maintain normal levels of productivity. Perhaps teaching that large introductory course every semester for fifteen years has lost its luster. Perhaps a semester off to re-tool the course may be just what is needed. Or, the opportunity to teach a senior capstone in its place might be intellectually stimulating and renewing. While changing assignments can be difficult, especially in small departments, it is important that other faculty not be burdened by such changes. This happens with sabbatical leaves where one faculty member gets recharged while others are driven into the ground because they must take on overload. This is simply not a wise investment. Rather, the sections vacated should be covered by adjunct appointments, by combining sections, or even by electing to drop a section, if possible. Some institutions may not have quality adjuncts available while others do not permit their employment. For the latter I would encourage administrative change to allow use of all possible resources to improve the institution. Again, this is an investment strategy and one must recognize that there is always a risk involved.

**New responsibilities for new experiences**: Faculty members who are in a rut may want to move outside of the normal array of faculty work. Perhaps there is an interest in administration, Honors Programs, recruiting students, working with special populations of students, or working on campus wide projects with faculty from other schools. These may be desired as a change of pace or as forays into potential new career directions. The chair can facilitate these interests by targeted service assignments and even actively seeking invitations for the faculty member to join certain groups or committees.

**"Hold Harmless" experiments**: Risk taking is often a daunting prospect especially for a faculty member who has not been performing at high levels. However, little is learned when one is not willing to put a new idea to the test. To encourage such enterprising activities a chair might want set aside short-term negative consequences in order to reap long-term benefit. A classic example of such a strategy is in the area of adopting new pedagogy in the classroom. In this case, the faculty member is inexperienced and may be a bit "clumsy" at first. Also, it may take time to adapt the new approach to the nature of the course and the personal characteristics of the faculty member. The initial impression that students may get could lead to low evaluations and, if such instruments are a component of the evaluation of teaching, the faculty member is penalized for attempting innovation. If this is a case where the faculty member is already in trouble for poor teaching, the result of the attempt at improvement makes matters even worse. In a situation like this the chair might ignore the initial evaluations providing the faculty member solicits feedback and makes adjustments to the approach thus refining the effort at improvement.

**Avoiding the "invest in the low performers" criticism**: One of the most consistent criticisms of post-tenure review is its intent to invest in extensive faculty development for under-performing faculty. This potentially significant expenditure is to take place when most institutions are suffering from fiscal shortfalls and, thus, this remediation will come at the expense of important existing programs and support for high performing faculty. Avoiding this scenario would be best accomplished by careful vigilance by the chair of faculty performance at least on a year-to-year basis. This places special emphasis again of the annual review process. Comparing the year-to-year performance and the success at meeting goals can provide early warning information that alerts the chair to diminishing performance that may not be problematic but may be predictive. Intervening early before the problem is widely detected can avert complaints about resources being unwisely spent.

**Mentoring**: There are instances where faculty performance can benefit from an apprenticeship with a respected and successful faculty member. A master teacher may be able to transfer some elements of effective teaching to a faculty member who is struggling. A successful grant writer might be a valuable resource to a faculty member who has excellent ideas but is unable to effectively sell him/herself on paper. The chair may make arrangements to get the parties together to effect positive change. This strategy may require some investment in terms of a "buy out" for the time of the mentor. Compensation may come in a variety of forms – released time, an assistant, a bonus – and institutions again need to be flexible in making small investments with potentially large returns.

**Interdisciplinary connections**: This approach follows from mentoring in some respects but differs in that it removes the work of improvement, at least partially, from the department. This may be particularly appropriate in situations where the home department has become a place associated with poor performance and where the faculty member feels under emotional duress. Moving the work to another culture and location provides evidence of a fresh start where there are no pre-conceived notions about the ability and effectiveness of the faculty member. This strategy also opens new lines of work and can provide avenues through which contributions with institutional impact can be made. This can lead to recognition and morale enhancement for the faculty member. The chair's role here is in identifying and arranging potential collaborators for the faculty member. Thus, attention to the work of others and connections with other chairs become vital in being able to establish synergistic and re-vitalizing partnerships.

**"Each other"**: An overlooked source of advice and best practice available to chairs comes in the form of the expertise available from other seasoned chairs. The challenge of improving faculty performance is universal among chairs but the strategies, both successful and failing, are not routinely shared among chair colleagues. Chairs typically meet as a group when called together by the dean. Typically the agenda is set by the Dean and the chairs are recipients of new information in these settings. The suggestion here is that chairs take the initiative to get together on occasion to consider common problems and share their experiences at solving them. The meetings are without other administrators to allow for frank and therapeutic discussion of matters that affect department leadership. Among the topics that will certainly arise are those clustered around faculty evaluation and mechanisms by which improvement might be achieved. This concept of "chair community" has other applications but post-tenure review may expand its utility.

# Attachment C

**The Annual Review of Dr. I. M. Erratic, Tenured Associate Professor**
**School of Fine St-Arts**

The Annual Review documentation of Professor Erratic reveals evidence in support of a disturbing pattern of professional behavior that is puzzling to his chair. Over the past five years, Dr. Erratic has demonstrated an apparent precipitous decline in the overall quality of his teaching effectiveness. Until five years ago, his teaching was generally viewed as being among the very best in the department. Indeed, over the course of his academic career, he had won several teaching awards in recognition of his innovative teaching techniques and his leadership within the department with respect to the introduction of problem-based learning. Based on his well-earned reputation, Dr. Erratic has been relied upon to routinely teach an average of five core courses per year within the department.

Over the past five years, however, despite very high productivity in the areas of research and university service, Dr. Erratic's teaching appears to have deteriorated dramatically. Students have complained to the administration on numerous occasions, claiming that Dr. Erratic comes to class unprepared, is unresponsive to their concerns, plays favorites among students, is unfair in his grading practices, and routinely blames them for being ill prepared to handle the rigors of a college education. He is also alleged to have made racist comments that have offended several African American students. Several faculty colleagues have also confidentially indicated to the chair that students had come to them with similar complaints. For the past three years, Dr. Erratic's student evaluations have been routinely below the mean for the school as a whole, and consistently at the bottom for faculty teaching within the department. His review documentation contains no plans to address these shortcomings.

The Department Chair has met with Dr. Erratic on numerous occasions in an effort to both understand and offer remedial help with the problem. Three years ago, she encouraged Dr. Erratic to apply for a sabbatical leave, hoping that "some time away from the classroom might provide Dr. Erratic with some time to update the content of his courses and re-examine his pedagogy." Dr. Erratic refused this offer, complaining that he did not want to "waste a sabbatical learning how to kowtow to students." Two years ago, the chair arranged for a confidential external peer review of Dr. Erratic's teaching, an experience that not only resulted in no discernable positive improvement, but also seemed to exacerbate Dr. Erratic's "negative attitude." Despite her best efforts, a year ago the chair felt compelled to inform Dr Erratic in writing that his performance was unsatisfactory and would have to improve or he would likely be judged to be performing at an unsatisfactory level at his next Annual Review. Dr. Erratic has stated publicly that he believes the negative assessment of his performance to be "politically motivated" by a segment of the faculty (including the chair) whose academic credentials pale by comparison to his own. The chair is now in the position of having to decide whether to Dr. Erratic's performance is unsatisfactory and thus the new policy of Post-Tenure Review would be started and the case would go to a Peer Review Committee.

The unit's post-tenure review policy indicates that:

> *To be judged "unsatisfactory", a faculty member's performance over a period of two or more consecutive years in any one of the three areas of teaching, research/scholarship, or service must fall into the lower third of his/her departmental reference group. In making this determination, the chair should consider extenuating circumstances such as health."*

For purposes of discussion:

1. Does Dr. Erratic's performance warrant a second "unsatisfactory" rating?
2. Are there extenuating circumstances that should be taken into consideration in this case?
3. How might the chair deal with Dr. Erratic's allegation that the assessment is politically motivated?
4. Should Dr. Erratic's "very high productivity in the areas of research and university service" be taken into consideration before the chair rates the overall performance?
5. Could the unit definition of "unsatisfactory" be re-examined?

# The Context as Key to Developing and Implementing Post-Tenure Review: The University of Nebraska-Lincoln Experience

**Gail F. Latta and Daniel W. Wheeler** [1]

## Institutional Context

The University of Nebraska-Lincoln (UNL) is the flagship university in a four-campus system governed by an elected, seven-member Board of Regents. It is both the only land-grant and sole Association of American Universities–member institution in the state. During the 1995-96 academic year, the University of Nebraska Board of Regents began discussing developing a policy on post-tenure review for all campuses to ensure senior faculty ranks were devoid of unproductive faculty. In response, the University of Nebraska-Lincoln Academic Senate Executive Committee formed an ad-hoc committee to draft a statement defining the context in which UNL faculty would enter into discussions with university administrators about post-tenure review.

The resulting document, "The Academic Context for Periodic Review of Tenured Faculty at UNL" (see attachment A at the end of this chapter), describes the existing annual performance evaluation and merit review processes for all faculty, as well as the mandatory three-year peer review of tenured faculty not yet fully promoted. It also included a discussion of the twin threats to academic freedom posed by post-tenure review policies by (1) giving inordinate power to administrators and/or governing boards, and (2) by removing the protections afforded by tenure in requiring senior faculty to essentially be re-tenured on a periodic basis. This statement was adopted by the full Academic Senate in fall 1996, and provided the context for faculty and administrators to begin discussing what, if anything, a post-tenure review policy could add to the existing faculty evaluation processes.

In the next academic year, 1996–97, the UNL faculty rejected (as unwarranted and overly labor intensive) a proposed mandatory post-tenure review policy that would have required all faculty to be assessed every five years by a peer review committee. Subsequently, the Academic Senate Executive Committee and the senior vice-chancellor for academic affairs negotiated a triggered, peer-review process linked to annual merit reviews conducted on all tenure-track faculty members, and to existing guidelines on faculty dismissal for cause. The trigger would be two consecutive unsatisfactory ratings on the faculty member's annual review.

The standards for satisfactory performance, under this policy, were to be defined for each department by its faculty, with approval of the appropriate academic vice-chancellor. The post-tenure review would be a review by as few as three "tenured faculty from within and outside the unit, who hold an academic rank at least equal to that of the faculty member to be reviewed" (University 1997a). The members of this committee are ideally selected by the faculty member being reviewed and his or her chair; if they cannot agree, a standing, elected faculty committee within the department or unit would be used.

The post-tenure review takes place in the academic year following the second consecutive unsatisfactory annual review. The review committee may find that the unsatisfactory rating on the faculty member's annual review is unwarranted, in which case, the review is concluded. If the committee upholds the unsatisfactory rating, a faculty development plan is designed to remedy the performance deficit(s). Subsequently, if the faculty member does not make consistent progress toward remediating the identified deficiency in the time spelled out in the faculty development plan, existing procedures provided for within the university bylaws for removal of faculty for cause would be initiated. Appropriate provisions for appeals are outlined for each of these circumstances.

This policy was approved by the UNL Academic Senate in spring 1997. In January 1998, the Board of Regents for the University of Nebraska system subsequently adopted a post-tenure review policy with minor wording changes to apply to all campuses within the system (see attachment B). UNL's post-tenure review policy was revised to incorporate the slight changes in the system policy, and the Office of Academic Affairs at UNL proceeded to guide campus implementation of the new post-tenure review policy.

## Implementing Post-Tenure Review

While the time frame for the trigger was defined in the post-tenure review policy, there were two aspects of policy implementation in which the policy prescribed campus-level responsibilities. One of these responsibilities was for the respective vice-chancellors of the Office of Academic Affairs and the Institute for Agriculture and Natural Resources to ensure that annual merit reviews of faculty were being conducted in a "rigorous and equitable manner" (University 1997b). This aspect of policy implementation has not yet been carried out.

The second area of responsibility for policy implementation was for departments to adopt written standards defining satisfactory performance for their faculty, including the specific rating(s) on the annual performance evaluation denoting unsatisfactory performance. Following some initial confusion about how to interpret this aspect of the policy, these tasks were successfully carried out. Resulting standards and annual performance ratings will trigger a post-tenure review of a faculty member who receives overall unsatisfactory ratings in two consecutive years.

### *Developing Standards*

In spring 1998, departments were charged to write — and submit for review — satisfactory performance standards. Faculty were specifically instructed to define "satisfactory," not "unsatisfactory," performance standards. This objective occasioned some confusion between faculty and administrators. Many departments set out initially to define "minimal acceptable performance standards," until receiving clarification from the senior vice-chancellor for academic affairs. In a memo to department chairs and academic senators, the senior vice-chancellor noted:

> . . . Certainly there is a gray area between performance that fully meets the expectations for satisfactory performance (i.e., your statement) and performance that is so poor that it can fairly be characterized as having a "substantial and chronic deficiency" (i.e., triggering a post-tenure review). (Edwards 1998: 1)

The senior vice-chancellor reasoned that in this gray area, one would expect the available faculty development resources of the university to be sufficient to return a faculty member's performance to a satisfactory rating before reaching "the (very low) level that triggers the post-tenure review" (1).

Similar confusion arose between faculty and administrators over establishing the rating(s) for triggering post-tenure reviews. The policy did not state whether unsatisfactory performance in *one* area of faculty responsibility was to be considered sufficient to trigger a post-tenure review, or whether it was necessary for a faculty member to exhibit *multiple* deficiencies before receiving an overall unsatisfactory performance rating. Since departments and colleges do not all employ the same evaluation instrument, this too was left to departmental consensus. Again, the senior vice-chancellor urged faculty to understand that:

> You are not writing an algorithm such that, when certain data are entered, it automatically churns out a "grade" on faculty performance; rather, you are writing a framework to inform the professional, academic judgments that will be made by peers and others, as well as to communicate your expectations to individual faculty members subject to evaluation. (1)

Once faculty accepted these interpretations of the policy, the development of departmental performance standards proceeded in a straightforward manner.

#### ***Approving Standards***

A small ad-hoc committee reviewed the departmental standards regarding consistency and conformity to policy guidelines. The committee comprised one associate vice-chancellor from each of the Office of Academic Affairs and the Institute for Agriculture and Natural Resources, and one faculty representative each from the Academic Planning Committee, the Research Council, and the Academic Senate. This committee found the majority of departmental policies to be acceptable; there were only five about which they expressed serious concerns, and only one which they recommended be entirely rewritten (this department had defined unsatisfactory rather than satisfactory performance).

The committee made a number of general recommendations to strengthen all the policies. The committee gave a summary of concerns to the senior vice-chancellor for academic affairs and the vice-chancellor for the Institute for Agriculture and Natural Resources, who in turn gave specific feedback to departments, recommending revisions to their documents. Most revisions specified the quality, significance, and success of faculty efforts in teaching, research, and service.

#### *Reaching Consensus and Assessing Faculty Concerns*

Although departments were not required to reach consensus across departmental lines, the review committee noted "there was clear evidence of consultation among departments and, in several cases, colleges developed college-wide expectations" (Ad Hoc Committee 1999). A survey of academic senators on this process sought to identify the strategies used to develop performance standards and how successful these efforts had been at achieving consensus. Faculty were also asked to identify what disagreements, if any, had occurred, and what level of commitment to the standards was achieved in the end.

The moderate response rate on this survey (29 percent) may be because departments with more than one representative in the senate only returned one survey, reflecting the views of all faculty in their department. In most cases (83 percent), senators reported a genuine attempt had been made, in their units, to develop performance standards based on a consensus among department members. Overall, 23 departments (79 percent of respondents) reported having "very good" to "substantial" involvement in developing the standards. A small number of departments reported the final faculty vote on the standards had not been unanimous, or no vote was taken, or the lack of discussion had been wrongly interpreted as consensus. These respondents felt some faculty had capitulated on the standards. A few responses indicated distrust and resistance or indifference to the idea of post-tenure review.

Even departments reporting general agreement on performance standards expressed an awareness that questions of interpretation and practice would emerge as the standards were applied. Senators suggested the specific language used in the standards needed to be debated by department faculty to achieve consensus, equity across departments, and accurate interpretation by department chairs and heads. Additionally, some faculty questioned how effectively teaching and service would be assessed. The validity of using student teaching evaluations as the primary measure of teaching excellence was specifically challenged. While not new, these issues carry additional weight within the context of post-tenure review because more than just merit and promotion rewards now hinged upon these measures of performance.

Some continuing philosophical issues also emerged as needing further exploration. A few faculty questioned why the policy applies to faculty who are not fully promoted, given they automatically undergo a peer review every third year. Others expressed lingering concerns about the threat post-tenure review poses to tenure and academic freedom at UNL. Faculty were also concerned the policy did not spell out the appropriate response on the part of a chair or unit head in the first year that a faculty member received an unsatisfactory annual evaluation. Questions also arose about what resources would be available to faculty and department heads for devising effective faculty development plans to address these deficiencies before a post-tenure review is triggered, and whether chairs and heads were prepared to develop such plans.

### *Adjusting the Implementation Timeline*

The results of this survey caused campus leaders at UNL to delay implementing post-tenure review by one year. This prevented faculty from being evaluated according to performance standards that had not been defined prior to the academic period being assessed. The delay was considered by many faculty to be the single most important signal that administrators truly intended to implement post-tenure review as a fair and formative policy.

## Consequences of Post-Tenure Review

A triggered approach to post-tenure review increases pressure on department chairs and heads, but there are two other significant pressure points. Linking post-tenure review to annual performance reviews (1) raises the stakes for faculty who obtain unsatisfactory annual performance reviews, and (2) increases the importance of peer input.

#### *Raising the Stakes*

Many concerns documented in the survey of academic senators reflected the growing awareness that UNL's post-tenure review policy significantly raised the stakes for faculty with respect to annual performance evaluations. No longer could faculty accept a reward system out of sync with the work that faculty were assigned to do on behalf of the university. Before post-tenure review, highly respected faculty members at the university had accepted being passed over for merit raises because the work they performed — while of high quality and of importance to the university — was not as recognized as was other academic work within the reward system. Under post-tenure review standards, these faculty might be at risk for post-tenure review.

Additionally, because the new standards for satisfactory performance were based on existing promotion and tenure guidelines, faculty were beginning to ask, "Did we set the bar too high?" The uniformly high standards of excellence required to achieve tenure and promotion had largely been redefined as "satisfactory," making anything less than outstanding performance subject to review. Some wondered whether this was appropriate, or even realistic.

#### *Peer Input to Annual Evaluations*

Faculty were also beginning to discuss the need to increase peer input to the annual performance evaluations. The annual reviews were traditionally done by departmental chairs and heads. Such a system under the post-tenure review policy could needlessly trigger post-tenure reviews, because chairs may not be fully informed of faculty contributions. Many faculty wanted to add peer input to annual reviews to avoid such circumstances. To date, however, no systematic assessment of existing departmental practices regarding peer input to annual evaluations has been conducted at UNL.

## Supporting Department Chairs and Unit Heads

Many faculty concerns identified through the survey of senators would present challenges for department chairs and unit heads as they carried out the next two rounds of annual performance evaluations. Chairs and heads had to work with their departmental and unit governing bodies to implement post-tenure review performance standards, and to simultaneously help faculty devise development plans to avoid triggering a post-tenure review. With more at stake, explicit performance expectations, and faculty calling for more peer input, chairs had to conduct effective reviews of faculty performance and credibly document their assessments. Chairs were expected to need training to fulfill some of these new roles. A survey of chairs and heads conducted in spring 2000 was used to design a series of workshops addressing different aspects of their roles vis-à-vis the implementation of the post-tenure review policy.

### *Assessing and Addressing Needs of Unit Heads and Department Chairs*

The survey asked unit heads and department chairs whether they would like to meet with outside consultants about the implementation of post-tenure review, and what, if any, specific topics they would like the consultants to cover. A summary of the findings of the senate survey was included with this survey. Thirty chairs and heads (50 percent) responded, with slightly more than half expressing interest in meeting to discuss post-tenure review implementation. A list of 19 topics was compiled from their responses, falling into roughly three categories of interest:

1. Understanding the role of the annual faculty performance evaluation in light of post-tenure review.
2. Conducting annual performance evaluations and producing documentation in a legal and defensible manner.
3. Strategies and resources available for developing faculty development plans for faculty undergoing post-tenure review.

Together with the issues identified through the survey of academic senators, these results provided a clear outline of campus concerns and needs pertaining to the implementation of our post-tenure review policy.

### *Workshops for Departments Chairs and Unit Heads*

These concerns were addressed through a series of workshops for department chairs and unit heads. Deans and academic senate leaders were also invited to attend these events, jointly planned between the Office of Academic Affairs, the Academic Senate, and the Office of Professional and Organizational Development within the Institute for Agriculture and Natural Resources. Other individuals were brought into the planning process as appropriate for each phase of development.

Two philosophical principles guided this work:

1. To achieve "efficacy, fairness, and overall contribution to institutional betterment" (University 1997b: 6), UNL's post-tenure review policy would have to be implemented not as an end in itself, but as one element of an overall institutional strategy to promote faculty vitality.
2. Faculty vitality results from a system that supports, recognizes, and rewards excellence, not a principally punitive system.

In this context, post-tenure review may be understood as one consequence of the institution failing to promote faculty vitality, not the primary mechanism for achieving it. This does not mean faculty should not be held accountable (they should) or that academic institutions are to blame if faculty are underproductive. The point is academic institutions cannot sustain vital faculty solely through post-tenure review. Faculty vitality requires a sense of efficacy, fostered by evidence the institution is committed to supporting meaningful and significant work based upon academic merit and not merely profitability, whether commercially, politically, or in terms of institutional clout or prestige.

### *Credible and Defensible Performance Evaluations*

One way to promote faculty vitality is constructive annual performance evaluations. Annual performance evaluations afford the institution opportunities to communicate what work is valued by the organization. To be constructive, these evaluations must be honest; to be effective, they must be grounded in standards that reflect institutional values; and to be meaningful, they must be linked to rewards.

The importance of credible and defensible performance evaluations that provide faculty with constructive, effective, and meaningful feedback coincided with specific concerns raised by both faculty and unit administrators regarding the implementation of post-tenure review. Thus, a discussion of the crucial role department chairs and heads play in conducting these reviews represented a logical starting point for planning a series of workshops.

#### *Links to Other Institutional Priorities*

We also used this workshop to position post-tenure review within the context of broader institutional interests and priorities. Two other projects pertaining to faculty evaluation and vitality were incorporated into this workshop. The first project was "Framework for Documenting Teaching Excellence," developed by the UNL Teaching Academy. The framework addressed faculty concerns about how faculty teaching performance could be meaningfully assessed beyond student evaluations. The document linked several dimensions of teaching to appropriate methods of assessments, thus providing tools to comprehensively gauge each faculty member's effectiveness as an instructor.

Chairs and heads were also invited at this workshop to consider the recommendations of a faculty task force report on the future of research and graduate education at UNL. The report asserted institutional success in these programs could be enhanced by strategically altering the university structure, operations, and culture, enabling faculty to conduct their research and graduate instruction more effectively. Presenting the report's recommendations to the chairs and heads at the workshop was a second opportunity to place post-tenure review policy within the overall institutional context. The resulting discussion emphasized strategies for promoting scholarly excellence by more effectively supporting all aspects of faculty work rather than punishing recalcitrant faculty.

#### *Legal Issues*

A second workshop was held to address department chairs' and unit heads' concerns regarding the legal ramifications of their responsibilities relative to the implementation of the post-tenure review policy. When surveyed, chairs and heads requested guidance about sufficiently documenting performance deficits and writing letters of notice appropriately to avoid legal entanglements for themselves and the institution. Questions were also raised about whether faculty evaluations and faculty development plans could be monitored fairly by the same individual, and how to prevent differentiated workloads from being used inappropriately to avoid review, when deficiencies were not remediated.

The resulting half-day workshop covered these issues and illustrative court decisions on faculty evaluation; the evaluation of teaching, research, and service; and weighing these three areas fairly. Other topics covered were issues pertaining to the Americans With Disabilities Act, methods of communicating results, the handling of appeals, notification of tenure, and letters of recommendation. This workshop covered the procedures of faculty evaluation, and provided chairs and heads with exposure to relevant court decisions without offering specific legal council.

## Faculty Roles Initiative

In January 2000 the implementation of post-tenure review at UNL was combined with other institutional change initiatives on faculty work life and vitality under the umbrella of the Faculty Roles Initiative. The initiative seeks to promote institutional excellence by focusing upon the health and well-being of faculty within academic units. As stated in the project's proposal:

> The proposed initiative would focus upon the creation of supportive work environments that will enable faculty to achieve their highest level of performance in the important academic work that is central to their assignments. A side effect should be better overall performance by the institution, but this initiative will begin and end with individual and unit working conditions. (Brinkerhoff et al. 2000)

The focus of the initiative is twofold:

1. To assess the overall quality of faculty work life within existing departmental units, the nature of scholarship, and the institutional expectations of faculty at UNL.
2. To work with departmental, disciplinary, and interdisciplinary units to develop effective alternative strategies for organizing, recognizing, evaluating, and rewarding faculty work.

The initiative is being carried out with the support of the vice-chancellors for the Office of Academic Affairs and the Institute for Agriculture and Natural Resources, and the Academic Senate. Assessment activities commenced in the fall semester 2000.

The Faculty Roles Initiative encompasses changes within higher education that promote scholarly excellence and diversification and the opportunities these changes present for enhancing faculty vitality by more effectively supporting faculty work and rewarding all forms of significant scholarship appropriately. It is deliberately proactive in addressing a spectrum of issues within the positive framework of recognizing new forms of scholarship, rather than the negative framework of highlighting faculty deficiencies. By providing support for faculty careers and re-organizing faculty work, the project seeks to *prevent* the ills post-tenure review is designed to identify and remediate. The goal is to institute changes to enhance faculty vitality before systemic problems result in declining faculty productivity and trigger post tenure review.

## Next Steps: What Lies Ahead?

Development activity continues at UNL along two fronts: (1) conducting the first round of post-tenure reviews, and (2) fostering departmental leadership and demonstration projects.

### *First Departmental Peer Reviews*

The 2001–02 academic year caps all post-tenure review planning and activities to date, as it is the first year in which departmental peer review committees will be formed to assess the performance records of faculty for whom a post-tenure review has been triggered. A questionnaire was distributed to all department chairs in spring 2001 on the outcomes of the year's annual reviews. The department heads and chairs were asked to indicate which departments would be conducting post-tenure reviews in the coming year. Responses will also be used to tailor appropriate consultation and training activities to the needs of faculty, chairs, and heads in those units.

Two areas of need are anticipated. First, it is anticipated that department chairs and heads and faculty serving on peer review committees will need assistance understanding the complex process and the expectations of all parties involved in conducting the reviews. Second, we will sponsor a workshop on how to develop effective faculty development plans, and outline the resources and services that exist at UNL for constructing such plans.

### *Fostering Departmental Leadership*

In addition to these targeted post-tenure review workshops, we will build upon previous workshops to continue nurturing leadership skills among department chairs and heads. These individuals will be encouraged to take a more active role in maximizing the contributions faculty within their unit make to the work of the department at all stages of their faculty careers. There is also interest in fostering a wider appreciation of faculty leaders as collaborative change agents throughout the institution. Together, chairs and faculty will be encouraged to try new approaches to organizing departmental work and fostering institutional effectiveness.

## Successes and Failures

### *Setting the Context*

Perhaps our greatest success concerning post-tenure review was setting the context for the initial discussion. By speaking openly about the potential threat to academic freedom posed by post-tenure review, and establishing the strengths of existing policies on faculty evaluation, we clarified for ourselves — and the public — the processes already in place to foster regular performance evaluation of all faculty, and to ensure accountability. This was key to the successful negotiations that followed, and the cooperation of faculty into implementing post-tenure review at UNL. Understanding the institutional context also allowed the campus to reject a costly, mandatory, and comprehensive approach to post-tenure review, and negotiate an acceptable window for a triggered, initiated post-tenure review policy.

### *Adjusting the Timeline*

Another key factor was altering the implementation timeline, which was extended to allow faculty to reach consensus about the standards for satisfactory performance. This was crucial to ensure fair and equitable evaluation for all faculty. Otherwise, some faculty might have been evaluated according to performance standards that were not defined prior to the period under review, placing them at a disadvantage in striving to achieve satisfactory ratings during the first year the policy was in effect.

### *Emphasizing Satisfactory Performance*

Instructing faculty to define standards for satisfactory performance, rather than "unsatisfactory" or "minimal" standards, also appears to have been a successful strategy. Doing so permitted more positive discussions about performance expectations, and established the role of professional judgment in the interpretation of individual faculty accomplishments.

### *Establishing Peer Review Procedures*

Explicitly defining the composition and procedures for appointing peer review committees, within the post-tenure review policy itself, was another successful strategy. Considerable time was spent negotiating this aspect of UNL's policy, prior to its adoption, when failure to negotiate could have resulted in the policy being rejected by either party. This subsequently made policy implementation much smoother. We believe it will also ensure greater equity for all faculty who must undergo such a review.

### *No Predefined Sanctions*

UNL's policy does not call for faculty to adopt predefined sanctions applicable in relation to specific performance deficiencies. Rather, each peer review committee — in conjunction with the chair and dean — decides upon appropriate sanctions, given the particular circumstances pertaining to a faculty member's deficiencies. We currently view this as a successful strategy, because it is difficult and time consuming to anticipate all the possible scenarios that might result in performance deficiencies, and it is possible that the predefined sanctions would become outdated or be inappropriate in relation to particular cases.

### *Link to Dismissal*

We consider essential the link between UNL's post-tenure review policy and procedures governing the dismissal of faculty for cause. This link gives post-tenure review serious consequences and lends credibility to the policy in the eyes of the public. If there is no clear link to provisions governing dismissal for cause, governing boards and external constituencies may challenge the credibility of post-tenure review. Equally important, this link ensures that post-tenure review is not permitted to bypass existing provisions for protecting the rights of faculty in conducting grievance investigations, as outlined by faculty governance bodies. Any policy permitting these procedures to be circumvented creates a serious threat to academic freedom, as well as potential inconsistencies that may be subject to legal challenges.

***Refocusing the Conversation***

Finally, we have succeeded in shifting the focus of post-tenure review from individual deficiencies and punitive measures to a productive dialogue about the quality of the institutional environment for nurturing faculty vitality. This is proving to be a rich terrain for fostering faculty-administrative collaboration. The shift was deemed appropriate because post-tenure review is but one of many factors currently affecting the nature of scholarship and the future of the professoriate. This approach has redirected attention from the less than one percent of faculty who may eventually be subject to the punitive procedures outlined in the post-tenure review policy to the greater than 99 percent of faculty whose performance enhances the institution.

***Faculty Resignation***

But UNL's implementation of post-tenure review has not been without some failures. Some faculty believe they have collectively capitulated to the administration on post-tenure review. The original convictions that faculty are already adequately monitored, evaluated, and managed remain strong. Many in the Academic Senate voted to accept the negotiated post-tenure review policy to prevent a less acceptable post-tenure review policy from being forced upon them by the governing board. In addition, some faculty did not participate fully in the development of performance standards for their units, either by choice or due to the strategies employed in their department or college. These undercurrents of unrest are expected to emerge again, in some form, as the first wave of triggered reviews proceeds in the coming academic year.

***Equitable Evaluations***

We consider a potential failure the variation allowed among departments regarding whether performance must be deficient in more than one area of faculty responsibility to trigger a post-tenure review. Although the definition of performance standards offered some clarification on this issue, little has been done to ensure that faculty evaluations are conducted in a consistent and equitable manner across the institution. In general, the significance of a deficiency will be weighed against a faculty member's particular apportionment of appointment, but this is also subject to variation. In some departments, faculty may choose to have their performance in different areas of responsibility weighted differently, even though their apportionment may be equal. Thus two faculty who each have 30 percent of their effort assigned to teaching might choose to have this aspect of their performance weighted differently on their performance evaluations.

#### *Resources for Remediation*

Finally, post-tenure review itself represents a failure to the extent it prescribes a poor use of scarce resources; i.e., throwing resources at remediation rather than at prevention, and putting time and energy into sanctions rather than rewards. The inclusion of provisions for a voluntary post-tenure review, while originally conceived as a means for faculty to secure necessary resources for retooling or making a successful career shift, would have afforded the policy some redemptive value. But, the potential for securing funding through a voluntary post-tenure review was stripped from the policy during its development for fear that it would hamstring already drained departmental budgets.

At this point, it is easier to judge success rather than failures in implementing post-tenure review. The coming year may expose weaknesses not yet detected in our policy and its implementation. Those who drafted the policy recognized that such judgments take time: UNL's policy calls for a review of its efficacy after five years.

### Lessons Learned

Some lessons may benefit other institutions as they consider implementing a triggered post-tenure review policy.

#### *Aligning Institutional Rewards*

First, our experience demonstrates that successful post-tenure review starts with — and builds upon — a sound annual review process. Ultimately, the legitimacy of performance evaluation depends upon the reward system to which it is linked. If an institution's evaluation and reward system does not accurately reflect its organizational values, it cannot serve to promote faculty excellence. Our initial study of faculty roles at UNL suggests many faculty feel a great deal of academic work essential to the advancement of the institution routinely falls to faculty but is not adequately rewarded.

Prior to post-tenure review, some faculty would do this necessary but unrewarded institutional work despite the negative consequences for them in terms of evaluations and merit raises. Post-tenure review has more dire consequences, for individual faculty as well as higher education institutions themselves, if these reward systems are not revised to reflect the range of scholarship and engagement encompassed in their missions. This is a serious issue for the institution, as many different types of faculty work are required to fulfill its mission. The university needs to clarify what is valued and expected of faculty, and to bring its reward system, including standards for faculty performance, into congruence with these needs, expectations, and values. This issue has resource, as well as policy, implications.

#### *Avoiding Comparative Performance Evaluations*

Similarly, we have learned that while faculty expect merit rewards to be comparative, they do not expect the same of annual performance evaluations. That is, faculty accept that merit raises are determined on a relative basis by comparing their performance with the performance of other faculty in their unit. But for the purposes of determining faculty performance ratings themselves, they expect their own accomplishments to be judged in relation to the stated performance standards, not in relation to other faculty member's productivity and accomplishments. For this reason, it is important that annual evaluations be linked to a faculty member's particular position, stated goals for the year, and the apportionment of his or her assignment.

#### *Addressing Systemic Factors Affecting Faculty Vitality*

Most important, we have learned that implementing post-tenure review not only seeks to address faculty deficiencies, it also reveals institutional insufficiencies. Post-tenure review is not an isolated issue but one aspect of a holistic strategy to promote long-term faculty vitality. What UNL has learned is that faculty vitality and productivity are linked. Certainly, faculty development efforts aimed at the deficiencies of individual faculty members represent one strategy for stimulating *vitality* among some faculty. But there are often other, systemic factors involved when a faculty member is underperforming, and these should be addressed as well.

Post-tenure review discussions focus on the inadequacies of individual faculty members, without considering how rapid changes in the academy, in the nature of scholarship, and in the higher education marketplace have made it impossible for faculty to meet the increasing expectations placed upon them. Faculty and university administrators must collaborate to reform how they organize and apportion faculty work to restore the possibility not only of success but of genuine vitality.

***Recognizing Unanswered Questions***

Implementation occurs even though questions remain. What challenges to post-tenure review will play out in the courts? Will UNL's policy withstand legal challenges? In reality, the question remains whether we have set the bar too high in departmental standards of satisfactory performance. Will chairs be judicious in applying these standards? Have we adequately provided for peer input to annual evaluations? Will faculty who contribute significantly to university excellence be unwittingly caught in post-tenure review nightmares? Moreover, will we be able to ensure equity across academic units in the conduct of annual evaluations, given the amount of variation our policy permits among annual review procedures and the reliance upon professional judgment in their interpretation?

What will be the impact of these post-tenure review policies on academic freedom? Will department chairs and heads — even inadvertently — use these policies to stop research that does not garner significant grant funds? Will institutions impose research agendas upon faculty in ways that compromise intellectual innovation and integrity? Have we put sufficient safeguards in place? What is the role of departmental goals in post-tenure review? Can post-tenure review be triggered for a faculty member who is doing high-quality research in unsanctioned areas of study?

## Recommendations for Other Institutions With Triggered Systems

Based on our successes and failures and the lessons learned, we offer the following recommendations for successfully developing and implementing post-tenure review.

1. Link post-tenure review to existing dismissal standards and grievance procedures, as this both lends credibility to the policy and closes significant loopholes that could otherwise lead

to legal battles.

2. Put performance standards in place before implementing post-tenure review. This will permit the institution to both win faculty confidence and avoid potential legal nightmares.

3. Prepare department chairs and heads for conducting efficacious annual reviews, and do not neglect the need for legal education relative to their role in faculty evaluation and post-tenure review implementation.

4. Post-tenure review is not an end in itself, nor is it necessarily a means of ensuring faculty productivity. Productivity is a function of faculty vitality that does not necessarily result from post-tenure review but results from efforts to support faculty development and create quality work environments.

5. Systemic issues often underlie individual performance deficits. Is faculty work adequately supported? Are faculty workloads realistic? Do adequate opportunities exist for faculty development in areas such as digital scholarship, instructional technologies, pedagogical techniques, grant writing, and community outreach? Are different aspects of faculty work appropriately evaluated and rewarded? Are faculty given a respectable voice in shaping institutional priorities? These issues are not necessarily addressed by post-tenure review.

6. Annual reviews of faculty performance require peer input. It combats problems relative to the reluctance of department chairs and unit heads to assign unsatisfactory ratings to faculty. In some cases, it is unfair *not* to assign unsatisfactory ratings to underperforming faculty. Peer input makes it clear that a chair or head will be supported in his or her actions. For this reason, post-tenure review can actually strengthen departmental culture, by strengthening the voice of faculty in evaluations and supporting the role of chairs and heads in triggering post-tenure review.

7. Faculty share responsibility for leadership and development, both their own and that of their department(s).

8. The motivations for implementing post-tenure review affect the way a policy is written and implemented and will determine whether the intended goals are met.

Implementing post-tenure review requires significant change in the culture of higher education institutions. At every stage of policy development and implementation, assessing and shaping the context for negotiations and changes in university culture are keys to ensuring success.

## Note

1. Gail F. Latta is professor of libraries at the University of Nebraska-Lincoln, and during 2001-02 is a faculty associate in the Office of Academic Affairs. She is project leader for the Faculty Roles Initiative, a former president of the UNL Academic Senate, and has a continuing appointment as faculty associate for faculty development in instructional technologies with the Teaching and Learning Center. As liaison for UNL's New Pathways II grant, Latta helped develop and administer campus assessments and plan workshops for department chairs. She has a B.A. in psychology from the University of Texas at Arlington and an M.L.S. from Texas Woman's University. (Contact her at glatta@unlnotes.unl.edu)

Daniel W. Wheeler is coordinator of the Office of Professional and Organizational Development and professor of extension and higher education at the University of Nebraska-Lincoln. He has a B.A. in biology from Antioch College, an M.S. in science education from Cornell University, and a Ph.D. from the State University of New York at Buffalo in foundations of education. Wheeler has also held positions at the State University of New York at Fredonia and the University of Nebraska at Omaha. (Contact him at dwheeler1@unl.edu)

## References

Ad Hoc Committee to Review Faculty Performance Statements for Post-Tenure Review. (January 26, 1999). "Summary of Concerns About Post-Tenure Review Statements of Faculty Performance." Lincoln, NE: University of Nebraska-Lincoln.

Brinkerhoff, D., S. Hilliard, P. Kennedy, N. Kenny, G. Latta, and D. Stanley. (January 31, 2000). "Proposal for a Faculty Roles Initiative." Lincoln, NE: University of Nebraska-Lincoln.

Edwards, R.C. (September 3, 1998). "Memorandum to Deans, Department Chairs, Directors, Heads, and Academic Senators, Re: Deadline Extended for Statements on Faculty Performance Expectations." Lincoln, NE: University of Nebraska-Lincoln.

Executive Committee of the Academic Senate. (1996). "The Academic Context for Periodic Review of Tenured Faculty at UNL." Lincoln, NE: University of Nebraska-Lincoln.

Faculty Roles Initiative, Gail F. Latta, Project Leader. (n.d.). "Faculty Roles Initiative: Charting the Future of the Professoriate at UNL." Lincoln, NE: University of Nebraska-Lincoln.

Jacobson, E. (February 23, 2001). "Post-Tenure Review." Lincoln, NE: University of Nebraska-Lincoln.

———, and G.F. Latta. (February 2000). "Unit Heads and Department Chairs Survey." Lincoln, NE: University of Nebraska-Lincoln.

Latta, G.F. (December 3, 1998). "Implementing PTR: Questions." Lincoln, NE: University of Nebraska-Lincoln.

———. (Spring 1999). "Survey of Academic Senators Regarding Implementation of the Port Tenure Review Policy." Lincoln, NE: University of Nebraska-Lincoln.

University of Nebraska Board of Regents. (September 30, 1997a). "UNL Post-Tenure Review Proposal." Lincoln, NE: Author.

———. (September 30, 1997b, amended 9/16/98). "UNL Post-Tenure Review Policy." Lincoln, NE: Author.

———. (January 1998). "Post-Tenure Review Policy." Lincoln, NE: Author.

UNL Teaching Academy. (Spring 2000). "Framework for Documenting Teaching Excellence." Lincoln, NE: University of Nebraska-Lincoln.

# Attachment A

## THE ACADEMIC CONTEXT FOR PERIODIC REVIEW OF TENURED FACULTY AT UNL

The Executive Committee of the Academic Senate

The role and structure of higher education in our society, and the design and rigor of educational programs in American institutions of higher education are currently the subjects of extensive public discussion. This healthy discussion allows for full public participation in examining expectations for higher education as it addresses the challenges of meeting society's educational needs in the next century. One focus of this examination is the tenure system. Some think tenure is a restrictive force inhibiting responsiveness to society's needs in a time of shrinking public financial support for higher education. Others think tenure insulates faculty from society's ability to hold them accountable. These perceptions need to be acknowledged, and seriously addressed.

In response to the public debate over tenure and, more specifically, recent administrative discussions at UNL on the topic of the periodic review of tenured faculty, the Academic Senate Executive Committee has reviewed the continuous appointment (tenure) system at UNL as it operates under University of Nebraska Bylaws & Guidelines. As a result of this examination, we have concluded that, in general, existing UNL policies and practices position the University well with regard to the need to negotiate changing faculty assignments and the necessity for rigorous review of faculty performance. We feel those who would challenge the present system should demonstrate inadequacies in existing standards and practices before asking that alternatives be considered.

Our response is not a rejection of informed suggestions for improvement before they are made; rather it is a sincere invitation to critics to point out where the current system of continuous faculty review at UNL falls short in achieving its academic purposes before making those suggestions. Legitimate calls for change should be based on evidence of weakness in the present system or a demonstration of the superiority of any proposed plan for periodic review of tenured faculty over the current system of continuous review. The faculty at UNL stand ready to participate in any discussion of the faculty review process motivated by academic concerns.

### THE ROLE OF TENURE

Academic discussion of post-tenure review must begin with a reaffirmation of the purpose tenure serves in upholding the goals and mission of the University. We are concerned that some discussions on the periodic review of tenured faculty have proceeded without a clear exposition of the significant role tenure plays in creating an environment in which teaching, research, thinking and expression may proceed, not free from evaluation, but under the protection of academic freedom.

Tenure was created to protect academic freedom. The purpose of academic freedom is well stated in Section 4.2., on "Academic Freedom," of the Bylaws of the Board of Regents of the University of Nebraska, dated June 13, 1992:

The University serves the people of Nebraska and the common good through learning, teaching, extension work, research, scholarship, and public service. Fulfillment of these functions requires the preservation of intellectual freedoms of teaching, expression, research, and debate. The right to search for truth, to support a position the searcher believes is the truth, and to disagree with others whose intellect reaches a different conclusion is the fiber of America's greatness. It is likewise, the strength of a great University, and its preservation is vital.

Tenure has helped to preserve an intellectual environment in which faculty with demonstrated records of scholarly and instructional performance can pursue the search for truth without threat of discrimination or reprisal. As past history has unfortunately shown, without tenure, the educational process in America's universities is at risk of coming under the control of special interests and unchallenged thinking.

The faculty of UNL are firmly committed to the idea that all faculty members must be rigorously tested before tenure is granted. After being hired, a faculty member's commitment and contributions to the University's tripartite mission of teaching, research, and service are rigorously tested for an average probationary period of six years. Probationary faculty are awarded tenure only after being recognized as highly competent, capable and contributing members of the University. This judgment is administered through a rigorous and coherent system involving many levels of review at the departmental, collegiate, campus, central administrative, and regental levels.

RESPONSIBILITIES OF TENURED FACULTY

Upon being granted tenure, faculty accept the academic obligations and duties outlined in Chapter IV. "Rights and Responsibilities of Professional Staff" of the Regents' Bylaws. Tenured faculty commit to remain competent and active in their fields of study, to convey their knowledge to society either through the formal classroom or outreach programs, to conduct research to expand the frontiers of knowledge, and, to "create and protect an atmosphere of intellectual honesty in the academic community."

RESPONSIBILITIES OF THE UNIVERSITY

When considering the productivity of tenured faculty, it is important to analyze the academic environment in which these faculty function. The granting of tenure constitutes a long-term commitment to the faculty on the part of the University. This commitment includes responsibility to preserve an environment in which:

Members of the staff shall not suffer sanctions or be discriminated against with respect to the duration of association with the University, pay or other emolument of their office, appointment, position, or their working conditions because of their enjoyment, or exercise, of their right of academic freedom. (Bylaws 4.2)

The significant kernel of this commitment relates to the creation and maintenance of an environment in which faculty initiative and excellence are facilitated and rewarded. In such an environment, faculty can feel confident to venture into unfamiliar or even unpopular teaching and research areas.

The University is a community that exists to promote discovery and learning. While recognizing its responsibility to respond to appropriate local and immediate requests for its services, the University must maintain this academic ideal in the face of vacillating political, social, or commercial interests.

The University must also ensure that faculty maintain high academic standards. In cases in which faculty are not maintaining high standards, the underlying causes should be determined before appropriate corrective strategies are implemented.

REVIEW OF TENURED FACULTY

How well tenured faculty members fulfill their responsibilities is evaluated on an annual basis, according to procedures specified in the University Bylaws and Guidelines for the Evaluation of Faculty, which call for the continuous, thorough review of faculty performance. These documents clearly state that a faculty member's performance is to be reviewed in relation to his or her current position description (including detailed apportionment of assignment), in relation to the department's and the University's mission. Sanctions administered in connection with such reviews, when the outcome is not positive, range from withholding merit raises to termination of continuous appointment in cases where adequate cause can be demonstrated, according to IV.4.11 of the University Bylaws.

We are concerned, however, when punitive and corrective consequences are the primary outcomes identified in discussions of proposed changes to existing evaluation procedures. Discussions on the periodic review of tenured faculty at UNL have sometimes focused primarily upon what would occur in response to negative review outcomes, i.e., the identification of mechanisms and resources which would be invested to redirect, rejuvenate, or retool unproductive faculty members through faculty development opportunities or reassignment of duties, and to strengthen the bases for dismissal. Of course, no faculty could support a system that protected unproductive or incompetent faculty; ineffective faculty members should be identified and encouraged to improve. On the other hand, at least equal attention should be given in these discussions to opportunities which might be created within the process of faculty review for recognizing and rewarding meritorious performance and initiative through faculty development opportunities, providing released time to pursue new areas of research, teaching innovation, or service opportunities.

Recognizing and rewarding faculty initiative should be as integral a component of periodic review of tenured faculty discussions as the remedial or punitive actions that have been suggested to address documented cases of non-performance. Following each annual review, a faculty member's department chair and/or other administrators are responsible for negotiating with faculty any changes of assignment necessary to ensure that future goals of the academic unit are fulfilled. The Guidelines for faculty review further call for a peer-review of tenured, but not fully promoted faculty, every three years, until the status of full professor has been attained.

Some academic departments are going well beyond the minimum requirements for faculty review. Faculty and administrators must join together to ensure that all units conform in their policies and practices to the standards and procedures outlined in the University's Bylaws and Guidelines in order to document each faculty member's work on an annual basis, thereby establishing a permanent record of service at UNL. The faculty recognize that administrators are also accountable for the review process because they are responsible for ensuring that the process is administered in a consistently rigorous manner across the University. If there are administrative concerns that annual reviews in any department are not rigorous enough, assessment of the situation should begin with an examination of how well existing guidelines are in fact being carried out.

CONCLUSIONS

Recognizing the importance of tenure to the preservation of academic freedom, and given the belief that existing UNL Bylaws and Guidelines, when implemented appropriately, provide for a rigorous system of continuous review of tenured faculty, the Academic Senate Executive Committee feels that the discussion on post-tenure review of faculty at UNL should acknowledge the following:

1. The University community must ensure that discussions of proposed changes to existing review procedures for tenured faculty at UNL take place within the context of a healthy discussion of the purpose and value of tenure for faculty, students, and society. Any discussions of policies affecting the review of tenured faculty at UNL must take place within a context which affirms this institution's commitment to tenure, and to the protection of academic freedom. Without the protection of the tenure system, this debate could not occur; and higher education would be in danger of coming under the control of primarily political interests.

2. University Bylaws and Guidelines must be rigorously followed in all units. Existing University guidelines provide for the full involvement of departmental chairs and college deans in negotiating

changes in faculty assignments on an annual basis. Additional procedures and guidelines for handling negative evaluations should be proposed only if existing guidelines and procedures are examined and found to be inadequate.

University administration and faculty share responsibility for ensuring that policies and practices follow current Bylaws and Guidelines. Review of existing policies and practices, as well as the instruments used for recording and reporting faculty performance is always in order, to ensure that provision is being made for faculty reward, redirection, and development.

3. UNL policy provides for substantive annual reviews of all faculty, as well as additional third-year peer reviews of all tenured, but not fully promoted faculty. If current policies for faculty review are found to be adequate, the only new element which might be considered would be a formative periodic peer review of fully promoted faculty to personal, departmental, and University goals. Of course, such a review would have to be made consistent with the goals of tenure, including the preservation of academic freedom.

4. Without minimizing the importance of the corrective function of evaluation, any additions to the current system of pre- and post-tenure review of faculty should have a positive focus, rather than focusing primarily on sanctions for negative evaluations. A suggestion that the effective outcome of additional measures for periodic review of tenured faculty at UNL would be the awarding of additional resources for faculty development and release time for redirecting those faculty receiving consistently negative evaluations, rather than the systematic identification and rewarding of faculty who continuously demonstrate outstanding performance, productivity, and initiative in carrying out their appointed faculty responsibilities is ultimately destructive of faculty morale.

5. Consideration should be given in these discussion to the magnitude of additional faculty time and administrative costs that would be required to implement additional review procedures. New, costly mechanisms for conducting additional faculty reviews should be avoided, if existing review procedures, when adequately enforced, are sufficient for achieving the goals of ongoing faculty development and reward.

# Attachment B

## POST-TENURE REVIEW POLICY

*(9/30/97, amended 9/16/98)*

*[This proposal would add to the "University of Nebraska-Lincoln Guidelines for the Evaluation of Faculty" a new section "C" on page IV.A.6; the current section "C" would become section "D".]*

**C. Special Peer Review**

1. **Purpose.** The special peer review process is intended to assist tenured faculty in achieving their professional goals and maximizing their contributions to the University throughout their professional careers, to provide assurance to the public that tenured faculty are accountable for their performance, and to provide continued peer involvement in the review of tenured faculty members. (It remains the responsibility of the Senior Vice Chancellor for Academic Affairs and the Vice Chancellor for the Institute of Agriculture and Natural Resources, respectively, to ensure that annual reviews referred to herein are conducted in all departments in a rigorous and equitable manner.)

2. **Applicability of Review Process.** The special peer review process is applicable to all members of the faculty who have been on a continuous contract pursuant to Board of Regents By-laws 4.4.3 for a period of three years or more. A faculty member shall not be subject to or eligible for a special peer review more than once every four years. A faculty member shall be reviewed in accordance with the special peer review process in either of the following circumstances:

a. A faculty member receives (after the third year of being on continuous contract):

(1). A written annual evaluation from the unit administrator that identifies a substantial and chronic deficiency (1) in the faculty member's performance and clearly states that if the faculty member does not make substantial, acceptable progress toward remedying the deficiency by the next annual evaluation, a post-tenure review will be initiated; and

(2). Notification deriving from the next annual review that the unit administrator has determined that the substantial and chronic deficiency identified in the previous evaluation has not been remedied, that a post-tenure review is appropriate, and that the dean concurs. Ordinarily, the faculty member shall be provided notification by June 30 that a review will be scheduled for the following academic year. Upon recommendation of the unit administrator and approval of the dean, a faculty member subject to post-tenure review under this section may be exempted or deferred for review if there are clearly extenuating circumstances (such as health problems) and an alternate plan for addressing the problems is adopted.

b. A faculty member requests a review in accordance with the special peer review process. The purpose of such a review would be to provide helpful evaluation and assistance to the faculty member in planning a prospective program by which the faculty member can maximize his or her contributions to the University and more fully realize his or her professional goals.

1

This document contains language that brings UNL's rules into compliance with the post-tenure review framework approved by the Regents. These changes

3. **Initiating the Review Process.**

a. Whenever a special peer review is initiated, either by the faculty member or the unit administrator, the unit administrator shall first consult with the faculty member and then shall establish a schedule for the conduct of the review. Ordinarily, the review shall be scheduled for the academic year, and preferably the fall term, following notification of, or request by, the faculty member.

b. For a review initiated under C.2.a above, the unit administrator shall construct a special peer review file containing a clear identification and description of the deficiency or deficiencies, copies of the faculty member's last three annual reviews, such other materials as are relevant, and a document suggesting ways in which the deficiency could be removed. For a review initiated under C.2.b above, the unit administrator shall provide the Review Committee with a file containing copies of the faculty member's previous three annual reviews and such other materials as are relevant.

c. The faculty member shall have the opportunity to supplement the special peer review file throughout the review process by including any information the faculty member believes to be material and helpful to the Review Committee or to administrators involved in the review process. The unit administrator shall cooperate with the faculty member to provide relevant information and shall periodically notify the faculty member of additions to the file. The faculty member shall be given access to all materials in the special peer review file. If the faculty member acknowledges a deficiency in performance, he or she is encouraged to include in the file a plan to remedy the deficiency or to otherwise maximize the faculty member's achievement of professional goals and contribution to the unit's mission, with specific goals and timetables for their achievement.

d. The faculty member and the unit administrator may include in the file a response to material provided by the other.

e. The unit administrator shall provide the Review Committee with a copy of the procedures and schedule for the special peer review.

4. **Appointing the Review Committee.**

a. A Review Committee shall be selected to conduct the review of the faculty member's performance. The Committee shall be composed of an appropriate group of tenured faculty from within and outside the unit who hold an academic rank at least equal to that of the faculty member to be reviewed. The Committee shall include some representation of the discipline and mission of the faculty member under review. Ordinarily the Committee should be composed of 3 individuals capable of providing a fair and unbiased assessment of the faculty member's performance.

b. Initially, the unit administrator and the faculty member shall meet and attempt to agree on the composition of the Committee, which must be approved by the dean.

c. If the unit administrator and the faculty member are unable to agree on the composition of the Committee, the Committee shall be chosen by an appropriate elected faculty committee within the unit, or, for departments with fewer than ten full-time faculty members, within the College; the composition of the Committee is subject to approval by the dean. Each unit, in its by-laws or otherwise, shall have previously designated the appropriate elected faculty committee for this purpose.

2

have been accepted by the Academic Rights and Responsibilities Committee and Academic Senate.

5. **Conducting the Review**

a. The Review Committee shall review the file constructed for this purpose and may meet with the unit administrator and the faculty member, either together or separately. The Committee may consult other sources of information not included in the file with the approval of the unit administrator and the faculty member.

b. Evaluation by peers external to the campus is required when research productivity is an issue: evaluation by peers external to the campus may be used when teaching and/or service/extension productivity is in question. If the Review Committee determines that evaluation by external peers is required or would be useful, the Committee shall notify the unit administrator and the faculty member. Thereafter, such outside reviews shall be obtained in accordance with the same procedure utilized by the unit to obtain outside reviews for purposes of making tenure decisions.

c. In accordance with the schedule for the review established by the unit administrator, the Review Committee shall make a written report of its findings and recommendations, if any.

d. If the special peer review is conducted at the request of the unit administrator pursuant to section C.2.a of this procedure, the written report of the Review Committee shall be provided to the unit administrator, the faculty member's dean, and the faculty member.

e. If the special peer review is conducted at the request of the faculty member pursuant to section C.2.b of this procedure, the written report of the Review Committee shall be provided solely to the faculty member. The faculty member, at his or her discretion, may keep the Report confidential, share it with the unit administrator, or share it with the unit administrator and dean. If requested by the faculty member, the unit administrator and dean shall provide a written response to the Report, indicating the extent to which he or she agrees or disagrees with the findings and recommendations of the Report and why. At the request of the faculty member, the Report and any response from administrators shall be made part of the faculty member's permanent personnel record.

The faculty member, the unit administrator, and the dean shall work together to implement those recommendations on which they mutually agree. Nothing in the Report shall be used in any university evaluation without the consent of the faculty member. However, the faculty member may not attempt to utilize only a portion of the Report or any edited version of the Report in other university evaluations.

6. **Preparing the Review Committee Report**

a. The purpose of the Review Committee Report is to provide an assessment of the performance of the faculty member subject to review and, where appropriate or necessary, to provide recommendations to maximize the faculty member's contributions to the unit and the University. The Review Committee Report is advisory. The Report shall include part (1) below and, as appropriate, parts (2) through (5):

(1). An assessment of the strengths and weaknesses of the faculty member's performance;

(2). Recommendations for ways, if any, in which the faculty member could enhance achievement of his or her professional goals and his or her contributions to the mission of the unit, including suggestions, where appropriate, for adjustment in the faculty member's responsibilities, goals and timetables for meeting the goals, and criteria for assessing the faculty member's achievement of enhanced performance.

(3). An evaluation of any proposed plan submitted by the unit administrator or the faculty member to remedy any deficiency in the faculty member's performance and any recommended modification to such a plan.

(4). Recommendations for ways, if any, in which the unit administrator could provide professional development support to assist the faculty member in enhancing achievement of his or her professional goals and his or her contribution to the mission of the unit.

(5). For a review initiated under C.2.a. above, any recommendations for sanctions to be imposed upon the faculty member for performance characterized by substantial and chronic deficiency.

b. The Review Committee, if it believes that inappropriate criteria have been used to evaluate the faculty member, shall also indicate that fact in its Report.

c. For a review initiated under C.2.a above, the Review Committee shall make one of the following findings, to be clearly stated in its Report:

(1). The faculty member has not identified substantial and chronic deficiencies. If the Review Committee finds that the faculty member's performance does not reflect any substantial and chronic deficiency or deficiencies for the period under review, the faculty member and the unit administrator will be so informed in writing and the review is thereby completed.

(2). The faculty member has substantial and chronic deficiencies. The Review Committee shall state and describe the deficiency or deficiencies in its Report, which shall include all the elements listed under 6.a, items (1) through (5). The Committee shall provide a copy to the faculty member and the unit administrator.

d. The unit administrator shall allow the faculty member being reviewed an opportunity to provide a written response to the Review Committee Report. Except when the review was conducted at the faculty member's request, the Report and any response from the faculty member shall be made a part of the faculty member's permanent personnel record.

7. **Completing the Review Process under a Finding of Substantial and Chronic Deficiency**

a. Upon receipt of a Review Committee report and the faculty member's response, if any, the unit administrator shall meet with the faculty member reviewed to consider the report and any recommendations therein. The unit administrator shall then provide the faculty member and the dean with a written appraisal of the faculty member's performance, together with all documentation pertaining to the faculty member's review, including the file constructed for the review, the Review Committee's Report, and the faculty member's written response to the review, if any. The appraisal shall include, where appropriate:

(1). the extent to which the unit administrator accepts or rejects the findings and recommendations of the Review Committee Report and the reasons for doing so; the unit administrator may reject the Review Committee's findings only for

4

compelling reasons, communicated in writing to the faculty member and the dean.

(2). a plan outlining the expectations of the unit administrator as to how the faculty member can remedy any deficiency in performance or enhance the faculty member's professional goals and contribution to the unit, including specific goals and time tables for achieving such goals and the criteria to be applied in making such a determination;

(3). the resources the unit administrator is willing and able to provide the faculty member to assist in implementing the plan;

(4). any adjustment in assignment or responsibilities of the faculty member; and

(5). any sanction to be imposed on the faculty member related to his or her performance. Sanctions governed by Regents By-laws shall only be imposed following the procedure prescribed in the by-laws.

b. The dean, after review and consultation, may accept, modify, or reject the unit administrator's written appraisal and recommendations, but where the dean's appraisal differs from that provided by the Review Committee or where the dean accepts recommendations that differ from those provided by Review Committee, the dean may modify or reject only for compelling reasons, communicated in writing. The dean's response shall be provided to the faculty member and to the unit administrator.

c. A faculty member dissatisfied with the results of the special peer review and the unit administrator's subsequent appraisal, or the dean's acceptance, modification or rejection of it, may pursue any appeal or remedy otherwise available to faculty members relating to matters that affect their employment status (2).

d. Progress towards achieving the goals and timetables set out in the unit administrator's plan, as approved by the dean, will be reviewed in subsequent annual reviews. If the faculty member fails to achieve the goals and timetables defined in that plan, those administrative processes defined by the Regent's By-laws (and different from special peer review) may be initiated as appropriate. Special peer review is not a prerequisite for initiation of those other administrative processes.

8. **Review of the Special Peer Review**

In the academic year following its fifth full year of operation, the Special Peer Review system shall be reviewed by a joint taskforce of administrators and faculty members. The taskforce shall assess the system's efficacy, fairness, and overall contribution to institutional betterment.

---

(1). The standards for substantial and chronic deficiency shall be determined by the faculty in each unit and, when approved by the appropriate unit administrator, dean and vice chancellor, shall become part of its evaluation procedures.

(2). By University regulations and tradition, faculty members have appealed adverse personnel decisions up the chain of administration from Deans to the Senior Vice Chancellor or Vice Chancellor for IANR to the Chancellor. This process would be unaffected by the regulations governing special peer review. In addition faculty have the option of invoking established University procedures administered by the Academic Rights and Responsibilities Committee. Allegations of violation of academic freedom, procedural irregularity and professional misconduct are currently handled through that Committee. In the unusual case in which a recommendation of termination is made against a tenured faculty member, established University procedures would require the case to be heard by an Academic Freedom and Tenure Committee.

# Balancing Institutional Processes and State-Mandated Post-Tenure Review

**Betsy E. Brown** [1]

Like many public institutions, Winthrop University has faced the challenge of integrating externally mandated post-tenure review into its existing faculty evaluation system. Winthrop faculty recognized ambiguities inherent in the post-tenure review mandate and developed a low-risk, low-benefit policy that highlighted the consequential nature of post-tenure review while linking developmental and reward systems to existing institutional processes. The institution used an AAHE post-tenure review minigrant to prepare faculty and administrators for the new review process and strengthen the annual review process.

## The Performance Funding Mandate

In 1996, the South Carolina General Assembly passed legislation linking all funding for higher education institutions to institutional performance on 37 performance indicators. The indicators range from average class size and faculty credentials to institutional spending patterns. Two indicators relate to faculty evaluation. Institutions are required to have a comprehensive faculty performance review process including assessments by the faculty member, peers, students, and supervisors, such as deans and department chairs. In addition, institutions are mandated to develop post-tenure review policies and procedures. The staff of the state's coordinating body, the South Carolina Commission on Higher Education, and institutional representatives developed a set of "Best Practices" both for the performance review system and for post-tenure review (see the attachments at the end of this chapter). [2] Each four-year institution had to develop policies and procedures based on these practices. Institutions were expected to submit policies for approval to the commission in time to implement them in 1999–2000.

Winthrop University is a state-supported, comprehensive teaching university offering bachelor's, master's, and specialist degrees in arts and sciences, education, business administration, and visual and performing arts. The university has long-established processes for faculty performance review viewed as effective by faculty and administrators. There is pre-tenure review for probationary faculty members involving peers, the department chair, and the dean. There is also an annual performance review including faculty self-assessments of teaching, scholarship, and service; student evaluations; and assessments by the department chair and dean. Finally, the tenure and promotion processes require peer and administrative evaluation at the departmental, college, and institutional levels. Winthrop faculty felt they were already adequately reviewed "post-tenure" and were skeptical of the value of this new review procedure.

During 1997–98, Winthrop established a task force on post-tenure review to develop a policy to comply with the state mandate. The task force was diverse, co-chaired by two deans (one was this author), and included department chairs and faculty members [3] from all academic units and the library. Despite faculty skepticism and the need for compliance with the state-mandated best practices, this group developed a consensus document unanimously approved by the faculty in May 1998 and by the Board of Trustees in February 1999. The task force succeeded in developing a post-tenure review process acceptable to faculty, the board, and the state commission by balancing the required components of the new review process with institutional values and existing institutional processes.

## Summative and Developmental Goals Conflict in Faculty Performance Review

Because the post-tenure review system had to comply with the state-approved best practices, the basic components of the system were already mandated.

1. *Periodic:* In addition to their annual performance reviews, all faculty would participate in the post-tenure review process; thus, the system would be "periodic" (every tenured faculty member reviewed at least every six years) rather than "trig-

gered" by one or more unsatisfactory annual reviews.

2. *Developmental and Consequential:* The best practices mandated "equal emphasis should be given to future development and potential contributions" (a developmental focus) and to past performance (a consequential focus), since faculty who received unfavorable reviews would be required to participate in an improvement process. If after two years they did not demonstrate satisfactory performance on a second review, they would be subject to existing procedures for termination with cause.

3. *Peer Reviewed:* Peer review was required, in addition to administrative review.

4. *Linked to Reward Systems:* Institutions had to "identify the means by which the post-tenure review is linked with faculty reward systems, including merit raises."

5. F*unds Provided for Recognition and Development:* Institutions were also required to "display a commitment to provide funds to reward high achievers on post-tenure reviews as well as to provide assistance to faculty members needing improvement."

The South Carolina best practices define a hybrid system of post-tenure review that Joan North called the "inspection" type, a summative evaluation with a developmental overlay:

> . . . in which an evaluation is required of all tenured faculty . . . regardless of achievement. While there is a desire for all participants to improve, the consequential teeth inherent in this approach make it clear that its primary purpose is to ferret out the laggards. The principle of "equal treatment" seems to tower over the principle of merit, since all tenured faculty must be measured against minimum expectations. Interestingly, many post-tenure review programs of the Inspection type profess to be developmental and downplay their summative soul. But when a university's review committee looks for satisfactory or unsatisfactory performance, with sanctions for poor performance, it is hard to disguise the summative nature. (North 1999: 11)

The ambiguity North detects in inspection systems is often reflected in externally mandated institutional policies and procedures. Campus-driven policies are likely to be clearer about the developmental or consequential purpose of the review.

## Underlying Assumptions

The Winthrop policies and procedures for post-tenure review reflect a number of assumptions growing out of the ambiguity between developmental and consequential purposes in inspection-type post-tenure review. Winthrop's task force members agreed on the following assumptions:

1. *Purpose:* Post-tenure review could not effectively achieve both developmental and consequential ends, despite the dual purposes defined in the state mandate.

2. *Relationship to Existing Processes:* As an external mandate, post-tenure review should complement, not supercede, existing faculty evaluation processes.

3. *Commitment of Funds:* Given limited resources for faculty development and faculty rewards, the institution should not link funds for merit pay or faculty development (except for those faculty found unsatisfactory through post-tenure review) directly to a post-tenure review process; instead, faculty development and monetary rewards should remain linked to existing evaluation processes.

## Consequences of Assumptions

Several features of Winthrop's policies and procedures demonstrate the consequences of these assumptions for institutional post-tenure review policies. [4]

### *Evaluation Threshold*

Although Winthrop's process includes reports written by peer review, the policy asks reviewers to rate their peers as either satisfactory or unsatisfactory, and does not ask reviewers to distinguish between other levels of performance. Given a choice of distinguishing among unsatisfactory, satisfactory, and outstanding or superior performance, the task force decided against more than two standards of evaluation. They felt asking peers to rate colleagues who were performing satisfactorily would create more dissension than benefit. As with other aspects of the post-tenure review process, the task force was unwilling to risk collegiality in a process they and their colleagues had not initiated.

### *Emphasis on Primary Responsibility*

Although in their report (which goes to the faculty member and the chair) peer reviewers evaluate faculty performance in all three areas of responsibility — teaching, scholarship, and service — the definition of unsatisfactory performance is linked to performance solely in the faculty member's area of "primary responsibility." For most faculty, this area is teaching. The use of a single criterion for determining unsatisfactory performance was troubling to the governing board; however, given that the process was intended to identify and possibly eliminate the poorer performers, the review should only be based on the faculty member's core responsibility. Some may have joined the faculty when expectations for scholarship were lower than expectations for teaching and service to students. Other faculty evaluation processes and the peer review reports, they argued, could more appropriately address performance in other areas of responsibility; tenure and promotion processes — and their links to rewards — should reflect the current mix of expectations.

#### *Cohort Mix*

Rather than beginning the six-year review cycle with those tenured the longest, each year's group of faculty to be reviewed is a cohort of those who have been tenured six, 12, 18, even 24 or 30 years regardless of the year of promotion. This process avoids targeting older faculty members in an attempt to "get rid of the deadwood."

#### *No Direct Links to Funds*

Winthrop's policy and procedures make no direct link between post-tenure evaluation and faculty compensation or funds for faculty development. The task force rejected a possible automatic salary increase or bonus based on post-tenure review. The existing reward system — though limited in terms of state and institutional resources — rested on processes developed within the institution, familiar to faculty and administrators, and more likely to achieve the purported "formative" goal of post-tenure review.

#### *Low Risk and Low Benefit*

Defining only a satisfactory/unsatisfactory rating system, linking unsatisfactory performance exclusively to the prime area of responsibility, developing a cohort model, and declining to link rewards directly to post-tenure review are decisions that, taken together, create a post-tenure review process with relatively low risk and correspondingly low benefit. Many members of the task force were convinced faculty would only accept post-tenure review if the risks and benefits were minimal. As one participant put it, "The size of the stick needs to be in direct proportion to the size of the carrot."

## Realism Versus Idealism

Advocates for the developmental value of post-tenure review will decry the compromises of this cost/benefit equation. Externally mandated review processes invite compromise by conflating two different types of review (summative and formative). Faculty are reluctant to redirect faculty time and institutional resources from familiar processes to an unknown one, or to impose unnecessary risks with the new review process. The Winthrop experience suggests that while externally mandated post-tenure review may serve institutional ends and states can define post-tenure review processes as "developmental" for all faculty rather than as punitive for poorer performers, faculty members are skeptical about these dual purposes.

## Winthrop's "Projects With Promise" Grant Activities

Faculty skepticism about the developmental aspect of a consequential review process is understandable. However, the skepticism reflected in an institutional policy need not be reflected in the post-tenure review process itself. To achieve that goal, Winthrop decided to apply for AAHE's "Projects With Promise" minigrant to:

1. provide training to prepare faculty members and administrators for participation in an effective post-tenure review process;
2. strengthen the existing faculty evaluation and reward system; and
3. develop a comprehensive evaluation process for post-tenure review that could serve as a model for other institutions in South Carolina and across the country.

Winthrop wanted to inform faculty about the new process, including how it related to existing faculty development and evaluation processes. In addition, the institution hoped to encourage faculty to recognize that the process could strengthen the annual review process.

#### *Faculty Workshops*

The grant supported developing materials and workshops for faculty to be reviewed and for peer reviewers. The materials were the post-tenure review policies and procedures, as well as institutional criteria and evidence for satisfactory performance in teaching, scholarship, and service taken from the faculty manual and other sources. Peer reviewers received additional materials tying their evaluation reports to the annual faculty review and reward processes, since the post-tenure review procedures stated these evaluations would be considered in decisions about faculty development opportunities and salary increases.

#### *Faculty Workshop Results and Outcomes*

Attendance was high at the first year's workshops, with more than two-thirds to three-fourths of post-tenure review participants and peer reviewers, as well as a number of deans and department chairs. More than 90 percent of each group rated the workshops as moderately to very helpful on the evaluation forms. They noted that the workshops:

1. clarified what the post-tenure review process entailed (and, conversely, what it did not);
2. enlightened faculty, peers, and administrators as they prepared for their roles in the process;
3. assured participating faculty that the review materials and the deliberations were more limited than those required by tenure and promotion processes; and
4. stressed the review as a career development tool.

Even though the policy requires only a satisfactory/unsatisfactory evaluation, faculty preparing their materials can use the process to discuss their career development goals and resources they might need to achieve them. Likewise, in their evaluation reports, peer reviewers have an opportunity to comment on their colleagues' meritorious accomplishments beyond the rating and suggest what resources might assist in their development. During the first year of post-tenure review, both faculty dossiers and peer evaluation reports went far beyond the satisfactory/unsatisfactory rating to address goals and resources for growth in all areas of faculty responsibility.

#### *Department Chair Workshop*

The grant also funded a workshop for department chairs on strengthening faculty evaluation through the annual review process — critical for post-tenure review to have a positive impact on comprehensive faculty performance review at Winthrop. Otherwise, post-tenure review could supercede existing review processes. Further, given the narrow focus of the post-tenure review criteria, chairs must provide a developmental component in the annual review of faculty. An external consultant conducted the department chair workshop. He placed Winthrop's process in the national context. In addition, he reaffirmed the components of an effective annual review process: (1) clear guidelines and criteria, and (2) written and verbal feedback including praise as well as suggestions. The participating chairs rated the workshop as moderately to very helpful. The chairs also suggested topics for future workshops, including the stages of faculty careers and implications for faculty development and evaluation.

***Developing an Assessment Process***

A third activity in Winthrop's grant was to evaluate the effectiveness of post-tenure review. After considering several approaches to achieve this goal, Winthrop adapted a survey instrument [5] developed by AAHE senior scholars Christine Licata and Joseph Morreale (who are also the joint editors of this volume). The South Carolina Commission on Higher Education agreed to add the survey to activities supported by a FIPSE (U.S. Department of Education, Fund for the Improvement of Postsecondary Education) grant to study the effectiveness of the state's performance funding legislation. The survey was distributed to all faculty being reviewed, peer reviewers, and administrators involved with post-tenure review during 1999–2000.

Surveys were received from more than 400 faculty members and administrators from 10 institutions. The survey allowed Winthrop to compare institutional with statewide responses. This analysis suggests the grant prepared Winthrop faculty for participation in the post-tenure review (see table on the next page). For example, 97 percent of Winthrop faculty agreed with "The process is clear" versus only 85 percent statewide (Brown and Prus 2000).

On separate questions given only to peer reviewers, 100 percent of Winthrop's peer reviewers indicated they felt adequately prepared (versus 91 percent statewide); the procedures were clear (versus 91 percent statewide); and the review was fair and objective (versus 78 percent statewide). While a number of

## Comparison of Winthrop University and Statewide Faculty Responses to Post-Tenure Review Experience

| | Winthrop | Statewide |
|---|---|---|
| The process is widely understood | 83% | 78% |
| The process is clear | 97% | 85% |
| The process is fair | 80% | 76% |
| The review criteria are clear | 90% | 82% |
| The outcomes are clear | 87% | 75% |
| Review committees are properly trained | 77% | 59% |

factors may have contributed to the differences between the responses of faculty at Winthrop and those statewide, these responses indicate the workshops succeeded in making all participants more comfortable in implementing the process.

## Conclusion

Prompted by an externally mandated, specifically defined set of guidelines for post-tenure review, Winthrop's experience suggests campus leaders must be realistic about the potential goals and benefits of post-tenure review. A process mandated by the state legislature to remedy a perceived lack of rigor in existing faculty evaluation processes is unlikely to be perceived by campus faculty as having primarily developmental purposes or outcomes. Those designing a campus policy need to acknowledge these inherent conflicts; post-tenure review should be placed in the context of a comprehensive performance review system in which specific goals for normative and developmental evaluations are achieved through different components of the process. Even with a mandated consequential review process linked to state funding for the institution, however, through broad discussion and appropriate preparation, campuses can ensure that faculty understand the purpose of post-tenure review and how its outcomes can feed into comprehensive faculty development and faculty reward processes. Winthrop's experience suggests that career and professional development may be better fostered through existing review processes than through externally mandated post-tenure review, and that recognition of this relationship can strengthen other developmental components of a comprehensive performance system.

### Notes

1. Betsy E. Brown was formerly dean of the College of Arts and Sciences at Winthrop University. She co-chaired Winthrop's Post-Tenure Review Task Force and was institutional coordinator for Winthrop's "Projects With Promise" minigrant. She is currently associate vice president for academic affairs in the Office of the President of the 16-campus University of North Carolina system. She has presented papers on evaluating the effectiveness of post-tenure review and workshops on improving faculty evaluation at a number of national conferences and college campuses. She received her baccalau-

reate degree in English from Appalachian State University and her M.A. and Ph.D. in English from the Ohio State University. She is a co-author, with N. Douglas Lees and Susan H. Barr, of three related articles on "Preparing Chairs for Expanded Roles in Post-Tenure Review" in *The Department Chair*, published in the Fall 2000, Winter 2001, and Spring 2001 issues. (Contact her at brownb@northcarolina.edu)

2. Available on South Carolina Commission on Higher Education's website at www.che400.state.sc.us/web/perform/csf_298.htm.

3. One faculty member was the leader of the local chapter of the American Association of University Professors.

4. The Winthrop University Post-Tenure Review Policies and Procedures are available on the institution's website: www.Winthrop.edu/acad_aff/Policies/post. html.

5. Information on the survey is available from Christine Licata at cmlnbt@rit.edu or Joseph Morreale at jmorreale@pace.edu.

## References

Brown, B.E., and J. Prus. (2000). "Post-Tenure Review: A Statewide Perspective." Paper presented at Strategies for Change: Meeting the Challenge of Performance Funding: The FIPSE South Carolina Conference on Performance Funding, Charleston, SC, September 20–22.

North, J. (April 1999). "Post-Tenure Review: Rehabilitation or Enrichment?" *AAHE Bulletin* 51(8): 10–13.

**Best Practices for a Performance Review System for Faculty**

1. The performance review system must meet the "Criteria and Procedures for Evaluation" (4.8.10) of the Southern Association of Colleges and Schools which stipulate that: (1) an institution must conduct periodic evaluations of the performance of individual faculty members; (2) the evaluation must include a statement of the criteria against which the performance of each faculty member will be measured; (3) the criteria must be consistent with the purpose and goals of the institution and be made known to all concerned; and (4) the institution must demonstrate that it uses the results of this evaluation for improvement of the faculty and its educational program.

2. The performance review system should be both formative (designed to be a supportive process that promotes self-improvement) and summative (assesses and judges performance).

3. The performance review system process and criteria should be explained to new hires.

4. All faculty, including tenured faculty at all ranks, are reviewed annually and receive a written performance evaluation. In this way, for those institutions with a tenure system, the performance review system should not pose a threat to the tenure system but extends and enlarges it.

5. The performance review system should have been developed jointly by the faculty and administrators of an institution.

6. The performance review system should allow for discipline-specific components.

7. The performance review system should provide opportunities for reflection, feedback, and professional growth whose goal is to enhance instruction at the institution.

8. The performance review system should include written performance evaluation data from four sources:
   a. Annually, instruction and course evaluation forms completed anonymously by students through a standardized institutional process and submitted for each course (not section) taught;
   b. Annually, evaluation which includes assessments from the department chair and/or dean;
   c. At least every three years, for tenure track faculty, internal peer evaluations, i.e., evaluation of faculty by their peers within the institution of higher education;
   d. At least every six years, for tenured tenure track faculty, input from peers external to the department and/or institution as appropriate to the role and function of each faculty member. External evaluators to the institution include national peers from the same field of expertise from other institutions of higher education, professional organizations and societies, federal agencies, etc. Specialized national accreditations and the CHE program reviews, which include external reviewers' assessments, could be incorporated into the external peer review component, where appropriate.

9. At an institutional level, the performance review system must include the following criteria as appropriate to the institution's mission:
   — instruction/teaching
   — advisement and mentoring of students

— graduate student supervision
— supervision of other students (teaching assistants, independent study students)
— course/curriculum development
— research/creative activities
— activities which support the economic development of the region or the State publications
— service to department
— service to institution
— service to community
— participation in professional organizations/associations
— honors, awards, and recognitions
— self-evaluation
— participation in faculty development activities/programs

10. The results of each performance review, including post-tenure review, must be used by the institution as part of its faculty reward system and faculty development system, and the system should include a plan for development when deficiencies are indicated in the review. Specifically:
    a. when an instructor (in the Tech system) or untenured faculty member receives an overall rating of unsatisfactory on the annual performance review, the faculty member may be subject to non-reappointment;
    b. when an instructor (in the Tech system) or tenured faculty member receives an overall rating of unsatisfactory on the annual performance review, the faculty member is immediately subject to a development process, developed by the specific unit, whose goal is to restore satisfactory performance. The development process will include a written plan with performance goals in deficient areas, with appropriate student and peer evaluation of performance.
    c. when an instructor (in the Tech system) or a tenured faculty member fails to make substantial progress towards the performance goals at the time of the next annual review or fails to meet the performance goals specified in the development plan within a specified period, that faculty member will be subject to dismissal (in the Tech system) or revocation of tenure for habitual neglect of duty under the terms of the senior institution's faculty manual.

11. The institution should develop an appeals procedure for those faculty who do not agree with the results of the performance evaluation and/or the resulting recommendations or requirements for improvement.

2

**Best Practices for Post-Tenure Review**

1. A post-tenure review system should incorporate all the indicators identified in the "Best Practices for a Performance Review System for Faculty" document.

2. The post-tenure review should be as rigorous and comprehensive in scope as an initial tenure review.

3. The post-tenure review should incorporate annual performance reviews accumulated since the initial tenure review or since the last post-tenure review.

4. Whereas the focus of an initial tenure review tends to be on past performance, equal emphasis should be given to future development and potential contributions in the post-tenure review.

5. Statewide, each tenured faculty member will have a post-tenure review conducted at pre-established, published intervals of no more than six years, unless the faculty member is participating in a development/improvement process in which case the review may be conducted more frequently.

6. If reviews for promotion (e.g., a tenured associate professor is reviewed for promotion to tenured full professor) fall within the appropriate time interval and encompass all the indicators in this document and in the "Best Practices for a Performance Review System for Faculty "document, they may constitute a post-tenure review.

7. The post-tenure review must include evaluations from peers external to the department and/or institution as appropriate to the role and function of each faculty member (usually to evaluate the quality of research), as well as internal peer evaluations, student evaluations, and administrative evaluations.

8. The post-tenure review must provide detailed information about the outcomes of any sabbatical leave awarded during the six-year post-tenure review period.

9. The institution must identify the means by which the post-tenure review is linked with faculty reward systems, including merit raises and promotion.

10. The institution must display a commitment to provide funds to reward high achievers on post-tenure reviews as well as to provide assistance to faculty members needing improvement.

11. If a faculty member receives an unfavorable post-tenure review, the faculty member is immediately subject to a development process as described in the "Best Practices for a Performance Review System for Faculty", as outlined in 10(b) and 10(c) of that document.

12. The institution should develop an appeals procedure for those faculty who do not agree with the results of the post-tenure review evaluation and/or the resulting recommendations or requirements for improvement.

# Transforming Post-Tenure Review Into Faculty, Department Head, and Departmental Renewal

**Barbara Hornum** [1]

The removal of mandatory retirement coupled with hiring freezes in the 1980s and early 1990s have resulted in faculties at many institutions who more than reflect the general graying of America. A number of colleges and universities have aging faculties who have no plans to retire. In the late 1980s and 1990s, attempts to facilitate early retirement (before age 70) met with dubious success. These attempts proved costly and frequently enticed faculty members whom colleges and universities wished to retain. Consequently, many colleges and universities have shifted from promoting "early" retirement to formulating processes of post-tenure review.

There are many models for post-tenure review, with a variety of goals and objectives. This chapter explores the efforts of one university to implement a post-tenure review process that is both developmental and participative and will provide opportunities for individual career flexibility in the standard areas of scholarship and research, teaching, and service. The formative emphasis can respond to needs held by the individual, the department, and the university.

## Changing Forces

As had many institutions, Drexel University hired a large number of its current faculty in the 1970s. Despite some new hires over the past five years, approximately half our faculty are more than 50 years old, with a significant percentage above age 62. This does vary between and within the various university units.

Since there is no mandatory retirement, we have an older faculty, with its resulting implications for the institution.

While age does not necessarily impair performance in teaching, research and scholarship, or service, length of tenure does present variables requiring assessment. New pedagogies have emerged, students have changed, even the nature of academic and campus life is different. Since the Boyer report *Scholarship Reconsidered*, the teaching of undergraduates is viewed differently than it was 25 years ago, often creating a situation of potential priority conflict for faculty and for departments.

In addition, a reward system emphasizing research rather than teaching undergraduates — especially freshmen and sophomores — impedes faculty awareness of developments in learning and cognitive styles, and on outcomes-based, student-centered education. Some faculty believe teaching detracts from work more valued and rewarded by the university. Whether true or not, this affects the teaching involvement of some faculty. Others, feeling their teaching efforts and high levels of student-centered activity have denied them promotion and salary increases, have become demoralized. Some faculty over the course of a long career go through the career equivalent of life cycle changes, reaching points in their academic careers when they wish to make shifts in emphasis. For these reasons, serious commitment to faculty renewal facilitates individual faculty revitalization, assists changing departmental goals and objectives, and benefits student learning.

## Institutional Characteristics

The Drexel University experience details a process of special interest to other private institutions where any form of post-tenure review is voluntary. It is set within the context of a rapidly growing, private, urban university wherein individual colleges, schools, and departments give their own unique formats to more generalized activities, such as annual reviews. The formative aspects of such reviews thus vary and are dependent on individual department heads for their administration, nature, and success. This is true of all levels of review from pre-tenure to post-tenure.

Nonetheless, the university focused on the need for department heads to work with new faculty to assist them as they moved through their probationary periods toward tenure. It was assumed tenured faculty would take care of themselves. Certainly, most faculty did just that within the specifics of their particular disciplines where there were some norms to follow. All of this reinforced the "silo mentality": Unless required by research or teaching to cut across disciplinary lines, many faculty members had few interactions across departments, much less across colleges. Few discussions about life at the university took place generally or examined some of the ideas that were coming from the Carnegie Foundation and similar arenas. When faculty did cohere, it was likely to be crisis centered and the cohesion lasted only for the duration of the crisis.

The most durable exception to this were faculty members who had been or were participating in the faculty senate. It is from this group that the planners for the Drexel version of post-tenure review were selected.

## The Approach to Senior Faculty Renewal

The president and provost requested exploration of post-tenure review as it might apply to Drexel. It was decided to use an already existing committee — the Faculty Development Committee — to develop a plan. The committee was composed of the associate provost and dean of undergraduate affairs (the author) and four faculty appointed by or from the Senate Committee on Faculty Affairs. This committee was familiar with Boyer's work and had participated in some national higher education conferences about the scholarship of teaching and learner-centered education. The committee had already decided to use the scholarship of teaching and learner-centered education as the focus of any form of senior faculty development. Drexel received support from AAHE. This grant provided internal credibility, particularly among faculty, and continues to provide an external network of people and institutions involved in various types of post-tenure review projects.

In October 1998, we initiated a pilot project: voluntary, formative, and developmental to focus on the renewal aspects of post-tenure review. The major goals and objectives of the project were simple. First, we wanted to reinvigorate long-term senior faculty members by emphasizing teaching undergraduates in the context of learner-centered education. Second, we targeted department heads, given their critical role in faculty development, to receive training in learner-centered education, in conducting formative annual reviews, and in assisting faculty members to develop short- and long-term objectives. Our vision was to create a partnership for each project department head and faculty member, essentially forming a team.

## The First Cohort

Our first cohort was composed of eight people who applied to the Faculty Development Committee. We began with three departments and one small college. [2] The department heads and their respective four faculty met to formulate a three-year plan for teaching enhancement and related activities. There were specific annual goals and objectives as well as some broader ones for the end of the third year. Those faculty who successfully complete their three-year plans receive an increase to base salary separate from any other increases. The amount is modest and, while an initial motivator, does not appear to be the major factor in either applying for or staying with the project.

## Incentives

There are other incentives built into the project that have received positive feedback from the participants. We wanted to develop a variety of incentives and rewards to both create and maintain momentum. We have held several workshops beginning in November 1998, shortly after the selection of the project participants. Workshops have ranged from fairly general ones on the framework for teaching in a learner-centered environment to specialized ones on revising syllabi or constructing teaching portfolios. The various training experiences and workshops held on campus were open to all tenured and tenure-track faculty as well as selected long-term adjuncts. To keep our emphasis on the formative aspects of post-tenure review, we did not want those involved in the renewal process to feel singled out or "exposed."

Additionally, we have provided subscriptions to publications such as *The Teaching Professor* that connect our faculty and department heads to national discussions of the core issues in teaching and in learner-centered education. Since one motivation is to embed faculty renewal within other activities, we trained department heads to do developmental annual reviews.

During the third year of the project, we presented one panel and two roundtables at a national meeting on faculty roles and rewards. Project members participated in workshops, attended sessions on the scholarship of teaching and engagement, and interacted with peers from other institutions. Attending professional meetings also strengthens the bonds between the members of the project cohort.

One intent of all internal and external activities was to foster dialogues beyond the typical departmental and collegial divisions of the university. These dialogues and the joint goal setting between department heads and senior faculty created a "teaming" that had not been anticipated. In turn, while we had expected renewal of individual faculty members, we were surprised at the sense of renewal expressed by department heads. One such department head characterized the renewal in the following way:

> I personally benefited from the AAHE minigrant by attending educational conferences. I found it refreshing to hear and think again about educational matters. A real danger for any administrator is to lose sight of our teaching mission. I particularly appreciated hearing talks where old-fashioned educational values were put forward and others where the business aspects were emphasized. Comparing these, I was reminded that the former is what I aspire to. I hope my administrative style will improve.

Department heads felt they had "new" allies and, in fact, are using the project faculty for a number of valuable department-wide administrative activities. Since department heads are essential to the success of any formative faculty development, they should be rewarded to ensure their continued motivation.

## The Department Head Benefits

Formative faculty development energized department heads as well. One professional benefit has been the clarifying of promotion and tenure guidelines, for example. Other benefits are intellectual stimulation and personal growth. The four department heads of the first cohort gained:

- deeper understanding of the scholarship of teaching and learning and of the importance of learner-centered teaching;

- expanded knowledge of resource literature;
- a recognition of and alternative solutions to some common problems cutting across disciplines and institutions;
- improved administrative ability; and
- renewed collegiality with their faculty, faculty in other departments, and administrators and faculty in other colleges of the university.

## The Faculty Benefits

The gains to the faculty are more individual. One faculty member, bored by teaching and feeling marginal in the department, was inspired by his improved teaching evaluations to become a departmental administrator. He now helps to develop the undergraduate curriculum and mentors other faculty. His own words reveal some dynamics of renewal:

> Another unanticipated outcome . . . was my election as a Senator representing the College of Arts and Sciences, as well as my own department. For me, "faculty development" took another turn at this point, and I became involved with faculty governance, whereby I began to appreciate the overall position of my field of learning for our students in the context of the entire university. There is a Faculty Senate Leaders National Summit I plan to attend at the 2001 AAHE [Conference on Faculty Roles & Rewards]. My goal is to help facilitate faculty participation in governance as itself another aspect of overall faculty development.

From a developmental perspective, it is exciting and rewarding to watch the varied directions in which remotivated individuals move. This developmental progression is underscored in a case study we developed from the experiences of one of our faculty participants (see the attachment at the end of this chapter). The AAHE New Pathways grant validated formative post-tenure review, thereby empowering faculty members and their department heads to modify their career paths.

## The Second Cohort

The second cohort, selected in early fall 2000, was as motivated to participate as the first cohort. The second cohort was different in that the department heads knew of the teaming benefits. The department heads of the first cohort probably shared their experiences openly with other department heads. The senior faculty members of the second cohort are familiarizing themselves with the theories and techniques of student-centered and active learning. They are learning how to apply these techniques within their disciplinary contexts to enhance teaching within their departments. As one individual stated in his application:

> My overall style of teaching has been the traditional lecture format. I am very organized and transfer my lecture notes to the blackboard and the students dutifully take down everything I write on the board. My exams cover my notes and those who like this style of teaching do well. But I would very much like to increase interaction with students in my courses to make learning more active.

A second faculty member wishes to improve teaching techniques and master pedagogy to adjust to the greater diversity of incoming students. All four faculty members in this group are experimenting with new teaching modalities to improve the learning experience for their students. Since the types of courses range from large lectures in business to small studio classes in design, we should have some good comparative data when the first year of self-assessments are completed in September 2002.

## Lessons for the Field

As we look at instituting post-tenure review — especially in a private university where it is not mandated — it is important to be clear as to its purpose or purposes. There must be mutual commitment from all parties and the development of realistic plans with good report mechanisms and follow-up. There must also be flexibility to accommodate the dynamics of change that may occur during the process, and a linkage between individual goals and departmental culture. The reward system may or may not involve money but it must involve recognition and praise. The Drexel University process, as both a strategy and a principle, is to institute post-tenure faculty renewal in a participatory, "bottom-up" manner. We believe that faculty should be active and reflective planners for their own futures. Both cohorts are now taking an increasingly strong role in planning for the future aspects of energizing our senior faculty members, and we expect that they will be helping to define and redefine the process for our university. The "teaming" aspect of the process is critical to its success. To help maintain department head commitment in the face of many competing pressures and demands, it is vital to have gains that accrue to the department as well as to the individuals involved. We know that this was sustainable for the first cohort. We hope it will be equally so for the second.

## Notes

1. Barbara Hornum is currently the associate provost and dean of undergraduate affairs at Drexel University. An anthropologist by training, Hornum believes changing the culture is the most durable way of implementing lasting change. Hornum initiated the formation of the Faculty Development Committee, which helps coordinate a number of faculty development activities including post-tenure faculty renewal and teaching excellence awards. She also works with the Faculty Development Center, a relatively new entity. She received her A.B., M.A., and Ph.D. in anthropology from Bryn Mawr College. Her research areas include comparative aging and planned communities in the United States and Great Britain. (Contact her at hornumbg@drexel.edu)

2. In one instance, we have a small college that has no individual departments. Its associate dean served the same function as a head and shall be included whenever the term "department head" is used.

## Acknowledgments

While I wrote this chapter (and any mistakes are mine), I would like to state that it could not have been written without the hard work and pioneering spirit of the Faculty Development Committee and the department heads and faculty of both cohorts. My sincerest thanks to John Hall, Bahram Nabet, Sheila Vaidya, Brian Wagner, of the FDC; to the first cohort teams Nira Herrmann and Herman Gollwitzer, Elizabeth Petras and Jim Calkins, Thomas Childers and June Verner, and Michel Vallieres and Teck-Kah Lim; and to the second cohort teams Karin Kuenstler and Rena Cumby, Jonathan Burton and Hazem Maragah, John Schaubroeck and Sid Siegal, and Shortie McKinney and Philip Handel.

## Case Study

Participant one was a physics professor heavily involved in research for 30 years. A little burnt out and desperate for a mid-career change in pathway, the participant was seeking approval and encouragement to switch his emphasis from research to teaching and service. In a department where success is (even now) mostly measured in the number of papers published and the amount of research funding achieved, the participant faced the likelihood of being treated as deadwood, an outcast, not a team player if the move was not "officially sanctioned." During annual reviews with his department head beginning in the early 1990s, the subject of a switch had been broached but was dropped like a hot potato each time it was raised. The participant was prepared to make the change and damn the consequences when, three years ago, the University won an AAHE grant to investigate developmental post-tenure review; the climate had changed. The department head, now convinced that he was no longer facing reprobation for having a certain fraction of his faculty devoting the major part of their time to teaching and interacting with students provided the overall objectives of the department were being met, asked the participant to sign up for the program.

The participant is now a "happy camper." His morale is up and he feels part of a team that appreciates his role . . . he has been freed to develop teaching tools, which enhance the learning experience of his students. He has found he has a little "showman" in himself and he has used that realization to charge his lectures with more energy than he had in the past. He has worked closely with the department head to prepare for the university's impending accreditation exercise, and he senses that the head is more comfortable when asking him to handle administrative and curricular chores. He has discovered, a little to his surprise, that he is not alone in seeking this transition in his career and that the university has a cadre of loyal and dedicated faculty who, in whatever they do, want only what's best for the university and its students.

The participant has attended AAHE conferences as well as workshops on how to develop teaching portfolios, and the insights gained during the process are informing his teaching activities. He is now able to supervise other faculty in writing their own portfolios and sees this as an enduring contribution toward the teaching-learning enterprise at the school. By merely "granting" the participant's wish to concentrate on a different pathway, the university has created a win-win-win situation: the school has a happy, productive, and re-energized employee, the faculty member feels useful, needed, more driven to improve every aspect of his service and more loyal to the institution, and perhaps best of all, his students have a caring and stimulating environment more conducive to active learning.

# Section III:
# Lessons Learned From Data Analysis

# Getting Out in Front: Cumulative Review and Development for Tenured Faculty

**Ronald J. Henry** [1]

The development of post-tenure review at Georgia State University followed an interesting path. The policy was developed before there was pressure to do so, and the intent from the start was to emphasize a formative approach. While substantive and thoughtful faculty discourse about the objectives and expected outcomes from such a review occurred, in general, this was not a highly contentious topic.

## Campus Initiative

Georgia State University initiated post-tenure review in spring 1995 after the university senate passed a policy on cumulative review and development for tenured faculty in February 1995. One argument for developing a post-tenure review policy was that many state university systems had such policies under active consideration. Because Georgia State took the initiative before required to by the state, the university foreshadowed the state's efforts. The University System of Georgia — comprising 34 colleges and universities including Georgia State University — passed a system-wide post-tenure review policy effective 1997–98.

We attribute the rapid adoption of the post-tenure review policy at Georgia State University to its design as an ongoing, periodic, proactive development opportunity for faculty. [2] We took the occasion of re-examining our tenure and promotion policy to add pre-tenure and post-tenure policies beginning in spring 1995. Subsequently working through policy implementation provided academic administrators and faculty an opportunity to see what worked well and what needed further fine-tuning. We did not expect the initial policy would remain unaltered. We planned to assess preliminary results, validate effective process components, and modify where necessary.

## Lessons for the Field

### *Phase-In*

The policy requires that a tenured faculty member be reviewed five years after the most recent promotion or personnel action. Since approximately half the tenured faculty was eligible for post-tenure review, the policy was phased in over three years. We charged the six colleges within the university to review at least one third of their eligible faculty by the end of spring quarter 1995 and gave colleges three ways to choose their first group — alphabetically, randomly, or chronologically.

In retrospect, we recommend faculty be selected for review based on random lengths of time since their most recent promotion and/or tenure review. We intended to include a range of faculty reviewed in the first year to demonstrate the value of post-tenure review to outstanding as well as problematic members. However, the chronological choice identified the most difficult cases: faculty who have served many years at the associate professor rank. Hence, we recommend alphabetic or random choice.

### *Modifications After Initial Experience*

The initial policy differed from the current policy in two ways. Originally, we suggested — rather than required — the candidates to provide a two-page statement on teaching, research, and service over the previous five years. With more than 160 candidates in the first two years, we became convinced the opportunity for reflective commentary was a significant advantage. Preparing the statement requires candidates to be thoughtful about their recent professional journey, making it easier to plan the next five years.

The second change to the policy was to broaden the statement of purpose for the review itself. As modified, the statement requires placing the contributions of the individual faculty member within the department or school's goals and responsibilities. Cumulative review is not just about the faculty member's individual achievements and development goals, but also is about the collective good of the faculty member and the department, and by extension the college and university. The revised policy reads:

> All units will conduct a cumulative review of a tenured faculty member. This review will be conducted either by the elected Promotion and Tenure Committee of the College/Unit or by an independently elected committee consisting of at least three tenured faculty. In case of the latter, the composition of the committee and procedures for its election will be determined by the faculty for each college or unit. This review should begin five years after the most recent promotion and continue at five-year intervals unless interrupted by a further promotion or impending candidacy for promotion within a year. This cumulative review should address accomplishments in teaching, advising, and serving students, in research/scholarly/creative activity, and in service. It will be based on available information; e.g., annual reports, student/peer evaluations of teaching, curriculum vitae, publications, etc. The only additional information that a candidate is expected to supply is a two-page statement of effectiveness in teaching, research, and service over the previous five years. This document should be accompanied by another page outlining projected five-year goals.
>
> Such review provides an opportunity to assess faculty development goals and achievements and provides assistance to faculty in ensuring continuous intellectual and professional growth and provides assistance to the unit in ensuring that all faculty members are contributing to the unit's goals and responsibilities. The cumulative review is distinguished from an annual review in that the former requires faculty and administrators to assess achievements and goals over a longer term, potentially at differing levels (e.g., multi-year projects, research, scholarship), and can facilitate longer-term growth and development. Such review might also be connected to determining eligibility to serve as a member of a college's graduate faculty. Guidelines for this review shall be specified in each unit.
>
> A cumulative review should be reviewed and commented on by the department chair, by the Dean, and the Provost. Faculty must receive a written report as to the results of this review. After completion of these assessments, a conference is held between the Chair/Director and the faculty member. This conference will produce a plan which focuses on professional goals and/or workload profile, for subsequent approval by the Dean. The Dean of each college will confer with the faculty member and will be responsible for monitoring progress through the regular process of annual faculty evaluations.

> Nothing in these guidelines alters the existing rules dealing with tenure termination. (George State University Statutes Article XI, Section 24)

***Recommended Procedures***

**Committee composition.** The process used at Georgia State University requires reviews by an elected faculty committee, the department chair, the dean, and the provost. Each college decides on the makeup of the elected faculty committee. Some colleges choose to have a college-wide or area committee. The College of Arts and Sciences, for example, has a committee for each area: (1) social and behavioral sciences, (2) fine arts and humanities, and (3) natural sciences and mathematics. Others choose a department review committee. We recommend that at least an area-wide review committee be used for the post-tenure review rather than a department-wide committee. An area-wide committee puts more distance between the candidate and review members. It also benefits small departments with only a few faculty eligible to serve on the review committee.

**Committee orientation.** The review committee writes the post-tenure review report. This report is normally authored by the chair of the committee, and may include minority or majority opinions. We recommend orienting committee members to their task. When the promotion and tenure committee serves also as the post-tenure review committee, some faculty had difficulty separating the different responsibilities. Post-tenure review, as practiced at Georgia State, has a strong faculty development component. Committee members are therefore asked to be formative rather than summative when reviewing materials. In the case study (Licata and Morreale 1999), a focus group of current and previous members of peer review committees "felt that the importance of the peer review committee was that it could be objective and provide real constructive feedback to faculty members as colleagues" (52). Further, chairs "asserted that its view was taken seriously by the faculty member and was often the decisive leverage needed to have faculty address deficiencies" (52).

**Role of dean.** The committee report and comments from the department chair, together with the faculty member's curriculum vitae and self-assessment of accomplishments and goals, are sent to the dean and subsequently to the provost. After the provost has added comments, all reports and comments go to the faculty member with copies to the other parties. At this point, the faculty member has an opportunity to respond to the review. After completion of these assessments, the chair confers with the faculty member. We recommend the dean also participate in this conference, as its goal is to produce a plan that focuses on professional goals and/or workload profile, for subsequent approval by the dean. The final report is placed in the faculty member's file in the main office of the college. The dean of each college is responsible for monitoring progress through annual faculty evaluations.

## Integration With Other Policies

While the post-tenure review policy was developed as part of a comprehensive promotion and tenure policy, its successful implementation depends on integrating the results into other policies. Integrating the post-tenure review policy with flexible workload policy and merit salary initiatives balances accountability and rewards (Abdelal et al. 1997). Further, faculty talents and interests must match with department, college, and university goals to realize strategic plans shaped by periodic academic program review. The process goes like this: Academic program reviews generate action plans. The action plans are used to determine funding in the annual budget cycle. The execution of the action plans is dependent on faculty talents. Faculty talents flourish when policies for faculty development, differentiated workload, and rewards are integrated. Therefore, we recommend the post-tenure review policy be integrated with existing policies for program review, workload effort allocation, and merit salary administration.

## Results From the First Six Years

Georgia State University has six years of experience with the post-tenure review policy, covering 359 reviews (see the table). These data are broken down by the workload profile. *Traditional* profile refers to faculty whose primary responsibilities are instruction and scholarship. Faculty who are not full professors but have a traditional profile are referred to as *Promotion Potential*. *Teaching/Service* refers to faculty whose primary responsibility is teaching or service. *Marginal* refers to faculty who are not effective in one or more of the areas. *Retired* refers to faculty who have voluntarily decided to retire.

In the first three years, 239 tenured faculty members were eligible for review. In the second three-year period, 120 faculty were eligible. Twenty-seven faculty elected to retire during the process and are excluded from this analysis.

***Actions Taken***

There are six possible ratings from a post-tenure review at Georgia State.

1. Excellent or very effective in all areas of instruction, scholarship, and service.
2. Excellent or very effective in instruction and/or service with moderate scholarship productivity.
3. Excellent or very effective in instruction and/or service with limited scholarship productivity.
4. Not effective in instruction.
5. Not effective and unwilling to accept negative assessment.
6. Decided to retire.

Faculty actions following the ratings range from celebratory/professional support to development plans or workload redirection.

The faculty who rank as excellent or very effective in all areas (instruction, scholarship, and service) are congratulated and asked how the administration can help sustain their effective performance. Those faculty who have moderate research productivity and very effective instruction and/or service are asked to construct with their department chairs a five-year professional development plan for improving productivity. Those with limited research productivity but effective instruction and/or service must formulate plans to modify faculty workload to match a teaching/service profile and adjust the basis for merit raises. That is, these faculty agree to teach more or to take on additional service functions in exchange for lowered research expectations and will be evaluated and rewarded accordingly. Because most had received low raises — having little or no research productivity — they often express relief at the altered set of expectations and the prospect of greater reward for activities in which they are effective.

Teaching/Service faculty often emerge as valuable contributors to achieving department goals. Faculty who are not effec-

## Post-Tenure Review Results by Workload Profile and Time Period

| | 1995–1997 | | 1998–2000 | | |
|---|---|---|---|---|---|
| | Number | Percentage | Number | Percentage | Total Number |
| Traditional Profile | 75 | 34.8% | 52 | 44.4% | 132 |
| Promotion Potential | 38 | 17.7% | 45 | 38.5% | 78 |
| Teaching/Service | 86 | 40.0% | 16 | 13.7% | 102 |
| Marginal | 16 | 7.4% | 4 | 3.4% | 20 |
| Total Active | 215 | 100% | 117 | 100% | 332 |
| Retired | 24* | | 3* | | 27 |
| TOTAL | 239 | | 120 | | 359 |

* Retired faculty are excluded from the percentages calculations.

tive in teaching are assigned mentors; some are referred to our Center for Teaching and Learning. Many faculty members recognize their instructional problems and are cooperative in trying to rectify them. There were only three recalcitrant faculty members who were unwilling to accept a negative assessment. We demanded five-year development plans. In other cases faculty chose to retire. Some faculty indicated they had been considering retirement and the review process had helped them reach a decision. Some did not start the review, while others withdrew when told to formulate a detailed five-year plan. These retirement decisions were voluntary responses to what the faculty members perceived as legitimate academic expectations. As such, the decisions generated little acrimony. (Analysis for the first three years experience for the College of Arts and Sciences was presented by Abdelal et al. 1999).

For the 1995–1997 group, 7 percent of faculty who completed their reviews were rated as Marginal. In the 1998–2000 group, only 3 percent of faculty were rated as Marginal. The first group had 40 percent of faculty in the Teaching/Service category, versus only 14 percent of faculty in the second group. Similarly, 35 percent of faculty in the first group versus 44 percent of faculty in the second group kept a Traditional workload profile. For the first and second groups, 18 percent of faculty and 39 percent, respectively, were in the Promotion Potential category.

The results vary between the first and second three-year periods. Fewer faculty have a Teaching/Service emphasis for the second three-year group, while more faculty are in the Promotion Potential category. The initial group included many long-time associate professors hired when the university placed less emphasis on research. Further, in asking whether the faculty having promotion potential from the initial group of 38 have now been promoted in rank, we find eight have retired and nine have been promoted. Most active faculty reviewed in the first year went through their second review in spring 2001.

Collecting and analyzing such data help interpret the effect a post-tenure review policy is having in accomplishing its goals. We recommend that data be collected and analyzed.

## Case Study Findings

Licata and Morreale (1999) conducted a case study on the impact of the comprehensive periodic post-tenure review procedures at the end of the three-year phase-in implementation at Georgia State. They interviewed 13 tenured faculty one-on-one. They held separate focus groups with deans, department chairs, and members of peer-review committees. They also surveyed all reviewed faculty. Nearly half of all Georgia State University's tenured faculty are in the College of Arts and Sciences.

Ninety-three (93) percent of administrators and more than half of faculty who responded to the survey viewed the policy as effective in achieving its primary purpose of assessing career developmental goals and establishing plans for continued growth. Eighty (80) percent of administrators thought the impact on performance was positive; none considered it negative. In contrast, only one-third of faculty thought the impact on performance was positive and one-quarter considered it to be negative. Differences also exist between perceptions by faculty from the College of Arts and Sciences and all other tenured faculty. Sixty-one (61) percent of faculty and administrators from the College of Arts and Sciences viewed the impact on performance as positive, but only 40 percent from other colleges.

Licata and Morreale (1999: 56) noted,

> On the whole, department chairs and deans were much more positive in their responses to the outcomes, impact, and benefits associated with post-tenure review than [were] faculty. While faculty, in general, responded more favorably than disfavorably to such outcome domains, their responses were usually in the "somewhat" or "slightly positive" range rather than in the "very," "highly," or "mostly" positive range as was the case with administrators.

As provost, I regard implementation of post-tenure review in the College of Arts and Sciences to be the most effective of the various colleges. This view is substantiated by a statistical analysis of the case study. [3] According to the analysis, we can attribute effectiveness to several features of the College of Arts and Sciences policy:

1. The dean participates in a conference with the faculty member and department chair.
2. The results of post-tenure review are integrated into the

college's workload and merit pay structures (Abdelal 1997).

3. The dean makes resources available as part of the five-year faculty development plan.

In general, leadership is key to successfully implementing the policy, and the dean of the College of Arts and Sciences has worked closely with the department chairs to develop trust in the process (Licata and Morreale 1999).

Faculty and administrators [4] have a number of recommendations to improve the current process:

- The process needs to be brought to closure in a reasonable and consistent manner. Timelines for receiving feedback are variable and too long in some cases.
- We need to improve overall institutional awareness of review results. The university community needs to know how we are addressing incentives and rewards for performance that meets or exceeds expectations as well as how we require improvement.
- Department chairs need help when they have "difficult conversations" with faculty. Chair development in personnel evaluation will have a much broader impact than in post-tenure review situations.
- Overall, we need better connections and alignment between annual and cumulative reviews, with consistent language for expectations, criteria, and standards.

## Conclusions

An evaluation policy for the development of all tenured faculty that deals constructively with those who have deficiencies as well as recognizes and rewards those who are effective has been successfully deployed at Georgia State University. We recognize cultural and political environments are crucial; nevertheless, we strongly recommend the formative approach to other institutions. In particular, implementation of this formative type of post-tenure review policy will succeed if it is closely linked with policies of flexible workload and merit salary compensation and there is institutional awareness of the results of reviews. Perhaps the most important aspect of post-tenure review is that it is not just about the faculty member and his or her achievements and development goals; it is also about the collective good of the faculty and the department; by extension, also the college and university. Post-tenure review can contribute strongly to an ethic of collective responsibility, which is essential for the ongoing vitality of universities of the 21st century.

## Notes

1. Ronald Henry is the provost and vice president for academic affairs and a professor of physics at Georgia State University since July 1994. Henry is involved in development of standards for P–16 education, and he is interested in application of quality tools to postsecondary education. Henry also is involved extensively in state and national education policy and action committees. He received B.Sc. and Ph.D. degrees in applied mathematics from the Queen's University Belfast (Northern Ireland). (Contact him at rhenry@gsu.edu)

2. The initial 1995 draft of a post-tenure review policy was modified slightly and the current version, passed by the university senate in February 1997, is found in the faculty handbook, section 307.04 at www.gsu.edu/~wwwfhb/fhb.html.

3. According to analysis by Jeffrey Jolton for a report on academic discipline/academic unit differences (Christine Licata, personal communication, 1999).

4. In the discussion below, "administrators" refers to department chairs, deans, and the provost.

## References

Abdelal, A.T., D.C. Blumenfeld, T.J. Crimmins, and P.L. Dressel. (Spring 1997). "Integrating Accountability Systems and Reward Structures: Workload Policy, Post-Tenure Evaluation, and Salary Compensation." *Metropolitan Universities* 7(4): 61–73.

Abdelal, A.T., D.C. Blumenfeld, T.J. Crimmins, and R.J. Henry. (1999). "Seasons of the Academic Life and Post-Tenure Review: How to Build a Constructive Rather Than a Punitive Approach." Paper presented at the AAHE Conference on Faculty Roles & Rewards, January 21–24, San Diego, CA.

———, and J.C. Morreale. (Fall 1999). "Post-Tenure Review: Outcomes and Impact — Case Study: University A." Washington, DC: American Association for Higher Education, New Pathways II Project.

# Redesigning Post-Tenure Review to Satisfy Accreditation Requirements

**Ann S. Hunter and Jonathan Lawson** [1]

Idaho State University (ISU) comes to post-tenure review with an unusual history and an absence of immediate external forces. Post-tenure review initiatives are commonly driven by mandates of governing boards or state legislators. ISU's experience is different in that it once had a rigorous process of conducting post-tenure review and then chose to simplify it.

Nearly 20 years ago, the Idaho State Board of Education mandated periodic performance reviews, which occurred every fifth year after tenure. Consequently, the institution established a rigorous post-tenure review process that operated much like the conventional promotion and tenure processes.

In the mid 1980s, the process was streamlined: Department peers voted on a faculty member's competency. This procedure was considered an improvement because it captured the vote of every single departmental faculty member without a committee hearing. Furthermore, the faculty member under consideration did not have to display evidence for peers to review his or her performance. The fifth-year ballot would trigger a full review if one-third of the departmental members or if an administrator challenged the faculty member's competency; this rarely occurred.

The institution's approach has come full circle — from an original, full-fledged, committee-driven, tenuring process, to a ballot or triggered review, and finally, to the present re-examining of what is the best system for current institutional needs. One could say ISU is taking a strategic approach and identifying external pressures before they become a mandate.

The present analysis is driven in part by the Northwest Association of Schools and Colleges requirements. Like many accrediting agencies, Northwest has increased its requirements for evaluating tenured faculty. Most specifically, Northwest requires a substantive peer review of all faculty — including those tenured — every three years.

An informal assessment across ISU's seven academic units indicated the policy was interpreted and administered unevenly among the academic units. Even if all adhered, substantive peer review of tenured faculty did not occur every third year in a way that met the requirements of the Northwest Association of Schools and Colleges.

Subsequently, a committee composed of faculty leaders and senior administrators has re-examined the post-tenure review policy at ISU.

## Institutional Setting

Idaho State University is a research university serving 13,000 students among six colleges, plus a separately funded College of Applied Technology. The main campus is located in Pocatello, and it serves five large and six small outreach centers throughout the state. Slightly more than half of its 550 full-time faculty are tenured or tenure track. Like most institutions, ISU hires part-time adjuncts. After examining tenure rules around 1995, the Idaho State Board of Education subsequently removed tenure opportunities from the College of Applied Technology. As a consequence, faculty react strongly to any tenure-related issue such as post-tenure review.

## Contextual Advantages

Idaho State University had four distinct advantages working in its favor as it sought to design a new post-tenure review policy: (1) no external pressure, (2) expansive leadership, (3) grant funds, and (4) rewarding for senior faculty.

### *No External Pressure*

The institution has benefited from the absence of an external mandate driving the post-tenure review policy study. Although a new and more stringent requirement of the Northwest Association of Schools and Colleges was the main catalyst, ISU initiated its study of post-tenure review about halfway through the 10-year accreditation cycle. Therefore, ISU had plenty of time to thoughtfully design a policy before facing the accreditation board.

### *Expansive Leadership*

A second advantage has been the breadth of institutional leadership developing the post-tenure review (periodic performance review) policy. The administration has engaged the faculty governance system. It is also the direct result of leadership from the academic vice-president, the deans of the colleges, and the faculty senate.

### *Grant Funding*

A third advantage has been that ISU obtained grant funding from AAHE to conduct its post-tenure review work. Linking the campus-wide study of post-tenure review to a national organization not only lent credence to the re-examination of post-tenure review, it also tapped a rich source of knowledge, experience, and support.

### *Commitment to Rewards*

A fourth advantage has been the commitment from ISU administrators and the entire team to the goal of making post-tenure review rewarding and meaningful for senior faculty. Although faculty expressed skepticism and disbelief, effective evaluation depends on tangible and intangible rewards.

## Challenges

In addition to improving faculty review, a major consideration has been to satisfy two external agencies. The Idaho State Board of Education requires annual reviews and fifth-year periodic performance reviews; the Northwest Association of Schools and Colleges requires substantive peer reviews every third year. At first glance, these requirements appeared to be straightforward; yet as the campus got further into the project, the team realized annual reviews and periodic performance reviews — or post-tenure reviews — are conducted unevenly across the colleges. The definition of "substantive peer evaluation" has been debated. For instance, is a department chair a peer? If a department chair conducts a comprehensive annual review without input from a faculty member's colleagues, does this constitute a substantive peer review?

The second consideration involves justifying a change of policy to doubtful faculty. As stated above, in 1995 the Idaho State Board of Education abolished tenure in the College of Applied Technology. Some senior faculty believed threats to tenure were embedded in the project and rejected overtures from the administration.

The third consideration entails how to identify meaningful rewards, and how to define excellent performance. The post-tenure review committee questioned whether salary increases are the most effective way to recognize the performance of outstanding faculty members.

The final concern encompasses identifying procedures for faculty who need or desire assistance with professional development. The committee believed this aid was critical even though few faculty would need remedial help.

## Four-Pronged Strategy

ISU's strategy has four steps: (1) inform, (2) communicate, (3) educate, and (4) involve.

### *Inform*

The team used several approaches to inform members of the academic community about the project. First, a webpage (www.isu.edu/itrc/forum/fo13.html) was established to post the text and timeline for the AAHE grant. This webpage also links to post-tenure review webpages at other institutions. The policy statement from the Northwest Association of Schools and Colleges on post-tenure review was uploaded. A mechanism for anonymous comment was included in the webpage. In addition, the academic vice-president regularly wrote letters to faculty members on the purpose of the project and circulated notices about public events associated with the study.

### *Communicate*

Communicating was both a "trickle-down" and a "trickle-up" process. Since an original member of the study team was a college dean, both the dean and the academic vice-president regularly updated the other deans about the study. In turn, deans conveyed this information to department chairs and program directors who informed their departments and programs.

Both faculty members and the faculty governance system were catalysts in the trickle-up communication process. The faculty governance system played an essential role in the communication process by using current and past presidents of the faculty senate who were co-principal investigators for the funding obtained from AAHE to apprise other faculty members. Their participation ensured discussion of post-tenure review would occur at the faculty senate level.

One of the post-tenure review committee's first goals was to evaluate faculty attitudes to cultivate an environment for thoughtful discussion. Focus groups were used for this purpose. A random sample of its 550 faculty members led to six focus groups averaging 12 per group who discussed specific questions related to post-tenure review. (See questions opposite.)

**Results of the focus groups.** It was through the focus groups that participants learned of the varying practices of fifth-year reviews across ISU. Most faculty members and department chairs were surprised by the variations in periodic performance reviews. In some cases, tenured faculty had only received annual reviews. Some departments and colleges included formal peer components as part of periodic performance reviews, while in others peer input was halfhearted at best. Most faculty members agreed that modifying periodic performance reviews could address such irregularities.

Focus group members unanimously expressed concerns about adding redundant work to the established annual reviews. There was consensus that faculty members are held to high standards of performance and productivity throughout all stages of their academic careers. Many spoke of being assessed formally by their department chairs and deans, while informally they are reviewed by their colleagues, who hold them accountable to departmental standards.

The study team learned department chairs needed resources to assist faculty struggling with burnout, technology needs, or developing instructional skills for new teaching methods, such as distance learning. The results of the focus groups were posted on the post-tenure review webpage.

### *Educate*

Education was a significant element of the post-tenure review study. In addition to sending members of the community to

## Focus Group Questions

1. How is post-tenure review currently practiced in your college?
2. What are the strengths and weaknesses of the current system?
3. What should be the goals of post-tenure review?
4. How should exemplary faculty be rewarded?
5. What support should be available to faculty whose performance is unacceptable?
6. How helpful are evaluation methods like electronic portfolios, videotaped lectures, and classroom visits?
7. What are the greatest concerns about change?

national conferences on post-tenure review, the team decided to conduct a forum to educate members of the academic community. Public forums were conducted two years in a row.

The first year, the campus forum comprised faculty members from the University of Kentucky and Arizona State University, where post-tenure review studies were driven by different circumstances. Other members of the forum were representatives from the Idaho State Board of Education, the Northwest Association of Schools and Colleges, and AAHE.

The first forum was moderated by the chair of the ISU faculty senate, who asked the panel questions submitted by faculty members. The forum also allowed for questions from the floor.

The second year, a campus forum for department chairs and program directors was scheduled. Department chairs and program directors wanted to learn more efficient and creative techniques for evaluating faculty members. An external consultant facilitated the forum.

***Involve***

Although each campus forum was expensive and required considerable planning, they were needed. The forums allowed faculty and administrators to think creatively about how to satisfy the requirements of the state as well as those of the accrediting agency.

The team used the information from the focus groups to design a survey for tenured and tenure-track faculty. The survey asked faculty to share views, experiences, and levels of satisfaction about the current review process. It included a question about preferred rewards for tenured faculty members who receive high marks (see attachment A at the end of this chapter). Results of the survey were posted on the post-tenure review webpage.

**Results of the faculty survey.** Of the 419 tenured and tenure-track faculty who were surveyed, only 29 percent responded. One possible explanation is a lack of importance to faculty. A second explanation is indifference. In this instance, indifference has a positive connotation: Since faculty members believe they are held to high standards of performance, they would be indifferent to adopting policies designed to observe it.

On the issue of potential rewards, the study team expected unanimous support for salary increases. Although there was strong support for them (80 percent), there was also support for funding for learning, training, or interning (59 percent); for sabbatical leaves (58 percent); for study grants (53 percent); and for a reduction in course load (46 percent). Forty (40) percent said meaningful rewards could include items such as laptop computers, books, or software programs.

The level of satisfaction with the current policy for reviewing tenured faculty was relatively high. Of those who responded, 59 percent said they believed the current process is somewhat or very effective in achieving its purpose at ISU. The current policy received somewhat lower marks (43 percent) on whether it helped faculty members become aware of their strengths, and only 32 percent said it helped in identifying their professional goals.

The faculty governance system was able to design a new policy for post-tenure review that integrates annual reviews with periodic performance reviews. The new policy satisfies the requirements of the state board and the accrediting agency. In this policy, each department is given the responsibility to formulate a procedure for collegial review, and the totality of any three consecutive annual reviews is the substantive review as required by the Northwest Association of Schools and Colleges.

## Summary

The Idaho State University team used a strategic approach to inform, communicate, educate, and involve all members of the academic community in developing a post-tenure review policy.

First, the team used faculty and department chair discussion groups (focus groups) to identify salient issues to be addressed by the ISU post-tenure review policy. Some issues were administrative: Hold every department and college to similar standards and practices. Others were conceptual: Clarify substantive review, and prescribe reasonable peer review. The team used discussion groups and a faculty survey to identify issues relevant to modifying ISU's periodic performance review policy.

Second, decision making involved faculty members — particularly the faculty governance system — at each stage of work. The study team included current and past presidents of the faculty senate. The revising of the policy was done by a subcommittee of the faculty senate, the Faculty Professional Policies

Committee. Third, the study team allocated resources to inform faculty through public forums with national experts and by creating the ISU post-tenure review website. A consultant was hired to conduct an evaluation workshop for department chairs and program directors upon their request.

The ISU work is not finished. A new policy to replace the existing policy has been crafted and approved (see attachment B). The policy builds on ISU's annual reviews. Unlike the previous policy, the new one requires evaluator(s) to identify areas of excellence and areas needing improvement. The policy requires that any three consecutive annual reviews combined should equal a substantive review by including (1) an assessment of teaching, service, and research; (2) the consideration of multiple factors; (3) collegial input; and (4) student input when appropriate.

When the initial policy came before the faculty senate, senators amended it to clarify collegial input. The amended policy (attachment B) includes the following statement: "The faculty of each department shall formulate the procedure for collegial review." The study team expects the new policy will be administered consistently across the campus. The revised policy defines substantive review, yet it assigns departments the task of deciding how and to what extent the review will include peer input. It is expected that assigning financial resources will benefit all tenured faculty — from the many whose performance is consistently superior to the few whose performance can be improved. The approach followed at Idaho State University was successful and offers other institutions a grassroots model to consider.

## Note

1. Ann S. Hunter is associate professor of sociology and director of the Ifft Social Science Methodology Laboratory at Idaho State University. She teaches undergraduate and graduate social statistics and research methods as well as demography. Hunter's research areas are Hispanic farm workers' access to healthcare and risk assessment. She has been on the faculty at ISU since 1991. (Contact her at oakeann@isu.edu)

Jonathan Lawson has been vice-president for academic affairs and professor of English at Idaho State University since 1995. In addition to his administrative duties, Lawson teaches in ISU's freshman seminar program and in the higher education emphasis in the doctoral program in educational leadership. Lawson came to ISU from Connecticut, where he worked at the University of Hartford for nearly a decade. (Contact him at lawsjon@isu.edu)

# Attachment A

## Questionnaire to ISU Faculty

**From the ISU AAHE Mini-Grant Committee on Post-Tenure Review of Faculty**
**October 1999**

This questionnaire solicits opinions of tenured and tenure-track ISU faculty members regarding our **current** post-tenure review process.

(Allow space here for directions).

1. Our post-tenure review policy is described as a *periodic performance review* in Part 4, Section IV.B.6 of the Faculty/Staff Handbook. Have you ever read this section?
   1 [ ] Yes
   2 [ ] No

2. Have you had any involvement with a *periodic performance review* in your department at ISU?
   1 [ ] No. If "no," skip 3 and 4.
   2 [ ] Yes. If "yes," continue to 3.

3. Was the process satisfactory?
   1 [ ] Yes
   2 [ ] No. If "no," why not? Please specify. If extra space is needed, attach a sheet with your comments on it.

4. How might the procedures be improved? Please specify. If extra space is needed, attach a sheet with your comments on it.

Presently, ISU's *periodic performance review* policy for tenured faculty members states that a faculty member's review will be carried out at intervals not to exceed five years. Furthermore, it will focus on five general categories: (1) teaching effectiveness; (2) research or creative activities; (3) professionally related services; (4) other assigned responsibilities; and (5) overall contributions to the department.

Please indicate whether you agree or disagree with the following statements relevant to this *periodic performance review* policy as it is administered in your department:

| | | Agree | Disagree |
|---|---|---|---|
| 5. | This process is taken seriously in my department | [ ] | [ ] |
| 6. | This process establishes an expectation of continuous professional growth | [ ] | [ ] |
| 7. | Present policy acts as a safeguard to tenure | [ ] | [ ] |
| 8. | Present policy places unreasonable demands on **departmental members** | [ ] | [ ] |
| 9. | Present policy places unreasonable demands on **department chairs** | [ ] | [ ] |
| 10. | Present policy places unreasonable demands on **Deans** | [ ] | [ ] |
| 11. | Present policy supports risk-taking in my professional activities | [ ] | [ ] |

1

12. As you understand it, what is the primary purpose for *periodic performance reviews* at ISU? Check all the ones that apply here:
    1 [ ] Assess individual performance in order to reward excellence
    2 [ ] Assess individual performance in order to remedy deficiencies
    3 [ ] Increase accountability to outside constituencies
    4 [ ] Review performance to determine if minimal standards are being met
    5 [ ] Review performance to determine if individual goals mesh with institutional goals.
    6 [ ] Other (please describe):

13. How effective do you think the *periodic performance review* process is in achieving its primary purpose at ISU?
    1 [ ] Very effective
    2 [ ] Somewhat effective
    3 [ ] Not particularly effective
    4 [ ] Very ineffective
    5 [ ] No opinion. Please comment using the space below or attach a separate sheet of paper.

14. Our *annual review* policy is described in Part 4, Section IV. B.1 of the Faculty/Staff Handbook. Have you ever read this section?
    1 [ ] Yes
    2 [ ] No

15. How effective do you think the *annual review* process is in achieving its primary purpose at ISU?
    1 [ ] Very effective
    2 [ ] Somewhat effective
    3 [ ] Not particularly effective
    4 [ ] Very ineffective
    5 [ ] No opinion. Please comment using the space below or attach a separate sheet of paper.

16. To what extent do you agree or disagree with the following statement? *The Annual Review process identifies excellent professional performance of tenured faculty members.*
    1 [ ] Strongly Agree
    2 [ ] Agree
    3 [ ] Neither Agree or Disagree
    4 [ ] Disagree
    5 [ ] Strongly Disagree
    9 [ ] Don't Know. Please comment using the space below or attach a separate sheet of paper.

17. To what extent do you agree or disagree with the following statement? *The Annual Review identifies unsatisfactory professional performance of tenured faculty members.*
    1 [ ] Strongly Agree
    2 [ ] Agree
    3 [ ] Neither Agree or Disagree
    4 [ ] Disagree
    5 [ ] Strongly Disagree
    9 [ ] Don't Know. Please comment using the space below or attach a separate sheet of paper.

18. If you have been tenured at ISU for five years or longer, then you have been subject to our *periodic performance review* process. Has this process occurred for you?
    1 [ ] No. If "no," skip to 24.
    2 [ ] Yes. If "yes," continue to 19.

2

Note: for Items 19 through 23:
SA=Strongly Agree; A=Agree; N=Neutral; D=Disagree; SD=Strongly Disagree

| | SA | A | N | D | SD |
|---|---|---|---|---|---|
| 19. The process was fair | [ ] | [ ] | [ ] | [ ] | [ ] |
| 20. The process helped me become aware of my strengths | [ ] | [ ] | [ ] | [ ] | [ ] |
| 21. The process encouraged self-assessment | [ ] | [ ] | [ ] | [ ] | [ ] |
| 22. The process helped me to identify professional goals | [ ] | [ ] | [ ] | [ ] | [ ] |
| 23. The process was a means for recognizing my accomplishments | [ ] | [ ] | [ ] | [ ] | [ ] |

24. Have you participated in the review of others who have gone through your department's *periodic performance review?*
    1 [ ] No. If "no," skip to 31.
    2 [ ] Yes. If "yes," continue to 25.

Note: for Items 25 through 28:
SA=Strongly Agree; A=Agree; N=Neutral; D=Disagree; SD=Strongly Disagree

| | SA | A | N | D | SD |
|---|---|---|---|---|---|
| 25. The process was fair | [ ] | [ ] | [ ] | [ ] | [ ] |
| 26. The process had clear guidelines | [ ] | [ ] | [ ] | [ ] | [ ] |
| 27. The process increased my **awareness** of work of colleagues | [ ] | [ ] | [ ] | [ ] | [ ] |
| 28. The process increased my **appreciation** of work of colleagues | [ ] | [ ] | [ ] | [ ] | [ ] |
| 29. The process built collegiality in my department | [ ] | [ ] | [ ] | [ ] | [ ] |
| 30. The process placed unreasonable demands on departmental members | [ ] | [ ] | [ ] | [ ] | [ ] |

Aside from the kinds of resources now available, what different types of resources could function as rewards for **excellent** performance in senior faculty professional roles? Check as many as you like.

31. [ ] Funding for learning/training/interning
32. [ ] Laptop computer for use in the field
33. [ ] One course load reduction for one semester
34. [ ] Research assistance by student aides
35. [ ] Resources for books
36. [ ] Resources for software or other equipment
37. [ ] Sabbatical Leave
38. [ ] Salary bump
39. [ ] Travel grants
40. [ ] Other (specify):

41. Do you think that the present policy for *periodic performance reviews* should be changed?
    1 [ ] No. Please explain. If you need more space, attach a separate page:
    2 [ ] Yes. Please explain. If you need more space, attach a separate page:

3

**Demographics**

1. How long have you been on the faculty at ISU previous to this current academic year?
   ___ ___ years

2. How long, not including this current academic year, have you held a faculty appointment at any four year institution?
   ___ ___ years

3. Are you a tenured or tenure-track ISU faculty member?
   1 [ ] Yes
   2 [ ] No

4. Have you received tenure at ISU?
   1 [ ] No
   2 [ ] Yes

5. What is your current academic rank?
   1 [ ] Adjunct, Instructor, or Lecturer
   2 [ ] Assistant Professor
   3 [ ] Associate Professor
   4 [ ] Professor
   5 [ ] Other (Please specify):

6. Do you now occupy an administrative position such as Department Chair, Program Director, or Dean?
   1 [ ] Yes
   2 [ ] No

7. In which unit are you a tenured or tenure-track faculty member?
   1 [ ] College of Arts and Sciences
   2 [ ] College of Business
   3 [ ] College of Education
   4 [ ] College of Engineering
   5 [ ] College of Health Professions
   6 [ ] College of Pharmacy
   7 [ ] School of Applied Technology
   8 [ ] University Library
   9 [ ] Other

8. What is your highest degree?
   1 [ ] Bachelor's degree
   2 [ ] Master's degree
   3 [ ] Professional degrees (e.g., ParmD, JD, and so forth)
   4 [ ] PhD, EdD, DA

9. At ISU, is your highest degree considered the terminal degree in your field?
   1 [ ] Yes
   2 [ ] No

4

If you would like to write any additional comments, please do so in the space below. You may also post any comments on our Post-Tenure Review Web page, at http://www/isu.edu/departments/aahemini/home.html. As before, your comments will be anonymous; no record appears, or is kept, anywhere of the names of persons who contribute comments to the web page.

Thank you for completing this survey questionnaire by October 15. When you are finished, please fold the survey and using the cover sheet with the address printed on the back, mail it to the Office of Institutional Research, Box 8368. anonymity.

# Attachment B

## *Revision of Faculty Handbook Annual Review Text to Comply With NASC Policy on Faculty Evaluation*

Each year the chair of a department (or unit head) must submit to the Dean of the chair's college (or appropriate superior) an evaluation of each faculty member in that department (or unit). Any evaluation must include at least administrative access to all primary or raw evaluation data. This evaluation, together with the opinion of higher administrators, will be used as one basis for the final recommendation relative to reappointment, non-reappointment, acquisition of tenure, or other personnel action, whichever is appropriate. The chair must communicate in writing an assessment of strengths and weaknesses to each faculty member evaluated.

Evaluation of faculty should be made in terms of the individual's potential effectiveness as a permanent member of the local academic community. The indices considered in annual faculty evaluations may vary by unit, from year to year, and by the faculty member's responsibilities and stage of career. However, the totality of any three consecutive annual evaluations should be substantive by adhering to the following criteria:

(i) address each relevant major faculty responsibility (e.g., teaching, service, research);

(ii) include consideration of multiple factors for each responsibility;

(iii) include informed collegial input on as many responsibilities as practicable; the faculty of each department shall formulate the procedure for collegial review;

(iv) and include student input as appropriate.

The annual evaluation should clearly indicate areas of excellence and areas needing development. The chair should identify and facilitate opportunities and resources for addressing those needs and rewarding excellence. At intervals not to exceed three years, the chair will review the faculty member's three most recent annual evaluations or other substantive reviews such as promotion and tenure and certify that a substantive review has been completed during the last three years.

# Post-Tenure Review in Texas: An Evolving Response to the Legislature's Challenge

**Debra P. Price, Dennis Longmire, Frank Fair, Laverne Warner, Paul R. Reed, William Fleming, and JoAnn M. Duffy** [1]

Post-tenure review came abruptly to the state-supported universities of Texas. As in other states, this process was not without trepidation. In 1996, a state senator proposed a "two strikes and you're out" revision of tenure. His proposal — "if someone receives two substandard evaluations in a row, then that person's tenure should be revoked" — challenged the institution of tenure. Texas faculty associations, joined by university administrators, campaigned to soften this blow to the tenure system. A number of key legislators worked closely with faculty leaders and administrators to craft a compromise acceptable to all parties.

## Legislative Mandate

At the close of the 1997 legislative session, the Texas Legislature passed Senate Bill 149. Senate Bill 149 required that post-tenure review be in place in all state universities in six months. [2] This bill charged the various university governing boards to devise their own systems of post-tenure review — now known officially as the Performance Evaluation of Tenured Faculty (PETF). Senate Bill 149 mandated several conditions.

- Advice and comment from faculty on the performance evaluation of tenured peers shall be given the utmost consideration.

- Every tenured faculty member must be evaluated "no more often than once every year, but no less often than every six years."
- Evaluation is "based on the professional responsibilities of the faculty member in teaching, research, service, patient care, and administration."

The discussions by the legislature that led to Senate Bill 149 focused on anecdotes concerning teaching and patient care rather than on specific, relevant hard data on faculty performance.

### *Legislative Guidelines*

Senate Bill 149 stated "revocation of tenure or other appropriate disciplinary action" was to take place only if "incompetency, neglect of duty, or other good cause is determined to be present." The bill's references to due process — including the innovative option of referring any case to a "nonbinding alternative dispute resolution process" — were reassuring to faculty. Additionally, Senate Bill 149 called for post-tenure review to "be directed toward development of the faculty member" and to "include peer review of the faculty member." These legislative guidelines gave the higher education community reason to believe the majority of faculty members already meeting their responsibilities might benefit from this process.

## Campus Implementation

To comply with Senate Bill 149 each institution in the various Texas systems formulated its own policy. In the six schools of the Texas State University System — Southwest Texas State University, Sam Houston State University, Angelo State University, Sul Ross State University, Lamar University/Beaumont, and Lamar University/Port Arthur — approximately 1,500 tenured and tenure-track faculty were affected by this policy. Because each campus wrote its own policy, procedures and criteria varied. In addition, many institutions allowed their departments to set their own criteria and formats. For example, some of the departmental procedures depended on the existing faculty evaluation systems, while others allowed a faculty member to showcase a range of accomplishments every five years.

## Understanding Stakeholder Perspectives

An interdisciplinary faculty team began to examine the effects of Senate Bill 149. The goal was to compile useful, comparative data on the post-tenure review process as it was developing on the various campuses of the Texas State University System. The team was also interested in understanding the legislative history behind Senate Bill 149 and in how specific stakeholders — including key legislators, system administrators, and faculty and administrators on the various campuses — viewed Senate Bill 149 and the process of post-tenure review. The results of that work are detailed here.

### *Collecting Data*

Two methods were used to collect the data: (1) We surveyed all tenured and tenure-track faculty in the Texas State University System [3]; and (2) we conducted interviews with key legislators, the chancellor, and the system attorney, as well as administrators and tenured and tenure-track faculty from each university in the system. In all, we interviewed dozens of stakeholders, and about 30 percent of faculty returned surveys (459 of 1,455). Here are the major findings:

### *Findings and Discussion*

From our campus interviews, we learned several key things about the annual merit review process.

- Prior to the legislative mandate, all but one university in the system required an annual review of each faculty member's performance. Although critical to the tenure and promotion process, these reviews were not the only determining factor.
- Most campuses tied merit increases to the annual review.
- For tenured faculty, there did not seem to be any development plan tied to the outcome of this evaluation. For non-tenured faculty, suggestions were frequently made for ways to improve performance so that tenure might be granted.
- Tenured faculty at five of the six campuses could be denied merit-based salary adjustments as a result of a substandard yearly review. The exception to this pattern came from one university that had few merit raises available.
- Tenured and tenure-track faculty at all campuses participated in annual reviews; but given the lack of merit increases, many faculty members failed to complete the required paper-

work. There did not seem to be any consequences for this action, just as there appeared to be little reward for compliance.

- Faculty members at the rank of full professor at one institution were not required to submit any yearly documentation.

## Annual Review Since Senate Bill 149

Changes to the review of faculty since Senate Bill 149 are varied. Two campuses have kept the yearly evaluation and added triggered reviews to comply with Senate Bill 149. In one case, two substandard evaluations trigger a development plan followed by dismissal if the plan is not executed. In the second case, three substandard evaluations trigger dismissal with no developmental plan ever being discussed.

The other campuses have implemented various procedures. Some procedures are based on existing faculty evaluations; others are more of an add-on. For example, on one campus, every tenured faculty member participates in the yearly review. This forms the basis for merit, tenure, and promotion considerations. Additionally, every fifth year, tenured faculty members present their accomplishments over that time to their department for consideration. This review does not directly affect tenure, merit, or promotion, but can trigger a developmental plan (see opposite).

## Impact of Post-Tenure Review

Survey and interview data revealed that much remains unknown about the impact of post-tenure review procedures. For many faculty, the process is too new to evaluate confidently. The following concerns surfaced.

### *Lack of Information/Uneven Implementation Concerns*

Many faculty seemed uninformed about post-tenure review and questioned how decisions would be made. For example, a faculty member expressed concern about the lack of formal guidelines for how an evaluation should proceed once it had passed beyond the peer review stage. This particular faculty member requested a "formal pass," — i.e., administration concurrence with peers' favorable evaluation — be put in writing, yet is still unsure whether or not any of the "higher-ups" even looked at the evaluation report.

## Features of Post-Tenure Review Policies

***Lamar-Beaumont***
*Policies:* combination
*Development Plans:* after second unsatisfactory review
*Type of Review:* peer and department head
*Policy Available Electronically:* www.lamar.edu/ handbooks/faculty/ page45.html

***Lamar-Port Arthur***
*Policies:* periodic
*Development Plans:* if six-year performance review is unsatisfactory
*Type of Review:* peer and department head
*Policy Available Electronically:* www.pa.lamar.edu/facultyhandbook.pdf

***Sam Houston State***
*Policies:* combination
*Development Plans:* yearly evaluations can trigger a plan, or unsatisfactory review at the end of every fifth year
*Type of Review:* peer and department head
*Policy Available Electronically:* www.shsu.edu/~vaf_www/aps /980204.html

***Southwest Texas State***
*Policies:* triggered
*Development Plans:* first unsatisfactory review triggers plan
*Type of Review:* peer
*Policy Available Electronically:* www.math.swt.edu/~handbook/ handbook99.pdf

***Angelo State***
*Policies:* triggered
*Development Plans:* after first unsatisfactory review, revocation of tenure after three successive unsatisfactory reviews
*Type of Review:* peer and department head
*Policy Available Electronically:* www.angelo.edu/ faculty_staff /publication.htm

***Sul Ross***
*Policies:* triggered
*Development Plans:* after second unsatisfactory yearly review
*Type of Review:* peer and department head
*Policy Available Electronically:* N/A

Not surprisingly, programs and procedures varied greatly from campus to campus and even department to department. Individual campuses need to make the process fairer, easier to understand, and less burdensome.

#### *Fairness/Academic Freedom Concerns*

Survey data also revealed a link between level and type of concern and rank, gender, and tenure status. The differences may be due to rank and tenure status rather than gender. Nonetheless, there continue to be concerns about academic freedom. Many faculty members were less well informed about post-tenure review and its implementation than were vice presidents, deans, and department chairs; not surprisingly, faculty were much more concerned about its fairness and effects.

#### *Dismissal Concerns*

There also were differences about whether dismissal of tenured faculty would become easier or harder. Some deans believe the post-tenure review process could add years to the time it would take to dismiss a faculty member. In particular, the development plans required when someone "fails" post-tenure review could add a complication that might make it more difficult to dismiss a faculty member. There was even a report of a faculty member "playing the system" (two substandard evaluations followed by an acceptable evaluation, followed by a substandard evaluation). Some vice presidents for academic affairs responded: "It should make dismissal more difficult. If we don't have all of the information we need, or if we haven't documented real attempts to help a faculty member change, then we shouldn't be able to dismiss them easily."

The Texas State University System attorney stated existing mechanisms for removing faculty for insubordination or dereliction of duty were rarely used because they could not survive a court challenge. The new post-tenure review policies call for documenting unacceptably low performance and for giving the faculty member a chance to improve. While these steps might add time to the process of termination, they make the process more likely to withstand a court challenge.

#### *Compliance Concern*

Interviews with legislators gave us reason to believe the initial intent was to eliminate tenure. The compromise legislation in Senate Bill 149 may have saved tenure for now, but policymakers assured us they would "be watching to see how university faculty respond."

### *Shifting Emphasis Concern*

Survey data may give us important insights into whether unintended consequences may arise. Legislators said their highest concern was teaching, and our surveys indicated faculty within in the Texas State University System do give strong weight to teaching in the evaluation process. But many faculty perceive post-tenure review as encouraging more research activity. Of those who indicated that the prospect of undergoing post-tenure review affected their professional activities, 53 percent had increased attention given to their research activities. The numbers involved are small, however, and so caution should be used in interpretation.

## Recommendations

Post-tenure review was initially decried as unnecessary and a threat to tenure. Now post-tenure review is accepted as inevitable. The task turns to the most effective and positive way possible to implement the policies. Accordingly, one of the outcomes from this study is a set of recommendations to improve the effectiveness of post-tenure review policies throughout the Texas State University System. The recommendations were given to faculty senate chairs and the vice presidents for academic affairs of the participating institutions (see opposite). They were also posted to a publicly accessible website (www.shsu.edu/~icc_drl/AAHE.html).

### *Revisit Post-Tenure Review*

Many respondents think it is "too soon to tell" how post-tenure review will influence academic freedom and efficiency. Similarly, it is too early to judge whether post-tenure review will permanently change academia. Accordingly, our first recommendation calls for the creation of a faculty committee on each campus to examine post-tenure review in five years. In the Texas State University System, post-tenure review policies were instituted hastily in response to a legislatively imposed deadline. There was only a brief time to research and ponder alternative approaches. Also, fully 41 percent of the responding tenured and tenure-track faculty were not involved in establishing the proce-

## Recommendations to Improve Post-Tenure Review [and Sources of Support for Each Recommendation]

1. Each component institution of the Texas State University System should appoint a committee to reexamine the procedures used on its campus for PETF. [Interview and survey data]

2. Each campus committee should consider whether mandatory development plans for faculty members should be triggered after they receive a rating of "Fails to meet minimum standards" for *one* academic year. [Interview and survey data]

3. Campus committees should deliberate on how to make the *central focus* of the PETF process be on *faculty development* and on how this development goal can be most *effectively* and *efficiently* accomplished. [Interview and survey data]

4. The committee needs to consider how, in order to achieve *effectively* the goal of faculty development, PETF needs to be, as much as possible, a *formative* process rather than a *summative* process. [Interview data]

5. Each campus committee should consider whether, in order to be an *efficient* use of faculty and administrators' time, that PETF — in general — should be applied to a faculty member on some periodic basis, with the period being perhaps every three, four, or five years. [Interview data]

6. The campus committee is charged especially with examining the role of the faculty peer reviews in the PETF process to make the peer reviews more effective and efficient. [Interview data]

7. The committee charged with reviewing the PETF process should give special attention to how to conduct the peer review of *teaching*. [Interview and survey data]

8. Campus committees should be charged with recommending procedures to monitor the impact of PETF. [Interview data]

dures. These committees as a result can help enable the faculty to revise post-tenure review procedures. Furthermore, establishing such committees signals to the legislators that the universities are taking reforming the tenure system seriously.

#### *Measuring Acceptable Performance*

Subsequent recommendations set forth two issues for the campus committees to address. The first issue is to identify incompetent faculty members and make possible the "revocation of tenure or other appropriate disciplinary action" (SB 149, Section [1] [c] [5]). How best to create and apply standards for minimum acceptable performance? Current standards vary and need to be assessed for clarity, consistency, and application. The range of variation is significant. For example, standards ranged from a numerical scale in a college of business to an entire campus system where the only response we received to repeated questions about minimum standards was that "whenever your supervisor says you are 'unsatisfactory,' then you are unsatisfactory."

We believe a rating of satisfactory versus unsatisfactory is insufficient to identify incompetence and neglect of duty as required by Senate Bill 149; the latter term is defined in the law as "continuing or repeated substantial neglect of professional responsibilities." We suggest identifying a minimum acceptable performance level to make it clear that any performance below this level will not be tolerated on a continuing basis.

Performance standards are inconsistent because they had been defined by each division, department, or program with very little consultation with other units. To some extent this is both natural and desirable. But similar programs need similar minimum acceptable performance standards.

Some campuses allow a faculty member two years of failing to meet acceptable performance thresholds before a formal development plan is initiated. We recommend a development plan be mandatory after the initial year of unsatisfactory performance. If failure to meet a minimum acceptable level of performance is taken seriously, then there can be no reason not to undertake promptly an active intervention plan to rectify the situation.

#### *Focus on Faculty Development*

The second issue focuses on making faculty development the central purpose of post-tenure review, and on how this development goal can be most effectively and efficiently accomplished. Through interviews, we are persuaded that the percentage of genuine "deadwood" is small. As a result, post-tenure review should help productive faculty become even more productive. This has one very direct implication. A large number of departments conduct post-tenure review by using a checklist of performance items that are to be rated "satisfactory" or "unsatisfactory." But a simple checklist cannot aid faculty development. If a faculty member receives a "satisfactory" rating — as the vast majority will — there are no specific recommendations to improve one's performance. Faculty members need feedback that is more substantive than a simple pass/fail grade.

Senate Bill 149 mandates "the evaluation include peer review of the faculty member" (Senate Bill 149, Section [c][2]). What constitutes peer review varies greatly, adding to faculty angst on this issue. A plausible solution is to appoint a small group of faculty members to serve as peer reviewers, who have been suggested by both the chair and the affected faculty member. Small departments could allow faculty members in a related discipline to count as peers, or the university can conduct reviews using disciplinary peers from other institutions.

Faculty members also cautioned against relying only on student rating forms to evaluate teaching performance. Peer review of teaching performance could enrich the evaluation process. Effective models for the peer review of teaching exist. AAHE has conducted a number of projects involving peer review of teaching, several inspired by Ernest Boyer's conceptualization of the scholarship of teaching. Peer review of teaching responds directly to the post-tenure review mandate of legislatures and governing boards.

#### *Final Issue: Monitoring the Impact*

Finally, the post-tenure review study committee on each campus should be charged to recommend procedures to assess the impact of post-tenure review. More than half of our survey respondents who had undergone post-tenure review reported they had not received any formal feedback. Any effective review process requires formal feedback. Second, according to our interviews with key legislators, the Texas legislature will probably revisit post-tenure review. Legislators will certainly take higher education's views more seriously if the institutions have gathered data on the effectiveness of post-tenure review. Data should include the number of faculty placed on mandatory development plans and dismissed for cause. Faculty who retire or leave for other reasons could be asked in exit interviews whether post-tenure review was a factor in their decision. The most important data are on the faculty development impact of post-tenure review. For example, our survey showed 27 percent of the peer reviewers have been helped to "identify areas of my professional role that needed strengthening." Such data demonstrate that post-tenure review is working the way the legislature intended.

## Conclusion

Process evaluation is an important but frequently neglected aspect of policy development. The legislature wisely gave Texas institutions considerable latitude in designing their post-tenure review procedures. The next logical step is to monitor the first cycles of implementation to assess impact and improve effectiveness and efficiency. In a subsequent study, we broadened our sample to include institutions such as Texas A&M, the University of Texas at Arlington, the University of Houston, and Texas Tech University. The same degree of variability in approaching post-tenure review within and across campuses appears at these other schools. We are developing a series of workshops (beginning in 2002) on strategies for creating consistent, effective, defensible post-tenure review procedures.

While we believe that acting on our recommendations will improve the implementation of post-tenure review at several of the universities we studied, the continuing challenge for us in the higher education community is to monitor the procedures we have in place at our institutions to ensure that they are as fair, effective, and efficient as possible.

## Notes

1. Debra P. Price is an associate professor of language and literacy studies at Sam Houston State University. One of her current research interests involves the politicization of literacy issues — and this relates to her interest in post-tenure review. She received her bachelor's degree from the University of Colorado-Boulder, a master's from Louisiana State University, and her Ph.D. from the University of Texas at Austin. (Contact her at edu_dpp@shsu.edu)

Dennis Longmire is a professor of criminal justice and director of the Criminal Justice Center's survey research program at Sam Houston State University. He has published numerous articles and scholarly publications focusing on public attitudes about crime, criminals, and the administration of justice. He has also served as associate dean for academic administration at Sam Houston State University's College of Criminal Justice. Longmire received his B.A. in sociology from Towson State University and an M.A. and Ph.D. in criminal justice from the University of Maryland. (Contact him at icc_drl@shsu.edu)

Frank Fair is a professor of philosophy and the coordinator of the philosophy program at Sam Houston State University. His research interests include decision making in dealing with environmental issues and the issue of capital punishment. Fair has received both the Sam Houston State University Excellence in Teaching Award (1989) and the Faculty Excellence in Service Award (1992). A long-time AAUP member, he served as the chair of the committee to create the new post-tenure review policy for the university and optimistically believes that post-tenure review can result in strengthening tenure as an institution. He received an honors B.A. in classical languages and philosophy from Xavier University (Ohio), an M.A. in philosophy from Boston College, and a Ph.D. in philosophy from the University of Georgia. (Contact him at psy_fkf@shsu.edu)

Laverne Warner is a professor of early childhood education and the senior tenured faculty member in Sam Houston State University's Department of Language, Literacy & Special Populations. She has received the Sam Houston State University Excellence in Teaching Award (1992), and she volunteered to be the first person in her department to undergo post-tenure review. Warner received her B.S. and her M.Ed. from Sam Houston State University, and her Ph.D. from East Texas State University. (Contact her at edu_lxw@shsu.edu)

Paul R. Reed is a professor of management at Sam Houston State University. His area of research interest is the strategic management of small businesses. He has received the Sam Houston State University Faculty Excellence in Service Award (1993), and he was president of the Texas Association of College Teachers (TACT) during the Texas legislative session that passed Senate Bill 149. He testified before the Senate and was instrumental in forging a post-tenure review compromise solution. He has his B.A. in history from the University of Notre Dame and his D.B.A. in management from Mississippi State University. (Contact him at mgt_prr@shsu.edu)

William Fleming is a professor of English at Sam Houston State University and has received both the Sam Houston State University Excellence in Teaching Award (1998) and the Excellence in Service Award (1996). He is 2001-03 president of the Texas Council of Faculty Senates. He helped in reviewing and revising the initial post-tenure review instrument for Sam Houston State University. Fleming received both his B.A. and M.A. from Sam Houston State University and his Ph.D. from the University of Toledo. (Contact him at eng_wpf@shsu.edu)

JoAnn M. Duffy is a professor of management and the director of the Gibson D. Lewis Center of Business and Economic Development at Sam Houston State University. Her research interests are in service management and health care productivity. Duffy was the first in her department to complete the post-tenure review process. She joined the research team at the end of the first stage of the project. She received a B.A. in social studies from St. Mary of the Woods College and an M.A. and Ph.D. from the University of Texas at Austin. (Contact her at mgt_jxd@shsu.edu)

2. To access the complete bill visit www.capitol.state.tx.us/tlo/billsrch/search.htm and search for bill149.

3. Information and specific details about the methods used to design the data collection instruments, plus the survey results themselves, are available at www.shsu.edu/~icc_drl/AAHE.html.

# Learning About Post-Tenure Review From Peer Institutions

**Susan H. Barr** [1]

## Post-Tenure Review in Virginia

Post-tenure review first appeared in Virginia in 1996 through legislative action (Senate Joint Resolution 139) taken following the report of the Commission on the Future of Higher Education in Virginia *Making Connections: Matching Virginia Higher Education's Strengths With the Commonwealth's Needs.* The report mandated evaluating tenured faculty:

> The faculty of the colleges and universities [in Virginia], working with the administration of those institutions, must take the responsibility to develop and support a process for regular evaluation of tenured faculty that leads to continuous improvement in their teaching, research, and service, or results in negative actions such as dismissal. (Commission 1996: 9)

The report also stated:

> Each board of visitors [2] should require the development of a process for regular evaluation of tenured faculty [including a reasonable, periodic schedule to fit each institution] that leads to continuous improvement in their teaching, research, and service, and that makes clear sanctions for unsatisfactory performance includ[ing] reduction in salary and dismissal. (9)

The guidelines for developing an effective post-tenure review policy were then outlined in the Senate resolution:

> It should be the product of a joint effort by the faculty and administration, integrated with the regular faculty evaluation policy; it should be developmental in nature so that a tenured faculty member who is not performing at the desired level has the opportunity to develop goals and a plan to meet the expectations together with the administration; and it should include a timetable

> to achieve the mutually agreed-upon goals. The review should be systematic and uniformly applied, provide for due process, and be connected to the existing means available to faculty to redress grievances.

Virginia's institutions of higher learning began to develop individualized post-tenure review policies following these principles. Virginia's system of higher education is the 11th largest in the United States, with more than 100 colleges and universities. [3]

## Institutional Context

Virginia Military Institute (VMI) is one of the public, land-grant, baccalaureate institutions in Virginia. Founded in 1839 by the Commonwealth, VMI is now a coeducational college with a student body of 1,300 cadets from 47 states and 22 foreign countries. With 100 full-time faculty, VMI offers majors in 13 disciplines in engineering, science, and liberal arts leading to a bachelor of arts or bachelor of science degree. Approximately one-third of graduates from VMI accept a commission in one of the military services of the United States.

## Post-Tenure Review at VMI

In response to Senate Resolution 139, VMI created two policies: the faculty merit pay plan and the plan for faculty development. The faculty development plan mandated the creation of a faculty development committee and a periodic survey of faculty to determine their developmental needs.

### *Merit Pay Plan*

According to the original merit pay plan — essentially the post-tenure review policy — each faculty member at VMI prepares an annual report presenting accomplishments in teaching, research, public service, and support of the Institute's mission (see attachment A at the end of the chapter). The academic department head meets with the faculty member to rate the faculty member's performance as exceptional, commendable, provisional, or unacceptable. The evaluation explicitly states the reasons for the classification. Merit pay raises are then allocated to faculty members who are rated exceptional and standard raises are allocated to those who are rated commendable.

Any faculty member rated as provisional and/or unacceptable twice within a five-year period meets with the department head and the dean of the faculty and receives a letter of reprimand to be placed in the personnel file. In addition, the faculty member will undergo a triggered in-depth evaluation. The review is conducted by a committee comprising the faculty member's department head, another department head in the division selected by the dean of the faculty, and, if the faculty member requests it, an external evaluator (a full-time VMI faculty member). The committee reviews evidence for the overall contribution of the faculty member to the Institute, then sends a report with recommendations to the dean of the faculty. The faculty member also meets with the department head and develops a written plan of action outlining goals, activities to meet the stated goals, and a timeline. Annual evaluations of the faculty member in succeeding years specifically review progress toward meeting the goals outlined in the plan. A faculty member who fails to achieve the stated goals within the agreed-upon timetable — usually one year after the completion of the plan — is subject to dismissal in accordance with the procedures specified in Appendix A, "Academic Freedom and Tenure," of the *Handbook for Faculty and Staff.*

Faculty members who are classified as provisional have salary increases held in abeyance pending a review by the dean of the faculty. If sufficient improvement is documented, the faculty member will receive the raise retroactively. Faculty who are rated unacceptable receive no raises.

### Faculty Development Plan

The goal of the faculty development plan is to improve faculty performance. Implementing an action plan as a result of a triggered review provides an opportunity for faculty to remedy a provisional or unacceptable rating. Thus, there is a connection between post-tenure review and faculty development at VMI.

VMI's plan for faculty development defines faculty development as:

> A collection of activities designed to encourage faculty members to improve and to grow by enhancing their expertise, skills, attitudes, and career path for the betterment of the students, the institution, and the individual. The plan calls for a Faculty

> Development Committee that monitors developmental needs and priorities of the faculty at VMI. The goal of the plan is "the enhancement of instruction in the classroom . . . [through] activities [like] curriculum planning, course design, applications of student learning theory, and . . . workshops on topics related to increasing teaching effectiveness." (VMI 1996: 1)

## The Project

In 1998, VMI sought to improve its merit pay plan and faculty development plan through an assessment of policies and processes at peer institutions. The focus of this effort was to compare practices and learn new strategies. [4] VMI evaluated its own merit pay plan by surveying tenured faculty at VMI [5] and by interviewing selected faculty members and department heads in 1999–2000. The Institute also sought to implement the faculty development plan and to re-assess the faculty's developmental needs.

Two of VMI's peer institutions — Lafayette College (PA) and Transylvania University (KY) — were chosen as partners in the project. We exchanged ideas with the partner institutions and hosted campus visits to explore policies of post-tenure review and their relationship, if any, to faculty development. All three institutions share a primary commitment to effective undergraduate teaching.

## Post-Tenure Review at VMI and Peer Institutions

At Transylvania and Lafayette, post-tenure review is summative and periodic (see attachment B). The policies were implemented thoughtfully as their boards of trustees considered increases in salary for faculty, increases in the number of tenured positions at the institution, additional funds for exemplary teaching, or other changes to benefit the institution. Some faculty reported a sense of "quid pro quo" for enhanced benefits to faculty paired with increased accountability by the board. The faculty at these colleges were motivated to develop policies of post-tenure review because they wanted to establish equity in expectations for junior and senior faculty. After several years of experience with post-tenure review at Lafayette and Transylvania, the policies have become embedded in faculty culture and are generally regarded favorably by faculty and administrators.

At VMI, a summative, triggered post-tenure review policy was created to satisfy a state requirement that the process be tied to merit pay. Perhaps because post-tenure review was externally imposed on VMI, uncertainty remains about the value of the review. A survey of tenured faculty in spring 2000 showed half of the respondents believed the process could be improved by (1) reviewing less frequently; (2) changing the chairs of the review committee; and (3) reducing the impact of student evaluations on the review.

The intent of post-tenure review in all three institutions is not to "target" ineffective faculty. In fact, post-tenure review processes in these three colleges have identified few faculty members who are not performing well. Likewise, post-tenure review has not been constructed as a mechanism for dismissal of faculty members. Dismissal for cause occurs through normal due process and is not included in post-tenure review policies and procedures. Early retirement is not a substitute for post-tenure review, given that a faculty member may earn tenure and still have 10, 20, or more years of service to offer the institution.

Faculty and administrators at all three institutions believe faculty development and revitalization are the desired outcomes of post-tenure review.

## Lessons Learned

Faculty and administrators from all three institutions expressed similar recommendations about their experiences with post-tenure review.

### *Anticipate Variable Reactions to Post-Tenure Review*

Faculty and administrators at Transylvania and Lafayette generally agree that post-tenure review sustains strong faculty performance in teaching and scholarship. One administrator at Lafayette said:

> I don't think [it's] an accident that we have [few problems]. I think it's a function of size, and the commitment to teaching is so strong here. . . . I've never seen a faculty that extends itself as much as this one. I think we're just blessed with the fact that we don't have deadwood.

At VMI, teaching and scholarship also remain strong, but the value of post-tenure review is nonetheless questioned: Forty-three (43) percent of respondents to the survey believe post-tenure review is worth the effort, but 39 percent do not.

Post-tenure review allows the faculty member and dean to reconnect with colleagues and share information about current activities and interests. At VMI, one faculty member expressed a sentiment shared by faculty at all three institutions:

> I'm more interested in what the department chair thinks of me as a colleague and as a professor. I think anything you can do to improve communication from the professor to the department chair . . . is good.

Faculty members agree the ultimate benefits of post-tenure review may, at best, be individual, as this faculty member at Lafayette College commented:

> The benefit depends upon how defensive the person is, how willing they are to change, how interested they are in hearing what the provost and the department chair have to say, how creative the provost and department chair are feeling at that moment . . . in terms of other options for the person.
>
> Some people leave this painful experience with a boost, and others leave it with a sense that they are really trapped in mid-life and whatever promise they may have shown at tenure-time hasn't quite materialized. They may have invested themselves . . . in various needs of the college and somehow they are not getting recognition for all that and [post-tenure review] may leave their morale worse than it had been.

#### *Prepare Chairs for Changes in Their Responsibilities*

Most department chairs in these three institutions agreed they had little formal training for their duties, including their role in post-tenure review. Prior service on tenure and promotion committees was often the only training they had. "I had no training whatsoever. I knew the detail was going to drive me crazy and it has," commented one chair at Transylvania University. They offer several suggestions for improvements in this area.

**Provide training.** First, provide a job description and formal training for chairs. [6] The description may appear in a handbook, on a website, and/or through workshops. Experience in various departmental and institutional processes is also helpful preparation for the chairs' duties connected with post-tenure review.

**Support the development of chairs.** Second, support the continuing professional development of chairs. As one dean put it: "The unintended consequence . . . is that . . . the faculty governance of the place is going to have to be predicated on professionalism of the department chairs." A faculty member at Lafayette reported "the school . . . has done a better job in making those decisions. The decisions . . . have become more professional."

**Assuage chair guilt.** Some chairs will assume guilt for their role in post-tenure review. One chair at Lafayette College allowed,

> I've seen people run through the halls saying "Can you believe what the ——— provost put in this letter to me" or "Can you believe what [the committee] said to me!" Because these become the administrative bogey people against whom you rail. They are not really your community — they are the enemies. And those of us who serve on that committee know how awkward it is to be believed to be that enemy. That corporate guilt you assume, having participated in any decision that makes somebody unhappy, for whatever reason, no matter how well chosen the words in the letter [is difficult].

### *Expect to Spend Time and Energy on the Process*

Post-tenure review at these three institutions demands different amounts of time. One senior member of the personnel committee at Transylvania University estimated each faculty member's review takes between 10 and 25 hours, whereas one faculty member at VMI estimated the time requirement to be about four hours. At Lafayette, the faculty member, department chair, and provost interact with the Promotions, Tenure, and Review Committee in a process characterized by one faculty member to be "fairly time-consuming."

The investment of time affects how faculty members view post-tenure review. Said these faculty members:

> One of the criticisms of post-tenure review is that it's a process that requires a lot of time and energy of people who already are maxed on time and energy, and that the numbers of people identified as weak don't justify the expenditure of all this effort (VMI).

> Some faculty take it seriously and spend a lot of time on their dossier, particularly their statement. That's an utter waste of time. But there is some utility in thoughtful people taking some time to think about what they are doing. And some faculty do that. Many faculty, I think, don't. (Transylvania University)

### *Examine Connections Between Post-Tenure Review and Reward Structures*

At Transylvania and Lafayette, post-tenure review is not directly tied to merit pay. Faculty at both institutions are satisfied with the indirect connection between post-tenure review and salary, and question whether salary should be implicated at all by the review. As one faculty member at Transylvania commented:

> What difference does it make to this faculty member who is dogging it, who perhaps is moonlighting or something like that? It strikes me that these people should be spoken to sternly by the dean, as individuals, and that their salaries should reflect the judgment of the dean and the division chair and the program director about their relative contributions to the institution. I would hate to see salaried matters being decided by a committee responsible for post-tenure review.

The direct link between salary and post-tenure review was also questioned by a department head at VMI:

> Post-tenure review . . . and merit all got merged into the same thing. Had we been able to separate those things more clearly, I don't think the faculty would have been as averse to it. I don't think they mind the idea of post-tenure review as an internal, collegial kind of notion, but they don't like merit pay at all, and those things were put together, so there was a lot of resistance.

### *Ensure Mechanisms for Revising Policies and Processes*

Institutions need to ensure periodic reviews and revisions of their post-tenure review policies. Currently, such regular appraisal is the exception rather than the rule.

At Transylvania and at Lafayette, existing committees have historically conducted the reviews of post-tenure review policies. Review committee members use existing governance structures to recommend changes to the policy.

Reviewing the post-tenure review policy at VMI was problematic, however, because an ad-hoc committee created the policy. As one department head said:

> One of the questions . . . is how this whole thing is evaluated . . . [for] people [to] decide if it works or not. There's nothing [set up] for that, is there? There's no formal mechanism. For example, if you wanted to say . . . what if we made this an every three years' process? There is no formal mechanism for you to even make that suggestion at this point in time.

### *Examine Connections Between Post-Tenure Review and Faculty Development*

The outcome of formative post-tenure review is "formulation of a professional development plan emphasizing future growth" (Licata and Morreale 1997: 5). In the best of cases, formative review can "assure that the talents of each faculty member . . . serve the students, the institution, the academic discipline, and the individual and . . . assist tenured faculty in their continuing professional development" (Portch et al. 1993: 17). However, whether or not faculty development is directly connected with post-tenure review is unclear for faculty members at these three institutions.

One faculty member at VMI says:

> I think the only way that [post-tenure review is developmental] is that it gives you an opportunity to toot your own horn. To make sure that the dean is aware of what you're doing. But other than that, no. I don't think it is. I see it more of a job performance.

Resources are not necessarily linked to post-tenure review. One department head at VMI reports:

> In theory it [is related to faculty development]. I've never sat down and said, "OK, we need to have so much laid aside to this, that, or the other thing." We do have proposals, and I do spend money . . . but you know that's been pretty separate from this.

There is also little, if any, connection between post-tenure review and resources for faculty at Transylvania or Lafayette. At Transylvania University, however, one faculty member acknowledges post-tenure review includes developmental elements:

> I think the other objective of post-tenure review would be to try to identify such folks early on that are "in crisis" or have some potential problems that could get larger down the road. Can't we identify them now and bring to bear our resources so that it won't become a crisis down the road? I don't know that we effectively do that with [post-tenure review]. . . . The only way that I see post-tenure review connected with development now is that one of the elements of the post-tenure process is a kind of personal statement which different faculty have taken to mean different things. But generally in that statement is some sort of exposition about plans for the future, whether they be scholarly or pedagogical plans. And so it does encourage faculty to think about where they're headed rather than just review where they've been for the last five years. That could quite easily plug into faculty development programs.

***Prepare for a Lack of Clarity About the Purpose of the Review***

Faculty members at these institutions have different opinions about post-tenure review and its link to early retirement:

> We shouldn't have a post-tenure review process. What every institution should have is an effective early retirement program. That's really what we are talking about, okay? People who are retired early without being formally retired are people who are just taking up space. You have to figure out a way to encourage them to leave. Clearly as they start approaching retirement, some people perhaps could be encouraged to retire a bit early. And then you have to be relatively close to it so that it's financially feasible. (Transylvania)

> No, I wouldn't agree . . . that [early retirement addresses post-tenure review] at all. . . . Just because you are post-tenure doesn't mean you can start thinking pre-retirement. How about your current performance up to the time where, if you choose, then you can retire? No, I don't think it should be just . . . a gateway to retirement. I would hope that everybody is reading the teaching evaluations, even if they don't say a whole lot. I would hope that people would read them and try to improve their teaching, or research, or collegiality. Whatever it is that you are working on. It seems to me that it's a good exercise just to see how you are doing. Or at least sit and see what the perception is of how you are doing. (VMI)

## Next Steps

The interviews and surveys at VMI, Lafayette, and Transylvania indicate each institution created policies and processes of post-tenure review that were uniquely motivated, institutionalized, reviewed and revised, and enacted. There are several common experiences among these institutions as well.

***Learn From the Experiences of Others***

Establish relationships with peer institutions whose experience with post-tenure review can provide meaningful guidance and prevent unnecessary missteps. Listen to how post-tenure review policies are perceived and how they function from faculty and administrators at peer institutions.

Although VMI read policies from other institutions as it developed the faculty merit pay plan and the faculty development plan, it has benefited the most from reviewing documents and conducting interviews with faculty and administrators of peer institutions. One result of the AAHE project on campus has been a reinvigorated discussion of post-tenure review and faculty development.

***Monitor and Improve the Process***

Have an effective mechanism for periodic review in any post-tenure review policy. By involving standing faculty committees with the dossiers and plans of tenured faculty and with the time required for reviews, many faculty will be aware of the time demands and be in a position to adjust the policy if needed. For example, at Lafayette and Transylvania, the number of years between post-tenure reviews has been increased after experience with the initial interval. At VMI, an ad-hoc committee created the policy, so no one had responsibility for monitoring post-tenure review and faculty development. Two faculty committees assumed responsibility for monitoring these policies as a result of the AAHE grant:

- The Academic Planning and Review Committee, a standing committee of the Academic Board at VMI, oversees the merit pay plan. The committee has proposed changes to the timing of evaluation related to the merit pay plan. In response to a suggestion from faculty at VMI, the committee has proposed the review committee be chaired by a department head from the same division who is not the faculty member's department head. It has also suggested the optional third member of the review committee be a tenured — rather than full-time — faculty member. The annual frequency of the reviews remains unchanged.
- The newly created Faculty Development Committee has begun to monitor the effectiveness of the faculty development plan and guide institutional priorities for faculty development at VMI. A subcommittee of the Faculty Development Committee is investigating ways to improve the developmental focus of VMI's plan for post-tenure review. The subcommittee has arranged for campus visits to two additional institutions to talk with their faculty and administrators about post-tenure review in general, about alternatives to student evaluations as a means of evaluating teaching, and about the frequency of post-tenure review. The report of the subcommittee will go through the governance structures at VMI for review and action.

Finally, because the Faculty Development Committee is now functional, it can monitor the process of faculty development at VMI and consider suggestions for improvements. The committee will continue to survey the faculty regularly to assess faculty satisfaction with development activities and make recommendations.

Plans are also under way to create focus groups of faculty at VMI who are at different stages in their careers. The groups will assess the different developmental needs of faculty. The focus group results will be given to the Faculty Development Committee to adjust annual and long-range faculty development initiatives.

Creating standing committees to monitor policies for post-tenure review and faculty development at VMI has been an important step to ensure the philosophical and functional elements of the policies remain current and evolve effectively and efficiently.

#### *Offer Professional Development to Chairs*

Department heads at all three institutions were not as prepared as they might have been for their roles. One administrator remarked, "I frankly think we could do better there." The chairs have new responsibilities in post-tenure review, as tenured faculty have new changes in expectations. It is important for institutions to provide training to chairs.

VMI trained chairs through a workshop. One suggestion from the workshop leaders was that VMI consider developing clear definitions of the four levels of performance in its policy — exceptional, commendable, provisional, and unacceptable — to ensure consistency across departments. The idea is being discussed.

## Conclusion

The lessons learned at these three colleges — learn from peer institutions, monitor and refine policies and processes, and provide training for department chairs and faculty — help all institutions with post-tenure review policies.

Through participation in AAHE's "Projects With Promise" minigrant program, post-tenure review was re-established as an item for periodic institutional and faculty consideration at VMI. Yet it remains important for all institutions to monitor trends and practical considerations in post-tenure review nationally and at peer institutions, to communicate changes and improvements to the institutional processes to all faculty, and to confirm the benefits and problems associated with post-tenure to the faculty as they become apparent.

## Notes

1. Susan H. Barr is dean of academic support and cadet services at Virginia Military Institute; formerly she was assistant dean of the faculty. Her research interests lie in the areas of faculty, student, and organizational development. She is a co-author, with Betsy E. Brown and N. Douglas Lees, of three related articles on "Preparing Chairs for Expanded Roles in Post-Tenure Review" in *The Department Chair*, published in the Fall 2000, Winter 2001, and Spring 2001 issues. Barr earned her Ph.D. in higher education and M.S. in biology at the University of Virginia; she earned a B.A. in biology from Bridgewater College. (Contact her at barrsh@vmi.edu)

2. Boards of Visitors are the governing boards of public institutions in Virginia, appointed by the governor.

3. State Council of Higher Education for Virginia website at www.schev.edu/.

4. According to Peter Blake at the State Council of Higher Education for Virginia (1999, personal communication), VMI's peer group was determined through a cluster analysis of the following variables: institutional type; total headcount; percent part-time students; percent bachelor's, master's, and doctoral degrees; SAT 50th percentile; percent degrees in art; percent degrees in engineering, business, education, biology/physics/math; percent degrees in first professional health; percent degrees in health; percent degrees in social science; percent degrees in first professional law; percent degrees in humanities; and percent of faculty with terminal degrees and research expenditures.

According to these criteria, VMI's peer institutions are Bucknell University, Lafayette College, Tri-State University, Transylvania University, Union College, the University of Evansville, the United States Air Force Academy, the United States Coast Guard Academy, the United States Merchant Marine Academy, the United States Military Academy, the United States Naval Academy, Valparaiso University, Wilkes University, the University of Minnesota-Morris, and the University of Wisconsin-Platteville.

5. VMI administered AAHE's Post-Tenure Review Outcomes Survey (Christine Licata and Joseph Morreale, Washington, DC, 1998).

6. Faculty handbooks from Transylvania University, Lafayette College, and VMI contain elements of job descriptions for department chairs:

(a) Length of term and rules for succession; (b) management responsibilities, e.g., monitor operations within the department, create positive atmosphere, serve as spokesperson, and enhance communication; (c) personnel issues, e.g., recruit new faculty, evaluate tenured and untenured faculty, advise untenured faculty on how best to grow and develop as a professional, conduct tenure process, and resolve problems; (d) program and students, such as encourage innovation within the discipline and in teaching, compel discussion of curriculum change, and assist with issues related to students; and (e) budget and resources, such as prepare budgets, allocate resources, and monitor and secure funding for physical plant and equipment needs.

## References

Commission on the Future of Higher Education in Virginia. (1996). *Making Connections: Matching Virginia Higher Education's Strengths With the Commonwealth's Needs.* The Report of the Commission on the Future of Higher Education in Virginia. Richmond, VA: State Council of Higher Education for Virginia. Accessed at www.schev.edu/html/reports/sjr139.html.

Licata, C.M., and J.C. Morreale. (1997). *Post-Tenure Review: Policies, Practices, Precautions.* New Pathways Working Paper Series, no. 12. Washington, DC: American Association for Higher Education.

Portch, S.R., et al. (1993). "From Frog to Prince: From Post-Tenure Review to Faculty Roles, Development and Rewards." *Change* 25(4): 17.

Virginia Military Institute. (1996). *VMI Plan for Faculty Development.* Lexington, VA: Author.

# Attachment A

## ANNUAL FACULTY ACTIVITY REPORT

This form is designed to provide information to the Department Head for annual evaluation procedures. It will be appended to the evaluation letter submitted by the Department Head to the Dean of the Faculty for the following purposes: (a) a self-evaluation of each faculty member at VMI; (b) a source of information for annual reports relating to the VMI Faculty Merit Program; (c) a more complete record of activity for each faculty member.

**PLEASE NOTE: Each of the text boxes on the following pages expands as you include text. Use as much space as you require in each box to provide thorough information in each area.**

| Evaluation Period Beginning | Evaluation Period Ending |
|---|---|
| | |

| | | | |
|---|---|---|---|
| Full Name | | | |
| Academic Rank | | Highest Degree Held | |

### TEACHING

**See Load Studies from the Relevant Evaluation Period for Teaching Loads**

1. Did you receive any **officially sanctioned** release time from teaching during this evaluation period?

| YES | | NO | |
|---|---|---|---|

| | |
|---|---|
| If your answer to #1 above is "yes," what was the amount and nature of this release time? | |

2. Course Development:

| | |
|---|---|
| New courses developed | |
| Current courses revised | |
| Relevant Classroom Innovation (new instructional materials, assessment techniques manuals, demonstrations, computer programs, etc.) | |

### SCHOLARLY ACTIVITY/PROFESSIONAL DEVELOPMENT

1. Books, articles, editorial/review or other written works published/in preparation:

| Title | Status | Contract? (publisher) | Co-authors? | Pub. date |
|---|---|---|---|---|
| | | | | |

2. Papers Presented:

| Title | Location (Meeting name) | Co-authors | Date day/month |
|---|---|---|---|
| | | | |

3. Grant proposals submitted:

| Title | Funding source | $ Amount | Funded? |
|---|---|---|---|
| | | | |

4. Meetings/workshops attended:

| Meeting/workshop | Location | Dates (day/month) |
|---|---|---|
| | | |

5. Professional awards received:

6. Relevant Consulting:

7. Ongoing Research:

8. Were sufficient funds available for you to participate in all the professional activities for which you had opportunities or in which you wished to participate?

| YES | | NO | |
|---|---|---|---|

| | |
|---|---|
| If your answer to #8 above is "no," what were you unable to accomplish as a result of insufficient funds? | |

**SERVICE**

1. Participation in professional organizations:

| Organization | Office held | Responsibilities |
|---|---|---|
| | | |

2. Institute-wide and departmental committees:

| Name of committee | Committee Chair | Meeting frequency | Responsibilities |
|---|---|---|---|
| | | | |

3. Cadet advising/counseling:

| Organization | Nature of your responsibility |
|---|---|
| Departmental advising | |
| New Cadet Advising Program | |

4. Co-curricular service:

| Organization | Nature and length of service |
|---|---|
| | |

5. Community service:

| Organization | Nature and length of service |
|---|---|
| | |

6. I maintain a professional appearance to include the wearing of the uniform:

| YES | | NO | | N/A | |
|---|---|---|---|---|---|

7. Additional comments regarding the wearing of the uniform:

## ACCOMPLISHMENTS/PROFESSIONAL DEVELOPMENT

1. List your major accomplishments of the year (you may include items listed above):

2. List your goals and objectives for teaching in the next year:

3. List your goals for research and service in the next year:

4. List your goals and objectives for professional development in the coming year:

5. Please describe any area in which you would like to improve:

6. What resources or assistance would be necessary for you to improve in the area described above:

## Attachment B

## Post-Tenure Review Policies at Three Peer Institutions

### Context for Creating Policies of Post-Tenure Review

Lafayette College:

- Board was considering increasing the percentage of faculty who could be tenured.
- Equity in the review of senior and junior faculty was a primary goal. Faculty committees developed policies that strengthened standards and processes for mid-tenure and tenure review and, at the same time, established regular and extensive post-tenure review of faculty who had already earned tenure.
- PTR began in the mid 1980s.

Transylvania University:

- Board was considering increased compensation for faculty that was paralleled by an increase in accountability.
- Equity in the review of senior and junior faculty was a primary goal. Faculty committees developed policies that strengthened standards and processes for mid-tenure and tenure review and, at the same time, established regular and extensive post-tenure review of faculty who had already earned tenure.
- PTR policy designed in 1991–92 and PTR system was implemented in 1992–93.

Virginia Military Institute:

- Policy was created in response to state directive to (1) establish policy of PTR and (2) connect the review to salary.
- PTR policy was designed in 1995–96 and implemented in 1996–97.

### *Model & Timing of Post-Tenure Review*

Lafayette College:

- Summative & periodic
- PTR occurs for the first time four years after the faculty member earns tenure. The four-year review serves the function of helping the faculty member prepare for the process of promotion to full professor. Once the faculty member is promoted to full professor, post-tenure review occurs every seven years.

Transylvania University:

- Summative & periodic
- PTR occurs every six years after a faculty member receives tenure. The process is conducted by a faculty committee that receives a self-evaluation from the faculty member, a report of classroom visitation by the division chair and colleague outside the division, and an interview with

the division chair who has consulted with divisional colleagues. The committee reports to the faculty member and to the dean. The dean interviews the faculty member. The dean prepares a report for the faculty member's file that includes areas of performance that are in need of improvement.

Virginia Military Institute:

- Summative & triggered
- A faculty member who receives two yearly classifications of provisional or unacceptable or one annual classification of each within a five-year period has an in-depth evaluation by committee and develops a Plan of Action that is the blueprint for improvement.

***Primary Elements of Post-Tenure Review***

Lafayette College:

- Self-evaluation by the faculty member is given to the department chair who, in turn, prepares a written evaluation of the professor that is given to the professor and the provost. The provost meets with the professor and submits a report of the conference to the professor, the department chair, and the faculty committee. The Promotions, Tenure and Review Committee typically delegates the responsibility for review of all three written reports to the provost.

Transylvania University:

- Personnel Committee receives a self-evaluation from the faculty member, a report of classroom visitation by the division chair and colleague outside the division, and an interview with the division chair who has consulted with divisional colleagues.

Virginia Military Institute:

- Annual review includes a self-evaluation that is submitted to the department head. The department head prepares a written evaluation of the faculty member, and meets with him or her.
- If an in-depth review is triggered, the department head and the dean of the faculty interpret the cumulative record of annual evaluations so that a total picture of positive contributions and deficiencies emerges. Inadequate performance is assessed through the department heads' evaluations, course evaluations by students, and peer evaluations. If continued performance is substandard, a review committee, appointed by the dean, may be formed and a plan of action is developed jointly by the faculty member and the department head in order to remediate deficiencies.

***Relationship of PTR to Salary and Other Resources for Faculty Development***

Lafayette College:

- No direct relationship

Transylvania University:

- No direct relationship

Virginia Military Institute:

- Faculty members who are classified as provisional have salary increases held in abeyance pending a review by the dean of the faculty. If sufficient improvement is documented, the faculty member will receive the raise retroactively. Faculty who are rated unacceptable receive no raises. The creation and implementation of the Plan of Action (essentially a development plan) provides a developmental opportunity to remedy a provisional or unacceptable rating and may include a request for resources to support the plan.

***Preparation of Department Chairs for Responsibilities Related to Post-Tenure Review***

Lafayette College:

- No formal preparation

Transylvania University:

- No formal preparation

Virginia Military Institute:

- No formal preparation

***Evaluation of Post-Tenure Review Process***

Lafayette College:

- No regularized evaluation; the period of time between reviews has been extended after experience with the original process

Transylvania University:

- No regularized evaluation; the period of time between reviews has been extended after experience with the original process

Virginia Military Institute:

- No regularized evaluation; process currently under review by members of the Faculty Development Committee

***Relationship of Post-Tenure Review to Dismissal for Cause***

Lafayette College:

- Separate processes

Transylvania University:

- Separate processes

Virginia Military Institute:

- Separate processes

# Section IV:
# Reflections on the Future

# Faculty Well-Being Review: An Alternative to Post-Tenure Review?

**Charles J. Walker** [1]

Post-tenure review is controversial for good reason. Faculty did not ask for it, nor have they always played a significant role in its evolution. Post-tenure review has not come from systematic research on faculty work, nor has it been shaped by well-established theories on human performance. It often stems from hearsay on a handful of delinquent faculty heard by administrators and legislators, not from the sincerely voiced dissatisfactions of professors nor their warnings about the worsening condition of the professoriate. Therefore, I predict post-tenure review will not be successful in most colleges and universities in the United States. It will fit the culture of some institutions and readily be assimilated; however, at most institutions, it will be actively rejected or passively ignored. Nonetheless, few institutions can reject the formative goal of post-tenure review, to bring out the best in faculty. Post-tenure review is one means to this end (Licata 1986; Licata and Morreale 1997).

When post-tenure review does not fit organizational culture, institutions will need alternative ways to develop their faculty. Administrators and faculty leaders will need a new paradigm to define and focus their work. They will also need guidelines to design feasible, effective faculty development programs. Without conceptual and operational definitions of faculty well-being, neither of these needs will be met.

The practice-based wisdom provided by other authors in this volume will help administrators learn what works; however, a model of faculty well-being — like the one presented in this chapter — will help them understand why programs work. For example, to import an exemplary post-tenure review program into the specific culture of their campus, administrators will need to know what adaptations are associated with high faculty well-being, on the one hand, and lower well-being on the other. Should post-tenure review programs be voluntary? Should peers be involved? What kind of rewards and recognition should be given? If competencies are to be strengthened, what specific skills and knowledge should be taught? Should students be involved? What kind of performance feedback will produce the most positive enduring change in most faculty? The model of faculty well-being presented in this chapter will help administrators decide between equally reasonable answers to questions such as these. However, to be effective, a program of post-tenure review, or its alternatives, must be mindful of the profession it is designed to promote. Research on the professoriate, reviewed next, suggests that it is a profession awash in change.

## A Review of Research on the Professoriate

If we listen to faculty and read the signs of change, the message is clear: The professoriate is deteriorating. In a recent study of 4,000 doctoral students by the Harvard Project on Faculty Appointments, 37 percent said their interest in becoming a professor declined since entering graduate school (Trower 2001). Of those obtaining Ph.D.s — particularly those in science — most chose to begin careers in corporations. They were swayed more by concerns about the quality of life than by pay and benefits. Again, according to data from the Harvard Project (Trower 2001), although new faculty rank pay and benefits highly, faculty pay and benefits have steadily declined since 1970 relative to occupations with comparable levels of required education. To choose to become a professor is to choose an income that is 20 to 30 percent lower than a comparable professional — a difference in income that totals more than $750,000 over a 30-year career.

Faculty work is changing for the worse, according to a four-year longitudinal study of new faculty sponsored by the Department of Education (Menges 1999) Within three years, all new faculty in the study showed early signs of diminished vitality, particularly when faculty values did not match the institutional mission (Walker and Hale 1999). A lot of faculty felt trapped with limited opportunities to relocate. Career inflexibility is one of the most frequently reported causes of dissatisfaction among college faculty (Blackburn 1997). To this picture, if we add the findings of a recent American Association of University Professors (1993) study that half the undergraduate students in the United States are now being taught by adjuncts and more than two-thirds of new faculty are adjuncts, it becomes clear that the faculty community as well as the profession itself are being undermined. The buffer against stress once provided by stable relationships with colleagues is weakening. Given all these changes, no wonder faculty are retiring early and in high numbers. In most occupations, older workers report the highest levels of job-specific well-being; however, this well-established finding on job satisfaction has not been observed with college faculty (Warr 1999).

Interventions to improve faculty performance — such as post-tenure review — focus on tenured older faculty. Yet according to research reviewed by Bland and Bergquist (1997), only six percent of faculty performance in teaching and scholarship is related to age. When the quantity and variety of work are considered, Bland and Bergquist conclude older faculty out perform pre-tenure faculty. Even when the criteria for performance evaluation are weighted to favor pre-tenure faculty (e.g., quality of journal publications or number of scholarly citations), research reveals no substantial performance differences between younger and older faculty (Blackburn and Lawrence 1986).

Performance and stage of professional development are not strongly correlated. The problems late-career faculty have also occur to faculty early or in the middle of their careers (Menges and Walker 1998). Therefore, low faculty morale and diminished vitality are more likely a product of the conditions of the professoriate than the character of professors. Without evidence that senior faculty perform more poorly than junior faculty, policies such as post-tenure review — that target older, tenured faculty — are vulnerable to charges of age discrimination. Ageism in the workplace is a major national problem; older faculty are not exempt from this prejudice (Finkelstein, Burke, and Raju 1995).

## The Meaning of Post-Tenure Review

In this context, what is the meaning and purpose of post-tenure review? How can a policy based on erroneous assumptions about faculty bring out the best in them? The goal and purpose of post-tenure review — the enhancement of faculty vitality — is worthwhile (Licata 1986; Licata and Morreale 1997). However, the method of intensive evaluation of tenured faculty focuses too much attention on individuals while ignoring other causes of diminished productivity, such as pay inequity or ineffective leadership.

The research literature on human performance and organizational commitment points to one conclusion: Organizations that take care of their employees get employees who take care of their organizations (Lee et al. 1992). Measures of the quality of work life and human performance are highly correlated (Iaffaldano and Murchinsky 1985). Faculty with the highest morale and energy are more likely to be found at vital colleges and universities (Rice and Austin 1988, 1990). Faculty with low vitality who relocate to vital colleges increase in vitality; on the other hand, highly productive faculty who move to less-vital colleges show decreases in their vitality (Pellino 1981).

Post-tenure review focusing only on individual faculty performance will not improve faculty vitality. A comprehensive review of the work conditions of faculty is required. Such a review would assess not only the performance of faculty but also the social and physical conditions under which they work — and might more aptly be called "a review of faculty well-being."

## A Model of Faculty Well-Being

The model of faculty well-being described in this chapter was derived from research studies on faculty satisfactions and dissatisfactions, and career development (Blackurn et al. 1986; Eble and McKeachie 1985; Eckert and Stecklein 1957; Finkelstein 1984); theories on human motivation, job design, and job satisfaction (Warr 1999); and the latest research and theories on psychological well-being (Kahneman, Diener, and Schwarz 1999; Ryff 1995). And because faculty vitality and institutional vitality are interdependent, the model of faculty well-being was also influenced by research on vital colleges (Rice and Austin 1988, 1990) and healthy organizations (Dunnette and Hough 1992; Senge 1990). For example, Rice and Austin found faculty flourish in colleges with:

- a genuine mission and clear goals;

- a distinctive institutional culture;
- productive faculty-administration relations;
- participatory governance;
- decentralized control;
- effective communication systems;
- competent support staff;
- sufficient technical and other resources;
- a heterogeneous, diverse community;
- ample and equitable rewards and recognition;
- opportunities for career flexibility; and
- effective leadership among faculty.

In contrast, Maslach and Goldberg (1998) found professional workers burn out in organizations when they:

- are overloaded with work;
- lack control of their work;
- feel insecure and lack trust in their leaders;
- are insufficiently rewarded;
- sense a breakdown of community;
- are unfairly treated; and
- report value conflicts.

Begin a review of faculty well-being by assessing the organization in which faculty work. Quantitative and qualitative data should be gathered at the department and school levels on the external conditions that cause faculty to flourish and perish. Then, these data should be analyzed to illustrate the work climate of specific groups of faculty and, more important, establish a context within which assessments of their performance can be interpreted.

Research on the well-being of professional workers, such as faculty, shows five internal conditions are essential: Professionals (1) must be experts at the tasks they do most often; (2) need challenging, meaningful goals set by themselves or legitimate, trusted leaders; (3) must have sufficient control of their work; (4) need to work in cohesive groups or have other reliable sources of social support; and (5) must get immediate, unambiguous feedback on the quality of their work from the people they serve or other sources. For faculty doing some research but teaching a majority of the time, I propose the following nine internal conditions must be established for them to experience high levels of well-being. Faculty must:

1. be scholars and masters in their discipline;

2. be knowledgeable, highly skilled teachers of individual students;
3. know how to lead and effectively manage groups of students;
4. pursue worthwhile, challenging goals in teaching and research;
5. feel sufficiently autonomous doing the work they value most;
6. have opportunities to receive social support from colleagues;
7. be recognized and rewarded by leaders for producing quality work;
8. have generative relations with students, reinforced with feedback; and
9. fully accept their current status and career as a professor.

I have used this model of faculty well-being to re-analyze past surveys of faculty (Walker and Hale 1999) and also to evaluate faculty development programs offered by teaching centers or faculty development offices. This model has served as the conceptual basis for the development of a self-administered inventory on faculty vitality, which yields scores on all nine dimensions of well-being: The Inventory on Teaching Climate and Faculty Well-Being has been administered to more than 600 faculty at 22 different institutions, and it has been on the Internet since 1998. [2]

To supplement these data, interview protocols have been developed for administration, staff, and faculty. To gain more insights into what strengthens and weakens faculty vitality, I have done field studies at four institutions (one junior college; two private comprehensive universities; and one public, doctoral-granting comprehensive university). [3] These data have yielded an interesting picture of faculty well-being.

## Research Results on Faculty Well-Being

There are differences in the well-being of individual faculty and the institutions in which they teach. Some institutions do not support the well-being of faculty. At these institutions, the scores of faculty on all nine dimensions of well-being are lower than those at the majority of other institutions. There are faculty who have low vitality: These faculty are more likely found at unhealthy institutions — usually in dysfunctional departments — but a few are at healthy institutions. In these instances, the individual is mismatched with the institution, does not desire to be a college professor, or a combination of both factors.

## Patterns in the Results

### *Type of Institution*

The well-being scores of faculty at small liberal arts colleges are slightly higher than others. For faculty at all types of institutions, scholarship and pedagogical skills bolster their vitality; a lack of rewards, weak social support, and insufficient autonomy undermine their vitality.

### *Stage of Career*

The overall pattern of results lasts throughout the lifespan of faculty. However, mid-career and late-career faculty more frequently report feeling less challenged and less recognized than do faculty early in their career. Only new faculty appear to enjoy moderately high levels of social support, but these scores drop to the lower levels reported by mid-career faculty within three years of being hired.

### *Gender*

No reliable gender differences in faculty well-being have emerged. The conditions of work have more influence on well-being than does the gender of the worker. However, at one formerly all-male college, I found new women faculty to have lower scores than their male counterparts on social support, recognition, and autonomy.

### *Academic Discipline*

Some data suggest differences in academic discipline on one or two, but not all, dimensions of well-being. For example, faculty in rapidly changing disciplines — such as computer science — appear to be less accepting of their careers than do faculty in traditional liberal arts disciplines (e.g., English literature). Faculty in applied disciplines such as accounting and nursing enjoy more generative feedback from students than do faculty in abstract disciplines such as physics or mathematics. This finding was more typical of two-year institutions. Faculty at four-year institutions may have more time to establish close generative relationships with students than do their counterparts at two-year institutions.

### *Career Acceptance*

Regardless of academic discipline, significant correlations exist among the dimensions of well-being. For example, the best predictors of career acceptance are social support, recognition, and autonomy. Faculty who work within a strong community of colleagues, get recognized by chairs and deans for their achievements, and have the discretion to do what they think is best in teaching and research are the most accepting of their careers as faculty. Two seemingly opposite dimensions — autonomy and social support — are indeed directly related. Faculty who work in highly cohesive departments also report the highest levels of autonomy. Mutual empowerment — not independence or isolation — strengthens autonomy.

## Seven Suggestions to Enhance Faculty Well-Being

Based on interviews with administrators, staff, and faculty and on surveys of faculty, I offer seven recommendations to raise the vitality of faculty and improve the quality of their work life:

1. Schedule open time slots (i.e., community time) on university and college calendars to give faculty and others an opportunity to get together to do practical things, such as holding in-person departmental meetings or doing university service work. Design schedules to free-up lunch hours, allowing administration, staff, and faculty to eat together, if they choose to. Schedule days within the yearly academic calendar expressly for administration, staff, and faculty development activities.
2. Create community spaces. In the design of new buildings, provide comfortable places for faculty, staff, and students to meet. When buildings are renovated, tear down walls to open up new common spaces for departments and other groups of faculty. Improve faculty offices to make them more attractive places to work privately or with small groups of students or colleagues.
3. Take departments more seriously by training chairs, redesigning their work, paying them more, decentralizing planning and budgeting, and expecting higher-quality performance from the faculty they lead.
4. At the department level, do a faculty work inventory. Then

ask faculty to rebalance the quantity and quality of their work (e.g., decrease quantity by 20 percent and increase quality by 10 percent).

5. At the school level, observe and log the day-to-day work of faculty, then use that data to redefine faculty work and the ways to assess, recognize, and reward it.

6. To counter "feeling stuck," establish active reciprocal agreements with other institutions within the United States and abroad for faculty exchanges. Redesign sabbatical and leave programs to make it possible for a higher percentage of faculty to renew themselves more often. Give leaves and sabbaticals before faculty need them.

7. Start and fund a standing committee on faculty well-being. The mission of this committee should be to improve faculty vitality and morale. To accomplish this goal, the committee should (a) annually measure faculty well-being at the level of departments and above, (b) evaluate programs of faculty development, and (c) suggest specific interventions to sustain and improve faculty vitality. Be prepared to start similar committees for administrators and staff.

These results and the other findings reported have implications for post-tenure review or any other program intended to bring out the best in faculty.

## Implications for Post-Tenure Review

Post-tenure review may be initiated for reasons such as policing delinquent faculty, "protecting" tenure, and conciliating legislators, but the best reason to begin post-tenure review is to improve faculty well-being. However, by itself, even formative post-tenure review cannot effectively promote faculty well-being. Instead, post-tenure review must be embedded within a comprehensive program of faculty development committed to improving not only individual faculty but also the social and physical conditions of their work.

At one institution, faculty in a humanities department were accused of not being on campus enough. An examination of their work environment quickly showed why they were "stealing time": their 10-feet by 8-feet windowless offices located in the basement of an old science building were stifling hot. Large asbestos-covered steam pipes passed through the offices. Their chair had been requesting improved offices for 11 years, but each time their dean filed their well-documented complaints under "deferred maintenance," a budget line that almost always was exhausted before the end of the year. Losing hope, some senior tenured faculty in this department who lived close to campus built comfortable home offices and met with students and colleagues at home at their own expense: "stealing time."

In another case, an education department with more than its share of "deadwood" faculty was accused by a provost of never meeting to do strategic planning. When I finally caught up with these professionals I discovered why. The faculty-to-student ratio was in fact 30 to 1, not 18 to 1 as advertised; when secondary concentration students were included, the ratio ballooned to 38 to 1. Because the student-teaching sites were scattered across a 40-mile radius, faculty started their days early, ended them late, and spent a lot of time traveling. There was no place to meet in the School of Education's building, and the 60- to 80-hour work-weeks made it impossible to capture a common meeting time. Unfortunately, the dean of the school never attempted to create open time slots for meetings through a revision of the course schedule. When these faculty did meet, they met evenings or on Saturday mornings in a dilapidated classroom. Turnover of staff in this department was high. Its four tenured senior faculty — while not deadwood — were certainly tired teachers constantly managing stress and avoiding burnout. How would post-tenure review promote their well-being?

Undoubtedly there are real problems in higher education. Post-tenure review may be a sincere attempt to deal with some of these problems; however, the problems are complex. They will not disappear when a handful of poor-performing tenured faculty are asked to change or leave. There is a better way to bring out the best, not only in faculty but also in administrators, staff, and students. Comprehensive annual reviews of the quality of work life of faculty hold the real promise of improving higher education. Most important, the processes they would initiate would be fairer and much more collegial; such reviews would bring campus communities together to hold up all faculty rather than to shame the fallen few. This is the path we should take. This is the direction we should go if bringing out the best in faculty and all the people they touch is our destination

## Notes

1. Charles Walker is a professor of psychology at St. Bonaventure University. He is a social psychologist known for his basic research on rumor as well as his applied research on classroom assessment and faculty well-being. At SBU he also serves as faculty developer and federal grant evaluator. Walker has developed the Inventory on Teaching Climate and Faculty Well-Being, available at web.sbu.edu/vitality/faculty_vitality/, and he works with institutions across the county on programs aimed at improving faculty vitality. He received a B.S. from the University of Pittsburgh and a Ph.D. in psychology from Adelphi University. (Contact him at cwalker@sbu.edu)

2. More information on the inventory is available at web.sbu.edu/vitality/faculty_vitality.

3. This research has been partially funded by AAHE's New Pathways II post-tenure review minigrant project.

## References

American Association of University Professors. (1993). "Report on the Status of Non-Tenure-Track Faculty." *Academe* 78: 39-48.

Blackburn, R.T. (1997). "Career Phases and Their Effects on Faculty Motivation." In *Teaching Well and Liking It*, edited by J.L. Bess, pp. 314-336. Baltimore: Johns Hopkins University Press.

Blackburn, R.T., and J.H. Lawrence. (1986). "Aging and the Quality of Faculty Job Performance." *Review of Educational Research* 23(3): 256–290.

———, S. Ross, V.P. Okoloko, J.P. Bieber, R. Meiland, and T. Street. (1986). *Faculty as a Key Resource: A Review of the Research Literature*. Ann Arbor: National Center for Postsecondary Teaching and Learning, University of Michigan.

Bland, C.J., and W.H. Bergquist. (1997). *The Vitality of Senior Faculty Members: Snow on the Roof, Fire in the Furnace*. ASHE-ERIC Higher Education Reports, no. 7. Washington DC: The George Washington University Graduate School of Education and Human Development.

Dunnette, M.D., and L.M. Hough. (1992). *Handbook of Industrial and Organizational Psychology*. Palo Alto, CA: Consulting Psychologists Press.

Eble, K.E., and W.J. McKeachie. (1985). *Improving Undergraduate Education Through Faculty Development*. San Francisco: Jossey-Bass.

Eckert, R.E., and J.E. Stecklein. (1957). "Job Motivations and Satisfactions of College Teachers: A Study of Faculty Members in Minnesota Colleges." In *Cooperative Research Report No. 7.* Washington, DC: U.S. Department of Health, Education, and Welfare.

Finkelstein, L.M., M. Burke, and N. Raju. (1995). "Age Discrimination in Simulated Employment Contexts: An Integrative Analysis." *Journal of Applied Psychology* 80: 652–663.

Finkelstein, Martin J. (1984). *The American Academic Profession: A Synthesis of Social Scientific Inquiry Since World War II.* Columbus, OH: Ohio State University Press.

Iaffaldano, M.T., and P.M. Murchinsky. (1985). "Job Satisfaction and Job Performance: A Meta-Analysis." *Psychological Bulletin* 97: 251–273.

Kahneman, D., E. Diener, and N. Schwarz. (1999). *Well-Being: The Foundations of Hedonic Psychology.* New York: Russell Sage Foundation.

Lee, T.W., S.J. Ashford, J.P. Walsh, and R.T. Mowday. (1992). "Commitment Propensity, Organizational Commitment, and Voluntary Turnover: A Longitudinal Study of Organization Entry Processes." *Journal of Management* 18: 15–32.

Licata, C.M. (1986). *Post-Tenure Faculty Evaluation: Threat or Opportunity?* ASHE-ERIC Higher Education Reports, no. 1. Washington DC: Association for the Study of Higher Education.

———, and J.C. Morreale. (1997). *Post-Tenure Review: Policies, Practices, Precautions.* New Pathways Working Paper Series, no. 12. Washington, DC: American Association for Higher Education.

Maslach, C., and J. Goldberg. (1998). "Prevention of Burnout: New Perspectives." *Applied and Preventive Psychology* 7: 63–74.

Menges, R.J. (1999). "Dilemmas of Newly Hired Faculty" In *Faculty in New Jobs: A Guide to Settling In, Becoming Established, and Building Institutional Support,* by R.J. Menges and Associates, pp. 19-38. San Francisco: Jossey-Bass.

———, and C.J. Walker. (August 1998). "The Vitality and Well-Being of Early, Mid, and Late-Career College Faculty." Presentation at the National Convention of the American Psychological Association, San Francisco, California.

Pellino, F.R. (1981). *Planning and Evaluating Professional Growth Programs for Faculty: Monograph Series 14.* Ann Arbor: Center for the Study of Higher Education.

Rice, R.E., and A.E. Austin. (March/April 1988). "High Faculty Morale: What Exemplary Colleges Do Right." *Change* 20(2): 50–58.

———. (1990). "Organization Impacts on Faculty Morale and Motivation to Teach." In *How Administrators Can Improve Teaching: Moving From Talk to Action in Higher Education,* edited by P. Seldin, pp. 26–41. San Francisco: Jossey-Bass.

Ryff, C.D. (1995). "Psychological Well-Being in Adult Life." *Current Directions in Psychological Science* 4: 99–104.

Senge, P.M. (1990). *The Fifth Discipline.* New York: Doubleday.

Trower, C.A. (2001). *Six Strikes Against an Academic Career: The Project on Faculty Appointments at Harvard University.* Available on Harvard University's website at www.gse.harvard.edu/~hpfa/.

Walker, C.J., and N. Hale. (1999). "Faculty Well-Being and Vitality." In *Faculty in New Jobs,* edited by R. Menges, pp. 216–239. San Francisco: Jossey-Bass.

Warr, P. (1999). "Well-Being and the Workplace." In *Well-Being: The Foundations of Hedonic Psychology,* edited by D. Kahneman, E. Diener, and N. Schwarz, pp. 392–412. New York: Russell Sage Foundation.

# A Profession at Risk: Using Post-Tenure Review to Create an Intentional Future

**William M. Plater** [1]

What has happened in the six or seven years since post-tenure review became a national topic of conversation among politicians, civic leaders, and journalists as well as academics? Why has post-tenure review become a shared concern across institutions of higher education in America, across faculty/administrative lines, and — more interesting — across institutional and public lines, through trustees, media, and even market analysts? What forces are at work in society at large that will impinge on the role of faculty and their ability to remain important? Are we paying enough attention to what is happening outside the academy to understand whether there is even a future for tenure? If we are purposeful, we can use our current experience in preserving tenure and our understanding of the forces of societal change to make post-tenure review the means of invigorating and renewing our profession.

## Looking Inside: Lessons to Be Learned From Implementing Post-Tenure Review

In commenting on what I think we have learned from the past six years and what I think we should anticipate in the next six to 10 years, I hope we can use this period of comparative calm to make a fundamental change in the way we go forward into the new century. We need to use this decade or so of experience to establish a new order that will serve our educational institutions well in what is certain to be a period of change brought about by the external forces: technology, increasing competition with private-sector suppliers, increased specialization of learning requiring certification of smaller bits of both skills and knowledge, changing demographics, globalization, and other less certain elements of change — revolutionary and evolutionary.

The first lesson we have learned from our experiences in developing plans for post-tenure review, in addressing the legitimate concerns of faculty, and in debating responsible critics including the American Association of University Professors (AAUP), is that tenure is fundamentally important. Its preservation — even if reshaped — is the overriding objective of post-tenure review and the several projects led by AAHE's New Pathways Project. The AAUP is right about the importance of tenure. I would argue for tenure's continuation — even in a changed form — because the reciprocal bond of tenure between the individual and the institution (note, the bond is not with a department, a discipline, or even a school — but with the whole institution) is the most effective basis of commitment.

But tenure — and what tenure represents — may no longer interest the public. So, let me be clear: Our primary lesson learned in the past few years is that we must preserve tenure by changing it. We must be specific about what its actual use will be in maintaining American higher education — from community colleges to research universities — as the world's best. If tenure is not essential for us to carry out our institutional missions, we cannot defend it as a right. Our arguments must be focused on the functional use of tenure as a means to an end — and not as a privilege, a status, or protection.

We need to understand what has happened and to outline where our common purpose lies in the future. To ground this outline in reality and particularity, I will draw on my own experience at Indiana University Purdue University Indianapolis (IUPUI) — but will also borrow from my knowledge of what has happened elsewhere.

To date, we have noted 12 tentative conclusions about the current state of post-tenure review that warrant reflection and further analysis.

### *1. Preserving Tenure Through Change*

As I have already stated, our first finding is we must preserve tenure by changing it and by using it to achieve institutional goals. Rich as the history and tradition of tenure may be, we simply must move beyond 1940 and embrace a self-imposed and enforced standard of public accountability, which ensures continuously improving faculty performance. Defending the status quo is neither defensible nor desirable in this new era of social organization.

### *2. Developing Post-Tenure Review as the Continuum From Hiring to Retiring*

We must view post-tenure review as part of a continuum of the individual faculty member's career, from hiring to retiring, and as a deliberate part of an overall structure of faculty assessment and reward. Those universities and colleges likely to succeed in implementing and sustaining post-tenure review will be those that can place it within a context of a hiring process, a promotion and tenure process, sabbatical leaves and other incentive programs, and even a structure for ending careers through a combination of gradual reductions and partial retirements. When post-tenure review is separate from the established and valued faculty review processes, then it is not likely to endure. Post-tenure review must become the continuum and matrix for these separate events to give shape, value, and meaning to a whole career. When faculty are hired, they should be guaranteed the protections and advantages of periodic review.

### *3. Make the Annual Review Substantive Through Post-Tenure Review*

Most colleges and universities conduct annual faculty reviews for salary decisions. At IUPUI, we have built our post-tenure review process on the annual review; two consecutive years of an unsatisfactory rating by the department chair will trigger a mandatory peer review and a required personal development program. Post-tenure review should enhance the annual review and make it more meaningful whether the mechanism for post-tenure review is triggered by one or more annual reviews or whether an annual review once every few years becomes more comprehensive and substantive. By asking each faculty member who completes an annual review to take it more seriously and to link one year's performance and activity to goals for the future and to past achievements, we will develop a more focused set of accomplishments for the institution as a whole. We have learned annual reviews can be neither routine nor superficial. When they are reflective and intentional, the faculty who prepare annual reports for review by their peers gain a sense of shared purpose and a connection with the people who must count on them. Viewed from this perspective, the annual review empowers the "reflective practitioner." It is active, not passive, and aimed at the future instead of "merely" a report or an historical record.

#### *4. Changing the Dialogue to Include the Margins*

We need to pay attention to who is participating in the discussions of tenure and post-tenure review. Tenured, mid-career faculty are, quite naturally, the most engaged in these debates, and they should continue to play a central role. As we watch momentum shift in the overall composition of the faculty due to our aging, however, we should note especially the role of colleagues at the margins.

We know many recently hired faculty are not on the tenure track, yet these colleagues have a vital interest in issues related to tenure. They face the prospects of a career different from those of us who entered the professoriate in the 1960s, 1970s, and 1980s. The new generation of faculty will live for decades with the consequences of decisions we make. Most pre-tenure faculty know much about the process for awarding tenure but less about what tenure means or the responsibilities it entails.

Fortunately, we see an interest in academic citizenship re-emerging among senior faculty — those colleagues near the end of their careers. Senior faculty have a sense of what is at stake not only for particular universities and colleges but also for the whole profession. Many welcome post-tenure review as an opportunity to put their careers, their accomplishments, and their hopes into a context beyond their own personal ambitions. We need to engage these colleagues, too, because they have the most experience with how tenure (1) enables faculty work, (2) helps achieve our missions, and (3) provides a social bond to a physical place and specific community. We have learned, incidentally, to be skeptical about promises of "virtual tenure," realizing that tenure and place are related even if we must think of "place" in ways that transcend geography. Tenure is more sustainable among a community of peers who truly know one another and their work.

#### *5. Make Peer Review the Foundation*

The value of peer review is also one of the important lessons we have learned. It is also a point of convergence with the AAUP. Those institutions most likely to implement post-tenure review successfully will rely on the judgment of peers to give credibility and legitimacy both to assessing faculty performance and to individual judgments. My experience makes me bold in saying the continued success of post-tenure review will depend on peer review because tenure demands this engagement as one of its responsibilities and because peer review will ensure tenure's continued importance. What is neither seen nor understood is not valued. As faculty work becomes more public, so will tenure — through peer review.

### 6. Make Our Work Public

Post-tenure review is making our work public. The conversation is being led by Lee Shulman, Pat Hutchings, Gene Rice, and Barbara Cambridge [2], among others, about making faculty work public through peer review and accountability. Faculty work is now subject to a more intense public scrutiny than ever. Chris Licata, Joe Morreale, Estela Bensimon, and Dick Chait [3] have used their discussions of tenure to confront faculty with the necessity of our knowing the breadth of the work of our colleagues through systematic — and periodic — review instead of only when a book is published, a grant awarded, or a teaching prize bestowed. Whether manifested by trustees who feel compelled to direct faculty work by specifying how much teaching will occur and in what form, or by legislators who provide incentives for increased research productivity, all faculty at all types of institutions are seeing their work discussed and evaluated by people other than department chairs and deans.

Through peer review, research results (even if not research processes and activities) have long been public. In fact, we usually cite peer review of research as the basis of success of American higher education over the past 50 years. We are now beginning to see teaching results become public as we focus on learning outcomes. The prospects for this parallel development are invigorating, and post-tenure review will be critical to giving teaching a status equal to research.

Professional service is next. Whether marching under the banner of "the engaged university" or stepping more gingerly to the tune of "civic responsibility," faculties and their institutions are beginning to declare what actually is their role in service. If we act wisely, we may prove critics such as Peter Edidin wrong in his pronouncement that "holed up on campus, the study of wisdom is struck dumb." We should welcome the opportunity to make our work and our value public as well as engaged.

### *7. Using Post-Tenure Review as the Means of Improvement and Change*

Post-tenure review will succeed and take hold, however, only when we agree on the intrinsic importance of post-tenure review as a process for the continued improvement, even survival, of the institution and the faculty collectively — not an externally imposed burden from the trustees or legislature. When faculty can embrace post-tenure review as a process we created, we control, and we use for our own ends, then we can be certain it will endure. The argument for post-tenure review as a means of preserving tenure depends on how we define the purpose of the review itself.

The proper definition must contain within it the notions both of assessment of individual performance against collective goals — the unit's mission — and of continuous improvement — the individual's mission. Most definitions of tenure are based upon the AAUP Statement on Professional Ethics, which elaborates the 1940 Statement of Principle and states that "professors devote their energies to *developing and improving* [emphasis added] their scholarly competence." Being satisfactory implies improvement.

On my campus, the single most important issue for us so far is developing a standard for satisfactory and unsatisfactory performance. While each school has the freedom to create its own definition, we have used the following definition as a campus-wide default:

> In general, determination of unsatisfactory performance will entail consideration of total faculty activity in the three [or four if clinical service is required] areas of teaching, research (or creative activity), and professional and university service including changes in emphases over time. Evaluation will be based on, but not limited to, such factors as: (1) failure to meet classes, to update course content and pedagogy, to receive satisfactory evaluations by peers, students, or others; (2) failure to remain competent in the discipline and to contribute to its knowledge base; (3) failure to apply disciplinary knowledge and professional expertise to society's needs and the profession (discipline) or to contribute to effective academic citizenship through service on committees and in other activities or through contributions to the overall well being of the school, campus, and the university; and (4) [for units which require clinical service] failure to serve patients or clients effectively or to receive satisfactory peer evaluations in clinical service.

At the core of this definition is the promise of tenure as set forth by the AAUP — that those who hold it devote their energies to developing and improving. This commitment seems to me to be unequivocal.

### *8. Focusing Faculty Development on Mission Makes Post-Tenure Review Practical*

Continuing development requires a clear understanding of the goals and objectives of improvement. I believe post-tenure review must be the means for faculty to get feedback on how they are doing and how their work relates to the goals of the institution. I think we have long given lip service to the importance of faculty development but not always invested in it. Even worse, we have provided opportunities without accountability or purpose.

At most universities, sabbatical leaves are a tangible benefit of tenure. Yet, how many sabbatical leaves have been granted without asking whether the investment is warranted by either past performance or the quality of the proposed work? How many of us routinely ask whether the investment of a teaching grant, released time for research, or supplemental pay for service will bring measurable returns to the institution as a whole, or whether the purpose of the award is related to the unit's mission? We all acknowledge sabbaticals as an investment — but in what? If it is not to bring a return to the community of which we are all a part, why should any of us be willing to pick up the slack left by a colleague's taking a year or semester away? I do not know of a single university or college that makes funds available to a department or school when a colleague goes on sabbatical; there may be some, but they are few. We support most faculty development out of the investment of our own time, and our colleagues who benefit have a responsibility to make the life and work of the whole community better. It is important to make faculty development intentionally a part of post-tenure review and of making faculty development a priority.

### *9. Guiding Post-Tenure Review by Mission*

Post-tenure review and improvement toward some community-shared end require we have standards of assessment. First among these must be mission. Will the process of reviewing individual performance against a standard other than the individual's own work over time lead to measuring a faculty member's work against some arbitrary — even capricious or political — standard? Arbitrary judgment is, in fact, a legitimate concern, but it can be defused by clearly defining the mission of the unit — be it a department, a school, or an institution.

Should a unit reward the work of a faculty member in research that lies outside the mission of the department? Probably not — but it need not and almost certainly cannot prohibit such work. Can a faculty member teach whatever she or he wants even if it falls outside the department's mission? I hope not, at least not as the unilateral decision of an individual, but I would never oppose a faculty member's volunteering to teach in a subject outside the department's mission and even bargaining through the host unit's leader for a "purchase" of time. Can professional service applied to activities that fall outside the unit's defining scope be appreciated? Yes, but they need not be rewarded if they do not contribute to the mission of the unit.

We have become familiar with program review of departments and schools. We accept the principle that external assessment of a unit's success in meeting its mission is benchmarked against appropriate institutional peers. Program review provides the context for placing the work of the individual faculty member into a meaningful context determined by mission.

We will prosper as institutions only to the degree we can focus our time and intellectual resources on the things that matter most. We need not be rigid or prohibit explorations of many kinds, but we can be clear to ourselves that we will recognize and reward those activities that advance our shared goals — our mission. We should be held accountable for both the quality and the extent of our contributions to the mission of our academic community through post-tenure review.

#### *10. Making Public the Results of Post-Tenure Review*

In relating faculty work to a mission and then assessing its value against this criterion — along with other criteria — I think we also have learned that reporting the results of post-tenure review is more complicated than we thought. While many external critics seem to want a score on individual faculty productivity and worth, we have begun to learn the review is much more subtle and important. A few years ago, I attended an AAHE Conference on Faculty Roles & Rewards where early adopters of post-tenure review were citing figures on how many faculty were reviewed and how many were disciplined or dismissed. I think we have begun to shift our thinking from such score keeping to the nuances of how faculty work really relates to mission — say in teaching undergraduates and in helping retain them to the second year and then to a degree — or to how faculty are continuing to evolve and improve their skills and interests to remain relevant and to lead.

In one university, the provost discovered many faculty in one particular technical field were no longer current with industry standards and practices; for example, many graduates in computer technology were entering work prepared to use COBOL instead of one of the computer languages used by industry. A whole department was comfortable with teaching what they knew, not what was needed. Because there was no accountability beyond the department, this failure of tenure went unnoticed until alumni and employers complained. We need to think carefully about what results we can report because, as in this example, the teaching of individuals might have been exemplary, but the collective work of the department was unsatisfactory.

As a dean of the faculties, I will be much more interested in data showing faculty are continuing to adapt and improve than I will be in finding out how many people have been deemed unsatisfactory or recommended for dismissal. It is my responsibility to develop measures that can be reported to the trustees and the public; these reports must be more than a list of firings. We need to develop measures against which we wish to be held accountable and that will contribute to the overall improvement of our institutions. We need to report what we have achieved, not how many faculty we have disciplined.

This is a time to educate and to set expectations for the results of post-tenure review. What are the accountable measures of post-tenure review? How do we report changes in emphasis, new directions taken, summative reflections, or even dreams? What are the proper measures of post-tenure review if not the number of faculty dismissed? We have learned post-tenure review must expand its vocabulary as well as its audience, and this is a topic that calls for further development. This is a point of converging interest for the AAUP and the Association of Governing Boards (AGB), as we shift our focus to results.

***11. Using Post-Tenure Review to Make Our Work Collective***

Evidence of continuous improvement and accountability will be increasingly important to accreditors ranging from regional bodies to specialized accreditors. The trend toward assessing processes and procedures as opposed to specific results is tied to the idea that our work and its results have to relate to our missions. If we can adapt post-tenure review results to the accreditation process, I think we can go a long way toward transforming the nature of accreditation from a burdensome response to outside interference to one of owning the very process itself. We might even begin looking forward to accreditation as an opportunity to boast about how much we have improved since the last visit, whether it was 10, seven, or three years earlier. Post-tenure review is a means for accumulating the work of individuals into the work of a whole faculty.

***12. Preparing Chairs for Post-Tenure Review***

Most of the lessons learned so far have been encouraging, if we can act on our reflections and begin to adapt our thinking to the needs of the future. There are some troubling lessons, however, and one of them is the impact of post-tenure review on the most precious and precarious of our academic leaders — our department chairs (and in some cases the deans of smaller schools). When we place the chair in the position of having to assess the people she or he is hoping to lead by encouraging a sense of collegiality, the balance between nurturing and evaluating may be too fine to sustain. It takes well-considered and well-developed skills to maintain the balance, and not all chairs have either the patience or the self-awareness to develop the skills they need. While we should spend more time on preparing chairs for the full role they must play as overall leaders in the unit, we should give immediate attention to the preparation of chairs for post-tenure review and overall personnel assessment.

These 12 observations are neither exhaustive nor definitive with regard to the experience of the hundreds of faculties engaged in implementing post-tenure review. Yet we are all discovering local success depends on a change in the national context and culture. This is why the AAUP is a critical participant. The AAUP is the symbol of tenure, and we need this organization to lead us all in changing the nature of tenure to preserve it and the ideal it represents — educating for the public good. Unless we can implement post-tenure review for ourselves — let alone the public — we cannot remain true to this value. If faculty who hold tenure are willing neither to improve continuously nor to be held accountable for their personal improvement, then tenure has become antithetical to the privileged position of universities and colleges in society. Post-tenure review is itself a principle as necessary as the first principle of tenure.

## Using Lessons Learned to Define an Intentional Future

There are major forces at work that will transform American higher education regardless of what we may do with respect to post-tenure review. I don't believe there will be revolution and I don't believe we'll see many colleges or universities disappear. I do think that the pace of change will accelerate in the next decade. Major shifts may occur. The impact will be felt most intensely by full-time tenured faculty. Post-tenure review and its role in linking faculty work to missions may be the most important mitigating factor to these forces. Post-tenure review will indirectly affect the new system of classifying faculty. The same forces reshaping higher education overall should also be factors in our thinking about how we implement post-tenure review nationwide. To the extent we recognize at least some of the most potent forces of change, we can better preserve tenure and use post-tenure review to enhance our effectiveness.

We must link tenure inextricably with important institutional values. The main values are quality, the importance of balanced and comprehensive work of faculty, governance and responsibility for the institution, the differentiated mission and identity of an institution tied to a specific physical place, and the value of a degree as a meaningful credential beyond certification of competencies. We must also come to terms with the reality that the new American academic workforce is no longer centered on tenured faculty. We need to act in concert with a shared common ground so that each institution's plans and goals will have the cumulative benefit of identifying ourselves as a distinct American entity and as a dynamic profession within the larger social, governmental, corporate, and institutional cultures.

## Next Steps: Seeing the Future

If we do not institutionalize post-tenure review, we are not likely to redefine and reposition tenure as essential. While the AAUP may seek to freeze tenure in time, the consequences in five to 10 years may be devastating, since tenure will be irrelevant if faculty are not held responsible for adapting to new knowledge, to a more competitive marketplace, and to serving a clientele whose learning continues throughout life. I believe that post-tenure review not only is the key to preserving tenure and thus differentiating us from other "eduprise" institutions, but it is also the means of creating the flexibility and adaptability we do not now enjoy. If we succeed, post-tenure review will transform and blend into our other processes of ensuring quality. If we really succeed, five years from now no one except educational historians will be interested in post-tenure review, because it will have become pervasive and ubiquitous, as periodic review of all academic appointees occurs within a framework of values determined by mission and accountability.

I would advocate our thinking collectively about three overarching trends or ideas that could affect our work together as we seek the niche for our own respective institutions.

### *1. Define Work in Collaborative and Collective Terms*

One trend is the recognition that there is a shift under way in faculty roles away from the individual to the institution — or perhaps away from the department or school within the institution. We must find ways to adapt the values we associate with individual work to the work of the unit. We must build an ethic of collective responsibility that takes priority over individual achievement. Despite the difficulty of persuading faculty to think more about how their unit can succeed collectively than how they can advance in their own profession, we have an opportunity to restore the original purpose of tenure, which was a bond of mutual benefit among a collection of individuals and a bond between the individual and the institution. The issue of personal responsibility within the context of the whole group's responsibility is, in fact, the point of tenure. By using post-tenure review to reaffirm these values and to help individuals place themselves within a context of a community, post-tenure review can play a greater role in preserving tenure than will citing 60 years of history or inherent rights or special status. Tenure must be functional and valuable to be preserved, and if it serves a pragmatic end then it can surely be measured and reported through post-tenure review. Those who hold tenure have a responsibility to see the work of the whole institution and to place the work of the individual — including those who are ineligible for tenure — within a context that transcends individual accomplishments.

***2. The Community — and Often a Place — Gives Tenure Its Value***

The second trend is that tenure is a concept of value and meaning only when it is attached to a place, or a specific community of values whose reason for existence grows out of a distinct mission. Tenure is often mistakenly assumed to be attached to a department or to a discipline or perhaps to a school. Instead, most tenure policies of which I am aware make clear that tenure is linked to the whole institution. Even in universities, such as my own, that practice responsibility-centered management, we know the institution must declare financial exigency — not a specific department or unit — before tenured faculty are dismissed. Each unit belongs to a community, and the community as a whole will protect the parts — whether these be departments or individuals. As a whole institution, physical location — *place* — becomes a powerful factor. Some faculty work in multicampus universities, few of which make tenure system-wide. Instead, we have tied the success of the campus to a geographic place and in turn each person within the community is linked to that place, even when the work of a few members of the community takes place at remote sites.

Instead of being a limiting factor, the overt and explicit linking of tenure with place can help preserve tenure and continue to differentiate our traditional colleges and universities from their virtual and corporate competitors. As already noted, this sense of place is another way of reflecting specific values and a distinctive mission. Post-tenure review can reinforce a sense of differentiated mission and unique place by assessing individual work in the context of the values and the mission of the place to which tenure is attached. Tenure is a matter of culture, and post-tenure review must respect this artifact of human nature.

Nonetheless, our sense of place must also be flexible enough to accommodate the establishment of community without geographic limitations. A community may extend to faculty located in other places when they are linked by effective means of social interaction (as we see evolving in media of electronic communication), a set of shared values, and a common commitment to a distinct mission. In an era of globalization, faculty may work in geographically dispersed locations yet form a community defined by the mutual responsibilities of tenure.

### *3. Tenure Is a Defined Set of Mutual Responsibilities*

The third concept is that tenure is a matter of mutual responsibility. Tenure defines a set of reciprocal bonds that in turn offers a stability of mission, of shared work, of values, and of a workforce linked to a specific place. When there is shared responsibility and a recognition that the success of each depends on the success of all, then an environment of trust and mutual support can be established. This trust, of course, depends on each member's contributing in a discernable way to the community — which means that peer review and assessment of such contributions are critical to its continued vitality, its improvement, and its adaptability to external factors. This is, of course, what post-tenure review is all about.

Each of these three big ideas is a tent with room for many actions and ideas. I think the next phase of our work together, whether through the New Pathways project, through organizations such as the AAUP and AGB, or through the emerging new Carnegie pecking order, will involve these objectives, and I do hope we can reference them and each other as we take our separate pathways.

## Next Steps

There are some next steps we can take now while we still have momentum and before external forces arise. These are actions within our means — the things we can do locally, in our own places. We should not rest until we can answer these questions to our own satisfaction, consistent with our vision for ourselves and true to our respective missions.

1. How can post-tenure review take advantage of the growing importance of teaching in universities and colleges? How can post-tenure review be linked to making teaching public and to

creating more tangible rewards for documented effectiveness in teaching?

2. How can post-tenure review help us develop effective means of differentiating the responsibilities of individuals from each other and for each of us over time? The outmoded concept of a single unit-wide teaching load, for example, hampers greatly the ability of a unit to deploy its human resources most effectively. Post-tenure review provides the best means we have to date to look at the total work of an individual and to relate it to the work of others as each contributes to the mission of all. How can post-tenure review liberate our individuality?

3. How can post-tenure review shape our thinking about the replacement of aging faculty with new kinds of appointments? The trend toward hiring more part-time people or lecturers with term contracts who do not enjoy the protections and responsibilities of tenure, or the hiring of academic specialists whose primary work may lie in advising or managing information resources or linking community agencies with learning, must be managed and be brought within the conceptual framework of tenure. While driven largely by economic forces, the trend toward a smaller tenured faculty should make tenured status special. What way is there to turn this trend to the advantage of both the institution and the faculty community of tenure and responsibility?

4. How can post-tenure review become a factor in helping preserve the values and mission of an institution through the shared responsibility of faculty for the well-being of the whole — transcending and enduring beyond changes in the office of the chair, dean, provost, or president? Every new administrator will have an action agenda, so what over-arching processes ensure that changes in leadership actually contribute to coherence and to mission?

5. How can the purpose of post-tenure review shift to continuous improvement for all and away from pruning the deadwood of isolated, ineffective individuals?

6. How does the responsibility of individual academic citizenship — surely an obligation of tenured faculty — get assessed in post-tenure review? If shared governance is a necessary as well as treasured hallmark of the university, who will ensure that it endures?

I hope that as a nation we can address these six questions within the next year or two and be prepared to take advantage of changes such as the new Carnegie classifications or the expansion of commercialized education so that tenure not only endures but helps restore control over our respective futures to local communities. Nothing can be more important or instrumental than establishing periodic review as normative for all academic appointees. We who have tenure should lead by our example, keeping our vision firmly focused on the pursuit of excellence. In the words of the AAUP, the professoriate should devote its energies to developing and improving itself, to creating an intentional future.

## Notes

1. William M. Plater is dean of the faculties and executive vice chancellor of Indiana University Purdue University Indianapolis (IUPUI). He has held this position since 1987. As the chief academic officer, Plater is responsible for faculty appointments and advancements, academic programs, and academic support services. He is a professor of English at IUPUI and teaches in the area of contemporary American literature. His research interests focus on contemporary fiction and the interplay of fiction with other genre. He has written on numerous topics related to technology, higher education, and planning as well as literature. He holds baccalaureate (1967), master's, and Ph.D. (1973) degrees in English from the University of Illinois at Urbana-Champaign. (Contact him at wplater@iupui.edu)

2. Shulman and Hutchings at The Carnegie Foundation for the Advancement of Teaching; Rice and Cambridge at the American Association for Higher Education.

3. Licata and Morreale through AAHE's New Pathways project; Bensimon through the Project on Faculty Evaluation and Compensation, University of Southern California; and Chait through the Harvard Project on Faculty Appointments.

# Conclusion

# Moving the Conversation Forward

**Christine M. Licata and Joseph C. Morreale**

> There is only one thing more painful than learning from experience and that is not learning from experience.
>
> — Archibold McLeish

Fortunately, as we come to the end of this volume, we can reflect on the lessons learned by our experienced practitioners and use these experiences to move the conversation forward.

In our first AAHE publication (1997) we advocated that institutions follow six strategies when developing a program of post-tenure review. We repeat them here because we believe the varied stories detailed in the preceding sections expand and enlarge significantly upon these original recommendations. Our original framework remains useful nonetheless, putting policy and implementation into the current context.

**Six Strategies and Precautions for Developing a Program of Post-Tenure Review**

**1. Clearly define and articulate the purpose of the review.**

Because the purpose of the review drives all other aspects and leads the way to appropriate language regarding outcomes and consequences, it is important to distinguish between formative and summative evaluations. While many evaluation theorists believe these two types of evaluations must be designed and implemented separately, many practitioners believe a system of faculty evaluation can accomplish both types of outcomes. Both camps agree that institutions must make significant efforts at formative help before summative consequences can be invoked.

**2. Involve both faculty and administrators in designing the process and procedures.**

Without collaboration, a post-tenure review program is doomed to faculty apathy and pro forma implementation. Everyone must take ownership of the process to enhance its usefulness and success.

**3. Sufficiently inform and guide those entrusted with carrying out the review procedures.**

Do not expect peers to be comfortable with this type of review or administrators to possess the necessary evaluation and development skills. The review process is only as effective as those given the responsibility to implement it. Comfort, commitment, and skill will vary. Results will vary. This is to be expected. Experience will enhance comfort and skill; commitment must always be reinforced.

**4. Develop a plan to measure the effectiveness of the review in accomplishing its stated purpose and to determine the overall benefit of the review to faculty members and the institution.**

We could find only three institutions with a "sunset" clause in their initial policies, where the policies are reviewed after a trial period to see what changes are needed.

Faculty perceptions of the benefit and usefulness of post-tenure review are critical. Consider surveying faculty members who have been reviewed — as well as other constituencies involved in the review — to determine their overall impressions of the usefulness of its procedures, the time invested, the outcomes observed, and the benefits accrued. Communicate the intent and results widely and effectively, and be prepared to modify the process based on the assessment.

**5. Do not expect post-tenure review to be a panacea for removing unproductive faculty or for staffing flexibility.**

Realistic expectations are important. Post-tenure review requires time and credibility to reap tangible benefits. Will it always work? Probably not. There will always be a few intransigent or recalcitrant faculty members who do not want to grow or improve. Likewise, there will always be a few chairs and department peers who fail to treat the review process with the seriousness it requires. This is normal. The challenge is to lay the appropriate groundwork with peers and administrators so that, on balance, the process does work and participants feel invested in it.

**6. Be prepared to deal with the myriad compelling operational issues requiring careful planning and follow-through.**

Strategic leadership by the administration is necessary to gain campus acceptance, develop sound review procedures, and implement the entire process fairly.

Gaining campus acceptance requires:

- Establishing principles to guide post-tenure reviews in the preliminary stages.
- Bringing all stakeholders into the discussion of post-tenure review early.
- Integrating the concept of post-tenure review into the existing promotion and tenure system and into other review cycles.
- Gaining allies among the leadership of the faculty and middle management.
- Inviting external practitioners who are knowledgeable and experienced on the topic of post-tenure review to address the faculty and administration and elicit discussion on the topic.
- Being open to suggestions from the faculty and demonstrating a willingness to compromise.

Developing the policy and procedures should include:

- Making the process simple and understandable to all concerned.
- Keeping the faculty at the center of any review system.
- Dispelling the idea that post-tenure review is a re-tenuring process.
- Being vigilant about developing process and procedures.
- Adding funds and resources — if financially feasible — to faculty development in response to post-tenure review.

Implementing post-tenure review is made smoother when steps are included to:

- Oversee the actual implementation of the post-tenure review process in each college or school.
- Make sure there is appropriate follow-up and feedback to the faculty under review.
- Constantly remind stakeholders of the purpose and expected benefits of the review.
- Keep careful records of the process and its outcomes.
- Conduct informal evaluations of the process through discussions with the deans and chairs.

- Develop a formal assessment process to evaluate the overall effectiveness of post-tenure review, and modify the review based on the assessment.

## Is Tenured Faculty Review Achieving Its Intended Outcome?

The institutional examples in this volume might lead one to conclude it is still too early to judge whether post-tenure review is serving more than just a symbolic or political purpose. While we have moved through the inquiry and practice phases, we have yet to complete the assessment and modification phases. Thus conclusions backed by data are lacking. Yet we have gained much from listening to these "experienced" voices.

What seems apparent to us is the post-tenure review movement has called attention to faculty work and how it is assessed. In this process, thoughtful questions about the purpose and credibility of tenure and annual reviews have been asked. The answers have varied and to some may even seem incomplete. Notwithstanding, we believe discussions with our constituents about how individual contribution is gauged and how to improve the way we support tenured faculty in their careers are essential to the academy's future. A recent poll conducted by the Public Higher Education Program of the Nelson A. Rockefeller Institute of Government at the State University of New York (1998) indicates more than one-half of all states now tie some of their financial support of public higher education to performance; all but a few appear likely to do so over the next few years. There is an increasing belief by policymakers that what is publicly supported should be connected to "specific institutional performance measures" (Education Commission of the States 1998: 26). So whether it is the issue of performance funding or post-tenure review, the imperative is the same. It is that "achieving closer collaboration between policymakers and education leaders" is an important policy objective (26).

The reports in this volume about the Arizona University System, Texas State University System, Oregon University System, the University of Massachusetts, and the University of Kentucky suggest that collaboration did occur through discussions centering on tenure and post-tenure review. The door to better communication between policymakers and higher education can be opened through such policy deliberations, but the conversation must be ongoing to meaningfully inform each other's perspectives. Others in this book have offered guarded optimism that post-tenure review will contribute to the ability of institutions and higher education to meet the demands for performance standards and accountability, or will at least contribute to ongoing discussion about these concerns.

Were we to prognosticate about what contributions post-tenure review has made and where it is headed, we would offer the following:

1. The effectiveness of post-tenure review in the institutions described here and elsewhere is dependent on context and process. This means the following basic operating principles are in place:
   - Evaluation purpose is clear and not duplicative of other processes.
   - Evaluation leads to tangible results.
   - Evaluation procedures respect departmental culture and institutional need for fairness.
   - Evaluation standards are well understood and consistently applied.
2. The challenges ahead include strategic action to:
   - Situate post-tenure review within a seamless and cohesive continuum of faculty review policies and faculty well-being strategies.
   - Put energy and value on faculty renewal as an institutional priority.
   - Balance faculty development potential with compliance requirements.
   - Focus stakeholder attention on realistic outcomes and shape stakeholder expectations about faculty work through meaningful and sustained conversations and information sharing.

But significant questions still remain, such as those suggested in the essays by William Plater and Charles Walker. Critical questions we continue to ask ourselves center on how flexible we want to be in influencing the work of senior faculty, in recognizing that career trajectories are not linear, in responding to changing institutional missions and challenges and in deciding what contextual factors can influence enhanced faculty vitality and well-being.

To assist your reflection on these issues, in addition to this volume we recommend *The New Academic Compact,* edited by Linda McMillin and Jerry Berberet. Taken together, the two publications portray perspectives that offer a way to think about faculty careers, the viability of tenure, and how post-tenure review and renewal might serve to bring individual and institutional needs together in symbiotic ways.

## Companion Resources

In our first publication, *Post-Tenure Review: Policies, Practices, Precautions* (1997), we discussed the status of post-tenure review in the mid 1990s and outlined models in practice and their distinguishing characteristics. At that time, there were few "experienced voices" in the field to draw upon, and most of the evidence about policy effectiveness was anecdotal.

In the current publication we provide practitioners with reality-based recommendations about post-tenure review and senior faculty renewal, including lessons learned through implementation.

A third AAHE volume also to be published in 2002 will report findings from an AAHE study of the impact and outcomes of post-tenure review within nine institutions with five or more years of experience conducting such reviews. That report will attempt to shed light on the question of whether post-tenure review is working as intended and what faculty and campus leadership perceive the benefits and problems to be.

A fourth publication summarizing the ways in which outcomes and results are actually tracked and reported by system offices and campus leaders is also planned for 2002.

These four companion pieces offer a comprehensive framework in which to view tenured-faculty review practices and provide thoughtful discussion of practical issues and important perspectives about what works and what doesn't.

## Enduring Voices

Will post-tenure review endure over the long run? We find from this research that as institutions adopt tenured-faculty review and focus energy on senior faculty vitality, institutional perspectives evolve. Institutions learn new ways to shape the review process and make it more effective in creating continuous faculty development. Interest grows in assessing policy effectiveness and making the policy work to the advantage of all. Miller has called the relationship between faculty and institutional renewal a "conservative paradox" because "it's only by continual growth and adaptation to a changing world that we (meaning faculty) conserve the values and principles that we hold most dear" (2001: 4). We agree.

From our work, we find much promise in the ability of faculty and administrators — like those in this volume — to strike the appropriate balance between reviewing and renewing. These efforts are also leading faculty and administrators to reform employment practices to better reflect the work patterns of tenured faculty and the fluid needs of their institutions. These efforts and those of all of our minigrant partners give us great hope that post-tenure faculty review and renewal can work side by side to help make our work more public and our work better understood and valued.

As institutions continue to take seriously increasing flexibility in allocation of work effort and widening the range among teaching, scholarship, and service, Huber's observation about balance is compelling. She cautions us that: "Boundaries between the conventional parts of academic life can easily blur and . . . balance is less about the relationships among different kinds of work and more about their integration" (2001: 23).

The creative conversations in this book center on the notion of compromise and integration. Through the themes of **Critical Beginnings, Strategic Checkpoints, Intentional Intersections,** and **Future Pathways,** our authors point out the essential and the expected along the journey. We trust that the lessons and sage advice contained here can help move the conversation on post-tenure faculty review and renewal forward and bring focus to ways of designing meaningful, visionary, and effective evaluation and development practices.

This voyage is far from over though. As we continue our work, we must remind ourselves it is the transactional and transformational nature of the journey, not the destination, that offers the most promise.

> The real voyage of discovery consists not in seeking new landscape but in having new eyes.
>
> — Marcel Proust

## References

Education Commission of the States. (1998). "Transforming Postsecondary Education for the Twenty-First Century." Denver, CO: Author.

Huber, M.T. (July/August 2001). "Balancing Acts: Designing Careers Around the Scholarship of Teaching." *Change* 33(4): 21-30.

Licata, C.M., and J.C. Morreale. (1997). *Post-Tenure Review: Policies, Practices, Precautions.* New Pathways Working Paper Series, no. 12. Washington, DC: American Association for Higher Education.

McMillin, L., and J. Berberet, eds. (Forthcoming). *A New Academic Compact: Revisioning the Relationship Between Faculty and Their Institutions.* Bolton, MA: Anker Publishing.

Miller, M.A. (July/August 2001). "Faculty as a Renewable Resource." *Change* 33(4): 4.

Public Higher Education Program, Rockefeller Institute of Government, State University of New York. (1998). "Current Status and Future Prospects of Performance Funding and Performance Budgeting for Higher Education: The Second Survey." Albany, NY: Nelson A. Rockefeller Institute of Government, State University of New York.

# Appendix

# AAHE Minigrant Projects 1998–2000

| Institution | Project Objectives |
|---|---|
| **Central Michigan University**<br>Mount Pleasant, Michigan | Problems in implementing post-tenure review involve perceived deficits in clearly articulated principles, standards, guidelines, on the one hand; and the lack of an evaluation component for the overall process, on the other. The former has created procedural problems for participants, while the latter limits its ability to more clearly know the effects of post-tenure review and respond appropriately to those effects.<br><br>• Objective 1: Develop a written Statement of Principles<br>• Objective 2: Develop written performance thresholds (standards)<br>• Objective 3: Develop written procedural guidelines<br>• Objective 4: Develop and carry out an evaluation plan<br><br>**Contact Person**<br>Dr. Richard Davenport<br>Provost and Vice President for Academic Affairs<br>Richard.W.Davenport@cmich.edu |
| **Columbia College**<br>Chicago, Illinois | • Development of procedures for faculty five-year reviews that allow for clarity, timeliness, efficacy, and a positive approach to the evaluation process. |

- Educating faculty, chairs, and academic officers in the newly reorganized evaluation process and its goals and objectives.
- Allaying fears and concerns about the evaluation process among faculty and chairs who see it as a potentially excessive workload with the potential to be punitive.

**Contact Person**
Dr. Caroline Dodge Latta
Professor
clatta@popmail.colum.edu

---

**Drexel University**

- Establish ways to reinvigorate long-term tenured faculty in terms Philadelphia, Pennsylvania of the teaching of undergraduates within a context of learner-centered education by building on the current annual review process but providing more structure.
- What we are proposing is a three-year development plan with an emphasis on undergraduate teaching that would be established by individual faculty and their department heads and reviewed by the Faculty Development Committee. This development plan would lay out a year-by-year proposal for each faculty member to improve the quality of teaching using a learner-centered focus, to attend workshops on teaching, and to begin to present and publish papers on pedagogy. Annual assessments would be done in terms of these individualized development plans.
- At the end of the three-year period, if the program were completed satisfactorily, the faculty member would receive a dollar-amount increase to base salary.

- Three initial categories of faculty have been identified for this initiative:
  - — Faculty who have been traditionally and heavily involved with classroom instruction and who are interested in expanding their knowledge of, and ability to apply, the new pedagogies;
  - — Senior faculty who are shifting some of their earlier career emphasis on research to teaching and wish exposure to new approaches to student learning;
  - — Professors who have "burnt out" and are teaching with decreased effectiveness and declining student interest who need to be re-engaged.

**Contact Person**
Dr. Barbara G. Hornum
Associate Provost and Dean of Undergraduate Affairs
hornumbg@drexel.edu

---

**Eastern New Mexico University-Main Campus**
Portales, New Mexico

1. Conduct a review of the current post-tenure review process.

2. Address the failure of this review process to reward faculty found "meritorious"; the University's review process is careful to require that the institution assist faculty found wanting in teaching; there is no complementary merit-based reward.

3. Strengthen a crucial component of this process: the evaluation of classroom teaching.

**Contact Person**
Dr. Patrice Caldwell
Executive Director of Planning and Analysis
Patrice.Caldwell@enmu.edu

**Idaho State University**
Pocatello, Idaho

- Review of current policies and procedures regarding post-tenure review with the objectives of establishing the beneficial outcomes of a non-burdensome but more substantive review;
- Create appropriate linkages between annual reviews of faculty and the more comprehensive post-tenure review;
- Add rewards for exemplary faculty and assistance for faculty whose performance should improve;
- Bring institutional policies into compliance with Northwest Association of Schools and Colleges (NASC) Commission's standards that require that "every faculty member at every institution be subject to some type of substantive performance evaluation and review at least every third year."

**Contact Person**

Dr. Jonathan Lawson
Vice President for Academic Affairs
lawsjona@isu.edu

Dr. Ann Oakes
Associate Professor
oakeann@isu.edu

**Indiana University Purdue University Indianapolis**
Indianapolis, Indiana

Develop an annual or biennial workshop for new chairs to complement existing training and to acquaint them specifically with campus policies, procedures, and chairs' responsibilities with respect to annual review, the promotion and tenure process, and faculty review and enhancement (post-tenure review). Specific objectives entail:

- Create a handbook inclusive of all materials that can serve as a reference for chairs — new and experienced — who are called upon to evaluate and to foster faculty development.
- Develop at the school level operational definitions of "unsatisfactory performance" and "chronically unproductive" — the conditions that trigger mandatory review of a tenured faculty member or librarians under the new policy.
- Lay the foundation for an interactive, Web-based training and reference system to be created following a year or two of intensive interpersonal interaction; the Web-based resource will enhance and perhaps replace the first two goals (above) in time.

**Contact Person**
Dr. N. Douglas Lees
Professor and Chair of Biology
nlees@iupui.edu

<table>
<tr>
<td>King's College<br>Wilkes-Barre, Pennsylvania</td>
<td>Review the current formative senior-faculty review program (established in 1989) to determine whether a need exists to re-invigorate the process, recapture the original objectives with new strategies, and possibly broaden the original objectives and desired outcomes.<br><br>Project objectives include the following:<br><br>• Determine the effectiveness of the revised senior-faculty review process as a continuing means of formative evaluation (survey of senior faculty, follow-up focus groups, and reporting by deans of Business School and of Arts and Sciences on professional outcomes accomplished in faculty professional growth plans).<br><br>• Explore possible ways of relating senior faculty review and professional growth plans to differentiated workload and other more novel outcomes (use consultant in process).<br><br>Contact Person<br>Rev. Donald Grimes<br>Vice President for Academic Affairs</td>
</tr>
<tr>
<td>Madonna University<br>Livonia, Michigan</td>
<td>• Strengthen the usefulness of the faculty review process as a tool for continuing professional development and for periodic performance evaluation by fully instituting the faculty professional portfolio system.<br><br>• Link performance review/goal setting to differentiated workload in order to allow individuals to choose different workload options at different points in their careers.</td>
</tr>
</table>

- Provide training for the faculty, department chairpersons, deans, peer reviewers, and administrators in their roles in the performance-review process and the expected outcomes of the new system, including creation of guidelines and benchmarks.
- Link faculty performance review to other important decision-making processes such as planning and program review.
- Develop materials for the annual new-faculty orientation detailing the goals, expectations, and process for the faculty professional portfolio.
- Assess the perceived effectiveness of and satisfaction with the faculty professional portfolio as a tool for professional growth and faculty review/evaluation at the end of two-year project.

**Contact Person**
Dr. Kenneth Rust
Associate Professor
rust@smtp.munet.edu

---

**Sam Houston State University**
Huntsville, Texas

Compile useful, comparative information on the PTR process as it is developing on the various campuses of the Texas State University System (1,100 tenured faculty). Information will be made available to individual campuses and the TSUS system office. The specific objectives of the study will be to collect reliable information concerning a number of particular questions related to PTR so that the sister institutions in the TSUS will have some benchmarks against which to evaluate their own situations.

Questions to be addressed include:

- How have faculty performance standards been established, and how is inter-departmental variation handled?
- How were first and subsequent groups of faculty selected?
- Has post-tenure review helped to identify "deadwood" and resulted in early retirements?
- Has PTR been successful in emphasizing a developmental approach for most?
- How do professional development plans vary from campus to campus?
- Has new review been effectively implemented, and how are peers defined?
- Are there any lingering concerns about academic freedom?
- Are there any issues arising from the PTR process that faculty members, their representatives, administrators, or system officials feel need to be addressed?

**Contact Person**

Dr. Frank Fair
Professor of Philosophy
psy_fkf@shsu.edu

Debra Price
Associate Professor of Language and Literacy Studies
edu_dpp@shsu.edu

**San Jose State University**
San Jose, California

A change in state policy in 1997 broadened post-tenure review to include scholarship and service but also added a voluntary enhancement option.

This change suggests a more positive and proactive view of the professional "life cycle," where tenured faculty are encouraged to engage in activities and processes focused on the enhancement of their professional practice and careers. However, the following certain needs/concerns of post-tenure faculty need to be addressed:

- Need for personal and professional renewal.
- Desire to be part of an intellectual community of conversation on campus.
- Worry about the separation (and alienation) of new faculty from senior faculty.
- Concern about lack of resources for even modest support for mid-career professional development (typically going to faculty and "stars").
- Request for opportunities to clarify and explore future career and retirement opportunities.

Four major project goals are to:

- Involve post-tenure review faculty in New Faculty Orientation programs;

- Establish a minigrant specifically targeting post-tenure review faculty;
- Extend career prospectus reflection model piloted with newly hired faculty to post-tenure review faculty;
- Fund a mid-year retreat involving post-tenure review and newly hired faculty.

**Contact Person**
Dr. Victoria Harper
Professor
vharper@pacbell.net

---

**Saint Bonaventure University**
Olean, New York

Conduct site visits and collect data on faculty well-being with the following goals:

1. To assess the effects that feedback from the *Inventory on Teaching Climate and Faculty Vitality* has had on faculty development programs and other practices that directly affect the quality of faculty work.

2. To find examples of practices that appear to maintain and enhance faculty vitality (i.e., best practices for faculty vitality).

3. To assess the effects that various expressions of post-tenure review have on faculty vitality and to find forms of PTR that promote faculty vitality.

**Contact Person**
Dr. Charles Walker
Professor
cwalker@sbu.edu

**Suffolk County Community College**
Selden, New York

Design and implement a systematic evaluation of the first three cycles (1995-1998) of Suffolk County Community College's tenured-faculty development process to improve the process and revitalize the original momentum. Specific objectives include:

- Identify the strengths and weaknesses of the process and determine the levels of satisfaction of the team participants and academic administration.
- Evaluate the quality of the assessments conducted according to SCCC's Tenured Faculty Development Guidelines.
- Determine the extent to which recommendations for remediation were implemented.
- Integrate this evaluation/revision into the overall process to be conducted every three years.

Participating campus constituencies will include:

- The 184 faculty, peer, and academic administrative team members who have participated in the tenure review process to date.
- The three deans of faculty who administered the process and participated in the post-review conference.
- Representatives of the Faculty Association; process is a part of the collective bargaining agreement.

**Contact Person**
Dr. Robert Arrigon
Executive Dean for Curriculum and Instruction
arrigor@sunysuffolk.edu

**Texas A&M University**
College Station, Texas

Develop multiple strategies to act as templates for Texas A&M University departmental PTR strategies, ensuring that diverse forms of scholarship are rewarded and considered in all promotion procedures.

Project objectives include:

- Identify and classify by discipline all obstacles that prohibit rewards for diverse forms of scholarship.
- Identify workable strategies that will allow progress in alleviating discovered obstacles.
- Develop workable strategies for administrative development opportunities for department heads and deans focused on responsible rewards for diverse forms of scholarship.

Participating campus constituencies include:

- Coordinator of Continuous Improvement for Academic Affairs representing the office of the Executive Vice President and Provost.
- Academic Program Council at TAMU (membership includes all associate provosts, all assistant provosts, and deans of all 10 colleges; Provost chairs the Council).

| | |
|---|---|
| | • Faculty Senate Ad Hoc Committee for Reconciling the Faculty Reward System With the Multiple Missions of the University.<br><br>**Contact Person**<br>Dr. William Perry<br>Associate Provost<br>bperry@tamu.edu |
| **University of Kentucky**<br>Lexington, Kentucky | Ensure that all higher education institutions have fair and effective post-tenure/faculty development policies in place by the 1999-2000 academic year. Objectives include:<br><br>• Foster university-wide discussion among faculty, administrators, and students about the need to develop structures for assessment and development of faculty after tenure, resulting in the implementation of a program by the 1999-2000 academic year designed to enhance post-tenure faculty productivity.<br><br>• Engage public and private higher education institutions around Kentucky in discussions of post-tenure review processes, including those with policies in place, those piloting policies, and those that have not yet considered policies.<br><br>**Contact Person**<br>Dr. James L. Applegate<br>Vice President for Academic Affairs, Kentucky Council on Post-Secondary Education<br>Jim.applegate@mail.state.ky.us |

| | |
|---|---|
| **University of Massachusetts System**<br>Boston, Massachusetts | Work with leadership of faculty unions and five campuses to:<br><br>• Assist the campuses in gaining faculty acceptance of post-tenure review;<br><br>• Create viable post-tenure review procedures by hosting a system-wide conference on post-tenure review jointly planned by administration and union representatives;<br><br>• Establish an external consulting team that would meet with individual campuses to review proposed post-tenure procedures;<br><br>• Conduct system-wide meetings of campus leadership.<br><br>**Contact Person**<br>Dr. Kate Harrington<br>Senior Associate for Academic Affairs<br>kharrington@umassp.edu |
| **University of Nebraska**<br>Lincoln, Nebraska | Ensure that the various elements of the post-tenure review process are complementary. Project will provide assistance to units in developing performance standards that take into account all aspects of faculty work.<br><br>Project will ensure that the annual evaluation process logically builds on the performance standards articulated and will provide unit administrators and faculty with guidelines regarding the development of career plans. |

Specifically, the project will:

- Assess the developmental needs of faculty and department chairs that grow out of the post-tenure review process;
- Prepare faculty and department chairs for the responsibilities post-tenure review places upon them;
- Provide practical approaches to utilizing the department as the unit for productivity and quality assessment in relation to both the annual performance and post-tenure reviews;
- Explore effective ways to tie faculty development, differentiated workload, later-life career planning, and other formative outcomes to post-tenure review and the development of professional development plans;
- Integrate ongoing University initiatives pertaining to faculty roles and rewards with efforts to implement post-tenure review.

**Contact Person**

Dr. Gail Latta
Associate Professor/Libraries and President-Elect, Academic Senate
glatta@unlnotes,unl.edu

Z. B. Mayo
Professor
zmayol@unl.edu
zmayo@unlnotes.unl.edu

| | |
|---|---|
| **Virginia Military Institute**<br>Lexington, Virginia | Enhance post-tenure review plan and faculty development plan:<br><br>• Improve the post-tenure review plan an the VMI Plan for Faculty Development through comparison with those processes at its peer institutions. Peer institutions to be consulted include U.S. Military Academy, Lafayette College, U.S. Air Force Academy, U.S. Naval Academy, Union College, U.S. Coast Guard Academy, Bucknell University, U.S. Merchant Marine Academy, Valparaiso University, Wilkes University, University of Evansville, University of Wisconsin-Platteville, Transylvania University, University of Minnesota-Morris, Tri-State University<br><br>• Evaluate the VMI Plan for Faculty Development and the Post-Tenure Review Plan by surveying all administrators, department heads, faculty members, and students to evaluate the efficacy of the two plans. Specific emphasis in the survey will be on how the VMI Plan for Faculty Development and Post-Tenure Review Plan intersect to improve teaching, the element of primary importance to both plans.<br><br>**Contact Person**<br>Dr. Susan H. Barr<br>Dean of Academic Support and Cadet Services<br>barrsh@vmi.edu |
| **Winthrop University**<br>Rock Hill, South Carolina | Strengthen existing faculty and reward system, which will, in turn, prepare faculty members and administrators for participation in an effective post-tenure review process.<br><br>Develop a comprehensive evaluation process for post-tenure review that can serve as a model for other institutions in South Carolina and across the country and that will include at least the following components: |

- Feedback each year from all participants on the value and effectiveness of the post-tenure review process;
- Collection of longitudinal data to document changes in faculty employment status and performance as a result of post-tenure review;
- Collection of longitudinal data to document changes in performance for faculty receiving "satisfactory" reviews;
- Development of a method to assess changes in performance for faculty who, as a result of "unsatisfactory" ratings, participate in mandatory development activities;
- Information on the financial aspect of post-tenure review on the institution's funding through the performance funding system.

**Contact Person**
Dr. Betsy E. Brown
Associate Vice President for Academic Affairs, University of North Carolina System
brownb@northcarolina.edu
(formerly dean at Winthrop)

# AAHE Minigrant Projects 2000-2002

| Institution | Project Objectives |
|---|---|
| **Appalachian State University**<br>Boone, North Carolina<br><br>**North Carolina State University**<br>Raleigh, North Carolina<br><br>**North Carolina Agricultural and Technical State University**<br>Greensboro, North Carolina | **"Maintaining the Momentum With Post-Tenure Review"**<br><br>1. Evaluate the effectiveness of various approaches to post-tenure review within a state system or within academic units of the same institution.<br><br>2. Explore practical approaches for establishing faculty professional development plans growing out of post-tenure review.<br><br>3. Strengthen peer review component within post-tenure review.<br><br>a. Collect data and review the effectiveness of post-tenure review policies and explore ways to improve processes.<br><br>b. Create more intentional links between post-tenure review and faculty development centers and other faculty development opportunities on the three campuses by assessing existing practices, sharing best practices, and combining efforts where appropriate.<br><br>c. Create meaningful and fair classroom visitation. Create meaningful and fair processes of evaluating portfolios, and train faculty members for this review activity. |

**Contact Person**

Dr. Peter Petschauer
Professor of History, Appalachian State University
petschauerpw@appstate.edu

Dr. Frank Abrams
Senior Vice Provost for Academic Affairs, North Carolina State University

Dr. Charles Williams
Associate Vice Chancellor for Academic Affairs, North Carolina Agricultural and Technical State University

---

**Atlantic Cape Community College**
May Landing, New Jersey

**"REVISIT Evaluations (Revise, Educate, Verify, Institutional Standards in Tenured Evaluations)"**

Develop and implement a new faculty appraisal system, which encompasses the evaluation of a wide range of instructional domains for effective teaching.

a. Promote an institutional environment conducive to the teaching and learning process through professional development of instructors; motivate faculty to improve their teaching performance.

b. Develop and recommend modifications for a multifaceted program of evaluation, encompassing the evaluation of a wide range of instructional domains for effective teaching.

c. Agree upon the new faculty appraisal system; emphasize educational experiences, both traditional and distance education modes.

d. Implement the new faculty appraisal system.

**Contact Person**
Dr. Josette P. Katz
Associate Dean of Instruction
katz@atlantic.edu

---

**California State University, Fresno**
Fresno, California

**"Developmental Post-Tenure Review"**

Develop and pilot guidelines for post-tenure review that incorporate strengths of the policies and practices already in place on campus and to produce a review process that is perceived by those involved as being useful and productive.

a. Adapt the development plan concept already in place (Probationary Plans) to post-tenure review.

b. Improve peer review and produce more self-aware teachers by incorporating elements of the peer coaching program into personnel-associated peer review.

**Contact Person**
Dr. Ethelynda Harding
Director, Center for Enhancement of Teaching and Learning
lyndah@csufresno.edu

**California State University, Long Beach**
Long Beach, California

**"Evaluation of Tenured Faculty as a Formative Exercise: Pilot Testing a Proposed New Campus Policy"**

Pilot test a proposed new policy on Evaluation of Tenured Faculty, carefully monitoring all phases of the process and receiving regularized feedback from all participants. The pilot test will help identify aspects of the process that need modification and areas in which faculty, and administrators need training.

a. Field test the new policy with volunteer faculty (15 faculty) within one or more departments.

b. Offer workshop and training sessions to support faculty and administrators involved in all aspects of the review process (45 evaluators).

c. Gather feedback to determine the extent to which the new evaluation of tenured faculty process meets the goal of supporting meaningful professional growth and development.

d. Modify the review process based on feedback received.

e. Develop and present case to the university community for the dedication of resources to support the professional development of post-tenure faculty.

f. Revise review process and present to the appropriate governance bodies for consideration, approval, and implementation.

**Contact Person**
Dr. Gary W. Reichard
Associate Vice President for Academic Affairs
reichard@csulb.edu

**California State University, Monterey Bay**
Seaside, California

**"Post-Tenure Review Policy and Process — Getting Started"**

1. Create a thoughtful and workable Post-Tenure Policy and Process.

2. Identify and plan for training needs associated with policy implementation.

   a. Compile, review, and compare existing post-tenure review policies from other CSU campuses and from other universities with similar definition and philosophy of faculty review/work process.

   b. Draft policy document in coordination with retention, promotion, and tenure policy and collective bargaining representatives.

   c. Gain approval by Academic Senate and administration.

   d. Assess campus-wide training needs associated with implementation; develop procedures for implementing post-tenure review.

**Contact Person**
Dr. Janie Silveria
Chair, Academic Senate, Faculty Affairs
Janie_silveria@monterey.edu

**Columbia College**
Chicago, Illinois

## "Exploring Methods of Evaluating Faculty for Post-Tenure Review"

1. Develop a paradigm for chair participation in post-tenure review, which will improve the process and help other post-tenure review systems across the nation.

2. Specific areas included in the chair participation program include: developing greater efficiency in helping faculty attain post-review goal; implementing procedures that invoke collegial exchange, and clarifying the chair's role at each stage of the process:

   a. Workshop for chairs: "Best Practices for Chairpersons in Managing Five-Year Reviews."

   b. Chair/faculty forum: "Exploring Methods of Evaluating Faculty for Post-Tenure Review."

   c. Two focus groups (chair/faculty) to assess impact of activity a and b above.

**Contact Person**

Dr. Caroline Dodge Latta
Professor
clatta@popmail.colum.edu

Dianne Erpenbach
derpenbach@popmail.colum.edu

**Drexel University**
Philadelphia, Pennsylvania

**"A Faculty Renewal Plan for Mid- and Late-Career Faculty"**

1. Establish a comparative assessment that will enlarge knowledge of which factors are general and which are unique in producing successful developmental faculty renewal.

2. Acquire a sharper awareness for faculty development experiences in order to improve ability to promote formative post-tenure review that acknowledges both individual and generalized patterns of growth and change.

3. Assist with growth of transformational leadership on campus. Transformational leadership — the ability to motivate people to do exceptional things — does not just happen. Department heads and senior faculty who should be involved in such leadership can be caught up in a variety of demanding routines that work against effective mentoring.

4. Expand the bottom-up process of faculty renewal. Promote and encourage faculty to be the proponents of ongoing and continual dialogues about the scholarship of teaching and the promotion of student learning outcomes as core elements in a process of continual faculty engagement. It is hoped that the faculty involved in the first and second cohorts will help prepare the ground rules for faculty renewal.

   a. Luncheon forums for members of cohort groups 1 and 2 to explore opportunities for ways to enhance teaching and student learning.

   b. Mentoring training for department heads and faculty from cohort group 1.

   c. Assessment workshop to cover development and use of comparative assessments.

d. Construction of teaching portfolio for cohort group 2.

e. Workshop/panel for department heads on transformational leadership.

**Contact Person**
Dr. Barbara G. Hornum
Associate Provost
hornumbg@drexel.edu

---

**Idaho State University**
Pocatello, Idaho

**"Stage Two: Modifying Current PTR Policy"**

1. Provide administrative support to the ISU Professional Policies Council and to the ISU Faculty Senate as they take up the tasks and concerns associated with post-tenure review.

2. Establish the meaning of "substantive peer review" relative to the requirements of the Northwest Association of Schools and Colleges (NASC) and the Idaho State Board of Education.

3. Determine how to integrate substantive peer review in a way that can be applied evenly to all tenured faculty.
   - Idaho State Board of Education requires annual review of all faculty. Appraise our annual review policy to determine whether, and in what way, a person's annual review(s) can be modified or reconstructed to become part, or all, of the PTR as required by NASC.

4. Examine whether ISU wants to create a mechanism for rewarding outstanding tenured faculty as a result of PTR? How to identify outstanding tenured faculty? What is meant by "outstanding"? Should senior faculty be evaluated on the same five criteria used to evaluate junior faculty for tenure? With equal weights? Or, can a senior faculty member be outstanding in just one (or two, or three) areas of specialization (such as research, or service)?

5. Determine whether ISU wants to create a mechanism for remediation of deficiencies of tenured faculty as a result of PTR? How to identify deficiencies? What is meant by "deficient"? What faculty development programs might be initiated? Is such a program desirable?

**Contact Person**
Dr. Jonathan Lawson
Vice President for Academic Affairs
lawsjona@isu.edu

---

**Kansas State University**
Manhattan, Kansas

**"Recognizing Departmental Mission and Professional Development Opportunities in Allocation of Faculty Work Effort: A Creative Approach to PTR"**

1. Aid departments in clarifying their missions and in identifying the critical areas to which faculty must contribute.

2. Tie the allocation of faculty effort to faculty strengths, as indicated by the evaluation and reward process.

3. Increase general awareness of the present opportunities offered by various units, departments, colleges, and university for professional development at all stages of a faculty member's career.

4. Develop multi-media presentation that explains practices and programs.

   a. Special presentations for faculty will disseminate information and encourage discussion on:

      - Diversity, Mission, and Academic Work.
      - Revisiting Faculty Roles and Responsibilities in a Changing Environment.
      - The Teaching Portfolio: New Lessons Learned.
      - Traits of a Teaching Scholar.
      - National Trends in Post-Tenure Review.

   b. Workshops with 25 departments to be held to discuss departmental missions, ways faculty can collectively meet their missions through individualized assignments, value placed on activities, support for faculty development and changes that may be required in a department's annual evaluation document, promotion and tenure guidelines.

**Contact Person**
Dr. Ruth A. Dyer
Assistant Provost
rdyer@ksu.edu

**Portland State University**
Portland, Oregon

**"Developing Faculty for the 21st-Century Urban University: PTR at PSU"**

Strengthen peer review component of post-tenure review process through a comprehensive review of current policy; understanding of why differential application occurs; and taking action in concert with Faculty Association to improve efficiency of PTR in faculty career development.

a. Assess historical changes in and current departmental participation in peer-reviewed career support processes by surveying faculty, chairs, and deans.

b. Develop statements of departmental expectations for faculty work, including expectations for teaching, scholarship, public service, professional service, and university service.

c. Evaluate and recommend changes in current policies and procedures to enhance faculty career development through participation in peer review.

d. Communicate project results locally and nationally.

**Contact Person**
Dr. James R. Pratt
Vice Provost
prattja@pdx.edu

**Saint Michael's University**
Colchester, Vermont

**"Senior Review in a Liberal Arts College Context"**

Examine results of PTR implementation and recommend approaches to strengthen its effectiveness. In this process, shape answers to these questions:

1. Exactly how should the peer review aspect of this review function? What is the line between developmental and summative peer review?

   - How can individual faculty development plans best emerge from this process — plans that are both challenging and realistic? What can be done within the context of the faculty regulations about difficult or recalcitrant cases?

2. How can the college connect these developmental reviews with effective means of support for academic renewal, for later career re-assignment in teaching, or for early retirement?

3. Which aspects of peer review have enhanced faculty support for the process thus far? Which have hindered it? Can the faculty culture be developed to ensure or enhance continued, widespread support?

4. What promising practices have emerged at other small liberal arts colleges in the implementation of post-tenure reviews? A consortium of related colleges might be initiated to discuss benchmarks and strategies.

**Contact Person**
Dr. John Kenney
Dean
jkenney@smcvt.edu

| | |
|---|---|
| **Sam Houston State University**<br>Huntsville, Texas | **"Post-Tenure in Texas State-Supported Universities: A Broader View"**<br><br>Expand original work with five regional campuses to include two major research institutions, two traditionally minority institutions, a major urban university, and urban campuses in UT system. Compile useful, comparative information on the PTR process as it is developing on the campuses of these state-supported universities in Texas.<br><br>a. Solicit participation from institutions through Texas Council of Faculty Senates and Academic VP's (TAMU, UT Tyler, UT Arlington, Stephen F. Austin State University, University of Houston, and Prairie View A & M have expressed interest).<br><br>b. Conduct survey with participating institutions and report reliable information concerning a number of particular questions related to PTR so that all participating state universities will have some benchmarks against which to evaluate their own situations.<br><br>**Contact Person**<br>Dr. Frank Fair<br>Professor of Philosophy<br>psy_fkf@shsu.edu |
| **University of Massachusetts System**<br>Boston, Massachusetts | **"Assessing the Impact: A Study of the Implementation of Post-Tenure Review at the University of Massachusetts"**<br><br>1. Evaluate the effectiveness of the post-tenure review process on each campus. |

2. Recommend procedural or policy modifications that might improve the process.

3. Assess and recommend possible policy changes for negotiation in Spring 2001.

   a. Meta analysis across system of implementation and results.

   b. Report findings with recommendations for action.

**Contact Person**
Dr. Kate Harrington
Senior Associate for Academic Affairs
kharrington@umassp.edu

---

**Virginia Military Institute**
Lexington, Virginia

**"Enhancing PTR Through Department Head Development of Evaluation and Feedback Skills"**

1. Improve the preparation of department heads for faculty evaluation and PTR.

2. Investigate effective ways to incorporate peer review into VMI's plan for PTR, discover additional forms of student evaluation, and examine alternative frequencies of PTR.

3. Provide academic department heads with an opportunity to discuss the connections among peer review, PTR, and faculty development with colleagues from other institutions.

- Chair workshop on effective faculty evaluation and developmental approaches that feed into departmental planning process.

**Contact Person**
Dr. Susan H. Barr
Dean of Academic Support and Cadet Services
barrsh@vmi.edu